# EMPOWER

## Praise for *Embrace* and *Entice*

# The
# Violet Eden Chapters

Book One: *Embrace*

Book Two: *Entice*

Book Three: *Emblaze*

Book Four: *Endless*

Book Five: *Empower*

www.**jessicashirvington**.com

# EMPOWER

## jessica shirvington

ORCHARD

*For Chris –*
*without your encouragement, I probably never*
*would've finished the first draft of* Embrace.
*Thanks, big brother! This one's all yours!*

ORCHARD BOOKS
338 Euston Road, London NW1 3BH
Orchard Books Australia
Level 17/207 Kent Street, Sydney, NSW 2000

First published in Australia and New Zealand in 2013 by Hachette Australia
First published in the UK in 2014 by Orchard Books

ISBN 978 1 40833 339 6

Text © Jessica Shirvington 2013

The right of Jessica Shirvington to be identified as the author of this work has been
asserted by her in accordance with the Copyright, Designs and Patents Act, 1988.

The author and publisher would like to thank the following for permission to use
copyright material: Guardian News & Media Ltd for a Carl Jung quotation originally
published in the Guardian, on 19 July 1975.
Every endeavour has been made on the part of the publisher to contact copyright
holders not mentioned above and the publisher will be happy to include a full
acknowledgement in any future edition.

The author and publisher would also like to acknowledge the following works from
which the author has quoted: Douay-Rheims Bible; English Standard Version; The King
James Bible; The Nag Hammadi library; The Holy Quran.

A CIP catalogue record for this book is available from the British Library.

1 3 5 7 9 8 6 4 2

Printed in Great Britain
Orchard Books is a division of Hachette Children's Books,
an Hachette UK company.

www.hachette.co.uk

'That you will gather the souls of the righteous and the wicked, place us on your great scales and weigh our deeds. That if we have been loving and kind, you will take the key from around your neck and open the gates of Paradise, inviting us to live there forever.

And that if we have been selfish and cruel, it is you who will banish us.'

**Roman Catholic poetry**

# CHAPTER ONE

*'But I have promises to keep, and miles to go before I sleep,*
*and miles to go before I sleep.'*

Robert Frost

**M**y sweater was coated in a layer of mist – again – a by-product of life in London. I barely noticed the constant drizzle any more. It's not as if the cold bothered me. Not when I was the very definition of cold.

What *was* bothering me was the smell. There is something rank about a meat market at night. Especially when you're wedged into the eaves wondering what, over the years, has been sprayed about and never cleaned away. I shuddered.

The Smithfield Market was currently in vogue, but a gritty sense of history thickened the air, giving it a density that made me sure this wasn't the first time the site had been used for wicked intent. And right now, it was hunting hour.

At least I was the hunter.

I watched quietly as the exiles came into the centre of the massive terminal-style space, vaguely interested to note that there were six of them, instead of the four I'd expected. No bother, I suppose. I still had the element of surprise on my side.

The past two years had taught me not to let the everyday hiccups get to me. Sure, the additional muscle would hurt, but only in the physical sense and I could cope with that. Rolling with the punches is necessary when you are a Grigori – a human–angel hybrid – a weapon against the ever-increasing numbers of exiled angels on earth. For me, even more so since they gave me such a colourful nickname. I'm the Keshet – the rainbow. I didn't ask to be, but I made my choices and I stand by them.

So, there I was. Although I was still trying to figure out exactly what being the rainbow meant, mostly I found that the desire to know conflicted with my continuing need not to think about it at all. One thing I did know was that somehow I could create space with the angels – an unknown place where we were able to take form and communicate. My angel maker – whose name I still didn't know – said it was a place of new possibilities. For what, I was not sure.

*But I know this is what I am. It is what I will be.*

The final two exiles sauntered up to the four already waiting. It used to be impossible for me to be this close to exiles without them going into a frenzy, sensing my presence. But I'd learned many lessons over the past year, the most useful of which had been how to keep my guards up and locked so tight that even exiles couldn't sense me when I was truly concentrating.

*Which – judging by the thin film of sweat on my forehead – is now.*

The exiles dumped the huge calico sack they had been dragging along the floor and pulled it open, revealing three mutilated bodies to join the two maimed ones already on display.

From my position it was difficult to tell how old the corpses were, and if the smell was able to give a clue, I wouldn't have known, the stink of death and flesh being an overall theme of the place.

It was no wonder the exiles liked it so much.

Normally, exiles wouldn't bother with the clean-up – leaving evidence was of no concern. *Normally*, the exiles enjoyed the mess and despair they left behind. But not these ones. These dark exiles were working for someone else. They'd been following a plan, using a hit list, and it was all too well-constructed for any one of them to mastermind. Our intel told us they'd been hired. Such behaviour would usually be considered beneath them, but apparently this group of exiles had decided the job was thrilling enough to suffer the humiliation of working for the highest bidder – even if that was a human.

As for the billionaire businessman, well, that's not my department, but someone will pay him a visit. Right after all the evidence of his wrongdoing – minus the exile activity – is handed over to the authorities and his bank accounts are heavily syphoned to pay for the futures of his victims' families. And our fee, of course.

*Which, thanks to certain people, is exorbitant.*

Two of the exiles were dressed impeccably: one in a steel-grey suit and sporting villain-typical slicked-back hair; the other wore a slim-collared black suit that hugged his tall figure and set off his of-the-moment tousled light brown hair. The remaining four were less striking in casual wear, though nonetheless picture perfect. All six looked over the bodies like fishermen comparing the size and quality of their haul.

My hand grazed my dagger, the blade that had been given to me after I first embraced my powers and became a Grigori warrior three years ago. I was never without it. I even had a sheath attached to my bed for a quick draw if needed.

I'd learned the hard way – through the death and suffering of people I loved and, strangely enough, through my own death and suffering – exiles stop at nothing. Their insanity and misguided missions know no bounds and they take pleasure in causing great pain and suffering to humankind.

At least tonight I would only face exiles of dark. A couple of years ago the two opposing sides, light and dark, had called a truce. Of course, I tried not to think back to that time.

I tried constantly.

The discovery of the scripture that could end all Grigori had found its way into my hands. That in itself was part of the reason the Assembly had rejected me. They blamed me for trading with the dark exile, Phoenix. My decision had allowed him to resurrect Lilith – his mother, the first dark exile – from the dead, and she had taken control of the Grigori Scripture. But at the time my choice had been a simple one. Phoenix had Steph, my best friend, and I wasn't about to take any chances with her life. I've never regretted that choice.

Not like so many others I've made.

In the end, that made it easier to walk away from a place in the Academy when Josephine decided to change her mind. Of course, that was after I'd given my life, Lincoln's soul had shattered and Phoenix had died – proving that not only was he the son of Lilith, but he was also the human son of the first man, Adam – all so that I could kill Lilith. And those reasons weren't even the ones I tried not to think about.

*But I can't go there right now.*

I caught myself: I was working and the last thing I could afford to do was acknowledge that I was thinking about *him*.

The six exiles started to shift the remains of the bodies towards the incinerator, tossing them with supernatural strength and no care. I half expected them to try and mince the meat and load it onto trays for sale tomorrow. I wouldn't put anything past them.

'Make sure you take the index fingers,' one of the suited exiles instructed. 'Mr George is expecting me to deliver them to him tonight.'

*That's a shame. Though I'm sure Mr George will receive a knock at his door nonetheless.*

'I still don't understand why we don't just kill him, too,' another said.

'Are you challenging me?' The exile who had spoken first stepped forward.

His questioner mirrored his actions.

*Here we go.*

'If I must.'

Exiles never back down. Their pride and egotism combined with their unique brand of insanity is just too much to ignore. Angels were not created to take corporeal forms on earth. Though they have existed for eternity, in human bodies they manifest emotions in ways their innate nature can never process. It makes them unstable. And almost unstoppable.

I wriggled into a better position and waited patiently, knowing that this would work in my favour.

Sure enough, the exile who had spoken out first also struck out first, engaging with the suited exile. It didn't last long.

The suit, clearly the older of the two and a true fighter – my guess was he had once been either a Domination or a Power – overpowered his opponent, snapping his neck and making quick work of removing his heart.

We had our methods of ending their immortal existence, they had theirs.

*Happy days. I now have one less exile to take care of.*

I checked the time and sighed. If I didn't get this show on the road I'd lose my window. And fighting alone was always my preference.

The drop to the ground was at least two storeys high, but I landed behind the group of exiles lightly, thanks to my angelic enhancements.

Breathing calmly, I let go of the power I was holding tightly within, just enough to lower my shields.

The exiles, who had been preoccupied with their boasting, stiffened instantly and spun around to face the new threat. It was almost comical, the look of surprise on their faces. I guess a Grigori had never snuck up on them before.

Responding quickly, the suited exile stepped forward, shoving two of them to the side, the five of them quickly forming a semi-circle around me.

*So nice of them to stand in single file.*

But the way he studied me – with trademark exile insanity and undisguised raw desire – made me think that this one recognised me. It happened from time to time.

I wanted to sit around and chew the fat. Really. I couldn't think of anything I'd rather do with my time than hear about how they intended to rip me limb from limb and how that would make them as great as gods and me the most pathetic of humans. But when you've heard it all before, and always walked away – or, at the very least, been carried – while they were returned for their ultimate judgement, it gets old. So, I cut to the chase.

'You have a choice. Make it or I will make it for you,' I said, knowing that of all Grigori, I alone had the right to put it like that. 'Consider wisely,' I reinforced. After all, I could return them like any other Grigori with one of our blades, but if I willed it I could also strip them of their angelic strengths and leave them human – a fate exiles considered worse than an eternity in the pits of Hell. As far as I was aware, I was the only Grigori who could do this without requiring the exile in question to first choose such a fate. Which, of course, never happened.

'You brought Lilith to her end,' the suit said, his head tilted to the side, as if confused.

*Yeah, that's right, little ol' me.*

*And it only cost me everything that mattered.*

I raised my eyebrows. 'Time's almost up,' I said, refraining from closing my eyes briefly as I felt a surge of power within, something that had been happening increasingly. I was getting stronger, and exactly what that meant and how to harness it wasn't the kind of knowledge I was excited to discover.

I could strip them all, make their choice for them and be done with it, but I'd only done it twice. Onyx had been my first and I'd seen the pain it caused him. I didn't like knowing I was the one who took away his choice. Who was I to do such a thing? The second had been a demonstration, and had resulted in the exile in question meeting a quick death. I can't say I regretted it – he'd been one of the exiles so happy to see me strapped to a crucifix and tortured for hours – but still …

Anyway, tonight was more like training, and I'd been taught to be thorough. So, when the suit threw the first exile at me – knowing he'd be nothing more than a momentary distraction while I took him down and he lined up the next one – I got to work.

I braced, grabbing my dagger and moving into position. By the time the exile came within range my dagger had sliced through his heart and he was no longer there. Simply gone. Where did their physical forms go? Beats me.

I was already spinning by the time the second one was sent flying through the air towards me. My foot stopped his momentum and threw him back. I was on him in an instant, my dagger going straight to his heart. It didn't *need* to be the heart to return them, just a killing blow inflicted by a Grigori weapon. You could slice into exiles all day long with your garden-variety knife or shoot them with a gun but neither option worked. I'd never seen a Grigori manage to rip out an exile's heart barehanded, and even though the trick worked for exiles taking out other exiles, something told me that it did not alter our rules. Permanent results for Grigori over exiles only came via the blades of angels.

*Or my blood.*

The third exile went much the same way and soon enough I was left being circled by the two suits. To my surprise, they actually worked together – exiles aren't good at that – boxing me into a corner. The brown-haired exile in the black suit moved in on me when the other one feigned a move to my right. I took a closed fist across the face and a foot to the stomach.

I heard a crack. Broken rib. But I didn't register the pain.

That kind of pain was barely a tickle compared to the agony I carried inside, every moment of every day.

My pause gave the other exile the chance to take a swing. His foot collided with my hand so hard that my dagger went flying across the room. I kept my eyes on my attackers but my ear on my weapon, listening to the reverberations as it slid along the concrete floor and eventually hit the far wall with a clang.

The exiles smiled.

I sighed.

Then I leaped into the air, gaining enough height to grip the brown-haired exile's throat between my knees. Twisting my body as I fell through the air, I dragged the exile down with me, his neck breaking with a loud crunch.

It wouldn't keep him down for good, but a broken neck buys time.

The exile in the grey suit grabbed me roughly from behind and threw me into the wall.

I groaned as I slid down the metal piping my back had hit. It was the opposite wall to my dagger.

*Damn it.*

It wasn't an ideal situation. And I wasn't fool enough to delude myself into thinking I could make it to my dagger. I was regretting my decision not to wear any other weapons tonight, but my dagger was the only weapon that, when sheathed, was invisible to human eyes.

*Think, Vi.*

I'd come down behind a wall of old crates. I was considering how I could use them to my advantage when I spotted a piece of the slim metal piping I'd broken in my fall. It lay by my foot.

I could hear the exiles moving towards me. They were cackling.

'We should take her body with us to the tournament tonight,' one said.

The other one laughed. 'That would definitely put dark in the lead.'

'And everyone would know that *we* were the ones who killed her.'

*Can anyone say: premature victory?*

Without stopping to think I pulled off the bracelet from my left wrist, using the specially designed clasp to cut open the flesh around my silver marking, currently swirling in the presence of exiles, and let it spill onto the end of the metal bar.

It took just a few seconds and as soon as I palmed the pipe, the exiles started to throw the crates aside then came into view, their smiles wide with anticipation.

I stood. I didn't return their smiles. I didn't bother to do anything other than what needed to be done.

I lunged, raising my elbow into the face of the black-haired exile as I spun, the metal pipe striking his companion through the heart. He was gone. I turned back to the first exile and, hoping that there was still enough of my blood on the pipe to do the trick and using my supernatural speed for all it was worth, I jammed the pipe straight into his neck.

His face wore an expression of pure surprise.

I'd seen that look before.

I sighed and my shoulders slumped forward, unfulfilled. This was my job, one that I would do for as long as I existed, which could be a significantly long time. But two years ago I'd accepted that there was no longer any satisfaction to be had in my world.

No fairytales.

Only the cold.

Turning towards where I thought my dagger had landed, my surroundings suddenly changed.

I was no longer seeing the warehouse. There were flashes of white, moving fast, pounding hooves. Horses. Silver streaked through the air like a dance. Swords. Slashes of red painted the sky. Something sharp and deadly ripping through flesh – wet and gruesome. Claws. Thousands and thousands of beings as far as I could see fought ruthlessly, with no sign of tiring. In the centre, two warriors battled beneath a blinding light. I could not make out their faces.

I blinked hard.

The image was gone and in its place Gray stood against the wall of Lincoln's warehouse, casually flipping my dagger in the air. 'Would you like me to applaud?' he asked.

Leaning against a metal support pole, he had that mid-twenties look I'd come to associate with the older Grigori – though I had no idea how old he really was – and was dressed in his usual black jeans, black T-shirt and black leather jacket. Black really was the only colour worth investing in – blood stains everything else. He sported about a week's worth of growth on his face, though his head was shaved, the scars that ran over the top of his skull telling of a history both terrible and secret. Grigori did not generally scar, so I knew that whatever had caused these had occurred before Gray had turned seventeen.

I swallowed over the lump in my throat and glanced around as I composed myself. The whole ... hallucination ... had lasted only a couple of seconds. I clenched my jaw.

*Christ. It was nothing. I'm just imagining things.*

I snapped my bracelet back in place over my marking and shot him a dry look. 'Should I be charging a spectator fee?'

My voice sounded normal but my ears felt like they were still ringing with the echoes of battle.

'Not if the show is going to be over so fast, princess.'

I glared at him for persisting with the stupid nickname. 'You know, you could've stepped in and given me a hand.'

'Sure,' he said with a solemn nod. 'And you could've waited until the meet time we'd all agreed on, too.'

I looked away briefly. 'So, why are *you* here early?' I asked, hoping to divert the conversation.

Gray tilted his head. 'Because I know you.'

I shrugged off the veiled accusation, even though it was true. To a degree.

'It was easier this way.'

He threw my dagger into the air and I caught it by the hilt and slipped it back into its sheath.

'Well you can explain that to the others, since they just arrived.'

# CHAPTER TWO

*'Children, it is the last hour, and just as you heard that Antichrist is coming, even now many untichrists have appeared: from this we know that it is the last hour.'*

**1 John 2:18**

$G$ray and I found the other Rogues waiting in the designated meeting place around the corner from the market.

Spotting us, Carter took one look at me and hoisted himself onto the bonnet of his car, shaking his head. 'Bloody hell, fellas, she's done it again.'

Milo and Turk set hard looks on me. The first time I'd been on the receiving end of their stares, it almost made me think twice about fighting solo again. But then, the alternative was even less appealing.

I wished I could explain it so they would understand. Hell, I wished I could understand all the reasons why it was easier to fight alone. I could say it was because of my blood. That since none of them – apart from Gray – knew what I could do with it, I was merely protecting one of my many secrets. Rogues were a law unto themselves, and I was still learning all the rules that operated under the guise of having none. I could also argue that if one of them was hurt I would feel responsible and have to heal them, creating a bond that, although nothing like that between Phoenix and me, still suggested some kind of ongoing commitment. Keeping my distance from people had become paramount to my day-to-day survival.

Really, though, I knew that it had more to do with not wanting to rely on anyone. And not being able to watch one of them take a fall.

Not that I was about to admit to any of that. These guys would eat me alive.

So instead, I shrugged. 'I got here early and saw an opportunity, so I took it. Don't we have somewhere else to be tonight anyway?'

Carter lit a cigarette, inhaling deeply. Of all the Rogues, Carter was the most … unpredictable. And the biggest. The guy was built like a freight train and had the strength of one too. When he pushed his hand roughly through his overgrown brown hair and narrowed his amber eyes at me, it was not in jest.

I rolled mine in response, to which I am fairly certain he growled.

'We all know *that* job ain't paying anything like this one,' he said, not even attempting to keep his voice down.

I folded my arms, unperturbed. 'You'll all still get your cut.' This was never about solo profiteering. 'This way we can get on with the other job and you'll all be able to start drinking earlier than planned.'

Milo threw me a wink and Turk ruffled his bleached mohawk. I read both actions as signs that they were happy enough with my offer. Carter, however, was still eyeing me off. He'd put on his full-length leather coat for nothing and was pissed he'd missed the fight.

I sighed. 'I'll buy you all a round,' I offered, to which Carter grunted but tossed his cigarette and slid off the bonnet.

'You'll be buying at least a few, purple,' he said, getting into the driver's seat as Milo and Turk filed into the back. 'Where we headed?' he asked Gray.

'Round the back of King's Cross Station. That big building they have all those billboards around,' Gray answered.

'The new Schrager hotel?' I asked.

Carter curled his lip. I suppose he didn't really care who the designer was. I might have left my artist days behind, but I still noticed things like that.

'That's the one,' Gray said. 'You know the drill. It's a London Academy job and they're paying us to be there as back-up. Tread on their toes and we don't get paid. Got it?'

Everyone nodded except Carter, who grunted and started his death-trap car. He didn't offer me a lift, which sucked, since now I'd have to ride on the back of Gray's bike. It was nothing personal, but I would have preferred the death trap. Of all the Rogues I was closest to Gray, but letting people into my space – and hanging onto them on the back of a bike classified as such – wasn't my idea of a good time. It reminded me of things I'd never again have.

Things broken beyond repair.

Taking part in Academy business was something I preferred to avoid, but this job had come in carrying an additional request from the New York Academy, and as much as I didn't owe them any favours, I agreed to the occasional contract. When Gray first told me about this one earlier today, I'd felt that chill on the back of my neck that I'd learned to respond to, and signed up.

'You really should invest in some helmets,' I said, not for the first time.

Gray gave me a flat stare and got on his Harley. 'Feel free to walk.'

*Like that was going to happen.*

I hooked my leg over the seat, careful to maintain a distance between our bodies, and made a scoffing sound.

'Well, don't expect me to heal you if you come off and land on your head.' As soon as the words left my mouth I froze, remembering the scars on Gray's head.

*Was that what had happened to him?*

Gray's shoulders shook for a moment before he flashed a knowing smile at me. 'Not even close, princess. And if I'm not gonna wear a bucket on my head when I fight exiles, I sure as hell won't be bothering when I ride my bike.'

As he started the engine and pulled out, I knew I'd lost my fight. Gray loved his bike and the freedom that came with it.

I couldn't deny him that.

We followed Carter's souped-up Fiat and pulled up behind him a block away from the building. We walked the final distance, spotting a group of about a dozen Grigori huddled together not far from the construction site, as planned. They were beneath a 'glamour', hidden from human eyes. It was reasonably constructed but I'd seen better and stronger. It worried me.

Exile activity only seemed to be increasing, and while Grigori were strong and capable, we were limited in number. Although new Grigori continued to come through, it took seventeen years from first being given the essence of an angel before we could embrace our powers, and then even more time to train. Our numbers were simply not holding up. Had the angels not foreseen this problem?

*They must have.*

And yet I feared that the time when we would finally be overpowered was closer than we knew.

I stayed behind the guys. They didn't think anything of me pulling on my worn Yankees cap – a gift from Zoe – and moving into the shadows. We were Rogues. Anonymity was our right. And a lot of Rogues had serious trust issues with the Academy.

The senior Grigori running the mission greeted Gray. I recognised Clive and his partner, Annette, from a previous gig we'd taken on a couple of months back – not that I'd ever spoken with them. Clive and Gray shook hands and talked quietly while I looked at the team they had assembled.

Another unsettling feeling swept over me. There were more than a dozen Grigori but the majority were young. Apart from the leading pair, only a few looked prepared.

Gray returned to where we'd been standing at the edge of the pack.

'Okay, they had a tip-off that this is a tournament site. We have the north entry and exit, which is the closest. We hold the upper level.'

I wondered if this was the same tournament the exiles I'd taken on earlier had discussed. Tournaments had been popping up all over the city lately.

'How many?' Carter asked.

'They don't know. Intel says it could be a big group.'

Milo gave a toothy grin. 'Yeah. Bet they're in there swapping recipes and baking bread.'

The guys chuckled.

'Why aren't there more Grigori here? And more senior Grigori at that?' I asked, grimacing, as I realised my critical observation made me sound a lot like my mother. But London was a big city with an independent Academy. I was surprised they hadn't sent in a more impressive show of force.

'Apparently they're spread thin at the moment with this type of operation,' Gray said and shrugged. 'That's why they called us in, I suppose.' He glanced at the others. 'Let's just do our bit, get our money and clear out.'

We all agreed, and I pushed my unease to the side and focused on the job at hand. Once we received the nod from Clive, we ran towards the northern entrance, which I was pleased to note was the closest, giving us the advantage of first eyes inside. Once the Academy Grigori started to filter into the building, any hope of stealth would be forgotten. They did not value our defensive shields in the same way Rogues – particularly our small group – did.

We slipped in through the side door and down a dark corridor that led towards another door. When Gray cracked it open we heard the sounds immediately, and tensed.

Flesh against flesh.

Ripping.

Beating.

Inhuman growling.

The sounds combined evoked death.

Slowly we stepped through the doorway and found ourselves looking down. The construction works had reduced the building to an outer shell that concealed nothing but a cavernous space.

Floodlights sat in the corners lighting up what could only be described as the exile equivalent of a fight club.

'Maybe we should just leave them to it,' Carter whispered, gesturing towards the sparring figures below.

It wasn't an altogether ridiculous idea. At this rate the number we'd have to face would soon be considerably fewer. In Exile Fight Club there is only *one* rule: the loser must die. And right then, there were four simultaneous fights going on and what looked like another two dozen exiles divided into two distinct groups, champing at the bit as they waited on the sidelines.

Over the past two years, since the alliances that had been formed between light and dark in their mutual quest to destroy all Grigori had dissolved, out-in-the-open brawling had become common practice. But the 'tournaments', ones like this – premeditated, orderly – were new.

For all the benefits, being an angel and incorporeal had one definite drawback – no blood and guts. Dark and light have an eternal rivalry but as angels they are limited in ways that some cannot accept. In human form their eternal fantasies play out. For exiles, earth and its offerings of life and beauty come a distant second to its promise of pain and death.

I pointed to the top of the scaffolding positioned in the centre of the work site. '*That's* why we can't leave them to it.'

Tied to the top of the scaffolding were at least ten humans. Gagged and with their hands tied behind their backs, they were bound to the metal structure, trapped as it wobbled precariously in response to the hits it was absorbing from below.

Killing humans was the aim and prize of the game. The team that managed to take out enough of its opponents to make it to the top and savage the humans won. And somewhere in all that, some sick bastard kept score.

My gifts allowed me to differentiate between exiles of light and dark and this helped to give me a more complete view of the organised mayhem below. Most of the exiles were dressed in fight wear but the styles spanned different eras. Exiles tended to get stuck in the fashion of the time at which they first became human, so while there was typical street wear, there were also army fatigues, Roman-style weapons, ninja get-ups and, of course, for those who insisted on rising above their peers to the end, perfectly pressed suits.

As empirically beautiful as each and every one of these exiles was, this was not some fight scene in a Hollywood movie and there was no sparring. It was a show of extreme violence as they launched no-holds-barred attacks on one another, knowing with complete certainty that every fight would be to the death.

We watched in silence as an exile of dark ripped the heart from an exile of light and those surrounding sneered and hissed with their own hunger for blood. Almost instantly, another exile of light had his heart torn free – and then any semblance of order evaporated as the remaining exiles of light began to randomly attack exiles of dark.

'Jesus Christ,' Gray mumbled, taking in the mayhem.

'On the upside, at least it's keeping their focus off that lot,' Carter said, pointing to the group of Grigori moving in on them from the far wall.

'This isn't going to end well, Gray,' I said under my breath. We were outnumbered and out-crazied. 'I'm going down there,' I said.

'Gray,' Carter hissed.

Gray looked over the carnage below, the humans waiting to be slaughtered on the scaffolding above and then to the young inexperienced Grigori preparing to throw themselves into the fray, before turning back to us. He knew that Carter was worried we'd lose our bounty if I was caught taking matters into my own hands. We'd been ordered to stay on the upper level. But it didn't take Gray long to see how this would play out if I didn't do something.

'Since when did she listen to any of us?' he responded with a shrug.

I flashed Carter a tight-lipped smile, quickly climbed over the railing and jumped the ten metres to the ground, hoping I wouldn't be seen by either the exiles *or* the other Grigori.

I landed hard on the concrete, jarring my knee, but moved quickly. Two exiles spotted me and came straight at me, their eyes alight.

I threw my blade at one and was in the air, somersaulting over the second and landing behind him with enough time to grab his head and snap his neck before he could turn away. I picked up my dagger from where the first exile had now vanished, spun and drove the blade through the other temporarily stunned exile, before dashing into the shadows. Catching my breath, I crouched and waited for the next exile to come close enough for me to deliver another silent, efficient attack.

In a battle zone, exiles forfeited their choices, and I took out five more the same way before the other Grigori even made it onto the far side of the basement level. I'd helped reduce the numbers a little but there was still work to be done. Turk, Milo and Gray leaped down from the upper level, the same way I'd done and I watched, my heart pounding, as each immediately engaged with their nearest exile.

Gray was an impressive fighter – fierce and unforgiving, the type who didn't hesitate or slow for a second until the job was done. His style reminded me of ... others. Turk was all brawn. He hit hard and got big results, whereas Milo was sneaky. He'd bring them in, bounce all around the place and then, in a flash, his blade would be in their neck; they never saw it coming.

Once they'd cleared the way, I waved them over to my dark corner.

'Having all the fun, I see,' Milo said, looking out at the rapidly increasing mayhem. 'What's that you got, five?' he asked.

'Seven,' I corrected, keeping my eye on the exiles. The London Grigori were now in full swing and the exiles' attention was broken between fighting each other and engaging with Grigori, effectively helping us gain the upper hand. I breathed steadily, moving further into the corner to get my bearings as I felt a familiar cold sweat run down the back of my neck. My eyes scanned the space anxiously. Something was wrong.

Gray settled beside me, also taking in the scene. My line of sight finally settled on the scaffolding hanging a couple of storeys above us. Clive and Annette were fighting two exiles. I watched the senior Grigori gain the upper hand, and my shoulders relaxed when I saw their blades, first hers then his, take down the exiles in a flash of colourful Grigori mist. Clive stood behind Annette, both of them looking out over the fight below to see where they were most needed next.

But my relief was short-lived.

The air left my lungs as I watched a man appear out of nowhere behind them; short, bald, wearing glasses and a light grey suit. In one hand was a briefcase I recognised. In the other, a long Samurai-style curved sword.

I opened my mouth to scream at Clive and Annette to turn around.

I was too late.

The sword moved fast and sure, impaling them both as its long blade was pushed through both their bodies from behind, piercing their hearts.

I saw Annette's look of shock before her eyes glazed over, and though I could not see Clive's face I saw his hand as he grabbed hold of Annette's in his last living act, and they crumpled to the ground.

Suddenly *his* calculated eyes met mine. Like he'd known I was there. Like he'd known all along I was watching.

Like … the entire display had been for me.

The corner of his mouth twitched and he bowed his head before stepping back into the shadows.

'What the hell was that?' Gray asked, still beside me.

'Throw me up!' I yelled.

He didn't hesitate, just cupped his hands and held them out. When I leaped into the hand-hold he used all his strength to catapult me high into the air. I landed on the balcony above, and ran towards Clive and Annette.

When I reached their motionless bodies, I looked around frantically, but he was nowhere to be seen. I dropped to my knees beside them, checking for their pulses. They were gone. No matter how much healing power I had, I couldn't bring back the dead.

Carter, who'd stayed on the upper level, was the first to reach me.

'Aw, hell, purple,' he said, crouching beside me. 'Are you hurt?'

I shook my head. 'He killed them before they even knew he was behind them.'

'You sure you're not hurt? You look white as a ghost,' he said. 'These two friends of yours, or something?'

I shook my head again. But Carter was right. I had seen something that had me shaking for the first time in two years. Something a part of me had been waiting for every day since *that* night.

*The exile who took my blood is back.*

And he wanted me to know.

# CHAPTER THREE

*'To live is not merely to breathe; it is to act ...'*
Jean-Jacques Rousseau

**W**hen I'd packed up and left the city with Mum and Dad two years ago, I'd really had no idea what lay ahead. Other than the eternal war. Although I had thought we would make it work all together, it didn't take long to realise that too much had happened.

I wasn't the only one who'd changed.

We moved a lot, bouncing between half a dozen of Mum's safe houses around Europe. Sometimes we travelled simply to go somewhere new, other times it was because I could feel that *he* was getting close.

Mum was no longer Grigori, and that meant a few things for us. First, while her experience and training methods offered me a lot of insight, she didn't have the strength or durability she once had. Second, and most frustratingly for her, it seemed that, like angels who exiled, when she became purely human she gave up many of her memories. She was still able to recall the important things, like her partnership with Jonathan and many of the battles they'd encountered, but every now and then I would ask her a specific question and she would just go blank.

Every choice has a consequence and this was one of hers.

As for Dad, as great as it was for me to see him so full of life, he constantly struggled knowing what I faced and had to fight against when I went out at night.

And then there was the love thing.

I was so happy for them. I barely recognised Dad without the haunted, sad eyes that I'd only ever known. With Evelyn by his side, he relished each day. I was proud of them; that they had moved beyond all the obstacles and found their own private bubble filled with love and passion and I sure as hell wasn't going to be the needle that burst it.

So I left, telling them it was to do my job.

Mum agreed that it was probably for the best, that I needed to take the fight to the exiles. She believed that the battles ahead would come to me whether or not I sought them and it would be better to be ready. But really, it was Dad who understood the most. I knew he recognised the look in my eyes as something similar to what he, too, had once displayed.

After I left Mum and Dad in Switzerland, I spent six months drifting from city to city, picking up odd jobs and failing miserably to pay my way. So, when Josephine tracked down my unlisted number and texted me with an offer of a paid-on-the-side job – fighting two exiles in Prague – I took it.

Since then, in return for her promise to keep our dealings private, I took the odd job when she didn't have local Grigori in place.

For a while it worked well enough. I was alone, the way I had to be, and always ready to move on – something I had to do often. As soon as I felt *him* closing in, I'd bail. And that first year it was really difficult, he was so persistent. There were times I only just managed to skip town before he reached me. But I kept moving, even when it felt like I was pushing through almost-set concrete, determined to keep my distance. I couldn't trust myself to slip up even once. No matter how much I wished I could look into his clear green eyes – the only place I'd ever found myself – one more time.

*Because once will never be enough.*

*A lifetime would fall short.*

For now, Barley Mow in East London was my home and place of non-Grigori work. Despite Mum's attempts to give me piles of cash and Dad's insistence that I at least keep hold of the Amex card that connected to his bank account. After everything that had happened, I needed to do this alone, to be independent, and that meant paying my own way. Even when I was down to my last twenty pounds. Somehow, I'd always found a way. And now I had a pretty good set-up. Although tonight's earlier escapades had no doubt cost me a chunk of next week's rent.

Walking into the small dark bar with Gray, neither one of us was surprised to see that Carter, Milo and Turk had beaten us there. We'd left the scene at the construction site by the time the clean-up crew had arrived, and although Gray had the advantage of a motorcycle – and rode like a madman – Carter simply didn't acknowledge that there was a speed between parked and flooring it.

Ryan and Taxi were there too, Ryan's full-belly laughter sounding out across the small pub, all of them sitting at our usual table in the back corner. Of all the Rogues I'd met since I'd stumbled across Gray one night by chance – and luck – this wayward group made up the ones I saw the most. Looking at the faces around the table, I guess you could call this dysfunctional, slightly bizarre group my friends. It wasn't like my friendships with Steph or Spence, though I barely saw them any more, it was different. What I had with these guys allowed me a comfortable distance.

And it was thanks to our frequent late nights at Barley Mow that I had found my job in the bar and my apartment upstairs.

As I approached, Carter was giving Ryan a foul look – clearly he had been the butt of some joke – but on seeing me his expression morphed into a smirk. He held up his half-finished Guinness. 'Karen's started a tab.'

Milo winked at me over the rim of his beer. And I knew that Ryan and Taxi would have included themselves in the free-round offer simply by association. I quickly tried to decipher just how many drinks they had managed to put away before we arrived.

*Crap.*

I narrowed my eyes at Carter as I went to the small bar to collect drinks for Gray and me and to explain to Karen, my boss and landlady, that the tab would be closing after the next round. The guys would drink the place dry if they didn't have to worry about the bill at the end.

Karen smiled warmly at me, her yellowed teeth noticeable even in the dim pub lighting. She'd been a pack-a-day smoker since she was thirteen, and at fifty-three she had no intention of stopping now. She passed me two beers, her bright orange nails so long they curled around the glasses like claws.

'Honey, you look like you walked into the wrong neighbourhood. Again,' she said in her husky voice, raising her eyebrows at the last.

I grimaced, realising how I must look. I probably should have gone straight upstairs to change first, but after everything that had happened at the tournament, plus being distracted by my overactive imagination at the meat market, I'd forgotten that I'd got a little messy earlier in the night. The guys, of course, barely sported a mark.

'Does it help that I also walked my way out?' I tried.

She shook her head slightly. 'The better question is: did anyone else?'

I couldn't help the small smile. Karen saw us all enough to know that there was … stuff going on around town that normal people had no business knowing about.

I grabbed my drinks. 'Trust me, that neighbourhood is now a safer place for us all.'

'Uh-huh,' I heard her murmur as I walked away.

I placed Gray's drink in front of him and sat down. I could tell he was talking business, and whatever it was, I already knew I'd want in. We all brought in the odd job, but it was Gray and his vast list of mysterious contacts who really kept us on the go.

Carter glared at me as if reading my mind. 'I think we should wait till Miss Steal-a-guy's-limelight has gone to bed for the night before we discuss this.'

'God, are you still whingeing? You got a fight tonight. You got paid, and,' I motioned towards his half-empty glass, 'in more ways than one. Move on,' I said, exhausted more by him than by the night's activities.

*And you're all still alive.*

'I'll take her to bed for you, if it helps out,' Taxi jokingly offered.

'Remind me why you're called Taxi again?' I asked.

He smiled so widely it was impossible not to smile in return. Turk had given him the nickname about forty years ago. They'd been living in apartments next door to one another in Islington – the same ones where they still lived now – and whenever Taxi picked up a girl Turk would know about it because he'd hear some poor now-sober woman hailing a taxi at the top of her lungs at the crack of dawn the following day.

'Violet, I promise I'll give you a ride home in the morning myself.' Taxi waggled his eyebrows.

Ryan hit Taxi on the head. 'Leave her be,' he said, giving me a nod.

Apart from me, Ryan, at thirty-three, was the youngest of the group – though like everyone else he looked barely a couple of years out of his teens. He was also the one whose dimples gave him a look of innocence, which was the exact opposite of Taxi and Carter, whose more angular features and lack of care towards personal maintenance made them seen menacing.

But it was Milo who always caught my eye and reluctant curiosity. While looking Grigori-young, he had a darkness surrounding him that was more than just his tall, slim figure, always-black attire and long jet-black hair. His eyes told a haunting tale, one that as a Rogue he had every right to never share. But we all knew that it had something to do with his particular gift. He was a Darkener – he had the ability to plunge someone into darkness, momentarily blinding them before launching his attack. It was a great defensive weapon against exiles, but it had left its mark on him in the depths of his sad eyes.

*Like me.*

Looking away from Milo and back to Taxi and Ryan, I recognised their slightly bloodshot eyes and lazy smiles. They had clearly been at the bar for a while and looked as if they had passed the one-too-many point a few drinks back. For Taxi, this meant crudeness. For Ryan, it meant genuine flirting.

I glanced at Gray and caught his subtle wink of understanding. Then he got on with business. And this was the way it was with Rogues. We didn't sit around rehashing the events of the night – we moved on to the next job. Gray had already reported to our employer about tonight's events at the meat market. The money had been transferred to us and the clients were having their own people deliver the news to the human in charge. Fine by us.

The Academy Grigori had stayed behind at the construction site to help the humans who had survived, bring in the clean-up crew and mourn the loss of Clive and Annette. We'd done our job, scouted the immediate area and cleared the rooftop, then taken our payment, shaken hands and bailed.

Now Gray had moved on to the details of the new job that had come in from his contact in Rome. An exile they'd been trying to find had fled Italy after taking out an entire church load of people during a single Sunday Mass in a small village just outside Florence.

The exile had posed as a priest.

I was still undecided when it came to my beliefs. I knew there was a place where souls were sent to suffer – my mother had been locked in the pits of Hell since the day she gave birth to me until the day I unwittingly freed her – and there were definitely stories out there with elements of truth. But God? One entity responsible for it all? Heaven? Peace? No, I wasn't sure about that.

What I did know was that dressing up in a priest's outfit and betraying people's faith and trust that way was very, very wrong. No way was I about to miss this hunt.

'They think he's in London and asked us to follow up.'

'Paying?' Carter asked.

Gray sniffed. 'Not a lot. If anything.'

Normally, Carter would argue to go back and settle terms before agreeing to take on the job but one look at my fingers drumming on the table told him it wouldn't work. If he wanted in on the fight, he'd have to get in on the ground level. So he settled for glaring at me and said nothing.

Ryan finished his drink. Karen had already delivered the final round to everyone.

'Taxi and I can start checking in with the London churches,' Ryan offered. 'See if there are any new clergy around or, you know, if there have been any massacres lately.'

Gray nodded. 'Okay. Let's start with that.'

Ryan looked at me and motioned to my empty glass. 'What're you having?' he asked, standing up.

I shook my head. 'A hot shower and bed,' I said, standing up as well.

He smiled, showing his dimples. 'I can work with that.'

Gray was suddenly beside me, wrapping his arm around my waist and pulling me close. I fought the instinctive urge to throw him into the far wall and kept breathing.

'Won't be any room for you, mate.' He glanced at the rest of the guys briefly. 'We'll talk more tomorrow.'

With that, Gray walked me through the back door and up the narrow staircase to my tiny apartment.

'Thanks,' I said once we were inside.

He shrugged. 'Not a problem.'

Rogues had a tendency to get a little handsy after a few drinks, and in our mix I was the only girl. I didn't think any of them seriously liked me, but alcohol often meant heavy flirting and a little too much presumption. Neither of which I handled well. But no one would tread on Gray's territory, so to keep me from having to explain things I couldn't, every now and then Gray would leave the bar with me to make the guys think we had something going on.

I knew we'd have to do the same thing again in a couple of months, and sometimes it annoyed me that it had to be done at all. But I didn't want to have to move on again. Not yet. So, this was the easiest and most peaceful way to deal with it.

'You gonna tell me what that was tonight?' Gray asked from behind me as I switched on my tiny espresso machine.

I knew he'd have something to say. He'd seen my reaction to the bald man, and he'd covered for me when I'd told the other Grigori I hadn't got a good look at the exile who had taken out their leaders.

Waiting for the machine to heat up, I kept busy, pulling out my blade and cleaning it. 'I've seen him before.'

'Who is he?'

'I don't know,' I answered honestly. 'But he's strong, powerful and ...' I closed my eyes, knowing that this last quality was the most frightening. 'He's smart.'

I let the information sink in with Gray. Exiles aren't often smart – it's hard to be when you're completely insane and ruled by emotions you can't control. But very rarely, an old exile comes along who can control the madness. Like Lilith.

'And he wanted to put on a show for you,' Gray said. It wasn't a question.

I gripped the hilt of my dagger tightly, guilt burning my conscience. He might as well have said that Clive and Annette were killed because of me. I pushed my emotions down, bit my lips and nodded jerkily.

'Is this only the beginning?' he asked.

I had a bad feeling we both already knew the answer to that so threw out a different question. 'Have you noticed how the tournaments are becoming less random?'

'Like they're gearing towards something? Yeah. You think he's behind them?'

I shrugged. We'd been hearing rumours from Rogues who passed through. Organised battlegrounds like the one tonight were popping up all around the world. Something was brewing. And seeing the bald exile gave me an all-round bad feeling.

'You hanging out here for a while or heading home?' I asked, turning back to the espresso machine to make my coffee and dodging the questions I couldn't answer. Sometimes Gray stayed a while and then went back down to drink with the guys. It didn't bother me either way. I knew he never once spoke to any of them about what was – or wasn't – going on between us. He just wasn't the type to use our situation to boast.

I could feel his eyes on me but I didn't turn. Eventually, I heard him moving about and I knew he was putting on his jacket. 'Nah. I'll slip down the outside stairs and head home.'

'Okay. I'll see you tomorrow at five, then,' I said, noting Gray's usual groan in response.

'Come on, princess. Surely I just earned myself a week's reprieve?'

I shook my head. 'No way.'

'Damn it, can't you find someone else? We've been going at this for almost a year now. I'm starting to grow girl parts.'

I bit back my smile and headed for the bathroom. Before I closed the door, I glanced back at Gray, who was opening the window to the fire escape that led down to the back alley. '5 p.m. Don't be late.'

# chapter four

*'For the gate is narrow and the way is hard that leads to life,
and those who find it are few.'*

**Matthew 7:14**

**W**inding down after a hunting night always took time. After my shower, I dressed in a pair of leggings, singlet and sneakers, then jumped on my treadmill.

I ran. A lot.

So much so that I'd had to get the life-warranty tread on my running machine replaced. Twice.

I used to run along the streets, working my way towards and around the parks. But more and more I preferred the solitude of my apartment. It might have been what most people would classify as a shit-box, but it was my shit-box. And I'd happily forgone most of my savings and floor space for my treadmill.

I started my workout, knowing that after seeing that bald-headed exile tonight and everything he'd stirred up, I'd be running for hours. Gray had asked me once why I ran towards the exposed-brick wall so my back was to the window. I hadn't bothered with an answer.

He knew I had nothing to run to.

And the world to run from.

Yeah, I still had my rules. No running, no quitting, and no believing in fairytales. And even though I had broken rule *numero uno* in the biggest way possible, I'd reasoned that it was a survival decision and so that made it okay. So, the rules stood.

Somewhere around 1 a.m. I had another shower and got into bed, hoping I'd run off enough energy and tension to get a few hours' sleep. I slept less and less these days, some nights barely managing an hour. If I was lucky, I was able to negotiate three or four. Apart from the dreams I'd started to have, eerily similar to the scene I'd imagined at the warehouse earlier in the night, sleep always left me unprotected. Tonight was no different.

When sleep was almost within reach, dream-like images filled my mind. I was moving, or rather, jumping from one distorted scene to the next, as if sifting through them.

The vision suddenly halted. I was looking over a courtyard. It was evening. The courtyard was lit with small lights climbing up the trunks of the delicate trees that bordered it. In a corner sat a man. He was wearing a charcoal-coloured suit, his jacket slung over the empty chair beside him. His crisp white shirtsleeves were rolled up revealing silver wristbands and bronzed forearms. He was alone and looked like he'd had a long night. He ran his hand through his golden hair, which I noticed was fractionally shorter and darker at the roots than it used to be. I inched closer, despite my desire to move away. His hand paused and he exhaled shakily.

He looked up, right towards my line of sight, and though he had my full attention I couldn't see into his eyes the way I so desperately wanted to.

He dropped his arm and stood up, slinging his jacket over his shoulder, and seemed to slump just a little.

'I miss you. So damn much. So. Damn. Much,' he whispered and then he walked out of the courtyard. Away from me.

As he had every right to do.

My eyes flew open as I breathed uncontrollably, only to find someone sitting at the end of my bed, casually throwing and catching an odd-looking ball with one hand.

I bolted upright, alarmed, my dagger already in hand, as my eyes focused on the intruder.

'Phoenix,' I gasped, lowering my hand. 'Not tonight,' I said, my voice shaking.

'Breathe, Violet,' he said, all too knowingly.

He gave me a moment and then started to throw and catch the ball again. 'Why don't you just ask me what you want to?' he suggested, not stopping his steady rhythm with the ball.

I pushed myself up further, leaning over the edge of my bed to grab my oversized sweatshirt. 'I have no idea what you're talking about,' I said, pulling it over my head. It wasn't easy to lie to angels. They kinda know.

*Doesn't mean I'm not going to lie, of course.*

He gave a small half smile and his chocolate eyes bore into mine, making me shift uncomfortably. I'd forgotten just how much those eyes could affect me. '*Yes*, is the answer. You *are* using your Sight when you find Lincoln. Just before sleep takes hold, a person's mind is most vulnerable and other … parts can push forward.'

*My soul, in other words.*

'What you see is real,' he reinforced.

My stomach lurched and I struggled to maintain my composure as for a brief moment the perfect stranglehold I kept on myself was loosened by his words.

*How do I fight my most defiant and deadly adversary when it is my own damned soul?*

*A soul that will never stop taking and punishing.*

I thought of Lincoln's whispered words. Had he known I was there tonight? All the other times? Had his words been for me? For someone else?

*It's been two years. It's possible.*

'I told you I'd come to you if I wanted to talk,' I said, fisting my hands in an attempt to reel myself back in.

Phoenix leaned his back against the wall and crossed his legs at the ankles. 'Yes. But I thought you might have forgotten that conversation, since I've barely heard from you in two years.'

'I haven't.'

I had only had contact with my angel maker in the past two years, and that had been limited to a few instructions or suggestions about cities he thought I should visit. I hadn't even seen Uri or Nox. I figured that it was because I was doing what they expected: taking out exiles.

He shrugged. 'Well, *I* needed to talk with *you*.'

'That's not the deal we made.'

He'd told me it was my call. It's not that I didn't care for Phoenix. I did. We'd been through so much and though he'd done terrible things, he'd also done good. In the end, he'd sacrificed everything. But it was just a reminder of ...

'I know,' he said, as if reading my thoughts. 'And I *have* stayed away, but it's hard ...' His voice dropped at the end.

I snorted. 'Don't think I don't know you've been lurking around.' I could sense him at times and knew he was keeping tabs on me.

He shrugged, showing no remorse.

'Why now?' I asked, knowing I probably didn't want to hear his answer.

'Two reasons. One, I miss talking to you.' His eyes flashed up, his gaze holding mine for a beat. 'You're the only person who has ever known me – for better and worse.'

When I failed to respond, he tossed the ball and went on. 'And, two, it's difficult to stand back and watch you disappear. Especially when you are using something I gave you in order to do so.'

'I'm not disappearing,' I said, my shoulders tensing. 'I'm very much here, working. I'm doing my job.'

He looked like he was about to argue, but stopped short. 'I looked in on Simon and Tom,' he said softly.

I felt the surge of his guilt and sadness. When Phoenix had given me a part of his essence, he'd also given me a mutation of his gifts. He was an empath and could move like the wind. For me, it wasn't exactly the same. I could move faster than before, and instead of reading and influencing emotions, I can turn them off – something that helped in my daily survival. However, when someone experiences a sudden influx of strong emotions and my guards aren't at full strength, I sensed a little something, and that was what I felt now.

Simon and Tom were two of the children we'd rescued from Lilith's cages. They were still too young to embrace, but Simon must have been getting close. Since many of the kids had no family left to raise them, the Academy had set up a makeshift home and school for them within their walls.

'How are they?' I asked. I thought about them often.

'Strong. Simon is fifteen now and will embrace in less than two years. He'll be an amazing fighter but he's …'

'Compassionate, too,' I said, already knowing this of Simon. His heart was so gentle.

Phoenix nodded, looking down.

I felt my own sadness at his reaction. Did he look away because he thought that I was not?

'He'll be a good addition to the Academy ranks,' I said, moving on.

'That's not what he thinks.'

'No?' I asked, my brow furrowing.

'No, he thinks the moment he has embraced he will be going out to find you.' Phoenix watched for my reaction, which I kept neutral, despite my panic.

'Why would he do that?'

'Because he's strong and strong warriors want strong leaders. He saw you in action, understands what you are capable of. I imagine in his time at the Academy he has seen much, but nothing that compares to …' He trailed off.

'I'm not a leader, Phoenix. I'm a weapon. And I take down everything and everyone in my path. If you care about his future, you should make sure he stays away from me.'

'And maybe you should let other people be the judge of that, Violet.' He said my name so softly, as if he were pleading with my heart. He sighed. 'Don't you ever wonder what he might have said if you'd just hung around a few more minutes that day?' And just like that the conversation veered into forbidden territory.

'Don't,' I warned. 'And coming from you, that's just ... Don't.'

'Why? Because I love you?'

I shook my head, more to myself than him. 'You love me but you want to know why I didn't stay with *him*?'

The lines around his eyes tightened in a pained expression but he didn't look away. 'Am I not allowed to want your happiness because it conflicts with my own?'

I flinched. 'You're an angel now. You don't feel emotions like that.' But he and I both knew I knew better. I just couldn't bear to hear those words from him. From anyone.

He half laughed, his hair flopping forward. The colours were more dazzling than ever, the streaks of purple so rich on top of the midnight black and the highlights of silver like shooting stars. 'I might be an angel, but I will always be fathered by man. Damned to never be enough of anything.'

It was one of the hardest realities for him. It meant that while he didn't suffer the effects of insanity when he was an exile, as an angel he still experienced emotions that were entirely human and so was left feeling constantly lacking. I wished I could explain to him that that was the very thing that made him extraordinary.

He tossed, caught, kept his eye on the ball as he went on. 'Violet, I know what I've done and that the time has passed for me to dare to fight for you. I know we will never be anything more than friends. But I'll always love you. That, I'm afraid, appears to be as innate as my darkness. And I know that this is true because it's more important to me that you are happy, than that I am.'

I gripped my pillow tightly, understanding the magnitude of such a confession from an angel of dark. I wanted to crawl over to him, to sigh deeply and let him hold me.

'Then you'll understand why I won't discuss this,' I said.

Toss. 'Yes.' Catch. 'But I'm in a difficult position because your choices have left you emotionally ruined and physically tormented.'

'Wow,' I whispered. 'Don't hold back.' I rubbed my palms into my eyes, feeling the cold that was always there press against me. Acknowledging it never helped.

'How bad is it?' he asked softly.

I looked away. 'Same as always. I can handle it.'

'Have you considered that perhaps you're not supposed to? That you don't have to bear the pain like some kind of punishment?'

I shook my head. 'Things are the way they are. Leave it at that, Phoenix.' I leaped off the bed and was at my sink in four short strides, grabbing a glass of water. After taking a shaky gulp I turned back to my angelic visitor. 'Please just go.'

He stood and took a step towards me before stopping again. He tossed the ball in his hands one more time, then threw it to me. I caught it and studied it. It was an intricate work of intertwined rope.

'What is it?' I asked, turning it in my hand.

He moved to the window as if pulled towards it, reminding me of my angel maker, who did the same thing.

*Does Phoenix miss the human world?*

'It's a Gordian Knot. No beginning, no end, a constant cycle that appears impossible to unravel.' He took a deep breath. 'There was a prophecy once that whoever undid the knot would become the ruler of Asia. Alexander the Great came along and instead of attempting to untie the knot, he simply took his sword and sliced right through it. And conquered Asia.'

'Okay. So, why are you giving it to me?'

He glanced at me, then back to the window, watching the quiet pre-dawn streets of London. I already knew there would be no sleep for me tonight.

'The Gordian Knot is now a symbol for the unsolvable and yet doable for the right person, with the right tools, who is willing to be quick and decisive.' He turned to me, his hands clasped as I looked down at the ball of rope again. 'Things are about to change, Violet. The question not one of us knows the answer to right now is, just *how much*?'

When I looked up, he was fading. Before he disappeared, he pointed behind me and winked. 'Door,' he said, and was gone.

That moment, there was a knock on the door. I looked at my watch, barely believing that there was now something else to deal with.

*It's 5 a.m., for Christ's sake!*

I walked to the door and checked the peephole. Shock doesn't really cover it. A sense of dread was close to what I felt as I yanked the door wide.

'What the hell are *you* doing here?' I demanded.

# chapter five

*'Be sober minded; be watchful. Your adversary the devil*
*prowls around like a roaring lion, seeking someone to*
*devour.'*

**1 Peter 5:8**

Onyx had barely sat down on one of the my wooden stools when I pounced.

'How bad is it?'

Steph was the only person who knew my address. She wouldn't have given it to Onyx unless something terrible had happened and she couldn't get to me. My mind ran wild and my first thought had been the worst, but I knew I would have felt that.

'Lover boy is fine,' he said, grinning as he answered the unspoken part of my question.

I ignored his comment. 'Steph?'

'Also fine, although still highly annoying. Even I can't bear to go on one more shopping trip with her.'

I swallowed nervously and nodded. Steph and Salvatore were getting married. *I* was the one who was supposed to be there, supporting her, like she'd always done for me. But she understood. Well, as long as I promised to be there on the day. Which I had. It would be my first trip back to New York since … And I'd been trying to ignore the fact that I had no idea how I was going to manage it.

Lincoln was one of Salvatore's groomsmen.

I bit my lip, thinking, and looked up at Onyx. He was wearing dark jeans and a fitted white shirt. He looked like I remembered; his hair black and heavily styled, his features dominated by his high cheekbones, but his eyes had most definitely changed. They were softer.

*Why him? Who would Onyx travel halfway around the world for?*

My throat tightened. 'Spence.' I wasn't asking any more.

Resigned, he nodded once.

'He's not dead. I … I think I would know,' I said quickly. I had healed him once, in Jordan, and though I wasn't certain, something told me it had left a residue, a kind of connection that tethered us in some small way.

'We don't think so either. But he's found himself in a mess, all the same. He's been distracted for months, insisting on mission after mission chasing every lead to do with those tournaments that have been happening all around.'

I nodded to let him know I knew of them.

'Last week he and his partner just upped and disappeared mid-assignment in Texas. He's been off the grid since,' Onyx explained, reaching into his coat pocket and pulling out an envelope, which he slid across the table. 'Till this turned up yesterday. When I told the girl,' he said, using Dapper's nickname for Steph, 'she told me where to deliver it.'

My hands were surprisingly steady as I picked up the well-creased envelope that had nothing but my name above the words, *For her eyes only.*

It was an envelope just like this that had changed my world almost three years ago. A letter my mother had left me.

'It came inside another envelope marked up to look like an energy bill and was addressed to Dapper's PO box,' Onyx said. 'It was postmarked more than a week ago, but we don't check it every day.'

'No one has read this?' I asked suspiciously.

Onyx settled a hard look on me. 'I'm the only one who has even touched it.'

I nodded. I had no need to question Onyx's loyalty. Not after what he'd done – what he'd sacrificed – with Lilith.

Besides, Spence and Onyx had been friends ever since Spence had been there for him the night Phoenix's exiles stormed Dapper's apartment, almost killing them both. Onyx didn't forget his debts.

*Spence.*

He'd wanted to leave with me but I'd said no. He was about to find his partner and I thought his place was with the Academy. He was a proud Grigori, and the Academy was the only family he'd ever known. Besides me.

*Had I been wrong to leave him behind? I miss him every day.*

More like a brother to me than anyone else, he'd been there for me every time I'd needed him. And more.

I started to open the envelope, already dreading what awaited me. I knew, like I'm sure Steph and Onyx did, that he wouldn't have tried to contact me this way unless it was life or death. The thought had my hands trembling.

I'd only seen him once since I'd walked away. He'd come with Steph to meet me in Prague, and he'd brought his partner, Chloe. She'd seemed nice enough, though wary of me – something I couldn't hold against her. With the amount of rumours circulating about me and that night at Lilith's estate, I was surprised she'd managed the meeting so well.

I unfolded the single piece of lined A4 paper while Onyx sat back in his chair, silently watching.

*Eden,*

*Christ, I hope this finds you. I'm gonna take the chance and send it to Onyx. There is no way the Assembly won't intercept if I send it to anyone at the Academy.*

*That night – the one that changed everything – I saw what happened before I pulled Lincoln out of there. I figured you never told anyone, mostly 'cause you wanted to put the whole thing behind you. So, I never told anyone either. But I never forgot him. Or what he took from you.*

*I've been looking for him ever since but never found a thing. It was like he didn't exist. But a few weeks ago, I finally saw him at one of these war nights exiles have started to have.*

*He's behind all of it, Eden.*

*The thing is, he saw me too, and I swear he knew me. He smiled, and that was all. But nothing has ever freaked me out so bad. I grabbed Chloe and ran. And now I can feel him coming. He's got exiles hunting us.*

*Nothing this exile does is by accident. It wasn't me who found him. It was all his doing.*

*I wish I had more I could tell you but all I know is that something nasty is going on. And shit, I sound like a girl, but I don't think I'm getting out of this one alive.*

*One more thing I thought you'd want to know: we've gone off-grid, which means Lincoln will already be looking for me. Eden, you know him, he'll be hell-bent on being front and centre but I don't think this is a battle he can win. Not alone.*

*We took off to Mexico but they're close and now I've got to find a way to get Chloe out of here. She's not like us, Eden. She's not ready for this.*

*I'm sorry to dump this on you. But I've got a real bad feeling trouble is going to find you soon.*

*Don't pack light.*

*Spence*

His handwriting was shaky over the final lines. Spence wasn't just scared, he was terrified.

*Oh, Spence. What have you done?*

I folded the note, not willing to share all of this information with Onyx yet.

'Has anyone heard from his partner?' I asked. If this letter was written more than a week ago, a lot could have happened since.

Onyx hesitated before speaking. 'Well, that's the other reason I'm here.'

I closed my eyes briefly, knowing that this was going to end up being a very tangled story.

'She's at the Academy in New York. When they found her she was in a bad way. She's in a coma. And since the last known person with her was Spence and she can't tell anyone what happened ...'

'They think he did it to her,' I finished incredulously.

'They're not ruling out the possibility. Grigori aren't immune to corruption, and Spence went AWOL. Plus, the one time Chloe did come around she refused to tell them what had happened.'

'Why the hell would she do that?' I snapped.

*Stupid girl.*

Onyx gave a small smile, knowing what I was thinking. 'She must have had her reasons. All she said was. "Find Eden".'

My stomach somersaulted. Only Spence called me Eden. I needed to speak to Chloe.

I braced my hands on my thighs, trying to settle my heart, some beats thumping hard, others fading to nothing. Spence had said that Lincoln would be looking for him. He obviously believed they had leads in New York that I didn't. If I started from scratch I'd be too far behind. And if Spence had found himself the kind of trouble it sounded as though he had, then I was going to need access to intel. And numbers.

I looked at Onyx. 'You came to take me back.'

Onyx raised his eyebrows. 'The girl thought you'd want in,' he said, again using Dapper's term of endearment for Steph.

I looked around my tiny flat: bed, treadmill, cupboard-sized bathroom and not much else. I'd hidden here for the past year. It was just a place. Not a home. No attachments. I knew what Onyx was here for – to take me to New York. To the Assembly. To everything I'd run away from.

And I knew exactly who'd be there.

Mouth dry, I walked over to my grimy window and grabbed the bag that was always half packed and ready to go.

Spence was family. I loved him – no questions, no strings – and I'd made him a promise that I'd always have his back like he'd had mine.

I made my way around the flat, shoving extra bits and pieces into my bag as my memory flashed back to that night. The estate. Lilith. Phoenix on the ground, lifeless. Lincoln, soul shattered, gone. Life draining slowly from my body.

And then there was Spence, who'd refused to let me go into the fight without him. Who'd been focused and strong. Who'd fought by my side and saved Lincoln from the fire when I could not.

Afterwards, he'd driven me to the cliff without question – he'd been the only person I could cope with being around. And it was Spence who'd carried me home.

Onyx watched me curiously as I jammed my passports – I had four – along with weapons and what clothes I could be bothered with into my bag before pausing and stuffing in more weapons.

*Spence* had *said not to pack light.*

I threw the bag over my shoulder and grabbed my mobile phone, sending a quick text message before looking back at Onyx.

*I can do this.*

'The girl was right,' I said.

Onyx tapped his fingers on the table a few times and nodded before standing. 'We have a plane on standby.'

I raised my eyebrows, but quickly let my question go. I didn't need to know how Onyx had managed to get his own plane. I flicked off my only light and left a note for Karen, telling her I had to leave for a family emergency. I also left most of the cash I had to cover my rent for the next few weeks. Just in case.

On the footpath, Onyx hailed a black cab.

'If I'm going back there, I'm doing it my way. Understood?'

Onyx beamed his familiar, wicked smile. 'Oh, I'd expect nothing less.'

I ignored his obvious amusement. 'Who else knows you're here?'

'Dapper, the girl and no doubt her Italian.'

I nodded, aware that if Salvatore knew he'd probably told Zoe too. 'Well, let's keep it to that,' I instructed, sending another quick text. 'And we need to make a stop to pick something up on the way to the airport.'

Onyx slid into the taxi, still smiling even as he shook his head.

'What?' I asked sharply.

'Honestly?'

I narrowed my eyes. 'Yes.'

'I'm just giddy with excitement,' he said, his eyes alight. 'It's as if someone has rebooted my favourite movie just for me and I get to sit back and watch all over again.'

'Still a bastard, then,' I mumbled.

He laughed openly. 'Why fight what works?' He leaned a little closer, and dropped his voice. 'But I'm sure you'll find that not everything has remained quite the same.'

I looked away, fighting my nerves. Did he mean the Academy? Or Lincoln? Or me?

I shook my head. With any luck I'd be in and out of that place in a day or two. I probably wouldn't even see him.

*Yeah. Right.*

I sat a little taller.

*Correction:* he *won't see* me.

'My way,' I reinforced.

'My dear, your way is *always* the most entertaining.'

My eyes narrowed in on him again as the taxi pulled over to the kerb.

'What are we collecting?' Onyx asked.

I looked out the window and saw Gray stalking towards the car, army-green duffle bag slung over his shoulder.

'Reinforcements,' I said, opening the door for him.

After a long look at Onyx, Gray settled his eyes on me. 'You're going to owe me for this, princess,' he said, dumping his bag by his feet.

I was conscious of Onyx's eyes darting between Gray and me, followed by a discreet but clear chuckle as he stretched back into his seat.

'Yes, rainbow,' Onyx practically sang. 'Most definitely, let's do this your way.'

# CHAPTER SIX

*'How well it suits all men, on the subject of chaos, to say that
it is a kind of darkness!'*
**The Nag Hammadi**

I recognised the jet the moment I caught sight of its sleek
black wings.

'Who managed this?' I asked suspiciously as the three of
us stood on the tarmac, bags at our feet, waiting to board.

Onyx snorted. 'Do you really think we could steal a jet
from under that tyrant's nose?'

I frowned, watching as the door opened and the stairs
came down. 'You failed to mention she knew I was coming.'

He rolled his eyes. 'I try to ignore her existence altogether.
How else did you think you'd be getting through the front door?'

Actually I'd had a similar plan myself. They just didn't
realise that I still had direct contact with the Vice of the
Assembly.

'Who are you talking about?' Gray asked from beside me.

'Josephine,' I answered, mixed feelings always rising
to the surface when thinking of her. We'd started off on the
wrong foot. She'd done everything in her power to stop
me from being accepted into the Academy and the general

Grigori community. In the end she'd changed her mind and the Assembly had voted again, this time in my favour – but by then it was a case of bridges burned and lives forever changed.

Though I would never say it out loud, there *was* a part of me that respected her. She did the things she did because of her commitment to her position on the Assembly. The problem was she was relentless with her demands and egotistical. Once Josephine decided on something, there was no swaying her or standing in her path, which was a problem, considering she was wrong as often as she appeared to be right. And that limited my respect for her.

'That bitch from Santorini?' Gray spat, looking like he was ready to get back in the taxi and head home.

'Yep.'

He pulled out his phone and started to tap away.

'What are you doing?' I asked.

'Putting a team on standby in New York. Last time I saw that cow she tried to lock me up.'

There were a few reasons Gray refused to deal with the New York Academy, but Josephine was the main one.

'You too?' I asked, my tone lightening.

Gray scowled at me. Rogues took their freedom very seriously.

'She *still* wants me behind bars,' Onyx said dryly from my other side.

I couldn't hold back a small smile, surprised how easy it was to slip into old habits with Onyx around.

Gray, still unhappy, eyed me suspiciously. 'And why would she give *you* a ticket in?'

Yeah. Gray was good at what he did.

I followed Onyx up the steps of the jet and looked back at Gray, contemplating how much I wanted to give away. 'We stayed in contact after ...'

'After you bailed on everyone?' Onyx offered eagerly.

I shot him a glare and tossed him my bag to stow.

He caught it with a grunt and smiled. 'Good thing we were able to avoid the metal detectors,' he said, the tell-tale clinking sounds of its contents clear as he hauled the bag into one of the overhead compartments.

'Somehow she got my mobile number,' I explained to Gray as he followed me aboard. 'She's the one who sends me jobs from time to time. If I'm not working on something else, I take them.'

This interested Gray. He realised some of the jobs I'd brought him and the other guys in on must have been for the Academy, too. I worried briefly that he'd be offended that he'd inadvertently worked for Josephine, but he just said, 'She thinks highly of you, then?'

I shrugged, taking a seat at the back of the jet, from where I could see everything. 'More like she figures I can get the job done. Either way I'm dispensable.'

Putting his bag away in the same overhead compartment Gray smiled, satisfied with my way of thinking. Neither of us was easily fooled. 'Does anyone else know about your arrangement with her?' he continued.

'No. And I want to keep it that way,' I answered, eyeing Onyx.

Onyx's smile widened. 'I give you my word, I will only tell two ... three people at most.'

I rolled my eyes. 'You haven't matured at all, I see.'

'Whereas you look decidedly aged,' he quipped.

If he thought that was going to upset me, he was wrong. I was pleased that the past two years showed in my appearance. I would turn twenty in a couple of months and it was only a matter of time before things in the ageing department slowed to non-existent. The last thing I'd wanted was to spend the next ten years looking like a teenager. I caught my reflection in the plane window as we took off. Yes, I did look older. I was slimmer, my cheekbones more defined. My eyes, still lacklustre hazel, betrayed having seen more than they should though I didn't look into them for long.

There was no doubt I was stronger, leaner and had changed in many other ways. I glanced at the reflection of my long dark hair, pulled back in a tight ponytail. It wasn't practical. And when my life had become about little more than training and hunting, I knew it would be the logical step to chop it off, but … I hadn't.

*Because he always liked it long.*

I shut down my runaway thoughts and refocused by planning how to spend the flight. The first half I decided to dedicate to drilling Onyx for every last detail he had about Spence's mission and whereabouts. Mostly, I wanted to know more about his partner, Chloe. We'd only met that one time. Even Spence hadn't known where I was living. Not because I didn't trust him to keep it a secret, but because I didn't want him to carry those kinds of secrets for me. It was hard enough asking it of Steph.

Keeping it from Griffin and Dapper, who I knew had been hurt by my leaving the city without explaining myself, was one thing but Lincoln … he was one of Spence's best friends.

Steph and I never spoke about Lincoln. She knew I couldn't. But I knew that after I'd left he had been hard on her on the few occasions he'd seen her. It had reached the point where Salvatore had had to step in. Words had been exchanged. With fists.

I couldn't bear to let the same thing happen between Lincoln and Spence. It wouldn't be fair. Lincoln deserved to know that Spence could always be honest with him.

The one time we'd managed to meet, Steph had taken care of everything to coincide with one of Spence and Chloe's Academy assignments in Prague. We'd had lunch at a hidden-away restaurant in Old Town and I'd been intrigued to finally meet Spence's partner. It became obvious that Chloe was daunted by the world she was now a part of, but I could understand that. She'd seemed strong in her own way and happy to follow Spence's lead. I could tell instantly that Spence was protective of her in that way that Grigori partners are – on a platonic yet deep and uncompromising level.

*The one at which Lincoln and I had epically failed to remain.*

Chloe had watched me cautiously and with fascination. I had wondered fleetingly if she was jealous of the obvious connection Spence and I shared, which in many ways reflected a Grigori partnership, but I quickly discovered she was simply too kind of heart to be that negative.

All in all, I'd liked her. And she had respected my privacy, not asking about all the rumours: that I am the only Grigori made by a Sole angel; that my abilities are more angelic than Grigori; that I can walk with angels. Hell, I'd even been told by a Rogue – who had no idea he was talking to the very subject of his gossip – that I was the second coming, and that I would be the great weapon of Hell. Even *I* still didn't know what I was. But he'd been right to call me a weapon. That much I knew was true.

Onyx, though strangely uncomfortable when it came to the subject of Chloe, wasn't able to shed much more light on the matter, other than confirming what Spence had implied in his letter.

'She sees the good in everyone,' he said, shaking his head. 'Even exiles. Spence worries that she isn't cut out for this life.'

The second part of the flight was spent with my eyes closed, rebuilding my walls and locking down all my emotions in the place that no one can reach.

Gray's talents had been my saving grace. Rogues tended to work with their defences at a higher level than the Academy Grigori. They had to; most Rogues were partnerless, whether by circumstance or choice. They didn't have someone on constant standby to supercharge their naturally enhanced healing abilities. But when Gray was dumped on the island of Santorini a few years back – another story he'd refused to share – and was forced to survive alongside the very powerful exile Irin and his Nephlim children, he'd taken Rogue strength to new heights.

He'd taught himself how to completely shut down the senses and become undetectable to exiles. It wasn't something Academy Grigori had ever thought to do, since our outward senses alerted us to exile presence as well. But thanks to Gray, I had learned the skill and discovered its many benefits. It helped keep me hidden, but it also worked like a glue of sorts, holding me together when the coldness tried to tear me apart from the inside.

In my efforts to meditate, I drifted off to sleep.

*Trumpets sounded. The thunder of hooves rampaged.
Thousands of horses – all white – charged towards the
terrifying dragon.*

*The scaled beast's roar was deafening, its spiked wings
spanning football fields. It was ferocious and intent on
causing maximum devastation.*

*As the dragon carved its way through legions of
warriors mounted on valiant stallions, it cleared a path for
the angel who commanded them all. The power the beast
exuded was tremendous, thickening the air and making my
lungs constrict. Warriors fell. Horses staggered to their
knees and rolled. Blood spilled and cries of agony rippled
through the almost tangible atmosphere.*

*I strained to see, my vision darting back and forth between
the angel and the dragon. Just as the way cleared, I gasped.*

I bolted upright so quickly I tipped out of my seat and onto my
knees. I leaped to my feet and made my way to the bathroom,
where I scooped cold water onto my face.

A dream. It had been a dream. A very real, very disturbing
dream. The same as the ones I'd been having for the past two
weeks. And, more troubling, the same as the flash vision I'd
experienced in the meat market.

All was quiet in the hour or so before we landed. Gray was
asleep and I presumed Onyx was too. I paced up and down
the centre aisle, releasing a few shaky breaths, fighting the
ghosts of my past.

When I passed Onyx he spoke quietly, startling me. 'You've changed.'

I kept pacing. 'Yes.' I swallowed. 'I had to.'

'Me too.' His response surprised me, stopping me in my tracks.

'I'm not sorry, Onyx,' I said, softly. 'A part of me will always carry the guilt of taking your choices from you and making you human, but if I hadn't you would've ...'

He nodded, sadly, showing me a truth in his eyes I'd never glimpsed before. 'I would've killed you and done untold things of horror.' He took a deep breath. 'They're not all bad, you know, angels malign – it's not that they're evil; they just see the value in the negative. Without it there is very little way to gauge the positive. As you know, for exiles – whether light or dark – clarity is not theirs. Everything – envy, greed, hatred, anger – it's all heightened. Exiles feel immense power and are driven by immense desire to simply act and effect change to their liking. It's their reality, and for them, it's addictive.'

I nodded, understanding as best as I could. I noticed that Onyx referred to exiles as 'they', no longer including himself in the same category.

Insanity and power are a perilous combination, which was why exiles of light were no better. The answer was always power and force, the solution always their own; and when they were in human form, that meant some form of physical violence.

'I still struggle within the confines of an only-human body,' Onyx went on. 'But that's not all you forced on me.'

I looked down, waiting for whatever nail he was going to drive in.

'You gave me clarity.'

I glanced up and he shrugged.

'Such a simple thing. It took months for it to finally settle and then even more time to come to terms with *what* I had become. Pride is brutal when stripped, whether it be from angel, exile or human. But it is also a gift when needed.'

I listened, dumbstruck by his confession.

'I'm not exactly sure what I am now,' he mused. 'I have an eternity of patchy memories, an inherent darkness that will never leave and, though I am mostly human, I am uniquely aware of what is not. And I have clarity. For the first time I have someone … I have *people* I would stand beside and fight with – not for my own purposes, but for theirs – because I choose to.' Onyx looked into my eyes for a moment and, I was suddenly certain, saw too much. 'Dare I say, because of you, I have come the closest in my existence to being … part of a family.' His voice caught on the last word. 'So,' he straightened, clearing his throat. 'No. No apology required.'

*Jesus, Mary and Joseph, Onyx really has changed.*

After a few stunned beats, I nodded. 'Thank you.'

His smile turned fiendish, and decidedly more familiar. 'No. Thank *you*. I can barely wait to get you to New York. I'd sell tickets to the event if I were willing to give up my front-row seat.'

'And what event would that be?' I asked, crossing my arms.

'Oh, come on. You and Lincoln in a room together? Soulmates. Once joined and now parted. Why, your story will be one for the new-age bible – the cautionary tale of dos and don'ts and the tragedy that lies between. No doubt we are headed for the greatest chapter yet.'

I shook my head. 'Sorry to disappoint. I'm going to get Spence and that's it. I'll be in and out, job done before there is any time for anything else.'

Onyx chuckled. 'Still deluding yourself, I see. Fabulous!'

When we touched down I sent Josephine a text:

*At JFK. Thanks for the ride.*
*Can I trust you to keep this to yourself?*

Her response was immediate:

*I won't tell a soul. But don't fool yourself.*
*He will find out.*

I sighed as I read her message, looking up to see Gray watching me carefully.

'Are you going to tell me why I'm coming along?' he asked.

He'd known it was important. And I knew he could smell a good fight ahead, so he'd come along, no questions asked, up until this point.

'Back up,' I answered. 'I never know what to expect from Josephine and I need someone who is definitely on my team.'

Gray nodded, understanding.

'And ...'

'Yes?' Gray raised his eyebrows.

'I need you to help me keep my guards up.'

Gray studied me for a moment. 'He's going to be there?'

I nodded. 'And I can't let my walls down. Not even for a moment.' I held his gaze, needing him to understand. It wasn't why Gray had trained me for these past ten months; that had been to help me fight so I could get close to exiles and remain hidden. But it had had a two-fold effect, which I imagined he'd suspected: it had also helped me block my connection to Lincoln. So much so that Lincoln had suddenly stopped tracking me. He'd always stayed close, pursuing me relentlessly, and then one day, when I was getting ready to bail on London … it all just stopped.

If I wanted to have any chance of surviving while being in his proximity now, I'd need to keep my walls up – I couldn't imagine what might happen if they were to come down. In many ways, Gray had taught me how to cage my soul.

'You're headed for trouble, Violet. You won't be able to control it twenty-four seven, especially at night.' He gave me a loaded look.

I didn't need to think further than last night to know what he meant. As Phoenix had explained, the time between rest and sleep was when my guards faltered. A definite problem.

I turned to Onyx. 'Any chance you have somewhere we can stay?'

Onyx, who'd been watching, enraptured, grinned. 'I have the perfect place.'

It was late evening and stepping out of the car outside the Academy buildings felt strange. I couldn't help but remember the first time I'd arrived there. How different my view of the world, and of life, had been then. Manhattan, such a densely exile-populated city, had completely overwhelmed my angelic senses.

I pushed down the immediate memories of Lincoln – how he'd kissed me in the very place I now stood; they way he'd taken the burden of the senses from me and released them. I still had all five, not that I openly shared that information. It was just one more thing I knew I might never understand.

At least now, thanks to Gray's help, they were muted. I registered the flavour of apple on my tongue, the sounds of birds crashing into trees. I smelled flowers, the fragrance so mixed it was as though I was in a city-sized florist, but without being overwhelming. Not even when the contradictdory sensations of ice and heat ran through my bones and blood, or when the images of morning and evening played in my peripheral vision was I taken away from myself.

I felt a boost of confidence. Yes. I could do this. I was stronger than ever. I was faster. I had more weapons. More control. And stronger defences. My powers in every way had developed.

And Onyx was right – I was most definitely *not* the girl I had been.

# chapter seven

*'Do not fear those who kill the body but cannot kill the soul.*
*Rather fear him who can destroy both soul and body in Hell.'*

**Matthew 10:28**

*G*oddamn it. He was everywhere!

I could feel his presence even on full alert and with my guards up, supposedly working as protective shields around my body and senses. My soul was unkindly defiant. But I kept it under control, confident that I was doing enough to keep myself hidden from the city's exiles, and most importantly, from him.

'This way,' I said, causing both Onyx and Gray to look at me questioningly as I led them around the back of one of the Academy buildings.

When we reached a small door that could only be opened from the inside, I knocked.

It was unlocked immediately, light beaming out brightly as it opened.

'Bloody hell,' Gray mumbled behind me.

'And I'm so thrilled to see you brought your friends, Violet,' Josephine said, lips pursed as she held the door open. 'I hope you understand that *he*,' she lifted her chin in Onyx's direction, 'is very much unwelcome within these walls. We do still have *some* standards.'

Onyx snorted. 'There is a saying that I do look forward to sharing with you one day soon,' he taunted.

I sighed, knowing it was a runaway train.

Josephine, of course, boarded. 'And I'm dying to know,' she said sardonically.

Onyx tapped his fingers lightly against his temple as if deep in thought as he glanced between Josephine and me. 'I believe it goes something like: "The Queen is dead. Long live the Queen."'

*Hell.*

I really did not need to start things off this way.

Josephine plastered a cruel smirk on her face. 'Well, I can imagine that thoughts of death do consume much of your time, Onyx. Is that a grey hair I spot?'

'Seriously?' Gray intervened. 'Did we just step onto the playground?'

I turned to Onyx. 'We'll meet you later on,' I told him, leaving no room for discussion. Then I looked back at Josephine. 'It's midnight and we've had a long day, Josephine. Gray comes with me or I don't come in, and we both know you wouldn't be standing at this door if you didn't want me here.'

Her eyes narrowed briefly but she opened the door fully and stood aside. 'I see time hasn't improved your manners,' she muttered. 'He can join you, as long as he can behave and show some civility.'

Gray ignored Josephine and nudged me. 'You're gonna owe me on the epic after this.'

I had a feeling he was right.

After Onyx stalked off, Josephine led us along a number of corridors before taking us in a coded lift up to the top floor of 'Command' building – into the heart of Academy territory.

She ushered us into a vacant meeting room and took her position at the head of a large oval table. The room was sparsely furnished, the ebony table, surrounded by a dozen boardroom-style chairs, taking up the majority of the space. The door and three of the walls were painted linen white, while the other wall was made entirely of glass and frosted white in typical Academy fashion. Gray and I took seats opposite one another.

Josephine looked exactly the same as I remembered. Her brown hair with strong auburn streaks was pulled back in a severe manner and she wore a deep purple pencil skirt and black fitted shirt. Her heels were off-the-charts high and she wore them with the ease of someone slopping around in slippers – though, of course, nothing about Josephine was sloppy. She was as immaculate and as cold-looking as ever as she settled her aqua-blue eyes on me.

'What do you know?' she started.

*Okay, so clearly we're not bothering with niceties.*

'Spence is missing. Chloe is in a coma but the one time she did come around she asked for me. And some people *mistakenly* think it's possible Spence has been corrupted.'

Josephine nodded. 'And while I'm sure that is not all of it, it's a good enough place to start, I suppose. And what is your intention from this point? You must realise that this is an Academy issue. Any decisions on how to proceed will be made through the Assembly.'

*In other words – through her.*

But this was where my status as a Rogue helped.

I leaned back in my chair casually, all but putting my feet up on the perfectly polished table. 'Well, we are going to have to discuss that. You see, I'm not Academy and I do not answer to the Assembly. But we both know you want me here, for whatever reason that may be.'

Josephine's mouth twitched. 'What are you proposing?'

'Why did you bring me here?' I countered.

Josephine looked down briefly and I could tell she was deciding how much she was prepared to say.

*Games. It's always the same with her.*

'Spencer was on a mission with his partner. It captured my attention. I'd very much like to know what he discovered and I believe you are possibly the best chance we have of finding him. Besides that, I also believe it is time some things were settled and having you here might do that once and for all.'

I watched her suspiciously. Did she know of the bald, briefcase-wielding exile? Did she know he was behind the tournaments? I was positive there was more to it, but she didn't trust me any more than I trusted her. Frankly, I was surprised she'd given me this much information.

'I'm here for Spence, pure and simple. I want to get him out of whatever trouble he's in. If I have to take down a bunch of exiles in order to make that happen,' I shrugged, 'that's just fine with me. You and the Academy can take all the credit and call the mission whatever you want. But I'll do it my way and on my terms.'

'And if I don't agree?' she replied sharply.

I raised my eyebrows. 'You know what I'm capable of. Do you, for one second, believe I won't walk right out of here and go and get him anyway? But I warn you, if it goes that way, any semblance of mutual respect between us will be over. We are not now, nor will we ever be, friends, but do you really want me as your enemy?'

Josephine glanced at Gray, no doubt wondering if having me as an enemy also meant making one of Gray, one of the most respected Grigori among the Rogue community. The flat smile he gave her seemed to be all the confirmation she needed.

'I never wanted you as an enemy,' Josephine said. 'I wanted you as part of the Academy, if you recall. I still do.'

'I recall everything, Josephine. We've all made our choices and we all live with the consequences. But right now, all I care about is Spence. And if you're hoping to use this as an opportunity to make me a part of this Academy, you will be sorely disappointed.'

I knew I was coming off bullish, but I needed to establish these things before we got any further. Josephine wasn't sitting here out of the goodness of her heart and most certainly not for Spence. She had an ulterior motive.

'You will not disrespect Academy procedure or the role of the Assembly while you are here. Nor will you attempt to recruit any Academy Grigori to your Rogue ranks,' she said.

'I never have,' I retorted, offended by the suggestion. 'And anyway, I won't be staying here.'

She raised an eyebrow.

'We've organised more ... neutral accommodation,' I explained, keeping my expression blank.

She saw through it immediately. 'He's running the mission.'

'Put someone else on it,' I fired back.

She shook her head. 'He's the best. Would you suggest we did less for Spencer?'

I took a breath. There was no question when she put it like that.

'Violet, there is no way to avoid him.'

'We'll see,' I replied.

'He's running a strategy meeting right now. If you want to find out what the latest is, I'd suggest you listen in.'

'I'd rather go to see Chloe,' I threw back, ignoring my racing heartbeat.

Josephine stood and started for the door. 'Priorities, Violet. Chloe is unconscious and is not going anywhere. The intel you need to help find your friend is just down the hall. What will it be?'

*Shit.*

I took a deep breath and pushed my scrambling thoughts aside. 'I'm not going anywhere I'll be seen.'

Josephine smiled. 'I thought you might feel that way. Don't worry, you're covered,' she said, pulling two black silk robes from a hook on the back of the door, handing them to me.

I held them up and noticed their hoods. I passed one to Gray who gave it the same once-over.

'Really?' he groaned.

I should've just legged it and found another way to track down Spence. But I knew I'd be taking a risk with his life and that he would never do that with mine.

*Damn it.*

'Really,' I replied throwing on the cloak and pulling the hood down to cover my face while I concentrated on keeping my guards locked tight.

'This way,' Josephine said, an unmistakable sound of victory in her voice. Suddenly I felt like everyone's plaything.

Each step down the quiet hallway broke me further in two. Half of me felt each movement like I was wading through quicksand, while the other half was tripping over itself to urge me on, knowing what was behind the door ahead.

Gray grabbed my arm as Josephine reached for the door handle. 'You can do this,' he said into my ear, his voice showing no doubt.

I nodded, relieved that he was here with me. 'I know.'

And I *would* do this. I had to. I'd spent the past two years doing nothing but growing stronger. I could stay in control of this situation.

*For Spence.*

We shuffled quietly into the back of another meeting room. Most members of the Academy might have been tucked into bed for the night, but here I could sense a couple of dozen people surrounding me. Ignoring the particular awareness that was overwhelming me, I peeked out from beneath my hood. The room was about twice the size of the one we'd just left and was full of Grigori. Some were seated around a central table, but most were without chairs and standing around the edges, providing enough of a crowd that we were able to remain unnoticed at the back of the room. Mostly.

Someone I couldn't see from my position was talking about Spence and Chloe, discussing their last known location before Spence had dropped off the grid.

'They were in Austin. But we found Chloe at the airport, so we have to assume Spencer was going somewhere from there. He could be anywhere in the world by now.'

Someone else went on to explain Chloe's current condition. While the long-winded run-down went on, I looked around a little more. The first people I recognised were Salvatore and Zoe. I smiled when I saw Steph positioned near the head of the table. It had been more than six months since I'd seen her. She'd let her hair grow a little longer and had given up her old spritzy style for an edgier blunt cut. It really worked for her. I also noted the diamond ring on her wedding finger I'd only seen before in pictures and my smile increased.

On the other side of Steph sat Rainer and Hakon, and Josephine had just moved into position beside them at the head of the table, seeming content at this stage to simply listen. Drenson, the head of the Academy, was not at the table.

Rainer moved her chair closer to Josephine as she looked towards Gray and me – the two cloaked strangers. Most people had remained oblivious to our entrance, but Rainer had noticed and was enquiring.

Before putting my head back down to maintain my anonymity, I saw Josephine swing a graceful but dismissive hand towards Rainer who, clearly unhappy, moved her chair back to its previous position.

Finally, though I forced myself not to look, my attention drifted to the right, my entire being humming with the effort.

Torture of any description would have been kinder. I took one agonising breath after another, but it didn't stop it; the distinctive impression of honey lazily trickling its way into my throat and settling over every inch of my body. I could sense the very spot where he stood, could imagine his posture, his eyes, his lips.

*Does he sense me? Would he still want me? Would he ask me to stay? Would he hate me and order me to leave? Would he show me the pain in his eyes that my Sight forced on me on those nights I unwittingly travelled to him?*

My hands started to shake.

*If only I could completely block myself from myself.*

The sound of his voice caused me to freeze. 'You're all speculating,' he said – the first words I'd heard directly from his mouth since the night I was strung up to a cross as Phoenix shot arrows into my body and Lincoln sent me all of his power through our soul bond. He'd kept giving it to me until there'd been nothing left. And just before he'd collapsed and I'd closed my eyes, he'd screamed his final words: '*I'm yours. Always. Always!*'

Those words had haunted me ever since.

I could sense him still, on the far side of the room. And hearing his voice, I couldn't stop myself from looking through the tiny opening in my hood. My eyes did not need to sift, they found him as easily as the sun finds day. He stood with his back to the room, hands in his pockets. Wearing a navy shirt that was tucked in at his waist, he was broader and clearly stronger than ever.

Slowly, he turned and I braced.

But as he faced the room, his eyes did not move in my direction. Not once. And with a broken breath, fraught with emotion, I realised he was oblivious to my presence. I glanced at Gray, who gave my arm a reassuring squeeze. My shields were blocking him.

Another person stood up at the far end of the table and I saw that it was Max. Morgan sat beside him, and beside her, I recognised Mia.

'Lincoln, it's the best we have right now. Until Chloe wakes up, at least.'

'When can we expect that?' he snapped, spinning his attention towards Salvatore and Zoe. I was shocked to see such harshness coming from him.

Zoe spoke up. 'She came around two days ago for a few minutes and that was it. She could wake up at any time.'

'And she said *nothing* when she woke?' Lincoln was watching them carefully, as if he knew she was keeping something back.

I held my breath.

Zoe crossed her arms and leaned back in her chair. I couldn't help but smile a little to see she seemed much the same with her light brown hair – currently with cherry-red ends – and military-style jacket. 'Just gibberish.'

'Gibberish?' he repeated, his tone now flat.

'Yep,' Zoe said, popping the 'p' casually, though I could tell she was wary of Lincoln's mood.

*He is different.*

Steph cleared her throat. 'Lincoln, we've narrowed down the likely possibilities by checking outgoing flights at the time he was at the airport and we've had maps drawn up. Also, since he was in one of the domestic terminals he was almost certainly headed somewhere in the States. We've set out the most probable options on these grids. I suggest that we put some conductors to work and see if they can scour the areas Scouts could also start fielding the perimeters for exile activity. You never know, locating a spike in exile presence might lead to something.'

Steph was … wow. I was so proud of her. She'd just taken on a full room of Grigori warriors. She was human and one of the youngest people in the room but where they failed to find direction she had offered it. They were so lucky to have her.

Lincoln, however, took a deep breath and I noticed that he didn't look at her once, even as he listened.

Finally, he nodded to her. 'Set it up.' Then he addressed the room. 'Spence is one of ours. He's stood by each and every one of you without hesitation at some point. He's family.'

My heart clenched.

Lincoln cleared his throat. 'I've heard the speculation, and while nothing will be overlooked, make no mistake: this is a rescue, not a hunt. We bring him home. We do it right. We do it smart. Call in your sources, contacts, allies; anyone you know. He's out there and someone knows where. You have until nine o'clock tomorrow morning, then we meet back here.'

I straightened as everyone quickly started to file out, leaving Gray and me wedged in a bad spot, making it difficult for a quick escape.

*Come on, come on.*

I looked up at Gray, who knew I needed to get out. But causing a scene to push through everyone was not a good idea.

'What now?' he whispered beside me.

My eyes darted around anxiously but I ignored the flight instinct that was gnawing at me and stood still. 'Let's wait for Josephine to get us out of here and take us to Chloe.'

We stayed in the corner. Steph spoke quietly to Salvatore and Zoe. I was tempted to approach her but knew it was smarter to wait until she was alone. None of them had noticed Gray and me yet.

Rainer and Hakon were visibly upset as they kept Josephine back in a hushed conversation.

I edged back into the wall as I watched Lincoln collect his files from the table and then stride towards the door, Mia in step behind him. It struck me how in charge he appeared, and even though his face looked so familiar, barely aged, he seemed somehow older.

He was going to walk right by us. Slowly, trying not to arouse any attention, I turned towards Gray to shield myself even more. But I flinched mid-turn when, from behind, a hand, blazing hot, wrapped tightly around my upper arm. A voice I knew better than my own spoke quietly into my ear from the other side of the silk hood.

'Would you think me such a fool that you could be here, in this city, this building, this *room* and me not know about it?'

I swallowed, frozen. I couldn't turn to face him. I couldn't lift my head. Even my soul was stunned.

Lincoln didn't seem to be bothered by our proximity, nor by my failure to respond. His grip only tightened to the point of almost painful. But it wasn't, it was just ... strong and maybe something else. My breath caught.

'Lincoln!' Josephine's sharp voice carried out across the room. 'I'll ask you to remove your hand from my guest.'

I felt Lincoln's body go rigid behind me. He dropped his hand from my arm and spun. I turned too, keeping my hood down to cover my identity from the rest of the room. From beneath, I watched what I could.

'You *brought* her here?' he asked, his voice disbelieving.

I watched Josephine's patent black high heels move closer as she strode towards us. 'An invitation was extended,' she answered smoothly.

I could see Steph's feet now too, as she moved towards us. I looked up a little to see her face, a picture of concern as she put the pieces together. She knew it was me.

'And three guesses who she brought with her,' Lincoln said, his words barely audible.

'Do you think she has no right? As I understand from the many stories I've heard, she saved Spencer's life once before.'

Lincoln looked down and half laughed, but there was no humour in the action. 'Yes. Well, whose life hasn't she saved?'

He spun back towards me. I dropped my head, reeling, and froze in place as his words hit me.

'Do what you must to satisfy whatever curiosity brought you here. Stay out of my way. I have people who rely on me and I don't have the luxury of being able to turn my back on them.' And with that final barbed comment he stepped out of the room, Mia following silently.

Josephine, noticing I still hadn't lifted my head, cleared her throat. 'Zoe and Salvatore, will you please make the necessary arrangements to escort our guest to the infirmary first thing in the morning? If you'll excuse me for now, I have to confer with the Assembly. Rainer and Hakon, could you please join me?'

I wanted to argue with Josephine, insist on visiting Chloe now, but speaking required more control than I had at the moment.

I could sense Rainer's reluctance to leave the room. She wanted to be sure it was me beneath the cloak. She'd been my mentor and we'd grown close when I'd been here last. But I couldn't show her. It was taking everything I had to hold still.

Once they had cleared the room and it was just Salvatore, Zoe and Steph left, Gray nudged my arm. 'That's your girl there, isn't it?'

When I failed to respond, he just nodded as if he understood. He pulled back his hood and spoke to Zoe and Salvatore. 'Couldn't show me somewhere I could clean up a little, could you? We had a long flight.'

'Of course. We'll show you to the guest bathrooms,' Salvatore said, in perfect English, grabbing Zoe's arm and dragging her to the door. Zoe stared at me the whole time, mouth agape.

I remained still.

When the door finally closed, I let out my breath and took a deeper one to replace it. And then my legs gave out.

Steph caught me, falling to the ground with me as I breathed in the lingering honey and absorbed the remains of the first touches of sun I'd felt in two years.

I was strong. I was a warrior. A weapon.

But seeing him, feeling his presence, crushed my heart all over again.

# Chapter Eight

*'Out of suffering have emerged the strongest souls; the most massive characters are seared with scars.'*

**Kahlil Gibran**

'**B**reathe, Vi,' Steph whispered in my ear.

I couldn't believe it. A few minutes in the same room as him had caused a complete wrecking effect on me. While he had remained just fine.

'It's okay. You're allowed to care,' Steph continued to soothe.

But that was just the thing. I *wasn't* allowed. I'd given up my rights to him. And he'd seemed so ... indifferent. And different. He was stronger but also harder. He was a leader now. No doubt a good one, but I couldn't help but wonder – was he a kind one? The leader I'd always imagined he would be?

*Christ, it hurts so much.*

I took a few deep breaths and reminded myself of all the reasons I couldn't storm down the hall, throw myself at him and beg for forgiveness. All the reasons things had to be the way they were. I pushed into my resources and found the switch I had come to rely on for simple survival and shut it all down, feeling my emotions slip away. It was a numbing gift that had come with a warning, but the need for it outweighed any potential negative consequences.

'I'm okay,' I said when I was sure I had a handle on things again. I pulled back my hood and gave Steph a small smile. 'I was just caught off-guard. Hey.'

Steph smiled back. 'Hey yourself. So, Onyx found you okay?' She bit her lip nervously.

I nodded. 'You did the right thing. It's Spence, Steph. Of course you did.'

She breathed out a sigh of relief and slumped a little beside me while I took another moment to pull myself together. 'Please don't tell everyone I'm here yet. I just … I can't face all the questions about … everything.'

'You don't need to ask. I've always kept your confidence. I always will.'

I reached over and pulled her into a hug. 'I know. And I love you for it.'

'Ditto,' she said, hugging me back. 'And at least we get to see each other. Maybe when we have Spence back and we've all taken turns kicking his ass we can go over my wedding plans. I picked up your dress the other day,' she said, her eyes twinkling with excitement.

I hid my cringe, not wanting to face the wedding issue yet. Or the fact that I was going to have to stand on the other side of the aisle looking at Lincoln while Steph married the man of her dreams.

I smiled. 'Let's just get Spence back first.'

She nodded, happy enough to let it go for now. 'Agreed. Why don't we get your rooms organised and I'll take you to see Chloe first thing. I figure the sooner the better since Lincoln won't take long to get a clear mind and figure out that will be your next move.'

I blinked. 'He seemed pretty clear-headed when he was speaking to me,' I said.

She scoffed. 'Oh, *please*. A hundred bucks says he's bent over hyperventilating somewhere right now just like you.'

She seemed so sure. I, however, wasn't.

'Anyway,' Steph went on, 'he's going to flip when he finds out Zoe and Sal didn't tell him everything Chloe said, but that's Josephine's problem to deal with. At least I know he won't bother *me*.'

'Why?' I asked, knowing I probably shouldn't.

She shrugged. 'He's always known I've been in touch with you. He made things pretty intense in the first few months, as you know. He and Salvatore had a run-in. Eventually they worked it out and made up, but ... he's never been able to be normal around me since. I think he believes that if I'd just told him in the beginning where you were he would've ... you know, fixed things.'

I shook my head. 'He wouldn't have, Steph. He would've just wound up more hurt. Me too. You did the right thing and I'm so sorry I left you to deal with this stuff,' I said, realising sadly that after we brought Spence back it might really be time for me to cut ties completely. I couldn't keep putting her in this position.

Steph watched me as if she could see my thoughts. 'When the alternative was never speaking to you again, it really wasn't a high price to pay,' she said sternly. 'And anyway, if I hadn't known where you were, Onyx would never have found you. It all worked out. Lincoln's just ... Lincoln.'

'I suppose,' I mumbled. But I was feeling better. Back in control. I stood up, pulling Steph after me, keen to close this conversation. I took the time to reposition my hood. People might already be gossiping that I was there but I wasn't ready to confirm it yet. 'No chance of seeing Chloe tonight?' I asked.

Steph shook her head. 'The infirmary's closed for the night. Besides, you look like you could do with some sleep.'

Despite the fact even my fingernails were exhausted I didn't think I'd be getting much sleep tonight. 'Do you know where Onyx is staying? He said Gray and I could stay with him.'

She smiled. 'You don't know?'

My eyebrows crinkled and her smile broadened. 'Onyx and Dapper own Ascension now.'

The bar hidden within one of the pillars of Brooklyn Bridge was closed for the night by the time Gray and I let ourselves in using the keypad code Steph had given us.

I barely made it three steps into the main bar before Dapper was in front of me sweeping me into a huge hug. A number of people – obviously staff cleaning up after the night – were staring wide-eyed and I knew it wasn't at me. Dapper wasn't exactly a cuddler.

I laughed out loud, surprising myself. 'I've missed you, too.'

He seemed to remember himself and stood back, clearing his throat. 'Yeah, well. People round here never stop talking about you,' he said with a tinge of his old gruffness. 'Makes it hard to forget all the trouble you cause.'

I found it hard to forget, too.

'When did you come to New York? What happened to Hades?' I asked. His old bar back in our home city had been his pride and joy.

Dapper grabbed my bag and started to walk me towards a narrow staircase behind the bar. 'Come on, let's get you settled in.'

Gray and I followed Dapper past the bar, where Onyx was sitting with a large glass of something toxic-looking in front of him. He raised it as we went by.

'Anyone tried to kill you?' he asked.

I rolled my eyes. 'Not yet,' I replied.

He shrugged. 'Blow anything up?'

'Not yet,' I said again, fighting the urge to smile.

'Eh. Still early days.'

I shook my head and kept walking.

'Think I might stay down here for a drink,' Gray said, eyeing the pretty blonde bartender as he pulled out the stool beside Onyx and dumped his bag.

'Suit yourself, but be ready to go first thing,' I said, knowing I probably wouldn't see him again before morning.

He gave me a salute and picked up the drink Onyx poured him.

'So?' I tried again, walking into the apartment with Dapper. 'Why the move?'

Dapper flicked on lights as we walked through. The apartment was different from his one above Hades, but it once again showcased his outstanding flair for interior design and love of Italian furniture.

'I've still got Hades,' Dapper said, taking my bag into a stylish bedroom, decorated in a cream palette with splashes of chocolate and lime. He opened a door to show me the neat en suite bathroom and took two folded white towels from the cabinet below the sink, resting them on the vanity unit.

'I'll head back there one day. But I decided to give New York a try for a while. Someone had to watch the girl,' he continued. 'Plus, she tried to steal half my books when she left. I figured it was easier to bring the whole lot.'

I smiled to hear Dapper speak so lovingly of Steph. 'So, you just bought Ascension?'

'I saw the opportunity.' He winked. 'Near-immortal regulars who can seriously hold their liquor make for good repeat business.' Then, before he seemed to realise it, he had enveloped me in another hug. 'It's good to see you, kid. Things just aren't the same.'

I wriggled free of Dapper's arms, overwhelmed by the emotion behind his words but also annoyed with myself for my reaction.

*Get a grip, Vi.*

Dapper gave a small nod as if he understood. 'You need anything, just yell out. Kitchen's down the hall if you're hungry, though don't get your hopes up. Onyx's idea of shopping consists of bourbon and Pop-Tarts.'

Actually, a Pop-Tart sounded kind of delicious.

'So, you and Onyx? You're happy?' I asked, surprising myself. Generally, I avoided these types of conversations and I knew Dapper wasn't a big sharer of personal information, but there was a part of me that was desperate to know.

Dapper stared into space for a time before a small smile tugged at the corners of his mouth. 'It hasn't all been a yellow brick road, if you get my drift, but yes,' his eyes softened. 'We're happy.'

I nodded, pleased that they had one another.

He waited a beat before asking, 'Do you want to talk about it?'

I knew 'it' translated to 'Lincoln', and to how I'd run away.

I looked down and unfastened the belt holding my sheathed dagger, setting it on the bedside table before looking back at Dapper. 'I'd really rather not.'

I sensed Phoenix in my room that night as I tried to sleep. I couldn't see him. I didn't need to. I could feel his anxiety but I was already on absolute overload and it was taking all my energy to hold back the cold and constantly keep my walls up.

I could feel his sadness eating away at him and it only intensified my own soul-deep pain. I wondered if we were doomed to feel each other's agony for all eternity. What a way to live.

'Just give me tonight, Phoenix. I can't deal with any more right now,' I whispered shakily to the empty room.

His presence faded away. Unfortunately the dreams, just like the one I'd had on the plane, did not.

The infirmary was on the level below the main operations, which occupied the top floors of the Academy skyscrapers, and was not far from where Josephine had once held my parents prisoner. It was early and Steph – dressed in a killer pair of apricot skinny jeans and an off-white peasant-style shirt – had met me outside the Academy first thing with a couple of to-go coffees.

*God, I've missed my best friend.*

'Where's Gray?' she asked.

I followed her through the back entrance and towards the private lifts, where I took the opportunity to throw on the cloak I still had from the previous night. I knew it was now a futile disguise, but that didn't stop me from clinging to it. I could already feel Lincoln nearby and my insides were flipping like a fish out of water.

'He and Onyx bonded over bourbon. I tossed a glass of water on his face before I left this morning. He won't be far behind.'

'Got it,' she said with a snicker.

I noticed as we walked through the halls that no evidence of the damage caused the day Lilith and Phoenix blew up the majority of the Academy remained. It all looked new.

*Pity you can't cover up memories with a fresh coat of paint.*

When we reached the entrance I wasn't surprised to see that the infirmary was well-guarded by Grigori. I didn't, however, expect them to immediately stand aside as we neared. At first I wondered if Josephine had informed them I would be coming down, only to remember they wouldn't be able to recognise me beneath my black hood.

It wasn't me for whom they stood aside so quickly. It was Steph.

'I see Lincoln isn't the only one who's moved up in the ranks,' I said. 'Last time I was here a human would never be allowed any authority.'

Steph smiled and I didn't miss her pride. 'Griffin gave his seat of power to me a while back. He didn't want to leave our city unprotected but the Assembly kept pushing for him to play a part here.'

I tried not to react to her mention of our home city and all the memories it stirred.

'In the end he sent me as a kind of proxy until he could find the right Grigori to take over from him there. Spence had already left to bring Chloe here for her training and I knew Sal and Zoe were keen for us to all stay together. I didn't have anything else holding me to home, so …' She shrugged. 'Here I am.'

'What about Jase?' I asked, knowing that she might not have stayed behind for her dysfunctional relationship with her parents, but she and her brother, Jase, had always been tight.

Her smile slipped. 'After everything that went down, he knew too much to leave it alone. In the end I gave in and told him and he … he just couldn't accept it. He didn't want to be part of this world and he didn't want me in it either. He gave me an ultimatum: him or Grigori.' She shook her head. 'I tried to explain that it wouldn't make any difference to just pretend exiles and Grigori didn't exist and I told him how I loved Sal completely and that meant I couldn't ever leave him.'

My eyes dropped.

Steph briefly covered her mouth with hand looking mortified. 'Oh, Vi. I'm sorry, I didn't mean it like that. You and Lincoln are different, I know that.'

I shook my head. 'I know. So, what happened?'

'It was gradual. He called me less and less. I spent more and more time staying with Sal, and Jase spent more and more time avoiding home. Finally, one day I called him and he didn't answer. He never called me back.'

'Oh, Steph, I'm so sorry. Why didn't you tell me?'

She grimaced. 'I don't know. We've spoken so little and I never really knew what you did and didn't want to hear. I guess I just tried to stick to the good stuff, hoping it might make you want to come back.'

Guilt gnawed away at me from the inside. 'I've been such a terrible friend. To you and Spence.'

'Don't, Vi. Spence and I above anyone else understood you did what you had to do. We've never blamed you for anything.'

I nodded, feeling ashamed anyway. 'So,' I said, reverting to our original subject. 'How did Josephine react when you showed up in New York?'

'She went nuts, of course. She called an Assembly vote to veto Griffin's decision, but Griffin has a lot of support and the votes in his favour won out. So much so that he's been approached more than once to consider moving for a seat on the Assembly, but he insists he isn't interested. Anyway, since then Josephine has had to accept my position here.' Steph grinned. 'We have our run-ins every now and then but I think I've grown on her.'

I absorbed all of this. I was so proud of Steph for standing her ground and carving out a place for herself in this reality. Mostly, I was impressed to see she really believed in her position within this world and not because I'd brought her into it, but because of her own endeavours.

'Do you ever regret it?' I asked. 'Wish you could go back to that day I told you everything and just not know?'

'Never. Not even for a fleeting moment,' she answered. And her sureness left me envious.

# CHAPTER NINE

*'God sends meat and the devil sends cooks.'*

**Thomas Deloney**

**a**s we approached Chloe's room, a closed door to our right drew my attention. Holding my coffee in one hand, my other rested flat on the door, but I made no move to open it. I looked over my shoulder to where Steph watched silently.

'Nyla?' I asked.

Steph nodded sadly. 'Rainer won't let her go. She says she'll know when the time is right and when all hope is gone. She says she'll feel it.'

I nodded, my hand slipping away.

Another wave of guilt crashed over me. I'd meant to visit Nyla when I'd last been here but I'd put it off constantly. And then it had all been too late.

I knew that before I left New York this time, I would return to this room. Even standing on the other side of the door I could feel an odd pull.

But right now, I needed to focus on Spence.

'Let's see Chloe,' I said, dropping my hand.

Steph showed me into Chloe's room, where Salvatore and Zoe were waiting.

'Holy shit, is it really you?' Zoe blurted the moment I stepped into the room.

I lowered my hood. 'I guess so.'

Salvatore came straight at me, encasing me in a warm hug. 'Welcome home,' he said.

I moved stiffly out of his teddy-bear arms. 'Thank you, but this isn't my home.'

He nodded sombrely, putting a protective arm around Steph. 'That may be the case. But it is your family.'

I didn't know how to respond, so I took a sip of my coffee and placed the paper cup on the table where a few vases of flowers and get-well cards were displayed, and turned to Zoe. 'Long time,' I hedged.

Silence met me.

I braced. Zoe wasn't the type to just forgive and forget and whatever she was about to dish out, I knew she was well within her rights.

Finally, she put her hands on her hips and narrowed her eyes. 'Well, it's about damn time you showed up,' she said, her expression blank for a few seconds before it morphed into an easy grin. 'God, if Lincoln had known all he had to do to get you here was put Spence in mortal danger he would've had him hog-tied and locked in a dungeon two years ago.'

My mouth fell open. I had no idea why everyone – well, almost everyone – was being so kind and understanding.

*I don't deserve this.*

The corners of my mouth lifted and I tried my best not to flinch when she pulled me into a tight hug. Apart from when I was fighting, I hadn't had so much physical contact in a long time. It felt foreign. Confusing.

*And nice.*

'I'm just here until we get Spence back,' I said, looking at them all.

Steph was the first to speak. 'And that's what we're all going to focus on,' she reinforced as I nodded.

Chloe lay unconscious in the bed. She was pretty in a traditional way. Neat blonde hair that, though currently dull, naturally fell in soft waves around her face. Even covered in bruises fading to green and yellow her gentle features were recognisable and her clear complexion shone through. But the amount of bruising still present highlighted how badly she'd been beaten.

'Was she really in the convent?' I asked, picking up on one of the things Onyx had mentioned on the plane.

Zoe snorted. 'Yep. Crazy, right? She would've ended up being a no-violence, life-of-chastity nun if Spence hadn't knocked on her door.'

'It must have been a hard decision for her to make,' I said quietly, knowing just how hard it had been for me to face a life of violence, and I certainly hadn't had the same life planned out as she had.

'Actually, she didn't hesitate,' Zoe said.

I glanced at her expectantly.

Zoe shrugged. 'Spence showed up, told her the way of things and she believed him straight away, didn't even ask for proof. It was enough to make Spence suspicious that she didn't have all her marbles, but when he asked she explained that she'd seen exiles before. A group of them had taken over her local church one day and held her captive as they murdered the priests in front of her.'

My eyes widened. 'Really?'

Zoe nodded. 'They would've killed her too, but one exile pulled her out of the church. She thought he was going to kill her, but then he just let her go.'

My face screwed up in confusion. Exiles do not take pity. Or value human life. 'That doesn't sound ...' I glanced back at Chloe, confused.

'And you know the exile who did it, too,' Zoe added, leaning back against the wall and pulling out a packet of M&M's.

When I just stared at her perplexed, she simply said, 'It was Onyx.'

'*What?* When?'

'Before he became human. He's really cagey about it and won't say much but we figure it was around the time he made the first alliance with Joel and the exiles of light.'

I glanced around the room to see Steph and Salvatore nodding in agreement.

'Wow,' I mumbled. 'So, she embraced, just like that?'

'Pretty much,' Zoe said.

'She's taken a while to get her head around some aspects, and her faith is an issue at times since Spence isn't exactly reverent, in any way,' Salvatore added.

I snorted. Reverent was the last thing Spence was.

'No shenanigans?' I asked, smirking.

'Unfortunately, no. But they seem to have found some kind of middle ground. They're good partners,' Zoe explained.

I nodded. 'What are her stats?' I asked.

Steph answered. 'Her mother died in a home invasion the day after Chloe was brought home from the hospital. Her angel maker is from the Angel rank. Her sense is sound. And her strength is perfect recall.'

'Recall?'

'Every single thing she sees is stored in her mind in exact detail.'

*Well, now I'm definitely waking her up.*

From what I'd heard of her story, Chloe's life had seen a lot of trauma and tragedy. Yet she seemed to still have an ability for both faith and fight.

*Lucky her.*

'Is she a strong fighter?' I asked.

'Fair,' Zoe said, with a diplomatic edge.

Sensing there was more, I pushed. 'Has she returned any exiles?'

'Not yet,' Steph said.

I wasn't surprised to hear the answer. It was why Spence would have wanted to get her clear of the bald exile – there was no way Spence would have been able to fight him and have Chloe's back too.

'Has she seen Onyx since she's been here?' I asked, intrigued by their connection. In an odd way, Chloe had been a part of all our dramas since the very beginning.

'Of course,' Zoe said. 'At first it was weird, but they seem to have some kind of bizarre understanding. They're never going to be besties, but she trusts Spence's judgement and accepts he is no longer what he was. Plus, I'm pretty sure something went on that night that only the two of them understand. Either way,' she said in a lighter tone, 'it doesn't hurt that she knows she's now the one with the power. If she wanted to take Onyx down, she could. He knows it, too.'

I sat on the edge of Chloe's bed, hoping to God she was strong enough to be the partner to Spence she now needed to be. 'Chloe, if you can hear me, it's Violet. You asked me to come and see you, and I figure you have something to say. Normally I wouldn't do this. It feels wrong unless it's life and death, especially without permission.' I placed a hand on her forehead and the other on her shoulder. 'But I need to find Spence and I'm betting on the fact that's what you want too,' I explained before pushing my power into her, finding her injuries and healing them.

It took some time. I could feel that she'd suffered a bad trauma at the back of her head and the internal bleeding was substantial. Without Spence to help speed up her healing it may have been a good while until she healed herself.

When her body convulsed Zoe took up position on the other side of the bed, holding her down. Finally Chloe's eyes shot open and she screamed. I slapped a hand over her mouth, not wanting to alert the entire building to the fact that she was awake.

I pulled my powers away from her. She wasn't perfectly healed, but enough.

I lessened my hold over her mouth as she became more aware of her surroundings.

'Chloe, it's okay. It's over. You should be starting to feel a bit better. Please don't scream again,' I urged.

Chloe nodded and I pulled my hand away as she took in a few deep breaths.

We let her take her time, but she didn't seem to need much because it wasn't long before words started to tumble out. 'I've been waiting for you.'

'You've been unconscious,' I said.

'In and out,' she said with a small smile. 'I just didn't want anyone to know.'

I nodded, impressed.

'Is he alive?' I asked tentatively.

She nodded and I knew it was true. As her partner she would know without any doubt. I could hear the combined sigh of relief from behind me.

'Where is he, Chloe?'

'I don't know,' she said, her voice catching on her obviously dry throat. Zoe held up a cup of water and Chloe took a few grateful sips. She then reached out and gently took my wrists in her hands, looking at the silver bracelets that concealed my markings. 'May I?' she asked.

Uncomfortable but willing, I nodded and unclasped the cuff on my right wrist to reveal the swirling silver patterns on my skin.

'They're beautiful,' she said. 'Like watching life in motion.'

'No,' I sighed. 'They're like watching death.'

Her eyes met mine. 'I can see how you would feel that, but that's not what I see.'

I swallowed and eased my arm back, refitting my bracelet.

'He gave me a message for you,' she said.

'What?'

Chloe looked around the room nervously.

I nodded her on. 'It's okay. You can speak in front of them.'

She took another sip of water then looked back at me. 'He said to tell you: it's a trap.'

I gritted my teeth. 'Chloe, is Spence in trouble because of me?'

She lifted a shoulder weakly. 'I don't know. We'd been sent out on a mission but Spence was … he was different about this one. He'd requested the assignment and been secretive about why. The only secrets he ever keeps from me are ones to do with you, so I figured …'

I nodded, trying to show her the apology in my eyes. She seemed to understand.

'Spence was using a glamour to get in close to a group of humans. They're working for this one exile and they're part of these tournaments going on everywhere.'

'I know the ones,' I said.

She nodded and licked her lips. 'We thought he worked alone at first, but we were wrong. Very wrong. We realised pretty quickly that we'd severely underestimated him. He's so much more powerful than anything I've … but Spence …'

'Spence what?'

She shook her head. 'I'm not sure what happened but he suddenly changed. And then we were on the run. I could feel them coming after us but Spence refused to tell me what was happening. He just kept telling me he was going to get me out of there.'

'Chloe, what happened?'

'We were weaving our way towards an old Grigori safe house in Mexico that Spence knew about. We were almost there but they found us. There were six exiles, plus their humans. Spence knew I couldn't …'

'It's okay, Chloe,' I assured her.

She swallowed. 'The exiles captured us and sent us off with the humans. But they weren't like ordinary humans. They were different.'

'How?' Steph asked.

Chloe's attention turned to Steph for the first time and she smiled warmly. I could tell they had formed a friendship.

'You know how when people are being controlled by exiles but they don't seem to be aware of it, they just see things like they're in daze?'

We all nodded.

'Well, these people – it was like they knew the truth and they were okay with it. They'd somehow accepted it and genuinely worshipped the exiles. If I didn't know better I'd think they were possessed or some kind of ...'

'What? Like a cult?' I asked.

'No. Like smart, wealthy people, all driven and working towards something. Like Scientology. They shot us with enough tranquillisers to take down a herd of elephants.'

'What did they do with you?' I asked, my stomach sinking. If they had Spence it was not going to be easy to get him back.

'They have places all over the world. They moved us every day, never staying in one place. They kept us drugged and moved us on a private plane. We left Mexico and went to Quebec, Toronto, Washington. On the fourth day, when they flew us to Austin, Spence made his move. We'd been getting stronger without them knowing – developing immunity to the sedatives. Once Spence had enough control it wasn't too difficult for him to take down the humans. He grabbed me and we ran into the commercial airport. He got me a ticket to New York and told me to leave. I thought we'd be coming here together but he wasn't having it.' Tears started to slip down her cheeks, and I gripped her hand even though my insides clenched with worry.

'He told me that I had to find you. He said to make sure I used your surname. He said to tell you he's still got your back and he knows he'll see you soon.'

Spence knew me well and I couldn't help but love that although he'd said it was a trap, he knew for sure that I'd go anyway.

*Now I just need to know where.*

'Can you sense him?' I asked.

'Only that he's alive. But I'm still pretty weak.'

With Chloe's permission I finished healing her. Tears streamed down her face but she didn't make a sound. When I released her hands she opened her eyes.

'Now can you sense him?' I asked.

She concentrated. 'He's in the country. He's south, but I can't tell you exactly where.'

'That helps,' Steph said.

I shook my head, still trying to make sense of it all. 'So, if Spence sent you back here, what happened to you?'

'Most of the damage is from the humans keeping us down. And when we got free of them I got on the plane like Spence said, but then I saw him through the window, moving around on the tarmac. A few minutes later I saw an exile following him.'

'Spence didn't know?' Zoe asked, seeing where this was headed. No Grigori could stand back and watch their partner be taken down.

Chloe shook her head.

'You got off,' Zoe concluded.

'Yes. But the moment I did, I was hit from behind.'

'And they just left you there?' Salvatore asked, voicing my

own suspicions. But for Salvatore, I knew it was more: he was seeking lies. It was his gift.

She bit her lip. 'I don't know why they didn't take me again. Or kill me.'

Neither did I. Discreetly, I glanced at Salvatore and registered his small nod. Chloe was telling the truth.

'Maybe they wanted to make sure you were found,' Steph offered. 'If someone was waiting for you the moment you got off the plane, maybe it was to make sure you really left. When you got off, they knocked you out, but put you where you'd be discovered, knowing the Academy would eventually find you.'

I looked up at Steph's worried expression.

'Because they knew she'd come to me,' I said, seeing where she was going.

*Because the bald exile had seen Spence that night. He'd been the only other one there at Lilith's estate. The only link to me besides Phoenix and Lincoln.*

'I think so,' Steph agreed.

'Spence is right. It's a trap.'

*And he's the bait.*

Steph tilted her head. 'You don't seem surprised.'

I wasn't. I'd been waiting for the bald-headed exile to come after me since the other night.

*And now I've put Spence's life in danger.*

'I've come to expect this kind of stuff,' I said, hoping my expression would tell Steph to let it go for now. I looked back at Chloe. 'Did you keep notes on the locations held by this human organisation?'

She nodded.

'Do they have a place in New York?'

She nodded again. 'Offices and tournament sites.'

'Where are the files?' I asked, hoping they were here.

Chloe tapped her head. 'It's my gift. I don't need to keep notes, I *am* the note.'

I rolled my eyes at her naivety. 'Until someone kills you.'

She blanched.

'Sorry,' I said. 'So, it works like a photographic memory?'

'Kind of, but it's triggered by my emotions. I remember everything because of how I felt at that moment and that creates a visual rehashing of the event, along with all of the smells, environment and feelings. I can relive a moment completely. I can share my memory with another person if they have a connection to it themselves and even tap into someone else's memories if they have a strong enough emotion from any one event.'

I quickly stepped away from the bed. 'I trust that's something that requires permission first?'

'Of course,' she responded, holding my gaze.

There are some memories that should never be rehashed.

'There's one more thing,' Chloe said, her eyes now showing her deep fear.

'What is it?'

'His name. I never saw him but I heard them talking. They call him Sammael.'

I bit down on the insides of my cheeks, needing the distraction. Having a name made it all that much more real. 'That's a good help. Thanks, Chloe,' I said, giving her a quick nod before I turned.

'Violet!' she called out.

I paused and turned back to her. 'I'll find him, Chloe. I promise.' I looked to Salvatore and Zoe. 'Can you hang around and get the list of properties, focusing on what they have in New York and south of here?'

Salvatore nodded instantly.

I tossed my empty coffee cup into a bin.

'Where are you going?' Zoe called after me as I walked out the door.

'To set a few things straight,' I said over my shoulder. 'Whatever is going on here, Spence needs me and there's no way in hell I'm leaving him out there alone.'

I made it to the lift before Steph took up position beside me, checking her watch. 'We'd better head straight there. Lincoln will already have the meeting underway.'

I nodded, knowing I was headed for round two.

The difference? This time I was ready.

# CHAPTER TEN

*'We are so accustomed to disguise ourselves to others that in
the end we become disguised to ourselves.'*

**Francois de la Rochefoucauld**

**S**ometimes we knowingly fool ourselves. Sometimes there is
no way to control what's going on, so we just lie to avoid facing
facts. The calm before the storm. Because there is no other way.

I strode purposefully towards the meeting room. My
emotions were in check, my hood was back in place, and
I ignored the inquisitive eyes as I walked through the halls.
But as soon as I entered the meeting room and felt the intensity
flowing from the presence at the head of the main table, I knew
there was little time left to hide.

Steph stayed with me at the back of the room. I peeked
through my hood, noting that Lincoln had angled his body
away from us. Another clear message. But it was a new day
and I wasn't going to let myself get caught up in his behaviour.
I was completely shut off, surrounded by nothing but my
ever-present coldness.

*Tick. Tick.*

'Our sources have told us there's a group of humans
organising an exile tournament this week in Manhattan.'

'Is there a chance they're connected with the group Spence and Chloe were investigating?' Josephine asked from beside Lincoln, before taking a sip from a china cup.

'There's a good chance,' Lincoln confirmed.

The door opened again and Gray moved into the room and took up position on my other side. He'd discarded his robe. When I looked up at his bloodshot eyes, he gave me a sheepish smile and shrugged. With an unveiled Gray beside me, the amount of unwanted attention on us multiplied.

*Tick. Tick.*

'Hakon,' Lincoln went on, holding up a sheet of paper, 'are you confident this is the right address?'

I heard Hakon, one of the highest-ranking Grigori and a member of the Assembly, speak up from somewhere on the other side of the room. 'It's a good source but that doesn't mean I wouldn't like to verify,' he said.

'I think we might be able to do that in a few minutes,' Steph said. She'd moved a few feet away from me. Not that it mattered. Lincoln didn't look in her direction.

'How?' he asked, feigning sudden interest in the file he was holding.

'Chloe is awake,' Steph answered, sounding meek for the first time. Before Lincoln could speak, she continued. 'She said the group they were trying to infiltrate had an office here. Zoe and Salvatore are getting the details from her now.'

The tension was palpable in the silence before Lincoln seemed to snap out of it. 'Fine. As soon as we get that, we'll assemble a team and raid the building. We'll run surveillance today and take them first thing tomorrow. It's not ideal but we need to ensure all the right people will be there. Office hours will be best.'

I took a deep breath.

*Tock.*

'A full-on attack is unnecessary.' My voice was so surprisingly steady I almost turned to Gray for a quick high-five.

'I beg your pardon?' Lincoln responded, tilting his head but still angling away from me.

I closed my eyes briefly then took a step forward, and lowered my hood. I ignored the sudden murmurs that filled the room and set my eyes on Lincoln, who had finally turned in my direction.

*So perfectly green. God, no memory could ever do your eyes justice.*

I cleared my throat. 'An attack will only alert the exile controlling all of this that we are coming in force.'

Lincoln held my gaze with little outward effort. I tried to affect the same response even as I felt the connection between us course through my entire being.

'That's hardly a problem as far as I can see; it might draw them out of the woodwork. And may I remind you that you are here as a guest. I'll tolerate that, but mind your place. This is not your mission and you will not be required to offer an opinion.'

If my emotions had not been shut down so tightly, his behaviour would have caused a flare of pain, and then anger. Lincoln knew how much I cared for Spence. He also knew that it wasn't smart to cut out opinion if it could lead to a good solution.

I took another step forward, my eyes narrowing on him slightly. I wasn't about to stand by and watch Spence get hurt.

'While I appreciate your *tolerance* I think you're missing the point.'

He crossed his arms over his chest. 'And what would that be?'

I glanced briefly in Josephine's direction, hoping in vain that she might speak on my behalf. But she appeared content playing the spectator, her eyes darting back and forth between Lincoln and me.

'If Spence had wanted *you* and *your* team to lead this rescue then he would have sent Chloe back with a message for you. Not to mention she's been hiding the fact that she's been drifting in and out of consciousness for the past couple of days waiting until I arrived.' I crossed my arms now, mirroring him.

You could have heard a pin drop.

Lincoln's face remained impressively impassive, given that I'd just challenged him in front of the entire room. 'Message?'

'He's alive.' I didn't miss his instant relief and I was comforted to see a glimpse of his familiar sincerity.

*He's still in there somewhere.*

I heard a gasp from the opposite side of the room and followed it to Mia. Morgan had her arm around Mia's shoulders as Mia hurriedly wiped her eyes. My brow furrowed but I turned back to the more pressing matters.

'We have a name to go on. Sammael,' I said. I swallowed before adding, 'You've seen him before.'

Lincoln raised his eyebrows.

I fought back the memories. 'Bald. Short, for an exile. Suit. Glasses. Br—'

'Briefcase,' he cut me off.

I nodded.

Lincoln glanced at Max and Morgan. 'Take his name up to the libraries and see what they can dig up on him.'

As soon as Max and Morgan were out the door Lincoln turned back to me, his mouth set in a straight line. 'What else?'

'Spence was tracking him when the tables turned on them. When he was separated from Chloe they were headed south and it looks like he's still somewhere in that direction. Still in the country. He told Chloe to tell me it was a trap.'

Lincoln threw a hand in the air. 'Well, there you go. Doesn't sound like he wants you after all.'

'And then he said he'd see me soon,' I fired back. 'I guess he knows me well.'

Lincoln's eyes narrowed at that statement. 'What are you suggesting, Violet?' His voice broke slightly on my name as if he struggled to say it.

I shrugged. 'Run your surveillance today. I'll take a few of your people tonight, if they're willing, to cover the perimeter of the building. Gray and I will go in and find out what they know about Spence and this exile. Once I know where Spence is I'll take a team with me to go and get him. Then I'll bring him back here.'

Lincoln laughed. 'You're delusional if you think that's going to happen.'

I shook my head and spoke before he could. 'Academy tactics are too obvious. They'll be waiting for you and they'll be ready. People will get hurt and Spence will be put in unnecessary danger. I won't allow that. I'm sorry.'

'For which part!' he roared, causing me to flinch before he quickly pulled his mask back in place. It was the first real emotion I'd seen from him and I had to force myself not to take a step towards him. Lincoln took a deep breath and then asked, 'How *exactly* do you think you're going to lead anyone from here? Why should they follow you?' He took a step towards me, showing the assembled Grigori he had no problem being in my space. 'I'm not saying you have no right to help find Spence. He obviously sent Chloe to speak with you for a reason. If you agree to do as instructed and stay out of our way ...'

*Out of* your *way, you mean.*

'I'll consider letting you come along.'

It was my turn to laugh. But I sobered quickly and took my own confident step into the centre of the room. I didn't miss the small step back that he took.

'Clearly you've misunderstood me at some fundamental level, so let me be crystal clear. Spence asked for me and I'll be leading this rescue, Lincoln, whether you like it or not.'

'If you're challenging his leadership there is only one way to do it,' Josephine said coolly from her place at the head of the table, drawing the attention of the entire room. 'You must challenge in physical combat.'

I glared at her. She smiled in understanding. 'There is a main-hall gathering scheduled this afternoon. If you wish to challenge you can do so there in front of the Academy and Assembly members. If you want our resources and power behind you and insist on taking point, this is the only way.'

This was not part of our deal, but I wasn't surprised she was already throwing curve balls.

Lincoln leaned back against the edge of the table and smirked. Judging by the number of similar expressions, he wasn't the only person in the room who didn't rate my chances against him in a one-on-one. My jaw clenched to see how sure he was of his abilities against mine, but I'd seen that small step back he'd taken. He was at least slightly wary. And I was highly aware of my strengths and weaknesses. I knew that what I carried within me was far more painful than anything else I could be made to endure, but I'd learned to control that pain. I'd had to.

Plus, Lincoln hadn't seen me in action since before Phoenix gave me his angelic essence. He was severely underrating me.

I felt the corners of my mouth lift, just as his dropped slightly.

'Fine,' I said mustering my willpower. 'Let's do it.'

Walking into the main hall was like stepping back in time. The memories of my Grigori testing and the mayhem that followed enveloped me momentarily before I shoved them aside.

Gray was beside me and already the hall was full on both the ground level and the overhanging balconies above. I'd never been in here prior to proceedings; I'd always been brought in as the entertainment.

*Actually, today isn't much different.*

'God, I'd forgotten how much fanfare this lot enjoyed,' Gray mumbled.

'You were once part of the Academy?' I asked. Gray made a point of not divulging his age or his history.

He shrugged. 'For a spell. Figured out very fast that it wasn't for me.'

I wondered, not for the first time, what had become of his Grigori partner, but I knew better than to ask. It was bad Rogue etiquette.

'When was the last time you were here?' I hedged.

He glanced at me, knowing my game. 'Well before you were born.' And I knew he would say no more.

'Did you manage to get a team together?'

Gray nodded. 'Carter, Taxi and Milo will be here in a couple of days. I've got some locals on standby if we need, too.'

'Is Carter going to be a problem?' I asked, well aware of how he felt about – and reacted to – any form of authority.

*Not to mention I'm not his favourite person at the moment.*

'He'll be fine. He gave me his word.'

'And you trust it?' I pushed. 'With your life?'

Gray set a level look on me. 'Even with yours, princess.'

I grinned, knowing full well that to Gray, my life rated well below his own.

At that moment Lincoln brushed past, knocking Gray's shoulder in the process. Gray watched as Lincoln continued without pause towards the front of the room.

'Not much of a welcome, mate,' Gray called out. I was surprised considering Lincoln and Gray had seemed to get along well when they'd first met in Santorini.

Lincoln halted and spun on his heel, looking Gray up and down once with hard eyes. 'I'm not your mate. And I didn't invite you here.'

Gray glanced to me and then his eyes narrowed in on Lincoln's, drawing some kind of conclusion. All I managed to draw up was a bad feeling.

Gray snorted. 'You Academy people are all the same. You think you know everything.'

Lincoln stalked back towards us, moving right into Gray's personal space, using his slightly taller frame for maximum looming effect. 'I know enough about you to have made up my mind,' he growled.

'I can see that, mate. At least, I can see that you think you have. So, tell me, have you been to London lately?'

The way he said it made me bristle. Lincoln stiffened at the same time. His eyes shot to me briefly as his jaw clenched.

'London is a city I go out of my way to avoid.' With that he turned and walked away.

My heart pounded.

*He's known where I've been. All this time. And he's stayed away.*

Gray moved close to me as I stood in a daze, putting the painful pieces together. I knew I shouldn't let it hurt. I tried to remind myself that it was what I'd wanted and that I should be glad that Lincoln had moved on. But right at that moment, my heart wasn't being practical.

'Hey.' Gray snapped his fingers in my face, causing me to blink. 'You want to win this thing?'

'Of course I do,' I shot back.

'At any cost?' he added, eyebrows raised in challenge.

'I have nothing to lose, so, yes. Why?'

He nodded but was silenced as the main doors swung open and the Assembly began to file in.

# chapter eleven

*'There is no greater sorrow than to recall in misery the time*
*when we were happy.'*

**Dante**

**W**ilhelm and Rainer led the way down the long aisle that
ran through the centre of rows of chairs arranged in the
massive opaque-glass-encased oval hall. Standing near the
front, I had a direct view of the Assembly members as they
walked in. Rainer caught my eye and nodded. It was her
way of giving what support she could. Though I noted she
also looked at Lincoln on the opposite side and gave the same
gesture. Wilhelm gave me a quick wink.

Hakon and Valerie came in next. Hakon still looked like
a hulk but he was different as well; he moved slower and his
expression was pained.

'What happened?' I whispered to Steph, who stood
beside me

'He never fully healed after the explosions Lilith and
Phoenix set off. They managed to save his leg but he's never
been the same. He doesn't often fight,' she explained.

I nodded. It was all I could do.

*That was my fault.*

'No one blames you for what happened,' Steph said, reading my mind. 'I don't think you understand how highly regarded you are by those who know you.'

I smiled sadly, failing again to muster a response.

That didn't stop Steph. 'And as for the rest, they don't know you. They hear the stories but they don't know what to make of them.'

There was a gap in the procession after Valerie. 'No Seth and Decima?' I asked.

Steph shook her head. 'I've never even seen them,' she pouted and I realised Steph was starstruck by two of the fiercest warriors I'd ever laid eyes on. 'I don't think they've returned since you were here last,' she went on, then leaned a little closer and lowered her voice. 'Rumour is they've petitioned for release.'

'Release from what?'

'Everything. The Assembly for one, but also from their angel makers. They're the oldest Grigori alive but word is that they're asking to die.'

'Oh.' I wasn't even sure that was allowed. But I could understand. After all they'd given, surely they deserved some say in the matter.

Josephine came down the aisle next. She still carried herself as though she were merely the Vice of the Assembly, but everyone knew she wielded the power over Drenson.

*Another reason I could never be part of their system.*

As Josephine strode towards the stage, a number of Grigori began to make a small gesture, clenching their right fist and raising it to their left shoulder.

'What's with the salutes?' I asked.

'It's old tradition,' Steph explained quietly. 'Not many Grigori from this century partake, but some of the older ones still do it. They're marks of respect. Though rank has always been the obvious dictator in the hierarchy, throughout the history of Grigori true leadership was earned and won, irrespective of rank. The first level of regard is to bow one's head. Second, the fist to the shoulder. And third,' Steph pointed to where a few Grigori knelt on one knee, 'complete service.'

I didn't fail to notice that there were significantly fewer gestures of respect displayed when Adele and Drenson made their way down the aisle at the end.

While Drenson and Josephine addressed the Academy, I looked around the room. There was so much power here, but that only seemed to give rise to an air of uncertainty. Drenson was not a good leader, and it felt as if the entire room was aware of that and therefore discouraged.

Valerie and Hakon, along with Rainer and Wilhelm, were strong Grigori, but they were not leaders. And with Seth and Decima – along with their battle know-how and wisdom – they were increasingly absent … I didn't like what I was seeing.

Unable to stop myself, I allowed my eyes to travel to where Lincoln stood, hands clasped behind his back. He had changed his top, now wearing a well-fitting white T-shirt, and appeared patient and attentive. But I could have sworn I saw a similar air of concern about his features as he looked over the Assembly members.

*Will he become an Assembly member one day?*

I hoped so. Maybe he would bring something to this place that it was sorely missing. The Lincoln I had known could make things right here. But the one who stood in front of me now? I didn't know him so well.

*Yes, you do.*

*No. He's not the same.*

*Liar.*

At that moment, Lincoln looked up and our eyes met for a flash. Just a minuscule moment was all it took for his piercing green gaze to cause the soul I had buried so deep to demand I move closer. Panicked, I looked towards the exit doors for a fraction of a second. When I looked back, Lincoln's focus had moved to his feet. His shoulders dropped as if he had let out a breath or sigh and I caught the slight shake of his head.

Showing nothing outwardly, I turned my attention back to the Assembly, but having seen Lincoln's reaction to me, his disappointment ... my chest constricted and I had to work hard to keep each breath even and calm. The question was: had Lincoln reacted that way because I looked at the door or because I didn't take the opportunity to leave?

I blinked away my scrambled thoughts as Drenson started to introduce the authority challenge between Lincoln and me. I saw Lincoln move towards the main sparring arena that had been left clear. He looked focused, strong and confident.

'So, about winning this fight,' Gray said discreetly from my side.

'Yeah,' I swallowed, suddenly nervous to be on display this way. Lincoln and me ... and sparring. I cleared my throat. 'About that.'

'You're going to have to play a little dirty if you want to beat him.'

'Why's that?'

'Because I've seen him in action. And with their big guy out,' Gray said, gesturing to Hakon, 'there's a reason the Assembly defer to Lincoln and let him lead in combat. Even with your speed he'll have strength over you. You'll hold the element of surprise but only for a short time. Plus, he's on home turf. So, you'll have to take him down hard and fast or you'll lose your window. You hearing me?'

I glared at him. 'Thanks for the vote of confidence, and your point is?'

He smirked. 'My *point* is that pissing him off will be the best distraction you could hope for. Just make sure *you* stay focused afterwards.'

'After *what*?'

I glanced at Lincoln. He stood in the fighting square, waiting for me. When I turned back to Gray to tell him I had to go, he grabbed me around the waist and pulled me flush to his body, kissing me hard on the lips and holding me there.

I was so shocked it took me a moment to push him away. I heard people nearby gasp and then I saw Gray smirk. More than anything I felt an overwhelming fury.

Gray grabbed my chin, squeezing tightly to hold my attention as he leaned in and whispered, 'Now, keep your shields locked tight, stay the hell focused and win.' He winked.

I leaned in a little further, my hand gripping his shoulder as my fingers dug in – hopefully painfully – to the soft spot. 'You're going to pay gravely for that.'

'No doubt,' he said with a devilish grin. 'But until then, use it.'

And I knew exactly what he meant and was already following orders, pushing my shields to the max.

It was underhanded, but Lincoln was the first person who'd taught me: you do what you've got to do to win.

I marched into the combat arena, not looking at Lincoln, and faced the Assembly. 'Rules?'

Drenson looked at me for a long moment, clearly unimpressed by what he saw. I was sure he'd hoped he would go the rest of his long life without ever laying eyes on me again.

*Yeah, well, the feeling's mutual.*

'First to move into a clear kill position,' he stated.

One round. Fine by me. Perfect, in fact. I nodded, turning to Lincoln. 'Ready when you are.'

Lincoln's arm shot out so fast I was surprised. But I dodged it, my speed beyond that of any other Grigori I'd known.

I smirked briefly when I saw the shock register on his face. But my optimism was quickly strangled when I glimpsed something else in those green eyes of his. Something almost like pride.

I didn't have long to ponder this, though, since I was already moving into a full-force round kick. It was another flashy display of my speed, and Lincoln never saw it coming. As soon as my foot made contact, I spun a second time, coming at him with another kick.

Lincoln managed to thwart my second attempt and then delivered a few good hits himself, gaining control. Gray had been right. His focus was adjusting to the fight and I knew I only had the upper hand for a few more moments.

Without hesitation I ran at him, leaping into the air and spinning as I did. My feet hit his chest with enough force to take him straight down onto his back. I surfed him like a wave and landed on top of him, straddling his waist.

I hit him hard across the face once, twice, further startling him, then both of my fists jabbed above his heart.

'Kill shot!' I yelled, jumping off Lincoln and putting as much distance as possible between us, trying to control my manic breathing. My body was flipping out while my soul was having some kind of hysterical fit. I needed to get out of this room, fast. It was all too familiar, being so close to him, smelling him, feeling him. And all while sparring, one of the things we used to do so well together.

I put my hands on my hips and addressed the Assembly.

'I'll take a team of six and we'll head out tonight,' I said to Josephine, but she wasn't looking at me.

My stomach flipped again.

'We're not finished here!' Lincoln roared from behind me.

I didn't turn. 'Oh, I think we are,' I replied, starting to walk towards the side door. 'Don't be a bad loser.'

'Terms of a challenge are that the participant cannot use internal powers to give them the advantage.'

I paused as I scoffed. 'I hate to break it to you but my speed and strength are not internal.'

His voice lowered. 'But the cowardly shields you and your Rogues are famous for relying on so much *are*.'

I flinched at his words.

*Anything but this.*

I turned, slowly. Lincoln looked straight at me. Emotionless.

*Does he know what he's doing? What this will do to me? Could he be this cruel?*

He raised his eyebrows. 'You want to beat me, you have to drop your walls.'

I looked up at the Assembly. Drenson was smiling. Josephine seemed surprisingly speechless. I gestured to Lincoln. 'I've already beaten him. This is bullshit!'

Drenson made a pathetically brief attempt to appear compassionate to my argument. 'Nonetheless, he is right. You have to prove you are of sound mind.'

'But I beat him physically. Who else has done that in the past two years?' I challenged, looking around the room.

'Even so,' Drenson said, increasingly unable to hide his enjoyment.

*Shit.*

*I can do this.*

*No! I damn well cannot!*

I couldn't remember the last time I'd let my guard down completely. I wasn't even sure I'd physically survive it. Part of me suspected that the only reason my soul had not shattered into oblivion the way it was probably supposed to was because I had naturally strong guards. I was broken into smithereens inside but my shields were like a protective glass jar holding them all together.

Ignoring Lincoln's eyes on me, I wrapped my hands around my waist, considering what would happen if I let the cold take hold.

*Pain. That's what.*

There would be so much pain. Even if I could physically survive it, mentally … The constant smarting I endured even with my defences on high made my existence barely tolerable – like sharp knives set on a constant cycle of stab and repeat. The idea of bringing down my walls …

*Oh my God.*

It would be like putting my body through a meat grinder and my heart through—

I stopped the thought.

Lincoln was a good leader. I truly believed that.

*Maybe I should just let him lead and go on my way, try to find Spence on my own.*

I glanced over my shoulder to Gray. Even he looked sick.

*Shit!*

I needed their damn intel. I couldn't take chances and I needed to be in charge otherwise I couldn't be sure to cover all bases. Spence had said that Lincoln would be out of his depth. I couldn't risk that.

'Fine,' I gritted out as I forced myself back into position.

Lincoln averted his gaze.

*Good. I hope you feel guilty.*

'When you're ready,' he said, making it clear he didn't feel too bad to proceed.

I couldn't believe he was going to do this to me. But I was almost certain he couldn't know. How could he? No one knew exactly what it would do to me. He was just playing the game, like I had. Win at all costs.

Slowly, I began to lower my shields for the first time in two years. My soul charged forward like the caged animal it was. And it was not happy with me.

The impact was immediate.

I knew my shields were not all the way down but there was no way I could go any further. My insides contracted painfully. The coldness that never fully eased its grip seeped into my blood and bones completely, like a poison, reaching all the way to my dysfunctional heart. The ache consumed me with such terrible grief that I screamed out in agony. My legs shook, about to give way. I stumbled but couldn't focus on anything around me.

An arm snaked around my waist from behind, its path warm and strong when there had been no warmth, no strength. Without being able to think or control my actions my body leaned back into the embrace, craving more. The sanity. The small reprieve. His other arm moved into position loosely around my neck and as I felt him press over my heart I wanted to cry out again, this time in relief.

'Kill shot.'

His voice was so steady.

My legs gave out completely, but he held me up, his hand gliding slowly down my rigid arm until his palm slid into mine. His fingers lined up with each of mine and then, unmercifully reminding me of moments I could never have again, his fingers slowly – warmly – closed and squeezed tightly just as his lips grazed my ear and he whispered, 'Put them back up.'

He braced me as I trembled and started to do just as he'd instructed, rebuilding the walls that protected me from the truth.

As soon as I was strong enough to stand, Lincoln stepped away from me.

I turned to face the Assembly again, refusing to look any weaker than was already obvious to the entire room.

I could feel Lincoln studying me. I glanced in his direction defiantly to see his brow furrowed as if he was confused by something. He opened his mouth to speak but just as quickly closed it and turned back to the Assembly.

'I'll lead a team out tomorrow,' he said, not looking back at me.

The room remained silent.

I took a deep breath, feeling more in control by the second. Overwhelmed by the whole thing and more than anything simply sad, I shook my head. 'You really have turned into one of them, haven't you?' And suddenly I was completely exhausted.

*What have we done to one another?*

Lincoln flinched and I looked up at Josephine. 'You're making a mistake doing things like this and I won't stay around to watch you put Spence's life in unnecessary danger. That's the beauty of being a Rogue. I'll bring Spence back when I have him.'

With that I turned around and started to walk out.

'You'll do no such thing!' Drenson yelled. I didn't stop. They didn't control me and I could already tell that Gray was walking out behind me.

'Violet!' Josephine called. I glanced over my shoulder and something about the way she looked at me, almost imploringly, made me pause. 'The way I see it, the outcome of that challenge was a tie. You and Lincoln will work together, assemble a team you both agree on and share the leadership.'

I shook my head. 'No. I can't work with him,' I said, knowing the full truth of my words.

'Then I guess it will come down to how much you want to find your friend, because we all know this is the best solution.'

With that she looked at Drenson, making it clear there would be no argument.

I looked around me. Gray rolled his eyes and Steph nodded me on at the same time that Lincoln glanced at Mia for counsel. A shot of jealousy speared me when I saw her give him an encouraging smile.

Finally, I shrugged. 'We should get into the building tonight.'

Lincoln shook his head instantly. 'We'll go during the day tomorrow and make sure no one slips away before we question them.'

I sighed and looked straight into his eyes. 'I get that you are used to charging through the front doors having nothing to fear, but there is a value to having the defences we do. These walls you were so keen to tear down keep us guarded from exiles. Trust me, if there are big players in that building they'll be there at night and if there are exiles, we'll find them before they find us. Give Gray and me an hour in the building tonight. If we don't come out with anything useful, storm the place until your trigger-happy heart is content tomorrow.'

He dropped his head. 'You say that like it's a possibility.'

'What?' I asked, confused.

'Contentment.' He said it like a throwaway comment and looked towards Mia again. 'We'll give this a go. Get the conductors on it. Set up a perimeter and we'll cover them for an hour.'

Mia nodded and moved away towards the doors. Lincoln turned to me, shooting a sharp glance in Gray's direction. 'You and your … *partner* should be ready to move in half an hour,' he said before marching out of the room.

I wanted to scream after him, but his words had hit so hard they had sucked the air right out of my lungs.

'Did he just call me your *partner*?' Gray asked, now beside me.

'He did,' I replied, still staring at the door Lincoln had just slammed in his wake.

# chapter twelve

*'The quarrels of lovers are the renewal of love.'*

Jean Racine

**W**hile everyone else went into research mode that afternoon, I slipped across the glamoured walkways, marvelling yet again as I walked between buildings on an invisible bridge over to the Academy classrooms in building D. I found Simon eating his lunch in the cafeteria.

It was strange to look at him. Just two years older than when I'd last seen him, looking malnourished and far younger than his age, he had changed from a boy to a young man. His blonde hair was styled into a messy heap and his glasses made him look more Clark Kent than Wimpy Kid. He glanced up from the book he was reading and when he saw me his fast-changing expressions from wide eyes, to mouth agape, to huge smile, made me laugh.

I sat down beside him. 'Hey there, stranger,' I said.

'You're really here,' he said, keeping his eyes on me as if worried I might disappear if he blinked.

'Passing through,' I explained. 'I wanted to see how you were doing.'

He put his book down. 'Great. I'm great. I mean, it's …

you know, life is different and I miss my family, but ... I like it here. I embrace in a year – well, actually closer to two years, but still ...' he said, stumbling over his words.

'I heard that. It sounds like you're pretty excited about it all.'

He nodded proudly. 'And once I embrace I'm going to come and work for you,' he said suddenly.

I found myself watching him with an odd sense of pride. Simon had been little more than a child, caged and doomed to a terrible fate at Lilith's hands. I had been there to save them, but even after they were freed, Simon had come back for me, his determination and calmness igniting my will to survive, even though I knew I'd lost everything. To see him now...

*See. It wasn't all for nothing.*

Simon was the perfect reminder.

I put my hand on his shoulder and looked him in the eye. 'I heard you might be thinking something like that, and that's part of the reason I'm here.'

Simon smiled.

'Listen to me, Simon. You have a great set-up here. You're going to have more training ahead of you once you embrace and before long you'll have a partner to think of too. Where I am ... it's not the right place for you.'

His smile slid away and I wanted to take it all back but I knew I couldn't. He needed to hear this.

'But you're the one,' he whispered.

'The one?' I asked softly.

His big blue eyes looked suddenly as young as they had the night he and the other children had lifted me through the fire. 'The one who changes everything.'

I bit my lip.

*And what exactly am I supposed to say to that?*

'Okay, well, how about we make a deal? You stay here after you embrace and complete all of your training with your partner then, and *only then*, if you still want to come and fight at my side, we'll talk about it again.'

His eyes narrowed and he pressed his lips together while he watched me. 'You promise?'

'I promise.' Now I just had to hope that by that time he would have lost any interest in getting mixed up in my crazy world.

'So,' I said standing up. 'Are you going to show me around and introduce me to your friends?'

Simon beamed, scrambling to his feet.

*Hell, even I know I'm quality show and tell.*

Lincoln insisted that Gray and I wear earpieces so he wouldn't miss anything.

*Let's hear it for bad ideas.*

I rolled my eyes, not seeing why the tech was necessary before reaching the clear-as-day conclusion that it was because he simply didn't trust us.

*Wow. The hits just keep on coming.*

The last of the daylight had just disappeared behind Manhattan's skyscrapers and Lincoln stood with Gray and me a few blocks down from the building we were targeting on 46th Street. Mia and two conductors lurked behind him as he shoved the earpiece and mic in my direction.

'Put them on.'

I glared at him as I snatched them, walking down the road a little to fit them – and put some distance between us. He was really starting to test my patience. And worst of all, I was mad with myself for being so completely affected by his nearness while he was so clearly immune to mine. Especially when I needed to be on my game.

I took a minute to get myself under control, pushing my emotions back. The city was abuzz in the way only Manhattan can be. Taxis dominated the traffic and lights flickered on in office buildings, where people would continue working long into the evening. Shadows loomed, moving towards me like creeping memories, just waiting for me to step into them, to ensnare me.

I jolted myself away from my thoughts and walked back to the group.

'There's a perimeter set up in the block surrounding the building and we have people on the neighbouring rooftops. Get in, do whatever it is you think you can do and get out. If I tell you to abort, you get out of there immediately, no questions asked. Do you understand?' Lincoln ordered.

'Of course,' I said. Gray cleared his throat, and though he nodded I could see his nostrils flaring. Gray did not take orders well.

'You have thirty minutes, starting now.'

'We have an hour,' I corrected.

'I reconsidered. If you haven't achieved anything within thirty minutes you're just kidding yourselves anyway. Thirty minutes, and that's it.'

Desperate for some form of mediation I glanced at the conductors. 'Are you supporting this?'

The female conductor – I didn't know their names – crossed her arms. 'If it were up to me, you wouldn't be going in at all.'

Mia remained noticeably silent with her eyes cast down.

*Perfect.*

'I can see why you keep them around,' I said to Lincoln.

'Yes.' He crossed his arms with a look of satisfaction. 'As opposed to your fan club they actually understand rank.'

I shook my head. 'They're not my fan club, Lincoln. They're my friends. They were yours once, too.'

He pressed his lips together, his eyes flicking to Gray. 'Many things were mine once. You're down to twenty-six minutes.'

I swallowed and started to walk. 'Let's go,' I said to Gray, who was already beside me.

'You're going to have to deal with that, you realise,' he said as we made our way to the side of the ten-storey stone building.

'He hates me, Gray. And he has every right. It won't help him to try and deal with anything at this point. I'm just here for Spence.'

'Yeah, well, I wouldn't mind if you clarified my role in all of this if you get a moment. I actually value my life.'

Gray was pointing towards the alley that ran behind the building when Lincoln's husky voice sounded in my earpiece.

'I don't hate you.'

My breath caught hearing the unmistakable pain that accompanied each tight word.

*Shit.*

I'd totally forgotten we were wearing mics.

'And I can assure you that I am well aware that you are only here for Spence. And *exactly* what your role is in all of this, Gray. So while we *all* appreciate hearing your conversation I would be immensely grateful if we could please get on with the task at hand.'

*Kill. Me. Now.*

Gray cleared his throat uncomfortably and mumbled, 'Sorry 'bout that.' Then he looked at me guiltily and pointed to his mic. 'Forgot,' he mouthed.

I closed my eyes and took a deep breath. When I opened them I started walking again. 'We should move around the corner,' I said, humiliated and desperate to end the conversation that Lincoln and God knows who else was listening in on.

We chose a well-shadowed area at the back of the building and began to climb the wall, leaping between windowsills, using the stonework as footholds to scale the building. It wasn't overly difficult. I considered what Lincoln had said earlier, referring to Gray as my partner. I could see how that would hurt, thinking I had replaced him as my Grigori partner – even though that was not the case at all. We worked together but in no ways like a partner team.

And then there was the kiss. It had helped me gain an edge in the fight against Lincoln, sure, but if I'd known what Gray was up to I never would've agreed.

I brushed that thought off quickly, telling myself that there was no way Lincoln would think there was more to the kiss than tactics. But maybe Gray had a point. Maybe I should at least set Lincoln straight on the partner issue.

*Or maybe I shouldn't.*

Maybe I should just let him think what he wanted to.

*It might make it easier for him – hating me. Maybe that's why he's been able to move on so completely.*

'Head in the game,' Gray murmured behind me as we slid through a top-floor window. I looked down suddenly, realising I hadn't even noticed we'd climbed the entire building.

I nodded quickly, silently chastising my runaway mind.

We climbed into an open-office workspace filled with sleek glossy desks and Aeron chairs – the type my father had obsessed over when he had his own office in the city. Clearly this company was doing well.

While I wiped my dirty hands on my black jeans we moved towards a doorway at the back of the room and found a small kitchenette. The area was deserted but all the lights were still on. Someone was home.

'Do your thing, princess,' Gray said, keeping a lookout.

'I really wish you wouldn't call me that.'

Gray grinned. 'And I wish I was lying on a beach in the Caribbean.'

I rolled my eyes but I was already concentrating on the well of power in my stomach. I mentally willed it up and out of me, sending it through the building.

I didn't like using my Sight. But I'd also made a point of learning how to control it in small doses. On some levels it had been successful and become a handy surveillance tool. I could scope an entire building, or even a city block, with little more than a thought. But still ... I was ever aware there was so much more in me that remained unexplored. And at that very moment, I could feel the power surge through me, as if it were looking for somewhere to go or even … for something specific to do.

Mum's warnings on the matter had been clear. She wasn't certain, and I continued to doubt her suspicions, but she believed that there was a chance that I was some kind of evolution-in-progress. As angels had learned to fall to earth and become human, I might be the first human who could evolve into an angel. She constantly warned me not to separate from my corporeal body for long, fearing that the lure might become so intense that I could forget to return, and I would lose myself.

Just the possibility that she might be right was enough for me to limit the use of my Sight, despite the pull.

The furthest I ever ventured was in that time just before sleep when my soul took over and sought him out.

*And that was never a conscious choice.*

Using my Sight, I roamed the levels of the building, quickly identifying a number of humans. There was, however, a darkened area on the level below us, which gave me a chill.

I returned to my body.

'There are about two dozen humans in the building. Half a dozen on this level and I think they're the ones we want. There's also a dark zone,' I said thoughtfully.

Gray was staring at me and I hit him on the shoulder, breaking him out of his daze. 'Sorry,' he said. 'It's just, you're one weird lass, you know that, right?'

'What's a dark zone?' Lincoln asked in my ear, causing goosebumps to rise on my arms.

'Something I can't see through. It could be titanium.'

'Hiding exiles within it?' he shot back.

'Possibly, but I can't say for sure, and anyway, it's a small area. It couldn't be hiding an army or anything.'

'I don't like it. You should come back out,' Lincoln instructed.

I looked at Gray and he pointed to his watch.

'We still have fifteen minutes. Out,' I said, pulling free my earpiece and shoving it in my pocket. He could listen in all he wanted but I couldn't do this with him talking to me. 'Tell me if he says anything worthwhile,' I said to Gray.

'Right now he's using several four-letter words,' Gray said wryly before leaning close to whisper in my ear. 'Do you think there *are* exiles in here?'

I nodded.

Gray threw a little bounce into his step. He was in the mood for a fight. I smiled at him. I was too.

It didn't take long for us to make our way down the corridor and towards what looked like a large boardroom. Through the glass doors we could see close to a dozen humans, sitting in an Armani, Prada and Gucci showdown of who had the slimmest tie and shiniest shoes. Chloe had been spot on; clearly these people were wealthy. And they didn't display that distant unaware look that usually accompanied humans under exile control. They looked motivated.

Time wasn't on our side thanks to our clock-keeper outside, but Gray and I settled back out of sight behind an open doorway and waited for a few minutes. It paid off when we saw two of the humans leave the boardroom and come towards us. We let the two men walk straight by us into a nearby office.

Before the door swung closed, my foot was stopping it and

Gray had his arm around the first human's neck from behind. I followed in time to see the second man already with his hands raised in surrender. They didn't scream or try to fight.

I hesitated. Alarm bells were already going off.

*They're expecting us.*

I looked at the man standing with his hands up. He was calm. No more than forty and typically good-looking in a tall, neat, tailored kind of way. He wore a gold ring on his wedding finger and on the desk before him was a framed picture of him with a woman and two children.

He smiled in a businesslike manner, one that said he was a smooth talker and accustomed to getting his own way. But his eager eyes told a less predictable tale.

'He told us you might come. I'd hoped I'd be the one to get to see you,' he said, his eyes skimming me and lingering on my wrists. 'He wants you to know that he's looking forward to seeing you.'

I knew he was talking about Sammael. I remembered that Lincoln was listening to all of this.

'Where is Spence?' I demanded.

The businessman smiled again, well aware he held a trump card. 'He has your friend and he wants you to know that if you want to see him again he will be in New Orleans the night before the next full moon,' he replied.

Gray groaned.

I glanced at him but he just shook his head. 'Nothing good ever happens in New Orleans.'

Gray nudged the first human towards the door. 'Let's take these two back with us. They clearly know more, and Lincoln wants to question them about the tournaments.'

'It's all him, isn't it?' I pushed, keeping my eyes on the man behind the desk. 'Sammael? He's running the tournaments through your companies?'

The man shrugged. 'There are a lot of wealthy people who are willing to bet large amounts of money. It's profitable entertainment.'

I stared at him in disgust. 'Humans *go* to the tournaments? Willingly?'

He nodded and pointed to his computer. 'Live feeds. One of which you two starred in recently, if I recall.'

They'd watched us in London. But that realisation paled in comparison to the appalling reality of what was going on in the tournaments. 'You watch people slaughter one another?'

He smiled coolly. 'They are all willing participants. We merely provide the arenas.'

'And what about the humans who are murdered for sport?' I spat out. 'Are they willing participants too?'

The businessman's expression did not falter, not even for a second, and it made me sick.

*Does he even* have *a conscience?*

'Violet, we should move them out of here,' Gray said.

I nodded, stepping closer to the businessman, but before I had a moment to react, he raised his hand, revealing a gun we hadn't spotted. He aimed it straight at Gray and fired, and I gasped when I saw he'd shot not Gray but the other human right between the eyes. In the time it took to look back at him, he had the gun to his own head.

'Wait,' I said, holding up my hands. 'Don't!'

'Death is no longer of consequence. He has promised our ascension regardless of our crimes,' the man said, right before he killed himself.

'Oh my God,' I said.

Gray was already moving, grabbing my arm. 'Not God's work, Violet. This is something else. We've got to get the hell out of here before they all come running and start offing themselves.'

I gaped at Gray. Did he really believe the other humans would do the same thing? I was damn sure I didn't want to find out. We hurried towards the corridor and headed back through the communal work area to the window we'd left open.

'Oh, and by the way,' Gray said. 'You were right. This is definitely a trap.'

'Gotta love being popular,' I said.

'Say that again in about ten seconds,' he said, looking over his shoulder.

Two exiles were behind us, moving in fast.

Working in practised sync, we spun to face the threat, Gray automatically lining up with the one on the right while I continued backing up, drawing the attention of the one on the left. The latter wore a business suit and looked unnervingly like Agent Smith from *The Matrix*.

*Weird.*

He took off at a run, heading right for me. When he got close enough I kicked his chest hard, halting his momentum. He quickly corrected his balance and spun, grabbing me by the shoulders and throwing me so hard I smashed right through the tenth-storey window. As I fell through the air I tried to right myself, and using my speed and strength I managed to get into a good enough position to roll through the impact of landing.

But that doesn't mean it didn't hurt like a bitch. Especially since a large shard of glass had joined the party and embedded itself in my shoulder.

I barely had time to stand before the exile who had followed me straight out the window – though with a touch more finesse – was there, lining me up for another round of hurt.

*Fine by me.*

In fact, I felt more in my element than I had since stepping foot in New York. Since embracing fighting had always come naturally to me. I let the exile come at me and didn't flinch when I saw another one round the corner, stalking towards us.

The first exile started to throw a series of hard punches my way. But even with the hampered use of my right arm – thanks to my new glass accessory – I wasn't worried. I knew I needed to draw the second exile in as close as possible before I made my move.

But the first exile took me by surprise, grabbing my ponytail and yanking it back so sharply that I cried out. I swung around hard and backhanded him across the face, but he barely flinched, and didn't let go. Instead, the psycho once-angel licked his lips and smiled, confident he now had the upper hand.

*Bask in your ego, buddy. It will be the last thing you do.*

From the corner of my eye I saw a figure charge around the corner running right for us.

*Lincoln.*

'Stop!' I yelled, hoping he would see that I had things under control. Okay, so it didn't look good. *Maybe* it even looked like I was at their mercy. But I wasn't. I just needed the other exile to take two more steps towards me and then it would be game over.

But Lincoln didn't even pause to see any of that. It didn't occur to him that perhaps his help wasn't actually *helpful*. He simply barrelled into the fray and leaped on the other exile.

Sighing, I swung my leg out and took the exile's feet out from under him while he still gripped my ponytail. As he fell he took a large clump of my hair with him. I stood over him and delivered a round of kicks to his side, stopping him from getting up before I grabbed my dagger and dropped beside him.

'Choose,' I ordered.

He laughed, and spat at me.

*Gross.*

'Soon there will be no choice for anyone,' he hissed.

The spitting thing tipped me over the edge. 'Not exactly an answer,' I said, finishing him with a blow to the heart. 'But I'll interpret.'

He disappeared.

I turned in time to see the other exile in an all-out brawl with Lincoln. The exile was holding a large piece of glass and he'd already managed to use it against Lincoln, judging by the gash on his forehead.

I shook my head, anger bubbling to the surface. I'd had the situation under control and if Lincoln had just trusted me for a few seconds instead of barging in to save me, none of this would've happened.

Wincing, I pulled the long shard of glass out of my shoulder and pulled back the clasp on my wristband, piercing the skin with the tip of the glass and watching some of my silvered blood join the already thick coating of red.

Just as Lincoln took a hard hit to his temple Gray jumped down from a nearby window and landed beside me.

'I see I missed more fun. Any others?' he asked.

I shook my head.

'Well, he'll probably wrap this up in a few,' Gray said, watching Lincoln fight. And yes, he was getting the upper hand. But …

'We don't have a few,' I said, knowing that more exiles and suicidal humans could turn up at any moment. I walked towards the exile fighting Lincoln, and lined him up. When Lincoln delivered a blow to the exile's side, causing him to stagger back, I took the opportunity and threw the shard of glass towards the exile's leg.

It was anything but a kill shot, but then, the glass *was* coated in my blood. The exile blinked, stumbling back into the wall, no doubt confused as to why he was suddenly so sure he was dying.

Lincoln quickly looked between me and the exile, who in the next moment disappeared just like his buddy had done.

I didn't need to look to know that Gray was already on the move behind me. He never needed to be told when it was time to leave.

Lincoln jogged after us. 'I didn't need you to do that. I had him.'

I spun, feeling my blood boil. 'No, Lincoln, *I* had him! If you'd taken two seconds to look at the situation before charging in you would've seen I had them *exactly* where I wanted them. It would've been finished minutes ago my way and without you needing to get hurt. Unnecessarily! *Jesus!* You just can't stop yourself!'

He looked at my bleeding shoulder, his eyes like daggers, his voice low and threatening. 'You were hurt and on your knees. Two exiles had you. On. Your. Knees. I was—'

I put up a hand, stopping him. 'I know.' I sighed. 'I know exactly what you were doing and it's fine. Just forget it. You can't help yourself and I accepted that a long time ago.'

Defeated yet again, even though I should have probably just been grateful for the in-the-face reminder of why there was no future for Lincoln and me, I left the alley ignoring his yelling after me to explain what the hell I was talking about.

# chapter thirteen

*'I would believe only in a God that knows how to dance.'*
Friedrich Nietzsche

It took an hour to debrief.

Lincoln, who had travelled in a separate car and disappeared as soon as we arrived back at the Academy, had ever so kindly left me to deal with Josephine by myself.

'They just *shot* themselves?' Josephine asked, again, as appalled now as the first time she'd asked.

I nodded, returning my attention to her after taking a few minutes to heal my shoulder wound. 'Well, one of them shot the other one and then himself. But it was like they were completely fine with it. As if death was of no consequence for them.' I shook my head, equally disturbed by the memory. There was something about the way the men had so fearlessly relinquished their lives.

'And they said Sammael has Spencer in New Orleans?' she went on, covering more of the same questions and gripping her pen tightly as she documented every word I said.

'That he *will* have Spencer in New Orleans,' I corrected. 'They must've recaptured him at the airport like Chloe suspected. I'd say they're on the move but, yes, he said Spence would be in New Orleans the night before the full moon, which is five days from now.' Steph had looked up the lunar calendar before I'd even made it back to the Academy. 'So, that leaves us with four to get to New Orleans and figure out what the hell is going on.' I stood up, rotating my shoulder, which still felt the phantom wound. 'Josephine, it's been a really long day. I need to get out of here for a while and clear my head. I'll be back tomorrow morning.'

Zoe had already taken Gray back to Ascension. They'd promised to stop by the infirmary on their way to bring Chloe up to speed. And I desperately needed some alone time.

'You're welcome to stay here, you know,' she said, sounding surprisingly genuine, though equally cautious.

'Thank you, but no.' I headed for the door, hoping she wouldn't push.

'Violet, what's it like?' Josephine blurted as I neared the door.

'What?' I asked. But I knew. She was pushing.

'Seeing him again.'

I turned. 'Why would you ask me that?' As far as I was concerned she had no right.

She leaned back in her chair, placing her pen on her desk. 'I ask because I'm partly responsible.' She pressed her lips together before continuing. 'I realise you all think of me as hard and arrogant. I've even been compared to exiles in that way. But the difference between them and me is that I am very aware of my failings and what they have cost me and those around me.'

I felt a rare twinge of pity for Josephine and wondered if it was genuine remorse I was hearing in her words.

'What do you want me to say, Josephine? That it rips me in two? That it makes me want to crawl into a dark hole and never come out when I see what we've become? That this incredible love we have has destroyed us? Do you need to hear me say those things when they can't and won't change anything?'

'No.' She took a deep breath and let it out. 'No. I was wondering if you might explain to me why things must be this way? I assume your reasons are valid, but I have never fully understood how you could force this distance between souls that have once been joined.'

My throat was closing over and I took the time to smother my emotions even as the coldness stabbed me from the inside. 'Because if I don't maintain the distance, I will lose the only thing that keeps me going.'

'And what is that?' she asked softly.

'Knowing that somewhere in this world, he's alive.'

After taking one look at me, Steph took me up to her room for a shower – scaling buildings was never a clean sport, let alone fighting to the death.

'It's so strange that Dapper owns Ascension,' I said.

'Yep,' she said, tossing clothes from her wardrobe onto the bed. 'He bought it about a year ago. Here,' she said, tossing me a little black dress, which looked like it flared from the waist.

'I'm not going out, Steph,' I protested. I reached into my bag for a clean pair of jeans.

Steph quickly snatched them out of my hand and stuffed them back in my backpack. 'Just put on the dress. Everyone's already at Ascension and Dapper is stupid-excited to show you the place in action, not to mention your friends, who just want a chance to see you and show you how happy they are that you're back. It won't take long.' She held the dress out to me again. 'Put. It. On.'

I stared at her for a moment.

Steph was having none of it, though, and simply stared back until I finally gave in and took the dress.

It felt strange knowing I'd be seeing everyone in a social environment, especially without Spence. Plus, the only time I ever sported a frock these days was when I dragged Gray to our classes twice a week, and even then I changed straight afterwards. Wearing a dress now felt like stripping away one of my pieces of armour.

A piece I worried I was going to miss greatly.

When we walked through Ascension's unmarked door we were instantly assailed by the cacophony of sounds of a night out – music, talking, orders being called out, laughter and glasses clinking. My guards were up but I still felt his presence the second we crossed the threshold. The woman on the door smiled warmly when she saw Steph, pulling her into a brief hug and giving me a curious once-over. I eyed the rack of masks behind her with every intention of taking both the mask and hair-colour glamour offered for anonymity, but Steph shook her head.

'People still do it, but why would you when the whole point is that people are here to see you? And anyway, Dapper keeps things so tight around here that disguises are less common. It's a safe place, Vi – free from the Academy and opposition. Try to relax.'

'Easier said than done,' I mumbled. This was a world I'd walked away from. One I'd never believed I would be a part of again. It had almost killed me to do it the first time and though I knew Steph was trying to help she just didn't realise how hard it was going to be when I left again.

I took my time looking around. Though I'd been here last night, Ascension was different when it was full of people – the place was a living force unto itself. I stared up at the tall columns that supported scaffolding-style walkways and spiral staircases that wound their way up the walls. There were doorways to small rooms and bars scattered intermittently. Grigori of all shape, size, rank and age filled the club and as I anxiously noticed the numerous sets of eyes tracking me, I realised that there were also plenty that weren't.

With each step I took in Steph's black-and-silver heels I felt the music working its magic on me. From the beat vibrating through the floor to the sounds of the bass, I couldn't help but relax in that way only music could inspire. It's the one thing I've never been able to let go of. No matter what, it has remained my secret.

Steph led me through the busy bar area to a large table where many of my old friends sat and beside which Dapper stood, dishcloth slung over his shoulder, a smile on his face as he leaned against Onyx's chair chatting with his patrons.

When Dapper saw us approach he frowned.

'What?' I asked, letting him pull me aside.

'Am I hearing things right? New Orleans?'

I nodded. 'Looks that way. We'll start assembling a team and making a plan tomorrow.'

'Violet, New Orleans is not a normal city. You're going to have to watch yourself there like never before.'

'Why is that?' I noted that the worry in his eyes was intensifying with each word.

'Witches.'

I grinned. I couldn't help myself. 'Really?'

Dapper didn't smile. If anything he paled. 'I don't believe in them either, but New Orleans is … Like I said, it isn't normal. Strange things happen there, and the power … it's wrong.'

I swallowed, absorbing an influx of Dapper's strong emotion. Fear tastes peppery.

Dapper wasn't messing around. Something about New Orleans really frightened him. I wet my dry lips. 'I'll be careful, Dapper.'

He nodded, back to his typical gruff self again and with a hand on my shoulder turned me towards the table. 'Well, I'm glad you're here tonight of all nights,' he said, but despite the new playfulness in his tone I caught the tinge of sadness in his eyes.

*He knows I'm not staying.*

I smiled nonetheless, keeping up appearances. 'Why?'

'Because tonight,' he said, looking up at the stage where a brightly clothed band was setting up, 'is salsa night.'

I couldn't help myself; I laughed out loud. I'd always loved to dance, but Dapper couldn't know that – none of them could. Except for Gray, who sat on the far side of the large table, looking rather green as he watched the band.

Morgan looked up at that moment and immediately yelped, leaping out of her seat and then jumping up and down. I shook my head, smiling. It was comforting to know that some things had remained the same. Even if, looking around the table, it also felt abundantly clear that I no longer fitted in.

'Oh my God, oh my God. I can't believe you're here! I've been trying to get to you all day!'

'Well, I'm here now,' I said, accepting her hug.

*Does everyone always hug this much?*

'Let her go, Morgan!' Zoe yelled, when it became apparent Morgan wanted to continue jumping up and down. With me.

Morgan quickly dropped me. 'Sorry!'

'That's fine,' I said, taking a seat and saying hello to everyone, pausing momentarily when I noticed Rainer and Wilhelm sitting on the other side of the table.

Salvatore wrapped Steph in his arms and sat her beside him. Seeing them so in sync with one another, a sharp bolt of longing shot through me. Zoe was there with two empty glasses in front of her already. Gray had wedged himself close to her and when I threw him a wry look he simply waggled his eyebrows. Onyx was on Zoe's other side with a bottle of bourbon, a shot glass and a wicked grin. I didn't need to ask what it was for. I didn't need to see *him*. I could have closed my eyes and still walked a straight line to where I could sense Lincoln in the far corner of the club.

I rolled my eyes at Onyx and gestured to the drinks as I asked Zoe, 'Doesn't Dapper have a problem with this?'

She shrugged. 'No police come knocking on his door here; no one knows it exists. Dapper figures if we're old enough to battle it out to the death then we're old enough to have a few cosmos too. But he usually cuts us off after a few.'

'Shouldn't you be working?' I asked Onyx.

He threw back a shot. 'I am. Customer relations. Are you enjoying yourself?'

A waitress came over and placed a number of drinks on the table. One in front of me. I raised an eyebrow.

'See?' Onyx said. 'Don't say I'm not looking after you.'

I shook my head and took a sip. Whatever it was it tasted citrusy and delicious. 'Thanks.'

'It's good to see you, Violet,' Wilhelm said from across the table.

'You, too,' I replied, doing my best to return his easy smile. 'I'm sorry I haven't managed to stay in touch,' I said to Rainer.

Her eyes softened. 'We know you've been doing what you had to. It's just … It's good to see you. We all felt your loss when you left New York, but when I heard you'd left Lincoln … Well, I'll admit I wondered if we'd ever see you again.'

'You were always going to see me again, Rainer. You of all people.'

She raised her eyebrows. 'Really? Now I'm intrigued.'

I glanced around the table, spotting something in the far corner of the room that made me flinch. I looked back at Rainer forcing my expression to remain neutral. 'I have some unfinished business that I want to talk to you about. Maybe in the morning?'

She nodded, understanding that this was not the time or place but I could tell I had her full attention. 'I'll be at the Academy. Come and see me in my office.'

'How about we meet in the infirmary instead?' I suggested.

Rainer watched me for a beat before quickly nodding. 'That would be fine, too.'

No longer able to stop myself, my gaze drifted to the back corner. Lincoln sat in a booth with Mia. They had their heads close, talking over drinks. Jealousy I wasn't entitled to feel struck my heart while something altogether possessive and fierce marched forth from my soul.

'What's the deal with those two, anyway?' I blurted to Steph before I could reel myself in.

Steph shifted in her seat and pretended to realign her skirt, all the while looking extremely uncomfortable.

'Steph,' I pushed.

She glanced up and sighed. 'I don't know. No one really does. They've been friends for a while, but the past few weeks they've been spending more time together. There's talk that ... that Josephine's pushing them to apply to become partners. So far they've refused.'

I swallowed. 'Why?'

It was a loaded question and Steph knew it. Lincoln was free to take a new partner; I'd made that much clear to him when I'd left the city. If he and Mia were a good match and worked well together, then the only reason he wouldn't want to be made her official partner was if they were ... Couples can't be partners.

*Unless of course they're soulmates and willing to destroy one another.*

'Honestly?' Steph asked, monitoring my reaction.

I ignored the little voice inside that told me to give this conversation a wide berth and nodded.

*Yes, I'm totally unstable.*

'I think it's because Lincoln would never consider another partner but you. But that's just my opinion.'

I gripped my glass and took a few deep swallows. I caught Morgan watching, and when she met my eye she quickly looked away.

'But not everyone's,' I said, reading between the lines.

I sat up straighter and grabbed the fresh drink that had just been placed in front of me, and lifted it to Onyx in thanks. 'Well,' I said, in an attempt to brush off Steph's words, 'he should do whatever he wants. For whatever reason he has. He deserves happiness.'

*And he does.*

*He deserves everything.*

I threw back my drink and did all I could to look like I didn't care that Lincoln hadn't even glanced in my direction.

*You can't have it both ways, Vi. Just stop thinking so damn much.*

I started on a new drink. Lincoln's indifference was a gift, really. It only made things easier and I should have been grateful. This way we'd be able to work together. We'd find Spence. Someone passed me a shot. We could stop whatever the briefcase man was doing. I threw back the shot and held my glass out for another. It would all be fine.

Dapper's hand landed heavily on my shoulder. 'I just cut you off,' he said as I pouted.

'Why? You know the alcohol effect will only last for about fifteen minutes.' The downside of increased healing abilities.

'And I'll have you know I work in a pub now. I'm very familiar with responsible service *and* consumption of alcohol.'

*Did I just slur?*

He shrugged. 'Come and talk to me in fifteen minutes, then. Or when you need a job.'

Feeling miserable, I diverted my attention to the band, listening to the music and watching the people moving on the dance floor. Dancing had always been the one thing that could take my mind off everything. It was bittersweet, of course, but in some ways felt like a deserved punishment.

Right then, I needed something and I needed it desperately. Something other than the constant cold and the ever-present pain.

'Gray!' I hollered across the table.

He looked up, already dreading this moment. Oh, he knew.

He shook his head slowly. 'No. No way. You promised never in front of people we know.'

I leaned forward. '*Nooo*. I promised never in front of the guys. And *the guys* aren't here.'

'No!' he yelled over the music, setting his jaw.

I nodded calmly. 'You still owe me and you know it.'

The whole table was watching our tennis-match conversation now.

'No. Way.'

I stood up, my hands braced on the table as I leaned all the way across. 'Make it good and you won't have to go to classes with me any more.'

Gray took a sharp breath. I knew he wanted out of those classes more than anything. Finally, he stood up, giving me a hard look before turning it on the rest of the table. 'If any of you ever speak a word of what you are about to see I won't be held accountable for my actions.' He looked back at me, scowling. 'And if you go back on your word I'll never bring you in on another paying gig as long as I live. Hear?'

I smiled, holding out my hand.

'What the hell was all that about?' Steph asked me.

I turned a sweet smile on Steph. 'Gray was just asking me to dance.'

He yanked me out onto the dance floor before she could respond.

'Back corner,' I said, wanting to be out of sight.

Gray rolled his eyes, yanking me along and altogether livid. 'Oh, you think?'

# chapter fourteen

*'Love is not a fire to be shut up in a soul. Everything betrays us: voice, silence, eyes; half-covered fires burn all the brighter.'*

**Jean Racine**

the moment Gray pulled me into a dance position, everything else slipped away and I all but sighed with relief.

'We're square after this?' Gray double-checked.

'Square.'

If he could go back in time he probably never would have agreed to go to classes with me, but Gray wasn't the type to go back on his word. So, twice a week for the past year, Gray and I had gone dancing.

He was atrocious at first, but once he got over himself and realised no one was going to point and laugh he started to improve; now he was quite good. And when it came to the lifts he was so strong he pulled them off with ease.

Our kind of dancing was by the book. I loved to get a little carried away when I was in my own space, but whenever I was close to another body I was hyper-aware, and Gray respected my … limitations.

He put me through a good workout, spinning me at every

opportunity. He tossed me around a few times and the people in our immediate vicinity moved back to give us more room.

By the end of the second song, I was covered in a thin film of sweat, but since I knew that this was the last time I was going to force Gray to dance with me, there was no way I would let him off the hook. I looked up to tell him just one more song only to feel my heart stall. My eyes fixed not on Gray's but on the blazing green ones just over his shoulder – firing into mine to a depth only they could achieve.

Seeing my face, Gray intuitively and cautiously stepped back, putting some distance between us. Lincoln stood rigid, jaw clenched, hands fisted by his sides.

Gray's eyes darted from Lincoln to me and I could see his mouth running over a string of mumbled curses. Eventually, when it became clear no one else was about to speak, Gray cleared his throat.

'How 'bout I go buy your friend over there a drink?' he asked.

Lincoln nodded curtly. 'How 'bout,' he said, his wild eyes not leaving mine.

Gray was out of there so fast he practically ran. I took a tentative step back, feeling the tension rolling off Lincoln. I glanced at my table of friends, whose eyes were all fixed in our direction, mouths hanging open. Onyx had swivelled his chair around to get a full view.

*Great. Nothing like a captive audience.*

And then, suddenly, I blushed. I hadn't meant to get carried away on the dance floor. I certainly hadn't meant for it to make Lincoln angry. He shouldn't have even been able to see us from the far side of the room.

As if reading my mind he took a step towards me. 'I went over to your table to tell you that you were right. It was a good call hitting them tonight and I was being stubborn.'

'Oh,' I said nervously, with a shrug. I took another sideways step, edging off the dance floor and towards our table, hoping that was all he came over to say. But as soon as I moved Lincoln closed the distance, his hand bracing tightly on my hip. Feeling the warmth of his touch, I stiffened in a hopeless attempt to guard myself. And then his voice dropped as he spoke close to my ear.

'You learned to salsa.'

I swallowed, my throat suddenly dry. 'I suppose.'

'Why?' he asked evenly, not moving away, his hand pushing into my hip.

I leaned back, trying to look away. 'A hobby, I guess.'

His lips pressed together but then he tugged me closer, speaking in my ear again. 'So, you can salsa. But is that all you can do?'

*He's too close. Too close! I can smell him. I can feel his warmth, his breath on my neck.*

'I ... I ...'

Not waiting for me to fumble through the answer, he stepped away, leaving me instantly bereft and held out his hand.

'What?' I blurted.

He half smiled. 'You still owe me a dance,' he said, his voice flat.

I baulked. 'What? That was ...' I couldn't even find the words. That dance was something we'd promised each other before everything had happened. It was ...

He shrugged, hand still out. 'Yes, well, there haven't been many opportunities since then.' He raised his eyebrows. 'Afraid?' It was a challenge.

*Damn it.*

I wanted to run and hide. Or just crumple to the floor and roll up into a ball. But another part of me was going to be damned if I looked like the pathetic girl who couldn't even manage to be in the same room as him. I'd already let him humiliate me once today.

My shields were up and if we were going to work together to find Spence it was about time he understood I was stronger than he realised. A little dancing would hardly undo me.

'Fine,' I gritted, lifting my hand towards his. 'But I believe it was *you* who owed *me* the dance.'

He snatched my hand and led me to the centre of the dance floor, spinning me out and then snapping me back into his chest. 'Then I'll be sure to do my best to not disappoint,' he growled.

*Jesus. Save me, someone. Now. Please.*

And so Lincoln and I danced for what was, strangely enough, the first time since I'd attempted to throw myself on him the night of my seventeenth birthday.

And of all the things I've dreamed about, it would have to have been on the top of my list. Almost. But in my fantasies, well, hell – even the most vivid imagination couldn't have conjured this.

Lincoln had once alluded to the fact that he knew his way around a dance floor, but this was …

He leaned in when I shot him a curious look. 'My mother loved dancing. All disciplines. For years I was her reluctant dance partner.'

Without another word he led me around the dance floor with purpose – pulling me, pushing me, controlling me, always one step ahead ready to catch me. He was fast and smooth and it wasn't just salsa. He mixed Latin with swing and threw in a good dose of plain old dirty dancing. If I hadn't been so damn well caught up in the whole thing, I would have paused to blush.

*No. Definitely not like dancing with Gray.*

It was close contact.

His hand on my lower back, fingers spread, pressing just so.

Hips jammed tightly together.

Knees bent.

Strong arms pulling me so tightly they arched my back.

Breathless.

Our bodies moulded together like they were designed for that very purpose.

My soul ached but my heart powered to life and for a moment, just an agonising split second, the coldness receded and I was … me.

Somehow my body melded even closer with his and Lincoln tucked the hair away from my eyes, tilting my head up to his. 'There you are,' he murmured.

*Where only you could find me.*

When the song finished, Lincoln cast his eyes to one side and it was clear he couldn't look at me. Slowly his hand slid from my waist and, chest heaving like mine, he started to walk towards his table. I wasn't sure if he realised his other hand still firmly gripped mine, but he didn't appear to be letting it go and for some reason I couldn't bring myself to pull away, so he dragged me along with him.

Gray was grinning from ear to ear when we approached Lincoln's corner booth, where he'd made himself at home beside Mia.

'Well, well,' he said. 'If it isn't my *ex* dancing partner. Can't say I'm sorry the partnership is over. Especially since now I can see all your naughty intentions.'

Mia chuckled and I took the opportunity to glare at her for a completely different reason.

Gray noticed Mia's giggle too. 'You, on the other hand,' he said, leaning towards her. 'I'd be more than happy to try some of those moves with you.' He smirked.

Mia glanced briefly at Lincoln, who had now let go of my hand and seemed unhappy in general. She rolled her eyes at him and then stood up, taking Gray's hand. 'A dance right now sounds like a great idea,' she said.

Lincoln and I watched as the two of them disappeared onto the dance floor. I felt embarrassed that Gray was hitting on Lincoln's—

'I'm sorry,' we said simultaneously.

I did a double-take, confused by his apology. I went on. 'Gray's a flirt. Actually, he's a sleaze. You might want to get Mia away from him at some stage tonight, otherwise he might think she's fair game.'

'Okay,' he said, his brow furrowed.

I couldn't bring myself to keep talking about Mia with Lincoln in this way, so I started to walk away.

'Violet,' he called out suddenly, but his voice was strained.

I turned back to him.

He swallowed, looking briefly out to the dance floor. 'I know we just danced, but aren't you upset that your ... that your boyfriend is dancing with another girl?'

I looked from Lincoln to the dance floor then back to Lincoln, feeling entirely confused. Without thinking, I blurted, 'That's the most disgusting thing I've ever heard! Gray isn't my, my ... Hell, he's barely qualified to be a friend.'

Lincoln nodded, his look decidedly dubious. 'A friend with whom you dance like *that*.'

I put my hands on my waist, struggling to see past the red. The fact that Gray was easy on the eye and drew his fair share of female attention was one thing but for Lincoln to honestly think I could register any kind of attraction to another person ... I took a deep breath, considering that it might be better to just let him think that, but for some reason I just couldn't stand any more lies. There had already been too many to count.

'I bribed him,' I confessed.

'Sorry?'

'He'd made a mess of a hunt and I saved his ass. And, considering by the time I did he was butt naked and hanging upside down, let's just say he owed me big time for both his life and his pride.' I shrugged. 'I forced him to go to dance classes with me twice a week from then on. He hates it with a passion but not as much as he hates the idea of the other Rogues knowing how close he came to a naked death.'

It was the most I'd said to him since arriving. Lincoln took a step towards me, his eyebrows drawn together. 'You're telling me you're *not* with Gray?'

I half laughed, not that anything right then was funny. Far from it. If only he knew how impossible the concept of being with anyone in that way was to me.

His frustration didn't ease. 'What about that kiss today?'

I dropped my shoulders and stared at him, my neutral expression saying it all.

He shook his head slightly and looked up. 'A distraction.'

'One that would've normally cost him a limb,' I said.

Suddenly exhausted by the long day and night on top of my previous sleepless night, I sighed. I gestured half-heartedly to where Gray was dancing with Mia. She was lifting his hands from where they had been moving dangerously low on her back. He was damn lucky he never tried that with me. I pointed to them.

'You might want to go cut in,' I said, even though the idea of him dancing with Mia like he'd just danced with me made me want to break in two. *After* breaking every bone in her body first.

I walked back to my table without another word.

Morgan was fanning herself dramatically as I approached. 'I have never seen anything so hot in my entire life!'

I grabbed my bag. 'I'm outta here.'

'I'll go with you,' Steph said, quickly standing and joining me.

As I walked behind the bar and through the door marked 'private' I could feel Lincoln's eyes on me, but I didn't allow myself to look his way again.

Once we made it into the back of house Steph walked me to my room.

'Thanks, Steph,' I said, wishing I could put into words how sorry I was that I'd taken off and left her behind, and how grateful I was that she didn't hold it against me even though she had every right to write me off as a friend.

'Want to talk about it?'

I shook my head. 'No. Thanks, but I just need to be alone for a bit. I'll see you in the morning, okay?'

Before disappearing back into the hall she paused at the door to ask, 'Roses or daisies?' When I stared back blankly, she added, 'For the wedding.'

'Oh,' I said, catching on. 'Daisies,' I answered, surprising myself. Steph had always been a roses girl, but I wasn't the only person who had changed over the past three years.

She smiled. 'Band or DJ?'

'Definitely a band. Something loungey and sweet.'

She nodded. 'Night, Vi.'

'Are you scared?' I asked quietly. 'The age thing?' Salvatore could live for many hundreds of years and continue to look young while Steph would live a normal human life.

'It's weird to think of all the unknowns, but I love him, Vi.' She gave me a knowing look. 'I have to believe that the rest will work itself out.'

# chapter fifteen

*'All is riddle, and the key to a riddle is another riddle.'*
**Ralph Waldo Emerson**

**I** woke with a start, surprised to realise I'd actually drifted off to sleep. It was one o'clock in the morning, which meant I must have had at least a few hours' shut-eye. Glancing around the unfamiliar surroundings I groaned, leaning back onto my pillow as the events of the past twenty-four hours came rushing back.

In such a short amount of time everything had come tumbling down around me, and now that I was alone with no one's thoughts but my own, they screamed at me that I was utterly screwed.

Unable to stay in my room any longer I headed to the kitchen, hoping I might find enough supplies to rustle up a late-night snack.

'I was wondering if I'd see you again tonight,' Dapper said from the doorway as I was half buried in the refrigerator. Then he checked his watch. 'Or should I say morning?'

He still had a dishcloth over his shoulder and looked like he'd just come upstairs after closing up.

'I couldn't sleep,' I said, dumping some bread and cheese onto the bench. 'Toasted cheese sandwich?'

He shook his head. 'That was quite a show the two of you put on earlier.'

I busied myself with making the sandwich while waiting. I knew he had more to say.

Dapper disappeared around the corner. I could hear him rummaging in his small bar, ice cubes clinking into a glass. 'You want a drink?' he called out.

'No, thanks,' I responded, pouring myself a glass of milk instead.

I was putting the cheese sandwich in the press when he resumed his position against the doorjamb, drink in hand.

'He came here tonight so I could heal him.'

I nodded. I'd noticed that the cut on Lincoln's forehead was considerably better. It would probably be gone by morning. Dapper had the ability to heal both humans and not-only humans.

'Thank you,' I rasped.

He rubbed the back of his neck, looking tired. 'I would've done it even if you hadn't asked me to be there for him before you left,' he said, referring to the favour I'd called in. 'Not that he comes to me as often as he should.'

'What do you mean by that?'

'He's stubborn, like you. He only comes to me when he has to. No way he would've come to me with tonight's injury if he didn't need to be in top shape to go after Spence. Normally he just sits and suffers through the broken bones.'

'Jesus,' I whispered. 'Why does he always have to take the hard road?'

'Are you really asking that? *You*?'

I shook my head. 'I wouldn't take the hard road if there was another option. But he's got someone here who can help him and he doesn't accept it. That just doesn't make sense. He doesn't always have to be the martyr.'

Dapper threw back the last of his nightcap and rinsed the glass in the sink. 'Have you considered that he doesn't do it because every time he accepts that this is now his life he loses a bit of what he had with you?'

'That's—' My eyes burned. 'That's not true, Dapper. Lincoln gave up on me a long time ago.'

'Oh, yeah?' he replied, raising an eyebrow. 'And when would that have been?'

'When he stopped looking for me. He chased me all around the world. There wasn't a day I couldn't feel him hunting me down in that first year. Then one day he just stopped.'

'And you wanted him to keep chasing?'

'No,' I said, sighing heavily. It hurt knowing that he was doing nothing but search for me, knowing I couldn't ever let him find me. It was a cruel game of cat and mouse with no victor to be had. I swallowed. 'It was for the best.'

He reached for his dishcloth and dried his glass. 'I remember when he came back. He sat in this bar for nearly a month. I've never seen anyone drink so much, not even Onyx.' He half laughed. 'And then there were the girls.'

I looked up sharply. 'Dapper, please,' I begged. I couldn't hear this.

He ignored me. 'They came from everywhere. All wanting to be the one who mended his broken heart and sorry soul.'

'Oh,' I said.

'Your sandwich is burning.'

I lifted the sandwich press and quickly transferred the burned-cheese melt onto the bench. I wasn't hungry any more.

When I looked up, Dapper's eyes were fixed on mine, waiting. 'He never looked at one of them. Not even for a fleeting moment.'

I swallowed something that tasted a lot like relief. 'So, what happened?'

'I'm not sure, exactly. One day Spence came in, the two of them got in a scrap and then Spence managed to haul him out. The day after, he just didn't turn up. The next time I saw him he was back with the Academy and a few months later he was running his own show. That's all he's done since. Just put his head down and worked.'

'That, I can understand.'

He nodded. 'I'm not surprised. There's only one person in this world for each of you. For as long as you're each not willing to take what you need, the other will inevitably suffer. It's a Gordian Knot if ever there was one.'

'What did you just say?' I asked, a shiver running down my spine.

'I said you two are impossible. Like a Gordian Knot. Do you know the story?'

'Yeah. I've heard it before.'

*Damn you, Phoenix.*

I knew he'd played a hand in this little coincidence; it had angel prints all over it.

'I think I might go out for a walk,' I said.

'Suit yourself. But if you're just after some fresh air, those stairs over there will take you to the roof. It's a nice view. And exile free.'

I nodded, before grabbing a sweater from my room and heading up the stairs as Dapper went to his and Onyx's room.

When I pushed through the high door and came out onto the roof, I was suddenly reminded of where we were. I was standing on the top of a Brooklyn Bridge pillar. 'Whoa.'

I moved to the edge and sat down with my legs hanging over. I'd only managed a few minutes of sky gazing before I felt the change in the air around me as gravity shifted and time slowed until the world around me was still.

My shoulders slumped and my head dropped forward. Of course. It was too much to ask for a few minutes alone.

When I turned around, remaining seated, I saw the whole gang present and accounted for.

I glared at Phoenix, who quickly held up his hands in surrender.

'Hey, you should be thanking me. Nox kept trying to turn up right in the middle of your dance.'

I grimaced. 'You all saw that?'

'Every single hip thrust and possessive look,' Nox said, dragging out his words.

'Even if you'd be better off dancing with someone else,' Phoenix threw in, his eyes moving away before I could catch them.

'You're probably not wrong there,' I admitted. Dancing with Lincoln had stirred too many of the emotions I worked hard to keep buried. 'Though dancing with *you* would be no wiser,' I added, to which he glanced up and gave a half smile.

I turned my attention to the others, noticing the grave expressions worn by my angel maker and Uri.

'How bad?' I asked.

*Stupid question. The fact they're all here is answer enough.*

'Very,' Uri replied.

'Anyone care to elaborate?'

'New Orleans is a ... complicated territory. Many bad things happen there,' Uri said.

'What bad things?'

'Things not meant for this world,' my angel maker answered.

'We recommend that you stay away from the city,' Nox added.

My eyes widened. 'You want me to hide from a fight. Since when?' I didn't bother to add that there was no chance I wouldn't go after Spence. I assumed that was already understood.

'To clarify, we don't *all* recommend you avoid the city,' Uri offered.

'*I* do,' Phoenix said.

Nox smiled. 'See. *He* does. And he knows you so, *so* well.'

I rolled my eyes. 'You do realise I can hurt you here,' I threatened Nox, reminding him that my blood – the very weapon the angels had instilled in me – was just as lethal to them when they chose to inhabit human forms as it was to exiles.

'We are all acutely aware of that,' my angel maker said, his perfectly articulated words sending a shiver down my spine.

I took in his chiselled jawline and seamlessly structured features, his perfectly neutral but purposeful clothing of grey pants and white shirt gracefully disguising a warrior's physique with none of the carelessness of Uri and none of the vanity of Nox. My angel maker was simply all about task and function. 'That in itself is part of the problem.'

'What's that supposed to mean?' I asked.

His lips pressed together, just enough to give away his slight hesitation. Along with Phoenix's frustration it only served to make me more curious. But Phoenix stepped forward, stopping my next question. 'They can't say, Violet. I can't either.'

I snorted. 'Since when do you follow the rules?'

He bit his lower lip. 'Being an angel makes it impossible for me not to. Why do you think so many of us exile? All I can tell you is that you already know part of it – so think back.'

'Back to when?'

'To the time you try hardest to forget.'

I looked away, knowing that this had something to do with the night we took down Lilith and the man with the briefcase.

*But I need more to go on.*

'I can give you everything you need,' my angel maker said, causing me to narrow my eyes at him.

'Did you just read my mind?' The corners of his mouth lifted slightly. 'Everything, huh?' I mused. 'How about starting with your name?'

'I already gave it to you.'

'Lochmet. Yes, but that's not your real name, is it? I know that my mother knows your name. She'll tell me if I ask.'

He nodded. 'Most likely. But you have not asked her because you know that you are not ready for the answer.'

I scoffed. 'Then how about you just answer once and for all what *I* am?'

'I answered that the first time we spoke.'

I thought back, shaking my head. 'No. All you said was that I was you and you were me.'

'And that is what you are.'

'So, I'm a warrior? But I'm human?' I swallowed nervously. 'I'm not an … I'm not becoming an angel, am I?'

He clasped one hand over the other gently in front of himself. 'Is that what you want?'

I didn't need a countdown to consider. 'No. I want to be human.'

'Then you must allow yourself to have the one thing that humans have that angels must not. The very thing angels envy most.'

'What?' I asked, dreading the answer.

'You already know. And when you surrender to it, when you allow yourself to be most vulnerable, you will be empowered and your time will arrive.'

'You're talking about love,' I said, knowing that it was the strongest emotion and gift of humanity.

*Except in my case.*

He bowed his head. 'You have the choice that we never will – to love fully and, most importantly, to be loved fully in return.'

I closed my eyes and whispered, 'But I've lost my love.'

'Love is never lost – only ever waiting to be found. You have been staring your answer in the face for a long time now, denying it and refusing to do what you must.'

I swallowed, glancing briefly at Uri. 'Surrender to it?'

'No, child. Surrender to yourself. Only then can you be the leader of your destiny.'

Not for the first time, I felt the weight of my angel maker's expectations and the great fear that I was not what he believed. Not enough. 'I'm not a leader,' I confessed.

'Said like a true leader,' he replied. 'And when your time comes, they will choose. If they choose to follow you, you will never doubt their loyalty for all your days.'

'Is that it?' I asked.

He nodded once.

I stood up and dusted off my clothes, now irritated. 'I don't even know why I bother. You need to learn how to speak without the cryptic. Then maybe I'll actually understand something you say before it's all over.'

My angel maker simply took in the view. 'It is the way it has always been.'

I rolled my eyes. 'Well, maybe it's time you evolved.'

To this, his eyes twinkled. 'We did. We made you.'

My mouth fell open.

'What do you know about the exile you saw that night?' Phoenix asked, and I could see the pain ripple over his features, remembering the night at Lilith's estate – the arrows, the death, the choices that were made that have forever changed us. 'The one who took—'

But I cut him off, holding up my hand, not wanting to hear him say it aloud. I wasn't ready to admit that I had let that exile steal my blood. Or that I'd always known, deep down, that it would come back to haunt me.

'His name is Sammael,' I said. 'He's behind all of this, somehow. He's controlling the tournaments and he has Spence. Why? What do you know about it?'

The angels all shared a look and I could see they were conferring on what they would say. I wished fleetingly that I could just beat it out of them. From the corner of my eye I saw Phoenix smirk and I glared at him. 'You *are* reading my mind!'

He chuckled. 'No. I just know you.' But then he looked back to my maker and after receiving a small nod, asked, 'Have you ever heard of the weighing of souls?'

I shook my head and hoped Phoenix would be permitted to shed some more light on the matter. Instead, he clenched his jaw in frustration.

*They aren't letting him say any more.*

'Ask Steph,' he said through gritted teeth, as if it was a battle just to utter the words.

And then they were gone.

Before I climbed back down into Dapper's apartment I texted Steph with an update before remembering the hour. I hoped I hadn't woken her, but then my phone beeped with a reply. Tossing up the idea of going out for a run, I headed into my room.

Only to find Lincoln there, standing by the window in the dark.

# CHAPTER SIXTEEN

*'And the angel said: "I have learnt that all men live not by care for themselves but by love."'*

**Leo Tolstoy**

'**W**e didn't finish our conversation,' he said.

I stayed near the entrance to the room, maintaining as much distance as possible and suddenly conscious of my daggy sweat pants and oversized black sweater that was so old and worn it had holes around the neckline. Of course, he looked … distracting, in faded jeans and a navy shirt, hanging unbuttoned and loose over a black T-shirt.

'It's 2 a.m.,' I replied, as if that actually mattered. 'And the less conversation you and I have, the better.' I stepped aside and held the door open, hoping he hadn't noticed the tremor in my hand.

Relief washed over me when he gave a small – conceding – nod and walked slowly towards the door. And then my stomach dropped when his arm whipped out and grabbed the edge only to slam it shut with both of us still in the room.

Standing close and breathing hard, he spoke in a low voice. 'Am I so insignificant to you that you won't answer a few simple questions?'

Defiantly, I walked over to where he'd stood by the window, re-creating the illusion of distance despite being acutely aware of how close we now were. How *alone*.

'Ask away,' I said, surprising myself but hoping this was the fastest way to get this conversation done with. 'If I can answer, I will. But then we move on. We need to work out what's going on in New Orleans and I need to stay focused on Spence.'

'Fine. First of all, clarify for me that you are not and have not been seeing Gray?'

I shook my head and kept my eyes on the windowsill. 'Not that it matters, but no. That's not a possibility for me.'

'Then why did I see the two of you walking out of some pub in Shoreditch a year ago with you in his arms while he yelled out to anyone who would listen that he was going home with you?' he accused. 'I *saw* him kiss you.'

I flinched.

*Should I let him believe it? Would it be better for him? To let him hate me this way?*

But I couldn't seem to conjure the lie. Instead I sighed, leaning against the wall. 'When I first moved to London I had no one. I was broke, surviving day to day, and I didn't want to use Mum and Dad's money. One night I was out hunting and I stumbled upon an exile in a hurry. I followed him to an old warehouse, where I found another three of them, and Gray hung up by his feet, barely alive. He was outnumbered and those exiles were their own special brand of sick. I could hear them talking about all the things they were going to do to him, and it was clear they'd already done a lot. The smart move would've been to wait them out and take them down but I could tell that Gray didn't have long left in him and I ... I recognised him from Santorini.'

I ducked into my en suite, where I ran the tap and splashed water on my face before coming back out, conscious of Lincoln's eyes on me the entire time.

'I hadn't spoken to another person, let alone Grigori, in months,' I explained, resuming my position by the window. 'So, I stepped in. I fought off three of them without too much trouble, but the last two had me and my dagger was thrown.'

I reached into my bag and withdrew a long, slim arrow with a sharp tip.

Lincoln's eyes went wide. I knew he was remembering the night Phoenix had done Lilith's dirty work and shot me with all those arrows.

'Yeah. It's my sick joke, I suppose. I usually have it fastened to my back.' I shrugged. 'It seemed fitting and it's always handy.' I spun the arrow to show how it split into two halves, making it twice the weapon. I rarely hunted without it.

'Grigori blade?' he asked, looking at the metal tip.

'Not so much.' I held out the inside of my wrist, unclasping the cuff and exposing the scar of the wound I'd first received in Jordan. I ignored his sharp intake of breath. The scar had been getting progressively worse each time I opened the wound. It was the only one that never healed completely.

'Your blood,' he murmured, almost painfully.

I tried for an easy smile as I put my cuff back on. 'I'm toxic, what can I say?'

When he didn't smile back, I kept talking. 'Anyway, I saved Gray and he saw me use it. I panicked that he'd tell other Grigori about it. The only people who really know about my blood are Spence, Griffin and Steph, though I figure Salvatore, Zoe, Onyx and Dapper have a pretty good idea. And you. You know.'

He nodded.

'And then, I healed him.'

Lincoln's nostrils flared at that. I tried to ignore it and the sensation it ignited in my stomach.

'And that freaked him out completely,' I powered on. 'But he remembered me from Santorini, and when I asked him, he agreed to let me hang out for a while and get in on a few paying jobs. He never told anyone about me and he knew I was ... that I didn't want to be social. Some of the Rogues can be forward at times and after I beat one to a bloody pulp it became clear that if I wanted to stay around, I had to work something out. One night when a couple of the guys started getting carried away, Gray just grabbed me and told them all I was out of bounds and that he was taking me home with him. They all just assumed he was staking some kind of claim, and, Gray being Gray, they accepted it. Every once in a while he'd leave the bar with me or put an arm around me and the guys would leave me alone.'

I was blushing, embarrassed to admit I'd let this happen, but I'd been desperate to be around people. Even if I couldn't actually be close to any of them.

'That night you ... saw. He ended up unconscious in the alley behind the pub for touching me like that. He never got carried away again.'

Lincoln, who'd remained deathly silent throughout the rehash, fell against the door, as if his legs had given out.

'What?' I asked, alarmed.

He seemed to be struggling to find equilibrium and shook his head repetitively. Finally he looked up, his green eyes so pained it hurt to see them. 'I travelled everywhere. For a year I was always one step behind. I found your parents in Spain. They let me stay with them for a few days, but it was torture, sleeping in a bed I knew you'd been in just weeks before. And, of course, they wouldn't tell me where you were. I ransacked the whole place to find the next lead.'

'I didn't know you stayed with them.'

He nodded, unsurprised. 'I followed you to Prague, Rome, Luzern, Brussels, always just missing you.'

I swallowed. 'I know.'

'I know you know. And I know that's why you kept moving, but I couldn't stop. How could I when I knew what we were? *Nothing* was going to stop me. When I finally traced you to London, it was so hard to get a pinpoint on you. Something had changed and I was afraid you'd been hurt. I'd heard rumours of a girl – a Rogue fighting solo and taking on groups of exiles at a time.' He half smiled. 'I figured you'd be reckless enough to do that. So, I tracked down Gray, hoping that he might have heard something or known someone who could help me find you.'

I nodded as it all came together. 'And then you saw us.'

He grimaced, his face now ashen. 'You'd learned to keep your shields up, but the moment I saw you I was able to break through them and sense you again. But you were ... in his arms. You had another life. And I wasn't part of it.' He ran a hand through his hair. 'I never would've believed it if I hadn't seen it with my own eyes.'

'But you did.'

He nodded. 'And now I force myself every day not to go after you again.' He swallowed tightly. 'Even when I feel you come to me.'

I mirrored the action, my mouth cotton dry. 'My Sight,' I said, understanding what he was saying. 'I ... I'm sorry about that. I can't ... when I'm asleep I can't always control it.'

He shrugged. 'Half the time I convinced myself I was imagining it anyway.'

His voice was so strained, I wanted to reach out to him. 'So, then you came back here?' I asked instead.

'Yes.'

'Well, it worked out for the best then,' I said. 'You've done really well.'

He pushed away from the door. 'You're not understanding, Vi.'

*He just called me Vi. Don't let it affect you. Remember!*

I cleared my throat. 'I think I caught most of it and I'm sorry that I hurt you and that things have gone the way they have. But you're better off. Trust me.'

'No,' he said, his eyes homing in on mine. 'You're definitely missing something. If I'd known you weren't seeing Gray. If I'd—'

I cut him off. 'It changes nothing, Lincoln.'

'It changes *everything*!' he thundered. 'I let you go because I thought you'd moved on! That I was ruined because I couldn't do the same but if you could, then I really had no right to stand in your way!' He was still yelling. 'But you're not fixed at all, are you? We're still us in all the terrible ways and none of the good!'

He was moving. I couldn't breathe as he stalked across the room, my back hitting the wall when I tried to retreat. 'There is no way I'm going to stand by and let you walk out of my life again.'

I was stunned, but Lincoln didn't hesitate. He grabbed me, a hand on either side of my face, and slammed his mouth against mine.

Every sensation I'd spent every second of every day trying to suppress flamed to life. Honey and the warmth of the sun enveloped me, and my body tightened in all that was bittersweet. It only lasted a few seconds before I threw him off me, breathless.

*But no one forgets heaven. Even if you only get it for a few seconds.*

And then I snapped, trembling from head to toe. 'Get the hell off me, damn you. You have no right to do this!'

But Lincoln showed no sign of backing down. I'd never seen him like this. 'I have *every* right and you know it. I gave up everything for you!'

And there we had it. The reminder I needed.

I bristled, my expression turning cold. 'No,' I said, suddenly calm. 'You *took* everything *from* me.'

He blinked. 'I gave my life for us!'

'You gave it for *you!*' I threw back.

'What the hell are you talking about?'

'You want to know why we can't be together? Fine! I can't ever be with you because you'll always be there to jump in and die for me. You'll die to save me and gladly leave me behind again. I'm barely here as it is, *barely* alive!' My voice broke, but now the words were coming, they weren't about to stop. 'Do you remember what it felt like when your soul shattered?'

'Yes,' he sneered. 'It isn't something I'll forget.'

'Tell me,' I demanded.

He visibly shuddered, his voice dropping. 'It was painful. Incredibly so. It surpasses anything imaginable. I can't put it into words.'

'Cold,' I said softly.

His brow furrowed. 'Yes. It was like an intense cold but so much worse, and everything felt twisted inside. Like it was all converging and exploding at the same time and then on top of it all was something so suffocating and inescapable because it was locked in my own body.'

I nodded. 'And how long did it last before there was nothing, before you were completely shattered?'

He swallowed hard. 'Minutes maybe. It could've been less or more but if felt like a lifetime.'

'And when you came back, the pain was gone?' I held my breath, knowing that this would answer one of my greatest fears.

'It was. Not that it mattered.'

A tear slipped down my cheek. As much as it was a relief to know his soul pain ended when I brought him back it was still horrible to know he'd had to suffer the pain even just for a few minutes. 'Just leave, Lincoln,' I said quietly. 'Please go.'

He crossed his arms over his chest. 'Nothing you can say will make me leave this room. Why are you asking about it, anyway, and who told you about the coldness?'

But even as he said it, the realisation dawned on his face. He stumbled back a step. 'No,' he whispered.

I couldn't respond.

'No, it can't be.' His head was shaking back and forth, the action a plea more than anything else.

I looked away.

'How?' he breathed. 'How can you have gone through it and still be here? I don't understand.'

It was a reasonable question. In his mind and anyone else's I must not have endured the pain of the shattering because I didn't disappear like he and Nyla had.

I let out a sad breath knowing that I couldn't leave it hanging like this. It was better to just get it done. Finished. I turned towards the window.

'After Phoenix killed me and brought me back, my soul couldn't find you. It hadn't experienced the disconnection in the way yours had but it responded nonetheless. The pain was there in all its glory but I didn't shatter completely, although there are times I wish for it.'

'*Are* times? *Wish* – as in *still. Now*?'

When I didn't answer, his tone became menacing. 'Violet, so help me God, answer me.'

I spun around to face him, my eyes locking with his and menacing in their own right. 'It never leaves. From the moment I was revived, it has never left. You call me a coward for turning off my emotions, but without my shields I'd be just as insane as any exile.'

Lincoln shook his head again, now frantic. 'They said ... Everyone said when I woke up that physically you'd been fine. And you look—' He held a hand out to me. 'Damn it, you're more beautiful than ever. How do you even stand up?'

'Because I have no choice.'

His mouth dropped open. 'But you do! We can fix this! *I* can fix this! Our souls are made to be joined. How can you have let this go on?' he screamed, looking so angry at the world, at me.

My anger rose up to match his. I clenched my hands. 'Because I'm not interested in a band aid! It will only end up killing me when it gets ripped off!'

'What the hell does that mean?'

I stepped towards him and pushed him in the chest. 'You don't get it – you never will! You want to run towards the fire to save me even when I'm the one carrying the bucket of water. You can't help yourself!'

Lincoln threw his hands wide. 'Because I fucking love you!'

My heart exploded, but I fought back my emotions and pushed against his chest again.

'It's not enough!' I yelled. 'I don't want someone to die for me.' My breath caught in my throat. 'Don't you get it, Linc? I need you to *live* for me. I *needed* you to let me risk my life when the alternative meant certain death for you. You left me!' I cried. 'And you did it with a full heart. You told yourself it was right, that you could make this sacrifice, but it was *you* who was the coward because you got to leave!' I smacked my own chest. 'I was the one left behind with the empty, broken soul.'

Tears were in his eyes. 'But you brought me back! It could've all been okay. Why'd you bring me back? Just to punish me?'

'What did you expect me to do? Bring you back and then just stand aside so I could watch you die for me all over again?

I'd rather live on the other side of the world, cold and in constant agony, and at least know that somewhere you still exist, because I know for certain that if you're with me – you're as good as gone.'

Lincoln's voice lowered. 'Tell me you wouldn't do the same for me. If I was in trouble, that you wouldn't give everything?'

'Not if it meant my leaving just so you could stay. I wouldn't condemn you to this life. I'd have your back to the last. I'd do everything I could bar simply taking your place. But *you* would, even if it weren't certain I would die without your stepping in.'

'That's why you left.' His shoulders dropped. 'That's why you were so upset with me tonight when I stepped into the fight.'

'I left because I promised my angel maker that I'd fight harder and give everything to hunting down exiles. It was our deal – my decision, no one else's – and I knew that all my future offered me was more blood. More death. I could live with that, I'd been given my three wishes, but I couldn't sentence all my friends to that future too.'

Lincoln fell to his knees. 'Three wishes?'

I'd said too much.

'Your parents?'

I nodded.

'The other two?'

When I didn't answer he yelled, 'Tell me!'

I swallowed. 'Phoenix. Though apparently I needn't have worried about him.'

'I heard he was an angel again. That he helped you.'

I nodded. 'He's a kind of guide now, but when he died I thought he'd gone to the pits. So, I asked for him to be okay. Turns out he already was.'

'Have you seen him often?' he rasped.

'Only a few times.'

Lincoln nodded. 'And the third?'

I sighed. 'What do you think?'

He looked up, ruined just like me. 'I think you gave up your family and friends and everything you have known and loved to become a warrior in return for bringing me back. And then you left me behind where I was expected to live in the shadow of your life and be reminded of you every day yet be without you just like you're accusing me of doing. So, tell me,' he said as he stood, 'did you give up everything just so that *I* could live?'

He'd twisted my words.

I shut down my emotions, sending out a silent thanks that Phoenix's essence had mutated in this way, rather than amplifying emotion as it did for him. 'You need to leave,' I said. 'I'm tired and we have a big day tomorrow.'

He stepped in dangerously close and his words were like a growl. 'I walked away that night in London. I was wrong. I should *never* have given up. I think of all that time we denied our feelings for one another – all of that lost time – and I think of the past year, lost too. And now, to know that you live every breathing moment in intolerable pain on top of the heartache of us not being together ...' He shook his head, breathing in deeply. 'I'll walk out of here and let you get some sleep, but hear me clearly when I tell you, *no*. In no uncertain terms, under no circumstances, Violet, will I *ever* leave you again.'

# chapter seventeen

*'You have been weighed on the scales and found wanting.'*

**Daniel 5:27**

the next morning Gray and I arrived at the Academy bright and early to find Steph, Sal and Zoe in the main cafeteria having breakfast. I made a beeline for the coffee, grabbed a latte and a tea – yes, tea – for Gray and joined them. It would be the first of several coffees this morning. After the events of last night, topped off by another series of odd dragon-filled dreams, I needed all the help I could get to stay on my game today.

Steph had a number of books open in front of her.

'You don't look like you got much sleep,' I said.

She looked me up and down. 'Well, when you throw around things like the weighing of souls, it makes a girl restless.'

I sat beside her. 'What did you find out?'

'Nothing cheery, that's for sure. The weighing of souls is a Judgement Day thing in the Bible. The day we will all have our souls weighed and each and every one of us will be judged. If it's as simple as Heaven and Hell after all of this, well, the weighing of souls is kind of like green light, red light, if you get my drift. Here,' she said, opening a book and reading. 'This is the Roman Catholic version – *That you will gather the souls of the righteous and the wicked, place us on your great scales and weigh our deeds. That if we have been loving and kind, you will take the key from around our neck and open the gates of Paradise, inviting us to live there forever. And that if we have been selfish and cruel, it is you who will banish us.'*

My brow crinkled. 'And this is all connected to the tournaments and Sammael how?'

She shrugged. 'Beats me, but this stuff is major. And it's not just the Christians.' Steph flipped through pages. 'It turns up everywhere, dating back to ancient Egyptian mythology, and the concept of final judgement is shared by almost all religions. If this all has something to do with what's going on now ...' Steph paled and clasped Salvatore's hand.

'Steph, breathe. It will all be okay,' Salvatore assured her calmly.

I nodded, taking a gulp of my coffee, leaving my hands wrapped around the mug. 'If the world was scheduled to end later today, Phoenix would've found a way to tell me. So, whatever it is, there's still a way for us to prevent it from happening.'

'Yes,' Zoe said, dryly. 'Because in Phoenix we know and trust.'

I stiffened. 'Things have changed. He's an angel now.'

'Which, by the way, does anyone else find just a touch hard to stomach?' Zoe asked casually.

'He gave his eternity to stop Lilith. Redemption is not for us to determine,' Gray said levelly from across the table where he'd been listening silently.

Zoe rolled her eyes. 'Jesus, it's just like having Griffin at the table.'

But I also noted the longing there. She missed Griffin and I understood; being around the old crew highlighted just how much I did, too.

Gray's eyes went wide with dismay and I almost lost a mouthful of coffee as I laughed. Griffin was not the kind of person Gray considered himself to be anything like. It was funnier still, because Zoe was right.

Steph nodded vigorously, oblivious to Zoe and Gray's conversation as she stared into space. 'Because,' she said, her voice high-pitched, 'we have a wedding coming up, you know. The world can't end before I get married. That would just be ... Vi? You *have* to save the world. You can do that, right?'

I put a hand on her shoulder and fought to keep my expression serious as I looked into her glassy eyes. 'Steph, your wedding day will be perfect. Nothing and no one will ruin it. Got it?'

She exhaled. 'Got it.'

Everyone went back to eating their breakfast, chewing on this latest information as much as their cereal – the big question being: where did Sammael fit in to all of this? Max stopped by the table to let us know Josephine had scheduled a meeting for later in the morning.

Steph shuffled her chair closer to me and lowered her voice. 'That's the fifth time you've looked at the door in the past thirty seconds. Expecting someone?'

I lifted my cup to cover my mouth as I spoke. 'No. Yes. I don't know.' I sighed. 'Last night after my group of visitors disappeared back to ... wherever it is they go, I had another one.'

Steph choked on her mouthful of orange juice. 'Details!'

I slumped further into my chair. 'Shh! Just rehashing a lot of things I would've preferred to have left buried.'

I was still reeling from the night before and I'd barely slept more than a few minutes here and there after Lincoln had left my room following his *never leaving me again* bombshell. It was safe to say I might never sleep again given the way the words were stuck repeating in my head like the song that just won't go away.

'Here he comes,' Steph said under her breath, her eyes flicking towards the cafeteria entrance. I turned slightly to see Lincoln striding straight towards us. When he stopped in front of Gray I tensed, worried for all the obvious reasons, but Lincoln just put out his hand.

Unsure, Gray glanced at me then slowly clasped Lincoln's hand.

'I owe you an apology,' Lincoln said, causing more than a few people to pause and listen in. 'You've had Vi's back for the past year when she needed someone. I shouldn't have jumped to conclusions.'

Gray shook his hand. 'No hard feelings.'

Lincoln smirked. 'Although I still owe you one for your dirty-handed tactics in the hall yesterday,' he said.

Gray shrugged. 'Tell me you wouldn't have done the same.'

Lincoln laughed. 'Perhaps. Nonetheless, you deserve my gratitude not attitude.'

Zoe snorted. 'Since when did you start rhyming?'

Lincoln smiled and it seemed different, almost boyish. 'Well, Zoe, you can expect a lot of things to change around here.' He looked at Morgan, who had just arrived and was sitting down beside me. 'Would you mind? I need to discuss a few things with Vi.'

The way he was now saying my name was so raw; the only time he'd used it like that had been at the cabin, when we'd thrown all caution to the wind. At least, that was what I'd thought. Lincoln had already devised his plan for everything by then.

I glared at Morgan as she cheerfully leaped out of the seat. *Traitor.*

It wasn't lost on anyone that there had been a definite shift in Lincoln's behaviour between last night and this morning.

'What are you doing here?' I gritted between my teeth, dreading what everyone was probably thinking.

'I live here.' Lincoln leaned in close but spoke freely, unconcerned with who heard. 'And I thought I made myself clear last night. I'm not letting you go again.'

'Someone should record this for Onyx,' Zoe threw in.

When I turned a horrified look on her she raised her hands in surrender. 'What? He'll only make us retell the whole conversation a dozen times if we don't.'

*Christ. She actually has a point.*

I pushed back my chair suddenly, putting distance between us and ignoring the sharp grinding sound that echoed through the large cafeteria. 'There's a meeting in the hall in a few hours to start assembling the team going to New Orleans.'

'Max told me,' Lincoln responded, accepting a coffee one of the staff had brought over to him.

*No one delivered my coffee.*

I nodded. 'Good. Well, I have something I need to do first.' Seeing his expression, I quickly added, 'In *private*. I'll meet you there.'

Deciding that was that, I collected my bag, swiped a croissant from the table and turned around, only to find Lincoln now standing, blocking my path with a twinkle in his eye. Before I could ask him to move out of my way, he grabbed me around the waist and dipped me, following me down, his mouth coming dangerously close to mine.

I froze, caught in the moment for a second before I came to my senses and pushed my hands hard against his chest. Now I was frustrated *and* embarrassed.

*And stuck with a pounding heart I have no idea how to calm.*

Lincoln had *never* behaved like this in public. Even when things were good.

'Next time you try that, I'll hurt you,' I threatened, regaining my balance and shrugging myself free of his hold.

'Don't you think we've done enough of that? Personally, I think it's time for something else.' He popped a piece of bread in his mouth.

*Seriously, who is this guy?*

'Such as?'

He finished his mouthful and smiled. And damn him because it was a mighty fine look on him. 'Getting on with the rest of our lives.' His smile widened to a megawatt beam. 'Together,' he added.

*And the Easter Bunny and Santa Claus will come and join us for Sunday lunch, too.*

I shook my head at him, suddenly weary. 'Don't do this.

It's not going to go the way you think. Steph?' I called, looking down at the wide-eyed people around the table.

She nodded, quickly grabbing her books and following me out.

The moment we hit the corridors she started quizzing me. 'What the hell happened between you two last night? You didn't ... I mean, did you?'

'No! Of course not. Lincoln just found out some stuff and he thinks it changes things.'

'But it doesn't?'

'No. It doesn't. My future is already set, and as long as Lincoln is in my life he's always only a heartbeat away from leaving me. I can't live like that.'

"Cause life as it is, is so grand?' Steph quipped.

When she saw my face her expression dropped. 'Sorry, my bad. It's just I hate to see you two like this. I mean, maybe you're right but maybe it would be a hundred or two hundred years before anything bad happened. That's a long stretch of happiness. No humans ever get that.'

I knew she was right, but ... 'You don't get it, Steph. You can't.'

'Oh, but I do, Vi. I was there when Phoenix brought you in a breath away from death. I stood on the other side of the door helpless while he killed you, only to then realise he'd also brought you back to a world without your soulmate. I pulled you out of that shower that had burned your whole body, and then – even after you saved all those children, defeated Lilith, redeemed Phoenix *and* saved Lincoln – I watched you walk away. You saved everyone but yourself, and I get that you're scared to let yourself be happy. I get that you're scared to lose everything, but you're ignoring what you'll get in return.'

I looked down, fighting the conflicting emotions running through me and was tempted to just reach in and shut them off. But I didn't. 'It's not that simple.'

'But it is,' Steph shot back. 'Let me ask you this: if you could go back in time would you give up that one perfect night you had with Lincoln?'

I thought of the constant agony I lived in every day because of our souls being ripped apart after they'd been joined that night. And even so, the answer came easily.

'No.'

Steph's expression softened. 'And are you really telling me you'd regret another night like that? Or a thousand?'

I looked up at her, lost. 'I … I have responsibilities. The angels are keeping things from me again and I know it's all coming to a head. I need to stay focused, and Lincoln will only complicate things more than I can handle.'

'Bollocks!' she scoffed. 'And you know it.'

I quirked an eyebrow. 'Gray?'

She nodded, seriously. 'His language really rubs off.'

I sighed. 'Steph, I don't even know who that guy was back there. He was so …'

'Hot?' Steph laughed. 'Actually, he looked a lot like a guy on a mission. One who has definitely considered the risks and formed a plan of attack. Gotta admit, it's refreshing. He's coming after you and let's face it, Vi, you might've managed to avoid him for the past two years but now you're face to face … any woman would be lost with the likes of him hunting them down.'

'Why do you think I left the city before he woke up?' I asked, feeling a small but sad smirk form. 'And should I pass that titbit on to Salvatore?'

She rolled her eyes. 'Oh, please! I'm getting married, not going deaf, dumb and blind.'

'It was definitely a new side to him,' I mused.

'Or maybe it's finally the honest version, without all the hang-ups. Everything is finally out in the open. I can't help but wonder what the honest version of you might be like, too.'

It was my turn to roll my eyes. 'I don't have that luxury any more.' Being with Lincoln involved a set of consequences I simply couldn't abide by.

'Oh, stop being a martyr!' Steph said, stealing my description of Lincoln yesterday, along with the croissant I was still holding, before she spun and stormed down the corridor as I watched after her, blinking.

The process of passing security to gain access to the infirmary took considerably longer without Steph to clear the way. When I finally walked into the medical rooms I wasn't surprised to find Chloe's empty. I'd managed to fully heal her yesterday and imagined they'd released her to return to her own room. It didn't mean a wasted trip, however, especially considering Chloe wasn't the reason for my visit.

I took a deep breath as I knocked on the door to Nyla's room. The moment Rainer opened the door she caught me off-guard, pulling me into a tight embrace. 'It really is good to see you,' she said, squeezing me one more time before letting me go. 'You've become something of an elusive legend around here. Especially with the children telling their stories of how your rescued them and parted walls of fire.'

'Don't believe everything you hear, Rainer. Kids embellish,' I said moving towards the bed where Nyla slept.

'True,' Rainer said. 'But they can also understand the true gravity of some things, better than most adults. And Simon in particular doesn't strike me as the type to exaggerate.' Her eyes dropped to her hands. I glanced over at Nyla, my heart tightening at the memories of that day in Jordan when Rudyard was taken from her. 'Violet, when we spoke last, before your trials, I was hard on you. I pushed your soul connection with Lincoln and I ...'

'You couldn't have known what would happen, Rainer.'

'Was there any alternative?' she asked, her guilt still showing.

I dug my nails into my palms in hope of distraction. But nothing diverts the coldness. 'We'll never know. Anyway, that's partly why I'm here.'

She looked up, but didn't say anything.

'I presume you know that I brought Lincoln back after his soul shattered?'

*Jesus. There's a reason I never speak about this stuff willingly.*

She nodded slowly.

'What I'm about to tell you stays between us, okay?' I added, holding her gaze.

'Understood,' she said, hesitantly taking a seat.

I sat down in the chair on the other side of the bed where Nyla lay perfectly still, the white sheets tucked seamlessly around her.

*Give me strength.*

'You've heard the stories, but not everything. When Phoenix killed and revived me, I came back to discover that Lincoln's soul had shattered. My soul didn't shatter completely like his.' I half laughed in the most never-going-to-be-funny way. 'I don't think it knew what to do, and with Phoenix's extra gifts making me stronger, I somehow survived. Barely. It's like being broken into a billion pieces and yet held together by some unforgiving force.'

Rainer gasped. 'Violet. I'm … I'm so sorry. Is it painful?'

I nodded. 'It is. Like nothing I've ever known. If I didn't have the gifts that Phoenix gave me, I don't know if my mind could survive the intensity of the physical pain.'

Rainer looked at me with such pity; that look was the reason I never told people the truth. 'That's why you're so different. So … disconnected.'

'I suppose,' I admitted.

*One of the reasons.*

'You're telling me to let her go,' she said, looking to Nyla.

'I'm telling you what you need to hear and understand before I say what I am about to now.'

She looked back at me, confused.

I continued, hoping this was the right thing. 'I've given this a lot of thought, and I've grown a lot stronger over the past two years. When I walked by Nyla's room yesterday, I felt something familiar.'

'What?' Rainer whispered.

'You. I felt recognition of you. But also Nyla. It's hard to explain.' I took a breath before I continued. 'I was able to bring Lincoln back and find him amid millions of souls because he is my soulmate. I think there's a chance you would be able to find Nyla's, too.' I took another breath. 'Because I believe you were born of the same soul. It's not the same as what Nyla and Rudyard were, but I think, as twins, you have a unique connection.'

The colour dropped from Rainer's face and I didn't know if it was in dread or hope.

'But how would I go where you went? Only you can do that.'

I licked my lips, praying I was doing the right thing. 'I think I can take you with me. It will be dangerous, and I don't know if it will work, but we could try. You need to understand, though, what you're possibly sentencing her to. She might come back and be okay, like Lincoln. Or ... she could be like me. She might not survive that, Rainer.'

Rainer stood and walked to the end of the bed, looking over her twin. 'That's a decision she's entitled to make herself. But I know Nyla, and I know that if she can fight, she will.'

I nodded slowly. 'Okay.'

'Okay? What does that mean? When can we try?'

I bit my lip, knowing that soon I would head to New Orleans and I had no idea what waited for me there. 'Lock the door.' I tried for a smile. 'There's no time like the present.'

Her eyebrows shot up. 'You can do it from here?'

'Like I said, I'm stronger than before, and doing it close to Nyla will only help.' I held out my hand. 'Hold onto it and don't let go. No matter what. I can't guarantee I'll be able to find you again if we lose the connection. And you'll only get one shot at this. Do you understand?'

Rainer nodded. 'I know the chance you're taking, Violet. I won't waste it.'

'You'll still have to find a way to connect with her. It has to be pure and only about her. Give her something that will call to her above anything else.'

She thought about this, watching me. 'What did you give?'

I pressed my lips together, my teeth biting down hard to distract me. Finally I answered. 'I gave my heart.'

# chapter eighteen

*'I simply believe that some part of the human self or soul is
not subject to the laws of space and time.'*

Carl Jung

**I** was nervous. And not just because I'd never tried to take
someone across the realms with me before – other than
Lilith, who'd been dead and, well, just different in all the
important ways.

Was I being foolish? Yes.

Was I taking a risk with Rainer's life? Yes.

And therefore with Wilhelm's partner as well? Yes.

Would I be blamed if things went wrong? Yes.

Would I feel responsible? No doubt.

Did I even want this to work? I didn't know.

Why was I doing this? Because.

Nyla was a warrior. She was loved completely by Rudyard.
I envied what they'd had.

So often I thought back to the night Griffin and I had gone
hunting with them. We'd come across a small farmhouse with
exiles and Nyla had gone into attack mode. It had surprised
me at first that Rudyard had stood aside and let Nyla take
the lead, placing herself in the most danger. I realise now that

I was too naive to see that his actions showed a great love and understanding. That was his greatest sacrifice, for her. For them.

I remembered his words: *'It will do her no favours if I throw myself in the line of fire just to be noble. Our relationship has gone beyond that.'*

And so perhaps there was a chance that Nyla, broken as she was, would still choose to fight. And if I could give her that chance, I would. Because I knew better than anyone the suffering that resulted from others making life-and-death choices on your behalf.

'Are you sure?' Rainer asked, obviously seeing myriad thoughts flit over my face.

I nodded. Something told me the days ahead would change everything. This exile, Sammael, frightened me. That he had Spence frightened me even more. Instinct screamed that I might be walking towards my final battle.

'There may not be another chance, Rainer. We should do this now. Close your eyes and breathe steadily; it can be unsettling.'

Rainer studied me for a moment before nodding and doing as I'd instructed. She'd read between the lines.

I took Rainer's hand and closed my eyes. Although I had avoided doing it, I knew how to cross the realms. It was similar to using my Sight; I just hovered in a different place. Somewhere between life and possibility, between flesh and imagination.

Becoming increasingly aware of my surroundings – not the room and people but the air, the atmosphere, the gravity – slowly, I let it all fall away, all the things that anchored my body to this world. It was a strange sensation – being aware of my corporeal form and of my hand holding Rainer's, knowing that I could take us somewhere new. Like Nox had once explained, it was like two worlds brushing together as curtains in the wind. When I was ready I simply faced the new direction and saw through the new window.

Finally, I opened my eyes and saw that we were in the abyss that I had once visited with Phoenix.

I looked around and wasn't surprised to see him standing to the side, leaning against what looked like a granite wall sparkling with thousands of diamonds. Dressed all in black he looked to be almost melting into the wall. Apart from the last few days, it had been a long time since I had laid eyes on him. It would be a lie to say memory did him justice. And it wasn't just his beauty, it was the rawness of the torment he carried about him; the kind that only aeons of time could etch out so masterfully.

Rainer opened her eyes, too.

'Oh, my God,' she whispered. 'Is this Heaven?'

I smiled, remembering asking a similar question once. 'Does it look like Heaven would to you?' I replied, asking what had been asked of me.

She shook her head. 'Not at all. Is it like purgatory? The in-between?' she asked, unaware that Phoenix was standing behind her.

I shrugged. 'Perhaps something like that. But I think it's more a thought, like a physical space to represent a kind of nothingness. I'm still trying to figure it out.' This place was not like the one I'd stood in last, where I'd had some kind of control. This was different. Not somewhere the angels or me could influence – this was ancient and eternal.

'Is this the angel realm?' Rainer went on, needing some kind of confirmation.

I realised that this was why the angels had let me believe it in the beginning, and I now understood the value. 'In a way.'

She nodded, accepting this, and I noticed Phoenix smile softly.

'I suppose it was only a matter of time,' he said from behind Rainer, startling her.

When she spun around I kept a tight clasp on her hand.

'Oh. Phoenix,' she whispered and I could see her conflicting emotions. Phoenix had been blamed for Rudyard's death, and for Nyla's state. It hadn't been his intention, but we all knew, even so, that it was his fault.

*And mine.*

He looked into Rainer's eyes, his remorse heavy, his guilt honest. 'I came to make sure the way is clear. I wish I could do this for you, but it is not permitted. Not even for her,' he said, glancing at me. 'I would give my life, my eternity, to right this wrong. But even for those of us who would give everything, it is not enough.'

'Phoenix,' I rasped, my cold heart thawing a little for him. I could see his anguish so clearly.

'If you could have her,' Rainer said suddenly, turning to me. Phoenix stiffened. 'If Violet could be yours in every way. If your heart could be full and your future complete, would you give *that*? Would you give her up to take away your sins?'

'Rainer,' I pleaded. 'Don't do this.'

'I deserve to know. And so does Nyla.' She did, but that didn't make it okay. The wounds between Phoenix and me were still raw. They probably always would be.

Phoenix abruptly dropped to his knees, his head bowed. 'I am angel malign. My essence is selfish. I see the value and benefit of darkness in its most alluring state. And I am human in heart, able to love and feel in all its punishing ways. I am man enough to sacrifice my existence for my sins. But my nature is also dark enough to know that should my greatest temptation lie at my feet for the taking, I would never be able to deny myself. So, perhaps we are all lucky that she is not capable of that kind of love. For me.'

I dropped down in front of him, keeping a hold of Rainer's hand. I ran my free hand through his beautiful hair in the first physical contact I'd had with him since he'd killed me. 'I'm sorry. I'm so sorry for all the pain I caused you.' A tear fell from my eye. 'If I could go back and change it, I would,' I whispered, my voice trembling. 'I've caused so much pain and suffering and it's ruined us all. You have to know that I never meant to hurt you.'

He grabbed me around the waist, pulling me to him, and buried his face against my shoulder like a child holding on for dear life. I didn't move away; I just continued to run my hand through his hair.

He was such a tormented creature. What would become of him here?

I looked up at Rainer, who was watching on silently. 'You cannot ask that he fight every part of his nature for his remorse to be true. Please. If he can't have your forgiveness, then neither can I. His mistakes are mine to bear just as much as they are his.'

Phoenix held me tighter and I felt this angel, this man, come apart. He was vulnerable, afraid and, more than anything, he was utterly lonely.

Rainer nodded. 'I can't say that I perfectly agree, but I trust in your heart, Violet. I have seen your goodness.' She looked at Phoenix. 'I believe you are sorry and I'm grateful for your honesty. I imagine if Nyla were asked what she wouldn't do for Rudyard, she would simply answer: nothing.'

I lifted Phoenix's face up and looked into his chocolate eyes, which were churning with emotion.

'This isn't the place for you, is it?' I asked, finally allowing my eyes to open and see what was becoming of him.

He shook his head, looking down again.

I tilted his chin up. 'You're here for me?'

He nodded.

'But I can't be what you want, Phoenix. You've known that all along.'

He nodded again.

Another tear fell down my cheek. 'Well, what the hell are we going to do with you?' I asked the universe in some kind of despairing plea.

He looked up. 'You could come here. You could. They would allow it. You could leave everything else behind. The cold. I know you feel it all the time.'

I studied his face as he watched me intently. There was even a part of me that was tempted by the idea of leaving it all behind and finding some semblance of peace. But what peace would there be without *him*? Like it or not, Lincoln and I were tied together; whether I was a human or an angel, I couldn't escape it. Nor could I leave him in a world without me when that was the very thing I couldn't bear for him to do to me.

'You already know I won't do that. You already know it all, Phoenix. You're an angel. You can see right into me.'

He was silent for a time. Then finally, he dropped his arms and stood, pulling me up with him.

He took a step back and cleared his throat. 'You will need to move quickly. The souls have felt your presence before, Violet. They will find you quickly and try to take it from you.'

I nodded, expecting as much. 'What about Rainer?'

He smiled sadly. 'She will be protected. Only you are here in your life form. You have brought her with you but her essence and form remain behind. Though if you lose her here, it will not be good.' He paused before adding, 'I need to warn you against this, Violet. Your maker will not be happy. There will be a price, and I have no idea how high it will be.'

'I know, Phoenix. This isn't on you. But this is what you can do to help me make it right.'

His jaw clenched and he nodded tightly. 'I can't help you, but I can be here, like last time, to push you back in the right direction when you're ready, but you'll have to make it back to me.'

I swallowed, looking out towards the nothingness that held billions of tiny floating shimmers: lost and broken souls, searching for what they once had, desperate to feel something again.

'Can you see them?' I asked Rainer.

She shook her head. 'I only see the darkness.'

I turned to Phoenix, who appeared deep in thought. 'And I only see the light because of it,' I said, acknowledging the value of the dark, and the role that the angels malign have in the universe. Telling him, in my own way, that I understood.

Phoenix flinched at my words and looked at me, his eyes instantly tearing. He quickly turned. 'You should get going,' he said, already walking away.

'You have a lot of intense relationships, you know that?' Rainer said beside me.

*Understatement of the century.*

'I know. And it has to end.' I looked up and took a quivering breath. 'But first thing's first.'

Together, Rainer and I walked towards the vast nothingness. Her eyes locked on the blackness, mine on the countless shimmering images, floating like stars, soundlessly searching.

The shimmers started to stir as we neared. 'Remember,' I cautioned, 'if you want to find her, you have to open yourself to her, find the piece of her that only you know.'

Rainer nodded. 'I've got it. We're twins, Violet. I'll find her.'

I nodded, though I knew that only time would really tell. 'Just make sure, no matter what happens, that you—'

'Don't let go,' she cut me off, squeezing my hand.

'Right.'

The reflections were moving in on us now. I knew how this went and that we wouldn't have long.

I stopped walking when we were far enough. 'Stay focused. You'll only get one chance at this, so make it count.'

Rainer nodded and tilted her head back, closing her eyes as she began to call to Nyla's soul.

*Oh, Nyla, forgive me.*

The shimmers encircled us. They were bolder than last time and I knew I would need to hold on to give Rainer the time she needed.

I gripped her hand tightly as they closed in on me, pouring through me, feeding on me, draining me. As the intrusions became violent I heard myself cry out as they crushed me from the inside and outside.

'Violet, you're bleeding!' Rainer said.

I looked at her. 'Keep going,' I ordered, ignoring the blood that I could feel trickling from my nose and eyes.

She nodded, refocusing.

Painful time is slow and gradual in its release.

The shimmers pounded through my being, grabbing like tentacles and sucking all they could from me. There was no way to fight back and I could not endure much more. But then I heard Rainer cry out.

'I can feel her, Violet. She's coming to me!'

And so there was no choice. I would hang on. I would give Nyla and Rainer their chance.

Blood ran down my throat and poured from my ears as pressure built with lost souls filling me, siphoning from me. My body jolted as the force of each intrusion became more aggressive and my strength to hold them back deteriorated.

'I have her! Violet, I have her!' Rainer was pulling me.

My legs were buckling beneath me. I wanted to fall down, I wanted to crawl or lie just for a time. Even if it was a gradual time.

But I couldn't take Rainer from Wil. And I had to get back to find Spence. So, my feet stumbled again and again as Rainer pulled me along. I heard her screams: 'Phoenix! Help us! She's not going to make it!'

Arms caught me as I fell back; a perfect game of trust.

He was there.

'She's not strong enough to cross the realms,' he said, sounding panicked. I wanted to reassure him but my mouth would not move. 'I can't ... I can't,' he floundered. 'Damn it! I can't heal her here and she can't ... We have to ... Oh, what the hell!' And it sounded like he'd decided something and I was grateful, because right then my mind could not work.

Suddenly, I was on a cold floor, choking on my own blood.

Rainer was by my side, calling my name, shaking me even as I felt her tremble. Something was bashing on the door and I felt an odd sense of déjà vu. Then a massive cracking sounded as the door splintered and the sun whooshed in, enveloping me.

People were yelling. One voice so commanding, screaming my name and ordering me over and over to live.

And even as the world went dark, I was painfully alive when I felt the most devastating kiss of warmth.

# chapter nineteen

*'We pay a price for everything we get or take in this
world ...'*

Lucy Maud Montgomery

**W**hen a person forces herself to live in a world that has no
sun, it is a dreadful existence. Most would be better off never
having known the sun existed than to be left cast into perpetual
shadow with nothing but the memories set on constant repeat.
Memories cannot – do not – recreate the sun.

It comes from every angle, attacks every sense and fibre of
our beings. The sun, more than anything, is the very assurance
that we are *real* and that there is life.

Awareness slowly returned and I was conscious of one
thing and one thing alone.

*I'm lying in the sun.*

And before I'd even opened my eyes, I was crying my
heart out, for the first time in two years.

My memories had never, *could* never have, done it justice.

'Don't cry, Vi,' the sun said. 'Don't cry,' he repeated, as he
smoothed the hair from my forehead and gently stroked the
contours of my face. 'Please wake up. Wake up so that you
can come back to me,' he whispered, as if *I* could be the one

special enough to belong to the sun. And even more, as if, by some miracle, the sun still belonged to me.

*But I'm not. And he doesn't.*

Lucidity increased by the second. It took only a few brief moments before my hand was briskly wiping away my unauthorised tears and my eyes were blinking open.

Lincoln sat on the edge of the bed, leaning over me.

'Hey,' I said, my voice catching.

'Hey,' he said, his voice soft.

He reached over and held out a glass of water with a straw. I sipped, and nodded when I'd had enough.

He stood then, and started to pace. At first I was struck by the pure relief that showed on his face and then, somewhere between trying to remember what he'd said as I woke up and seeing that his expression was morphing into something decidedly more furious, I began to sit up, moving into a more defensive position.

Right on cue, Lincoln spun towards me, one hand up in helpless confusion. 'What the hell did you think you were doing? You were half dead when we found you!'

*He really has developed a hot temper.*

I rolled my eyes. 'I'm fine.'

'You are not damn well fine. I've spent the past twenty hours in here trying to heal you and you're still black and blue.'

I grimaced, wondering just how banged up I looked. But then his words registered. Twenty hours? Wait. 'You ... you healed me?'

'Of course I healed you,' he said, his irritation growing.

I could feel it now, his power, his *self* running through me, fixing me. It was wonderful in the worst possible way.

'I wish you hadn't done that,' I mumbled.

'Why?' he asked, his anger giving way to sadness. 'Do you *want* to die?'

'No. But we're not partners any more. You shouldn't have ...'

Lincoln laughed sardonically. 'God, you are so twisted it's not funny.'

*He's not wrong.*

'I never said any of this was funny.' It was then that I noticed I was wearing a gown instead of my clothes. I blushed, looking away from Lincoln. Had he undressed me?

The door opened and Gray walked in, smiling when he saw me awake. 'On the mend, then?'

I nodded and then sent him a sharp look. 'Did you let him heal me?'

Gray scratched the back of his head. 'Well, I didn't bloody well stop him, if that's what you're asking. I suspect a herd of elephants would've had more luck at that. The man can be quite insistent when he wants to be. No one was allowed within ten bloody feet of you,' he said, his British accent thickening.

I continued to glare at him.

His eyebrows went up. 'I'm flippin' serious! There's a doctor out there with a badly broken nose to prove it. And anyway, I figured you'd want to be up and about to get on with saving your friend, and for that you really are going to need to be vertical.' He smiled mischievously. 'Though to be frank, I won't deny that there is one horizontal activity I think you'd highly benefit from.'

My mouth dropped open in shock. I didn't miss Lincoln's smirk from his position at the end of my bed.

Gray broke into full belly laughter. 'I see my work here is done. Should I let the troops know we'll be pushing ahead?'

'Of course,' I said just as Lincoln said, 'No. She needs more rest.'

I glared again, giving equal attention to Gray and Lincoln.

Gray backed towards the door. 'Sorry, mate,' he said to Lincoln. 'But now that she's awake, well, let's just say, I know what she's capable of when she's pissed off.' He ducked out the door and as he did I spied my clothes folded neatly on the armchair.

Lincoln held the bridge of his nose and closed his eyes.

*Is he counting?*

'Is Rainer okay?' I asked.

He nodded. 'She's back, Violet.'

He wasn't talking about Rainer. Nyla was back. It had worked.

'It might take her a little longer to wake up than it did me since she was gone for so long, but her brain activity has returned and Rainer says she felt the transfer work. You brought her back.'

I let out a deep breath. 'I hope it was the right thing to do. You should … call Griffin. He'll want to know.'

'Steph's already spoken to him. He's preparing to come over and should arrive in the next day or so. He said to tell you it was about time you got back in the game.' He cleared his throat. 'And … that you did good.'

Tears stung my eyes but I held them back. I'd woken up crying – a display I wasn't about to repeat.

I pushed myself up further, spending a little time on healing the worst of my injuries. I'd patch myself up properly later. 'Can you pass me my clothes?' I asked, pointing to the folded stack.

Lincoln handed them to me and I pulled my jeans on beneath the sheets. I settled for just my T-shirt when I saw the state of my sweater. I was sure Steph would lend me something else. 'Turn around,' I said.

Lincoln did as I asked while I stripped off the hospital gown and threw on my top. By the time he turned around I was pulling on my boots.

'What happened at yesterday's meeting?' I asked, worried I missed the arrangements.

'It was rescheduled for today. They should be heading to the hall now, in fact.'

I stood up, trying to hide the shaking in my legs. 'Well, we'd better get going, then. They can't assemble our team unless we're there, right?'

Lincoln huffed, clearly not finished with this conversation – or lecture. I ignored him and walked carefully to the door, unable to hide a few sharp winces.

'You know I could help with that,' he said from behind me, his voice suddenly low.

I froze, knowing exactly what he meant. When we connected our healing powers were much stronger, but it was always confronting, sharing our emotional as well as our physical abilities.

I shook my head. 'I'd prefer not.'

*I am a pathetic liar.*

'Hmm,' he said, brushing against my side before opening the door for me. 'We'll see.'

When I passed him to go through the doorway, he

grabbed my wrist, holding it tight. 'Next time you decide to do something so reckless, at least tell someone you might be on your way to die. You know, just so we can find you,' he said, unable to disguise the bitterness in his tone.

I licked my lips. 'Sure. Next time I'll do that,' I snapped, trying to pull my arm from his grip.

'Be sure you do. Maybe then it won't be so hard to tell you that what you did was just damn amazing.'

My breath caught. I stared as Lincoln simply dropped my wrist and stormed ahead towards the hall.

Only when I heard the chuckling did I notice Steph standing in front of me.

'What's so funny?' I asked.

She shook her head. 'You two. You're just so ... annoying.' She laughed again.

'We can't seem to stop yelling at each other.'

'Maybe you should try doing something that doesn't involve talking,' she said with a wink.

I looked to the ceiling. 'Please. Not you, too. Come on, we'd better get to that meeting before Lincoln has another reason to yell at me.'

She snorted. 'You have some housekeeping to take care of first.'

I looked at her, confused. 'Such as?'

'Such as where Phoenix is going to be staying.'

'Steph, Phoenix is an angel. As in *incorporeal*.'

She rolled her eyes and pointed behind me. 'Well, Vi, honey, you might want to explain *that*, then.'

My heart skipped a beat and my breathing practically stopped completely as I turned slowly on my heel to see

Phoenix, in the flesh, sitting on one of the waiting-room chairs with his elbows on his knees and his head slumped forward, looking at the ground.

'What. The. Hell?' I breathed.

'If that was our only question it would be easy. He hasn't said much, but according to Rainer you weren't going to make it. So, Mr Self-sacrifice here brought you back.'

'He … he …'

Steph placed a supporting hand on my shoulder. 'He exiled, Vi. For you.'

# chapter twenty

*'But woe to the earth and the sea, because the devil has gone*

*down to you!'*

**Revelations 12:12**

'**O**f course he did,' I mumbled, feeling closer than ever to losing my mind. 'Of course he did,' I repeated, delirious.

*How can this all be happening?*

My crazy laugh caused Phoenix to look up. He was tired and, for the first time since we'd met, he looked unsure.

Steph murmured, 'I'll let them know you're on the way,' as she left.

I sighed as I sat down next to him. 'Tell me this wasn't for me,' I said softly.

His lips twitched before he looked back down to his feet. 'This wasn't for you.'

'They won't let you go back again,' I said.

He nodded. We both knew it was true.

'What are you going to do?' I asked.

He shrugged. 'I have no idea.'

I closed my eyes. Once again everything was completely out of control and it all seemed to be because of me. I should have thought it through more before racing ahead to save Nyla.

*What have I done?*

'I'm sorry,' I whispered.

'Don't be,' he said. 'You and I know it was only a matter of time.'

I blinked. 'I realised you weren't happy but I don't think either one of us knew you were going to do this.'

He shrugged again. 'There's no perfect place for me. At least as an exile I have choices. There was a time when I believed being an angel was who I was.' He looked at me briefly before dropping his eyes again. 'I've changed.'

*Haven't we all.*

I rubbed my face, tired too. But I knew I had to say it. 'Phoenix, I can't ... you know that I ...'

He leaned back, looking ahead blankly. 'That you love Lincoln?'

I flinched. 'It's not that. I just can't be with anyone.'

He half smiled. '*Because* you love Lincoln.'

'I'm not the girl you first met. And with all the history between us ... I don't know how we handle this.'

His smile widened. 'Is that your way of saying you don't want to be my BFF?'

He'd caught me by surprise and I pursed my lips to hold back my smile, but it came anyway.

With that, Phoenix stood up and put his hand out for me. 'Don't worry. I'm not planning a repeat of history. I don't think the world would survive.'

'That's probably true,' I said, deadpan, but as we walked up the stairs towards the hall, I chewed my lower lip.

Phoenix reached out and gently touched his thumb to my chin. 'It'll be okay. How about we just concentrate on getting your friend back and this problem solved? Then we'll get drunk and work out what to do with the rest of my eternity.'

I smiled. 'Okay,' I said, realising that I was glad he was here to help. 'So, they actually let you in here?'

'I do have an arsenal of persuasive skills,' he said with his more familiar cocky smile. 'And I *did* return with a few of their valued possessions, so, for now, no one has tried to kill me.'

'Has Lincoln seen you?' I asked hesitantly.

'We shared a moment. Grunts were exchanged.'

When I just stared at him, he sighed. 'Violet, he doesn't like me. He never will. The feeling is entirely mutual. But we have an understanding, and since I returned you, it bought me some time before he insists that I beat him into the ground.'

I rolled my eyes. 'If anyone is beating up either one of you, it will be me,' I said, stopping again outside the doors to the hall, breathing deeply as I redirected my concentration. Phoenix chuckled beside me.

'You know,' he said, 'I know what you're doing, and you're not helping yourself like you think you are.'

I glanced up at him as soon as I had my emotions under control and muted. I knew my eyes were cold and hard, but I was fine with that. 'Thank you for saving me. What you did was ... incredible. But I'm warning you, don't interfere with this stuff, Phoenix. I mean it.'

'I know you do,' he said, shaking his head and holding the door open for me. 'But that doesn't make you right,' he added as I walked past him.

The hall was already full. The Assembly were in their places – although I noticed that in addition to Seth's and Decima's vacant seats, both Rainer and Wilhelm were also absent. I could feel Drenson's eyes on me as I walked towards the front of the room where Steph was waiting for me. As I moved I noticed a couple of Grigori drop their heads as I passed.

Zoe and Salvatore were beside Steph and when I reached them, they pulled me into tight embraces.

'Thank you, Vi,' Zoe said, her voice thick with emotion that I heard but, fortunately, did not have to feel. 'Nyla is the closest thing I have to family. Thank you so much.'

I nodded and moved away from them with a small smile. Phoenix had taken up position just behind me, next to Gray.

'When you are ready, Violet,' Drenson said, sounding distinctly irritated. 'May I remind you that there are many people in this room who have more pressing issues to deal with than your reunion with friends.'

I decided not to bother with a response. Instead I stood and stared at the man who, I was realising more and more, was not a nice person and was a terrible leader.

Satisfied he'd belittled me, Drenson redirected his attention towards Phoenix. 'He must be removed. This is Grigori business and he is an exile who has already launched one attack on this building.'

Lincoln stepped forward from the other side of the room. 'He is an angel who fell to save a Grigori life. You call him an exile, but what exile has ever done such a thing? We owe him a debt of gratitude, and he has also offered to help us find Spence. I've asked him to come with us.'

Drenson's face bloomed red and his jaw clenched. He flinched when Josephine placed a hand on his shoulder. She didn't speak, but her touch seemed to be enough. He turned away from Lincoln and moved his shoulder to shrug off Josephine's hand.

'As I was saying,' he went on, as if the previous exchange had not happened, 'we have received reports from Grigori in Mexico, Texas and Georgia who have all witnessed dramatically increased exile activity in the past two days. It seems these recent battleground wars between light and dark have developed into a kind of travelling tournament. One of the humans working for the exiles was captured in Florida last night and our Grigori managed to extract Sammael's name from her, confirming that he is behind the tournaments, before she …' He trailed off.

*Before she killed herself.*

My eyes were on Josephine who, at the mention of Sammael, had paled.

I glanced at Steph, who looked deep in thought.

Drenson put his hands up to stop the murmured speculation that had already begun. 'There are many stories about Sammael and his terrible deeds but he, like every other exile, now wears a human body. He is in *our* world and we will stop him. We can safely assume at this stage that Sammael is holding Spencer captive, and since there is a chance Spencer is also holding intel we could use, our primary objective is to recover him. Lincoln and—' He cleared his throat, 'our visitor, Violet, will run the task force. Some of you will be put on standby, others will be sent to neighbouring cities to collect further intel and work with local Grigori on containing the human element we are now dealing with. Questions?' He returned to his seat, and something about the arrogant look on his face put me on alert.

'Yeah,' called someone from the back. 'Since when are we letting a Rogue lead us?'

Drenson cast a smug look in my direction.

*Oh, hell.*

Josephine surprised me by standing up. 'Because the *Rogue* is the best-equipped to get this job done.'

'Is it true she can cross into the angel realm any time she wants?' another voice called out.

'Is that how she brought Nyla back?' a girl asked from the upper level.

'How can we trust her when she doesn't even want to be one of us?'

'She has no code!'

'She abandoned her own partner!'

*That one hurt.*

I stepped forward, unwilling to let this go any further, and faced the crowd, relieved that I had my emotions in check. 'I don't answer to the Assembly or the Academy. That is a choice I was free to make. And I had my reasons. I fought with you all against Lilith's exiles. I fought until I almost died. I fought with you after the Assembly rejected me and told me I was not good enough. You're all free to make your own choices as I have done and after this is finished you will never have to see me again, but Spence is one of *my* people. I don't care who I have to take down on my way, I *will* get him out. That is the reason your Assembly found me unworthy of being one of you. And I'm A-okay with that because I don't intend on changing. So, if you have a problem with me, or think you are better-suited for the job, take your shot now. I've got a few minutes to spare between people trying to kill me, but make sure you have your partner on standby ready to heal you, because I don't have enough time to be careful.'

I stood tall and looked back to see Phoenix's amused grin. Gray was beside him, looking resigned, hanging his head. Clearly he didn't think I'd done as well as I'd thought.

And, clearly, he was right, since half a dozen Grigori walked towards the sparring area ready to fight. I shrugged, not missing Drenson's self-satisfied smirk or Josephine's irritation.

*Petty politics.*

The five men and one woman who'd stepped up to fight were all well-established warriors. They all fought hard. But my emotions were shut off and the constant judgement was only making me restless.

Lincoln had moved closer to the sparring area, but he kept his distance, watching silently, and I was relieved that he didn't attempt to control the situation. These Grigori needed this. One by one I took them down, trying, despite my earlier warning, not to hurt any of them too badly. It was a purely selfish decision. I still had no idea what we would face in New Orleans and figured it was best to keep all fighters capable of performing their duties.

Just as I turned around to the now-quiet Grigori I let in enough emotion to feel pretty damn good about myself ... then my eyes fixed on a woman standing by the doors. My internal congratulations came to a sudden halt.

Decima, the mightiest and most ancient of all Grigori warriors apart from her partner Seth, strode towards me, panther-like.

I adjusted my stance, preparing for sheer brutality.

She stopped in front of me. My pulse quickened, knowing that this fight was about to hurt. A lot. Out of the corner of my eye I saw Lincoln step forward; I dared to take my eyes off Decima long enough to shoot him a hard look, effectively stopping him in his tracks.

Decima tilted her head as she studied me with interest. 'I am not here to challenge you. You have grown, I see. It intrigues me and I admit that I do not know if you would better me in combat, but I do not think so.'

*That makes two of us.*

'Go on your mission. Bring back your friend,' she instructed.

'Then why are you here?' I asked cautiously.

'Because I heard a name I have not heard for centuries. I came to tell you that if you come up against Sammael, you will not win.'

*Oh, got it. You're here for a morale boost.*

'You cannot beat him in strength. Not the way I see you fight. Sammael has fought without heart for much longer than you.'

I flinched at her accusation. Was I heartless?

'If you cannot be human, you cannot defeat him,' Decima said, her ancient eyes looking through mine as if my ultimate demise were near.

I stared back at her. 'I know who and *what* I am. I'm a weapon and I'll be used as such. If Sammael wants a fight I guarantee you, Decima, he will have one.'

Decima laughed, the sound like troubled wind chimes. 'Still a child in so many ways. Let me keep it simple for you – sometimes one is best understood by the world when the world can first measure the value and power of one's greatest enemy. You may not know who Sammael is, but I have no doubt you have heard of his nemesis the angel Sammael fought and almost dragged to earth with him?'

I swallowed, a chill running down my spine. My mouth had gone suddenly dry and my eyes darted to Phoenix, who would not look at me.

'Who?' I asked.

Decima did not look happy to be the one to share this information. If anything, she looked resigned. 'The Viceroy of Heaven. Commander of all the armies. The one to whom our last judgement stands. Sammael's arch-enemy is the Prince of the Elect, Michael.'

My brow furrowed, processing everything she'd just said. 'But I ... I thought God had the final judgement. Or Jesus.'

Decima tilted her head and then gave an aloof smile. 'And there are those who would believe that Michael and Jesus are one in the same.'

I shook my head, confused. 'But isn't Lucifer supposed to be Michael's enemy?'

'Lucifer is Michael's perfect opposite. As Michael is the Prince of Light, Lucifer is the Prince of Dark. They serve a purpose, their functions at the opposite ends of the spectrum, but they have always remained true, unlike Sammael who believed his purpose entitled him to more than his function.' Decima pulled her hood over her head and gestured to someone to open the doors for her. 'I will leave now. Seth waits.'

She began to walk down the aisle, people moving away from her as she did.

'Wait!' I called out. 'What *was* Sammael's purpose?'

When she reached the door, she paused, though she did not turn around. 'Sammael was the angel of death.'

*Splendid.*

# Chapter twenty-one

*'… in Heaven and in Earth, are a double Nature; in Heaven*
*they are unchangeable and incorruptible; but on Earth they*
*are changeable and corruptible.'*

**Hermes Trismegistus**

**D**ecima's brief appearance and inspiring speech left even
fewer Academy Grigori pleased about my presence. I wanted
to point out to them that while she might have stated that
I couldn't win, she didn't suggest any of them could either,
but it was probably time to keep quiet.

I waited for whatever was coming. Drenson was smiling,
which meant he had more cards to play. But before he had a
chance to speak, Lincoln walked towards me and stopped at
my side, turning his attention back to the Assembly.

If it were possible, the tension in the room immediately
went up a notch. I sent him a sideways glance. 'You don't
have to do this,' I said under my breath.

He didn't respond, but I knew he'd heard.

Lincoln was making a stand. By my side. And it felt like
a knife wound to my heart. Even after I'd walked away and
left him, he was still willing to stay beside me as my partner.

He was loved and respected within the Academy and he was a tool of the Assembly. His support could not go unnoticed.

'I can speak for myself,' I insisted.

He sighed, but only handed me a piece of paper.

I glanced down to see the list of names of the proposed team. It showed almost everyone I would have wanted, including Phoenix. I wondered why Mia's name was missing then put it together that it must be because she was partnerless. There were also a few names I didn't recognise.

As if reading my mind, Lincoln said, 'Shadu and his partner are tech experts. You met the conductors on Santorini, and the others you don't know are unquestionably loyal to the cause and strong fighters. They will follow you as much as me.'

I believed him.

'What about Chloe?' She had a right to go after her partner.

Lincoln smiled softly. 'She's a given, Violet.'

I nodded, absorbing this. 'I have three Rogues who will meet us at the airport. They won't answer to you and they don't answer to me either. But they have their own set of skills and Gray will probably be able to keep them in line.'

'Probably?' he echoed, eyebrow raised.

'They're good fighters, Lincoln.'

He nodded, taking the list from me and handing it to Josephine. 'This is the lead team we will take, plus three others who will meet us at the airport. I'd also ask that those who are not assigned to other duties be ready to step in. We have planes on standby worldwide to transport Grigori at short notice once we have a pinpoint on Sammael's whereabouts and have Spence in our possession.'

'Are you requesting an army, Lincoln? A little much, don't you think?'

I glanced in Phoenix's direction while Lincoln considered the question. It was clear by the intent glare Phoenix had fixed on Josephine and the hard set of his jaw that he didn't think an army was too much at all. As I watched, he took a few sly steps closer to where the Assembly members sat.

We wanted to get into New Orleans on our own terms, which was why we weren't taking more people, but after everything we'd just heard from Decima I was starting to think it wouldn't be long before reinforcements would be necessary.

'Yes, Josephine. I'm requesting that we be fully mobilised in the event that aid is needed,' Lincoln answered.

Josephine held his look for a moment, her gaze curiously drifting in Phoenix's direction before settling on me as she responded. 'If that is your standing, you have our support.'

After leaving Josephine to dish out the orders and Drenson to sulk, Lincoln and I left the hall, followed by Steph, Phoenix, Gray and Mia.

'I'll have to stop by Ascension and get my things,' I said.

'Let me grab my bag and I'll go with you,' Steph said. 'I want to pick up some books and talk to Dapper. I'm going to stay in Manhattan for now and see what else I can find out about Sammael. I'll catch a later plane,' she added.

Lincoln nodded, looking at Steph briefly. 'Thank you, Steph. Sal and Zoe will keep you up to date, no doubt.' He took a breath. 'Feel free to contact me with any new information.'

Steph's eyes widened.

'What?' he asked cautiously.

She bit back a smile. 'Nothing. It's just been so long since you've looked at me, I'd forgotten how green your eyes are.'

When Lincoln looked like he'd rather take a knife to himself than be stuck in that conversation, Gray saved him.

'I'll head to the airport to meet the other Rogues and we'll join you there. Escort me out of the building, love, so no one tries to lock me up?' he asked Steph.

Steph nodded, her eyes sparkling with humour. As soon as they turned the corner, Lincoln let out a breath and Mia, who'd been standing by quietly with her head down, offered to show Phoenix where he could get some fresh clothes and supplies.

As they turned to leave, I grabbed Phoenix's arm. 'You influenced Josephine, didn't you?' When he just stared at me blankly, I pushed. 'When she asked about needing an army, I saw you move closer to her. What did you do to her emotions?'

His chocolate eyes bored into mine. 'I gave her a touch of insight into a possible future for this world and what that would feel like.'

I swallowed, suddenly unsure. 'And what was that?'

'Fear,' he said, stepping back and away from me. He gave Lincoln a curt nod before turning on his heel to follow Mia.

'He knows more than he's saying,' Lincoln said, watching them walk around the corner.

'Yeah. But he'll tell us when he's ready,' I said, knowing it was true. Then, suddenly aware that Lincoln and I were now alone, I added, 'I should get going, too.'

Lincoln stepped into my space, and despite every intention of doing so I failed to move away.

His thumb smudged across my cheekbone in a way that was so familiar it made my breath hitch, and my memory plagued me with a reminder of all the other things he could do when his hands were on me.

*How have I survived without his touch?*

I stared at him, lost in the moment. He must have sensed my uncertainty because he inched closer, his thumb repeating the motion, then moving down to my lips. Suddenly his shoulders dropped forward, and his forehead rested against mine.

'Come back to me,' he whispered.

'I'm right here,' I said, my chest unbearably tight.

'No. You're not.'

He was right.

'I miss you.' His fingers curled around the nape of my neck and into my hair.

I closed my eyes for one more second, drinking him in. But a second was already too much, too dangerous. 'I can't do this,' I said, stepping back and looking anywhere but into the green. 'Steph will be waiting for me,' I mumbled, already hurrying down the corridor.

Lincoln didn't follow. But I could feel his eyes on me, watching me walk away.

I crossed over one of the Academy's walkways and turned the corner, almost bumping into Mia who was leaving a room.

'Oh,' she said when she dodged me. 'Sorry.'

'My fault,' I said. 'Phoenix?'

She nodded. 'I just left him to get what he needed.'

'Oh. Okay,' I said, quickly moving on.

'I was coming to look for you, actually,' she said before I'd made it two steps.

I bit my lip hard and turned around with a small smile. I guess if she was going to do this it would be better to stake her claim on Lincoln in private rather than rip me apart in front of an audience.

'Should we get some fresh air?' she asked, gesturing to a side door.

I nodded, following her outside onto a large covered balcony, its floor littered with pot plants and its ceiling overhung with trailing ivy. We walked to the railing, and looked out over the bustling Manhattan streets.

'I'm sure you've heard the rumours, and I thought we should talk,' she said.

'It isn't necessary,' I replied.

*What do you want me to say?* 'Yes, *I've heard you've grown close to my soulmate. I wish you both the best.*'

'Josephine pushed us to consider being partners but I think she knew that Lincoln would never be interested, and that I was still grieving for Hiro and not ready.'

I nodded, feeling terrible for her loss. 'Mia, you don't need to explain this to me.'

'But I do,' she said, her tone now adamant. 'I care about Lincoln, a lot. We've grown close and I think he liked that I was separate from all … your mutual friends. I think he was able to relax a bit with me.'

'I get it,' I said quickly, hoping she would stop speaking soon. Even with my emotions locked down this was becoming too much.

'No, you don't. I know there are rumours that we're together. Lincoln knows too. But there has never been anything like that between us. I mean, I admit there was a time I might've had a bit of a crush on him, but that was years ago. Way before you came along.'

I looked up to see Mia's sincere expression.

She shrugged. 'We don't want to be partners. Lincoln would never consider it even if I could. He already has a partner and in his eyes that has never changed. But he didn't want to keep explaining to people why he made the choices he did. People watched him and doubted his strength because they only saw him as the Grigori who lost his soulmate and wouldn't let her go.'

I swallowed the lump in my throat.

'Violet, he just figured that if people thought—'

'That you two were together it would solve both problems,' I finished for her.

She nodded, looking relieved. 'Yeah. But we never added to the rumours or did anything to start them. We just agreed not to stop them.'

I rubbed my face, exhausted. Lincoln had used a mask relationship with Mia in much the same way I had with Gray. I could understand that. It was a survival issue.

'Actually,' Mia said, sounding sheepish. 'I kind of like someone else.'

I raised my eyebrows. 'Anyone I know?'

'As a matter of fact, yes,' she said, biting her lip.

I thought of her reaction to finding out Spence was still alive, and the careful way she had watched over everything to do with his rescue. I'd assumed it was to stick close to Lincoln, but ...

'Spence?' I asked, my voice high.

She nodded, smiling. 'I'd very much like to get him back soon. That's the other reason I wanted to talk to you.'

Instantly, I knew what she wanted. Academy rules stated that partnerless Grigori were not permitted on missions. It had been the bane of Spence's existence until I'd come along. But once Griffin knew I could heal him, Spence had been allowed to play his part.

I wondered fleetingly if Dapper had given some kind of assurance to the Assembly that he would heal Lincoln in my absence and if that was why he hadn't been prevented from pursuing his role. I suspected, however, that it was more likely some arrangement he'd struck with Josephine.

I looked at Mia, her feelings for Spence now painted on her face. And though it was selfish, I couldn't deny the relief I felt that they were not for Lincoln. She wanted to be there to get Spence back.

'Get your stuff together and be on the plane.'

She nodded warily. 'They won't be happy.'

I half grinned. 'Story of my life. I can heal you as well as any partner can. If you're willing to endure the pain of being healed by me, I'll be there to do it. As far as I'm concerned that solves the problem. I'll see you at the airport.'

She threw her arms around me quickly before backing away, to my relief. 'Thank you, Violet. And … I'm glad you're here. For both of them.'

I looked beyond her, to the surrounding buildings. 'I'm not staying,' I said, not quite sure who I was trying to convince any more.

'Well, you should. They both love you, and so do other people here. And love is worth fighting for.'

I glanced at her briefly before heading for the door. She didn't realise that I did fight for it. Every day. I fought myself.

But then she surprised me. 'And other times ...' she called out behind me. 'It's worth giving in.'

An hour later, Steph and I sat across from Onyx and Dapper in their apartment above Ascension. My flight was leaving soon and my bad feeling had already taken off. Everything was about to change, I just had no idea how much.

'So, you just decided it would be a good idea to go marching into a universe of lost souls and pluck her out?' Onyx asked, taking a deep drink of whatever was in his crystal tumbler.

'Rainer *plucked* her out, I was just the taxi service,' I explained, accepting the coffee Dapper passed me.

Onyx shook his head and took another – large – sip and I noticed how his shoulders dropped when Dapper placed a discreet hand on his back.

'Rum?' I asked, unimpressed.

'Oh, don't even,' he snapped. 'I brought you back here to get Spencer, not risk his life by endangering your own.'

I flinched.

'Hey!' Steph piped up, sitting forward now. 'That's not fair and you know it.'

Onyx glared at Steph and then back at me. 'Isn't it?'

'Onyx, enough,' Dapper chided. 'How is Nyla doing?' he asked me softly.

I pulled my eyes away from Onyx, who was staring daggers at me. He was such a contradiction.

'Rainer's watching over her until she wakes up. Only time will tell.' I'd popped my head in the door quickly before leaving the Academy, but I was so conflicted about whether we'd done the right thing, I hadn't been able to get out of there fast enough.

I tucked a few strands of hair behind my ear, keen to move on. 'Dapper, do you know anything about an exile named Sammael?'

'Not much, I'm afraid. Like you've been told, he's supposedly the arch-enemy of the angel Michael. But no one knows what he's been doing for the past several thousand years. Some thought he'd been killed, while others claimed he'd found some kind of land and made it his own. All we know for certain is that he's a purist.'

'In what way?' Steph asked.

'He's an exile of light and he believes in their superiority over dark. He drives the war.'

'The tournaments?' I asked.

'It would seem.' Dapper began to flip through a book in front of him, pulling out some loose-leaf papers and handing them to me. 'Take these with you. It will give you some of the history on New Orleans. I've been looking through them and it seems possible that this might be the land once spoken of.'

'Why there, though? I mean, why America and not Europe or Asia?' Steph asked.

He shrugged. 'It's a good question. Maybe he had foresight to know what America would become and saw the value in controlling a port city. Maybe it was something else. The land is some of the newest territory in the world – rising up out of the water only five or six thousand years ago. And now, it's gradually sinking again, as if …' he slowed, ruminatively.

'What?' I asked, dread building in me.

He shook his head, then changed tack. 'Sammael found a way to cross the realms after he'd first exiled – did they tell you that?'

'No.'

'Most believe he only exiled because he knew the way to return.'

'Why exile if he only planned to return?' Steph asked.

'Because he knew that once he assumed a physical form the angels would need to appear that way to him in the cross-over as well.'

I nodded in understanding. The angels always appeared in human form when they saw me.

*Sammael had wanted a physical fight.*

'Somehow, he opened a gateway and used his magic to summon a great dragon, riding it to a battlefield between the realms.' I shivered when he mentioned the dragon, remembering my dreams. 'He fought Michael and was defeated. Michael stripped part of Sammael's power so he could never open the realms again, but Sammael escaped before he could be thrown into the pits, swearing he would rebuild the world, and man, in *his* image.'

'What do you mean when you say "cross-over"?' I asked, my voice tight.

He nodded, sagely. 'I believe it would not be dissimilar to the cross-over you are able to create with the angels.'

At least he couldn't do it any more. But then, that left him here, with us. And he had Spence. 'So, even Michael couldn't defeat him completely.'

Dapper smiled sadly, as if he too suspected what lay ahead: nothing good. And a lot of blood.

'Sammael is said to be a magician with the ability to go beyond mere illusion to something much more tangible. It's possible that this land he inhabits was never intended for this world.'

My mouth fell open. 'You mean he *made* it?'

'Unlikely. But perhaps he brought it up from beneath the sea.'

'Why? Why there?' Steph asked again.

'Because it was so close to his slaves and worshippers.' Even though Steph seemed to understand this, Dapper saw my complete lack of comprehension and elaborated. 'Read the pages I gave you. But in short, New Orleans is just across the water from Haiti, where Voudon was born – a religion that worships the dead. There are some who argue that it was Sammael – the angel of death – who created the religion and brought it to New Orleans, turning it into Voodoo.'

'Voodoo? Devil worship?'

He shrugged. 'Like everything, there is both light and dark. Sammael would've seen it as appropriate – to create a religion to feed off the power of the dead. New Orleans has had a colourful history, changing hands more than once between the French, Spanish and Americans, but perhaps it is Sammael who has truly owned the city all this time.'

'Do you know anything about this?' I asked Onyx.

He looked away, as if embarrassed. 'If I did, it's gone from my mind. My memory conjures nothing but fury and fear every time I hear his name.' Dispensing with sips, he settled instead for throwing back the rest of his drink. 'When I think of New Orleans, I feel nothing but bloodlust.'

I stared at him.

*Wow. Thanks so much for your contribution.*

He shrugged, getting up to refill his glass while Dapper tracked his movements with a concerned expression.

I shook my head. 'Why was he helping Lilith if he's so adamant about the division between light and dark? Why would such a powerful exile stand by while Lilith made her power play, especially since she was the first dark exile?'

Dapper raised his eyebrows. 'Lilith and Sammael have crossed paths more than once in human form. They formed a secret alliance, among other things. Phoenix will be able to tell you more. But it's safe to say it was a volatile relationship based on keeping one's enemy close.'

I nodded. 'I'll speak to him.' I paused, looking up at Dapper. 'What does Sammael want?'

He sighed and took off his glasses. 'I don't know. I've put word out to some of the other Patriarchs to see if they know anything else. But when all else fails, you can assume he's after what the rest of them are, just on a bigger scale. Death, Doom and Destruction.'

I left shortly after, with one thought on my mind.

*If Sammael just wants destruction, why did he take my blood?*

# CHAPTER twenty-two

*'It is the strange fate of man, that even in the greatest of evils*
*the fear of the worst continues to haunt him.'*

Johann Wolfgang von Goethe

Carter, Taxi and Milo were already on the plane with Gray by the time I boarded. I was the last to arrive, having chosen to make my own way in. But I'd needed the solo time to get my head – and heart – straight.

I passed the Academy Grigori who'd congregated at the front and paused when I saw Phoenix sitting at the midway point.

'You okay?' I asked.

He smirked in that way of his. 'Your pals at the back tried to jump me when I boarded, but I think we made friends.'

I glanced beyond him to where the Rogues were sitting. Milo had a large bruise forming on his temple. I rolled my eyes but found myself smiling back at Phoenix. 'Please play nice.'

He sobered and glanced out the window. 'I'm trying.'

I nodded awkwardly, knowing that he was saying a lot in that statement.

'Thank you,' I said, causing his eyes to flash up and meet mine. I wanted to cry when I saw the pain that churned within them and wondered if he saw something similar when he looked in mine. 'For saving me. I never said thank you.'

'Definitely beats killing you,' he said, as if pondering this very idea himself.

*We really are a twisted bunch.*

'I'm glad,' I said, suddenly aware of more than one set of eyes on us. I shifted from foot to foot. 'I'd better go and ...' I gestured to the back of the plane where the guys were sitting.

'Yeah,' he said, looking back to the window. 'You'd better.'

Making my way down the aisle, I noted that they looked incredibly uncomfortable despite their outward bravado. I shook my head when I saw Milo.

'You just couldn't help yourself, could you?' I said, pointing at his bruised face.

He smiled, cheekily. 'It's like a compulsion I can't control. I see an exile and I have to have it.'

I bit my lips to hold back the laugh. 'And did you learn your lesson?'

Milo nodded. 'Fast bastard, isn't he?'

To that, I couldn't hold back the chuckle. At least Milo looked like he'd got it out of his system.

''Bout time you turned up to your own party, purple,' Carter said by way of greeting.

'Boys,' I nodded to them. 'Miss me?' I stifled my own surprise when I realised that *I* had missed them.

Carter snorted while Taxi and Milo chuckled. 'You know we did,' Milo said.

'This gig paying?' Carter asked, cutting to the chase when I sat in the spare seat across from him.

I shrugged and glanced over at him. 'Well, I guess that depends on what value you put on the world as you know it.'

'Oh, please, spare me. Are you seriously going to pull some save-the-world crap on me?'

I rolled my eyes. I'd known it was a long shot. 'I'll figure something out,' I grumbled.

'Damn right you will,' Carter threw back.

'Did you get anywhere on the exile priest before you left?'

Carter snorted. 'We only had two days before Gray sent us off to rescue you.' He gave a toothy grin. 'Of course we got him. The SOB couldn't stop himself from trying his moves at a Sunday Mass – daft bugger was so senseless he tried to help himself to Westminster Abbey. Last thing he ever did.'

I smiled, pleased the exile priest was out of the way. And by the look on Carter's face he had enjoyed being the vehicle of deliverance.

'Why do they go for religion?' I asked.

Carter leaned forward. 'Come on, purple. That's the easiest question of 'em all. They all want what they can't have. They think they should be the ones who are worshipped, they think they should be in charge.'

'And what if one of them has actually created a new religion?' I asked.

Carter raised his eyebrows. 'Well, he wouldn't be the first, but it's kind of like the ultimate finger to the sky, you know.'

I was surprised by Carter's response. I lowered my voice. 'Do you believe in God, Carter?'

'Hell, purple, I haven't even had a beer yet.' He sighed, seeing I was still waiting for his answer. 'Look, ask yourself this: if there isn't, do you really wanna know? 'Cause I sure as shit don't.'

I licked my lips. 'Good point,' I admitted.

'I'm full of them,' he said, winking at me before looking towards the sound of approaching footsteps. 'Who are you, then?' he barked.

I didn't need to look up to know Lincoln was standing in the aisle. 'I'm running this mission with Violet,' he said levelly.

I closed my eyes briefly, tucking a loose strand of hair behind my ear, while pushing my emotions down.

'Carter, this is Lincoln. He's ... He was my partner.'

'*Is*,' Lincoln interjected.

Carter gave Lincoln a long visual assessment and then turned back to me. And burst out laughing. 'Pretty boy here was *your* partner?'

'*Is*,' Lincoln corrected again.

Ignoring Lincoln, I nodded at Carter even as I glared at him.

He choked on his next bout of laughter, wiping his hand down his face. 'Well, no wonder you came running to us.'

I stood up, ignoring whatever Lincoln had started to say. I hadn't even been able to bring myself to look at him yet but that didn't stop an internal raging at Carter's words. I moved right into his personal space, knowing how much that vexed him.

My voice was surprisingly steady. 'You don't get to say that, Carter. You don't get to pretend like you know me or have any idea why I've done the things I've done. You definitely don't get to comment on why I left my partner. He's a stronger Grigori than you will ever be and not just because he fights harder. It's because he's *better* than any of us. So, listen carefully when I tell you this: Don't. Go. There.'

I was so close to Carter's face I saw the flash of fear in his eyes.

'Yeah, yeah, I hear you, purple.' He glanced over to Gray. 'Hell, man. A bit of warning that this dude's her trigger switch mighta been nice.'

'And miss this? Never,' Gray said as I plonked myself back into my seat to the sound of his and Taxi's laughter.

Finally, I looked up to see Lincoln staring at me, his eyes glassy.

*Oh, hell. How am I going to put this one out?*

I expected him to sit down and start going over our non-relationship again, or at least the plan for when we arrived in New Orleans, but after a moment his brow furrowed slightly and his eyes cleared, looking into me in a way no one else ever has or will, as he drew his own conclusions.

*Crap. Crap. Crap.*

Finally, he just bit his lip, smiled warmly at me, then turned and walked back to the front of the plane where Zoe, Salvatore and the others had all been pretending – unsuccessfully – not to gawk.

Phoenix, who was sitting at the halfway mark, didn't hide the fact that he'd watched the whole thing.

*Jesus. This is going to be a long flight.*

I did the only thing I could do. I tucked myself into a corner and went to sleep.

# chapter twenty-three

*'Passion is unjust,*
*And for an idle, transitory gust*
*Of gratified revenge, dooms us to pay*
*With long repentance at a later day.'*
**Theognis of Megara**

## PHOENIX

I am in agony.

My mind races with options but they're all hopeless. And painful. Every breath feels tight. Impossible. And I know it shouldn't hurt this much just to breathe, but it does.

I'm back. I'm in human form again. I should want a glass of wine; a day lying in the sun; a thunderstorm, for Christ's sake – all the things that I once treasured about being corporeal. But even after everything, there is only one thing on my traitorous mind.

Christ. I can smell her.

Reach out and touch her.

She's been sleeping for the past hour, tossing and turning; she wouldn't even know if I did.

Not that Lincoln wouldn't be on me in a flash. He might be sitting at the other end of the plane but he's not fooling anyone. Every molecule of that man is attuned to her. Just like me.

But, the difference is, she doesn't want me.

The truth? She never has.

The torture? I've always known.

Still, I look at her and ache. Still, I lose my breath. And worse, I don't care about myself any more. I just want her pain to stop. I want her to be happy. Even though I know who makes her the happiest.

Is this love?

Of course it is.

The worst kind.

And I can't have it any more. I can't survive it. She knows that as well as me. Eternity is too long a time to lie to myself. And yet, how can I consider an existence without her? She is all I have ever known of true desire.

All I have ever known of my true self. Lust incarnate. It should be so easy, human form again. I should be working her out of my system, but the mere idea of another woman makes my skin crawl.

Maybe if they weren't all so predictably lost to my leaking emotions ... but they are. Even here, on this plane with these Grigori warriors, I can sense the females keeping their attention on me, though they don't understand why.

They don't care for me. None of them. The only one who ever did was Violet. Even if it was fleeting. Even if it never compared to how she feels for him. Even if I've known it all along. It was still the purest thing I have ever felt.

And how did I repay her?

I've damn well broken her, too. It all comes back to me. My choices. My darkness. And now she carries a part of me within her. And it destroys me that she is using it to slowly kill herself.

Now death himself wants her and I have to help her fight. Sammael is pure evil, with a plan. he won't stop until he is put down. But, can she do this?

hell, she'd better. Otherwise I won't be the only one who is ruined.

She has no idea how important she is.

I rake my fingers through my hair and am fighting the urge to scream, to go on a rampage that once I would never have denied myself. Instead, I force it back: the malign. But I know it's just a matter of time. It's in me. A part of me.

Darkness.

Eventually, it will rise. And it will target its attention in the very same direction as my heart. My jaw clenches. I won't survive hurting her again.

Somehow, it must stop.

Suddenly she is sitting beside me. hell, I need to pay more attention.

'Phoenix,' she says, and I want to scream because just hearing her say my name hurts and lowers me to an all-new level of wretchedness. And I want to cry because I think that it might be all that my future holds: waiting for her to say my name, and then screaming in agony when she does.

'Sammael?' she begins. She looks pale. And though she can shut down her emotions, I'll always be able to sense enough – perhaps even more than she can herself. Something has upset her.

I nod.

'Did you know him?' she asks.

I shake my head, still struggling to make my voice work. I hate myself. 'Lilith knew him,' I finally manage. 'Very well.' I let a little innuendo slip into my answer, shielding me like a mask.

It makes her nervous and she inches away from me.

Better.

'I see. he was there, wasn't he?'

I nod again, but she already knows.

All that is now happening is because of me. Because of everything I did. If I hadn't brought Lilith back, Sammael would never have known that Violet existed. Given what I think he is after and could possibly achieve, it brings the term 'the weight of the world on your shoulders' a very literal meaning.

I manage to speak again. 'he owed Lilith; she was collecting.'

Violet's forehead crinkles and her breathing tightens and I know she is remembering that night. Is she remembering my role? Seeing me standing before her, loading the crossbow and shooting her with arrow after arrow. Is that all she sees now when she looks at me?

Christ, I just want it to end. There was a moment there when I was facing Lilith – her hand gripping the blade in my gut – where I thought it was all over and I remember looking beyond my mother and into Violet's eyes. I remember exhaling.

But it isn't over. It never will be. There are no retirement plans for exiled angels – just the promise of more. My 'forever' can't feel like this – empty. My only hope is to find some form of satisfaction. And that will only come from finding hers. I could almost laugh. The crying shame of it all is that her happiness is directly connected to another man.

Yeah, life's a sneaky bitch.

And the kicker? I'm not even sure it will work – that it will help me at all. But I know, beyond a doubt, that it will heal her.

'he took my blood, Phoenix,' she says, finally admitting it and because I've done nothing but watch over her since that night,

I know that this is the first time she has said it aloud. And that hurts too. That she would trust me enough to confide in me and yet it changes nothing. She doesn't want me.

'Yes. And I imagine he has used most of it by now.'

'The dreams?'

When I simply hold her gaze she draws in a sharp breath and I know I'm only confirming her worst fears; the ones she has kept suppressed even from herself. And I understand why. having someone like Sammael force himself inside your head, control what you see … It's a vile poison.

She shivers and I have to fist my hands to halt their gravitational pull towards her.

'You just had one, didn't you?' It's the only downside of being back in her world: I don't get to instantly know what goes through her mind, but I'm willing to bet that that's why she looks like she's just seen a ghost.

She presses her lips together and nods.

'Tell me,' I say, keeping my voice relaxed, even as I try to prepare for how bad it might be.

She swallows hard. 'There are trumpets sounding from everywhere. And it feels much more like a memory than a dream. Just not mine, you know?'

I nod her on.

'The dragon was there and I watched as it carved through lines of warriors all dressed in white, all … magnificent.' She breathes the last word in awe. 'But it's always the presence in the centre that the dragon focuses on, and so do I. I try to see beyond the army of white, but I can't see him.' her head snaps up as she puts the pieces together. 'It's Michael, isn't it?'

'Yes,' I say. 'You are seeing the angels at war.' Which makes me want to grab her and run. But there is no place I can keep her safe.

'This time, there was this awful battle cry and then I could see the one riding the dragon, with a huge sword in his hand. I recognised him instantly,' she said quietly, her shoulders shuddering at the memory of the dream. Every part of me wants to reach out and comfort her, but I don't.

'he screamed out ... It was pure ... bloodlust and it urged the dragon forward.' her breath quivers and I know what she is about to say. 'It was Sammael. And when I realised that, he changed. his armour suddenly turned into his suit and he was wearing his glasses when he looked right into my eyes. There was blood on his lips and he smiled. At me – through the dream.' She jolts and finds her way through the memory and back to me before she continues.

'he's controlling the dreamscape, isn't he? he's really there with me.'

I don't answer. I don't need to. A part of her has been waiting for all of this since the moment he took her blood. And she knows as well as I do that these games he is playing are all to ensure that he succeeds in luring her into his trap.

'Phoenix,' she begins, her voice catching, and I wait for her to ask. Finally she is ready. She swallows again. 'Why does he want me?'

I don't look at her. Instead I grip my thighs so hard I can feel them bruise.

'Because you're the rainbow. The link between the realms.'

'The covenant,' she whispers.

'Partly. But there's a chance that it's much more,' I say.

She doesn't push. Instead, she simply accepts it. 'Well, he's never going to get the chance to do whatever it is he has planned.'

'You think you're that strong?' I ask, intrigued. I know she is. I know she hasn't even begun to accept how powerful she is.

I risk a glance in her direction and she licks her lips. I look away quickly.

'I'm a better fighter than ever. The full force of the Academy is behind us. We can beat him.'

I look out the window. 'And what if it was just him and you?'

I can feel her smile and I make sure not to look because I know that it will carve me in two just to see it.

'Then it would be a good day.'

I understand. It would be her preference even if it meant unimaginable pain for her. It was an acceptable price to pay so she would not have to stand by and see those she loves hurt.

Especially him.

I've watched her these past two years. I've understood her pain, and as a consequence of sharing my essence with her I even feel a shadow of it. It is unlike anything humanly or angelically bearable.

how she survives it, I will never know.

# chapter twenty-four

*'Do not turn to mediums or necromancers; do not seek them*

*out, and so make yourselves unclean by them ...'*

**Leviticus 19:31**

The first time I went to New York I was overwhelmed by the number of exiles populating Manhattan. Arriving in New Orleans was not dissimilar. And yet it also reminded me of a particular sense of foreboding that I could only associate with my first impressions of Santorini.

We had travelled to Santorini to try to stop Phoenix opening the gates to Hell, and I had discovered that the island was under the control of a lone exile: an ancient by the name of Irin who had fathered a number of children with a human woman he would eternally mourn.

Irin's children were Nephlim, and their power had been similar yet different from that of an exile. They had the ability to access the minds of Grigori. I didn't know if it was a skill unique to Irin's offspring, but I wasn't keen to find out.

As we loaded into the four-wheel drives that would take us to the Grigori safe house, I couldn't deny the prickling sensation that ran from my spine to my toes.

'There are Nephlim here,' I said to my carload, which included Zoe, Sal, Gray and Mia. It hadn't gone unnoticed that Mia had chosen to travel with me instead of Lincoln, and I knew that it was her way of reinforcing that her relationship with him was nothing more than friendship.

*And I continue to have absolutely NFI how to respond.*

More unsettling was the fact that Phoenix and Lincoln had ended up in a car together. The last time those two went off alone, I ended up part of an elaborate resurrection plan.

*You can't blame a girl for being nervous.*

'Is that what that creepy slick feeling running all over my skin is?' Zoe asked, screwing up her face.

I wasn't sure about that. I knew what she was referring to but I worried that that was something else altogether. 'All I know is that there are a lot of them. Exiles too. And they're very old.' Not quite as ancient as Irin, but still, there were seriously powerful exiles here. I swallowed, gripping the door handle as we took a sharp turn. We had already been warned the drive would be 'defensive'.

'And they're all exiles of light,' I added, feeling the weight of my statement fill the vehicle.

'*No* exiles of dark at all?' Gray asked carefully.

I let him see my eyes and that was all he needed.

'We need to keep Phoenix hidden,' I said. Apart from the fact he had betrayed all exiles – who took vengeance very seriously – by helping us stop Lilith, now that the rivalry between light and dark was in full force I knew that we had put him in danger just by bringing him to New Orleans.

Gray pulled out his phone and started to type.

'What are you doing?' I asked.

He didn't pause. 'There's an emergency code. A group of Rogues got together about sixty years back. We set it up and kept it running. There are two codes. One to prepare. One to mobilise.'

I nodded, my mouth dry. The Rogues would only come together if the situation was, well, unprecedented.

To be sure, I checked. 'Have they ever been activated before?'

'Not once,' he said, putting his phone away.

Zoe, who was sitting next to Gray, raised an eyebrow. 'Which one did you trigger?'

He looked at her and I couldn't help but notice that his eyes seemed to soften slightly. 'There's something very bad here.'

Sal nodded. 'He's right. There is something …' He closed his eyes. 'Like a shield of lies covering the land, but that's not it. More like … intent and ignorance.' He opened his eyes. 'This place is like a world separate from our own.'

Zoe shuddered. 'I can feel it, too. The trees, they're not right. I know this sounds strange but it feels as if they're here against their will.'

I thought about what Dapper had said, how this land had been raised from the water. If Sammael had brought this land from the ocean then perhaps what Zoe said was right. If it had stayed where it was, trees would never have grown.

*And people would not live here.*

Zoe pulled out a packet of M&M's and offered them around. No one felt much like a sugar hit. When she looked at Gray, her eyes intensified. 'Which one did you activate, Gray?'

His eyes flicked up and met mine before he sighed. 'It'll take them at least twenty-four hours to get here.'

He'd mobilised them.

*Jesus.*

I rolled my eyes and slumped back in my seat; it was that or reach over and smack him over the head. And, Zoe was already in motion.

'You just risked Spence's life!' she said, hitting him again for good measure.

Gray's upper lip started to bleed. Zoe never pulled her punches.

'Hit him for me too, please,' Mia requested from Zoe's other side.

Zoe was happy to comply.

I wanted to be mad at him. I wanted hitting him to make it better. But deep down, I knew he was right. This place ... it was flooded with exiles and Nephlim. We were going to need back-up. Spence would agree.

And the way I saw it, it just meant I was going to have to find Spence sooner rather than later. Fine by me.

While they bickered in the back, I turned to the driver, who was one of the few local Grigori stationed in New Orleans.

'It's Roman, right?' I asked.

He nodded stiffly.

'You've been awfully quiet,' I said.

Roman kept his eyes on the road and his foot flat on the gas. 'I need to get you to the city safe house first. Then we can talk all you like.'

I noticed that his hands gripping the steering wheel tightly were dirty and his jeans and grey sweater looked in need of a wash.

'They're hunting you?'

'Always,' he admitted.

I nodded. 'Where are we going?'

'We'll stay in the French Quarter tonight and move you out to the ships in the morning.'

Lincoln had already arranged for us to use naval ships in the Mississippi River. Two Destroyers would arrive tomorrow. Having Grigori positioned in all military ranks did come in handy.

'So, I take it you know why we're here,' I said.

His jaw clenched. 'You're here to rescue your friend.'

'You say that like it's a lost cause,' I pushed.

His lips pressed into a flat line and I noticed the thick pink scar that ran down the side of his neck. Burn scars, maybe.

'I arrived here six months ago. I can't even remember what life is like outside this place and I'm certain I will never know it again. There were twelve of us who arrived, only to discover that all of the Grigori who were supposed to be here were missing.' His eyes flicked to mine. 'There are three of us left.'

I nodded, understanding his pain. 'Your partner?' I asked.

'Gone.'

I nodded again, and my next words were a statement, not a question. 'You think my friend is dead.'

He turned into a narrow street and then took another sharp left into an open driveway. The tyres ran over loose gravel, which flicked beneath the car until we pulled to a sudden stop and he looked at me.

'I think your friend is dead.'

*At least he's honest.*

Ours was the last car to pull in. Lincoln and the others were waiting by theirs but Phoenix stood apart from the group, further down the driveway. He was looking towards the street and I could tell he was using his abilities to try and gauge how threatening our surroundings were.

*Extremely damn threatening!* I wanted to yell. But I didn't since it was taking all my concentration fighting off the urge to be sick. I had worked so hard for the past two years to avoid this ... sense of responsibility. But now Phoenix had exiled for me and there he was, right in the middle of everything. Because of me. And if something happened to him, it would be my fault.

Roman cut the engine, but I didn't move.

Christ, I was practically hyperventilating and I hadn't even begun to think about how much worse it could get.

But then Lincoln was there, opening my car door, and I couldn't ignore him completely. I stared at him. Yeah, it got much, much worse. The whole thing was starting to feel a lot like déjà vu, and in the most terrible way.

Lincoln's eyes stayed on mine, sensing my fears, but when his hand reached out to touch me, I shook my head and quickly took a step back. After giving me a long look, Lincoln let it slide and I shoved my emotions back down and forced a neutral expression as introductions were made. Now more than ever I needed to stay focused on the job and on getting Spence back.

Along with Roman were partners Ray and Leila, who appeared to be in charge of their small team.

'Why don't we get your gear inside and then grab something to eat? There's a place down the road that's safe and has good food,' Ray suggested.

Lincoln nodded. 'We'll set up a team here to watch the house. They can go out in groups when we return. It'll also give us a chance to talk first,' he added.

Ray nodded and instructed Roman to stay behind to help get everyone else settled.

While Lincoln asked Zoe and Sal to oversee and head up the security of the house, I pulled Phoenix aside.

'You need to stay in the house where you won't draw any attention to yourself,' I instructed.

He smiled grimly. 'You felt them too?'

'Just enough to have me seriously freaking out. Clearly this is their territory and if they sense an exile of dark here they'll go mad. We can't afford for them to storm this place.'

He nodded, suddenly interested in the shrubbery. 'And here I thought for a moment you were worried about me.'

I opened my mouth to snap back, to tell him that he knew damn well I was worried about him. But the words just stuck in my throat and instead, I sighed. 'I'm worried about everyone, Phoenix. You included.'

'And what about you?' he asked, looking up and holding my wary eyes. 'Are you worried about yourself?'

My throat ached with the need to have some kind of release – a scream or a cry. Either one probably would have helped. 'Don't do this,' I said instead, quietly, glancing over my shoulder and catching sight of Lincoln watching us intently. The ache dropped to my heart. 'Just stay in the house, okay?' I pleaded.

'Don't worry. I'll behave,' Phoenix said, not looking at me again before throwing his bag over his shoulder and heading into the house.

Lincoln and I left the house with Ray, Leila, Gray, Carter and Chloe. Carter had looked positively miffed when Lincoln asked him to come with us, but I wasn't. It was a tactical move. Lincoln had marked him as a potential problem and was including him in the inner circle to ensure he didn't cause any trouble. Carter was eating it up, hook, line and sinker.

As we followed Ray and Leila down the street I took a few minutes to process – or at least move past – my conversation with Phoenix. I was relieved that Lincoln didn't ask questions and had chosen to walk with Gray. He was giving me some space.

*Still knows me. Still thoughtful.*

From what I caught of their conversation, Gray was using the opportunity to smoothly bring Lincoln up to date on his recent call to mobilise the entire Rogue community. Hearing snatches of Lincoln's heated response, it was safe to assume he wasn't happy Gray had made this choice before consulting him. But, like me, I could tell he also knew there was little point in dwelling on it now.

'Whoa! What *is* this place?' I asked, after turning the corner. I was suddenly dodging crowds of people and thrown off kilter by the scene in front of me. I tugged Chloe's arm, manoeuvring us to the side. The street was alive with music and mayhem. People spilled out of clubs and bars for as far as I could see.

Leila smiled, guiding us all to a less crowded area. '*This* is Bourbon Street.'

When it became obvious I was nervous about being in such a public place, she continued. 'This street is always busy to the extreme. Exiles are everywhere, but humans are too,' she said pointedly. 'Plus, half of them are drunk and it helps confuse the vibe. If exiles sense us and start a hunt, it's easy to get away, and we have a number of exit strategies. We're safer here than somewhere secluded, trust me.'

I nodded, my mouth agape as I looked around. I *had* been curious to see New Orleans. I'd heard the stories of its epic nightlife, but nothing could have prepared me for the first taste of craziness. There were so many people, of all ages, and they were all here to party. We passed bars, clubs, restaurants, cabaret places and jazz playhouses. Some guy even tried to drag Chloe inside for a pole-dancing lesson, which sent Carter into hysterics. People not only lined the street but also the balconies that hung over it, all throwing out colourful beaded necklaces, which we had to dodge as we walked through.

And, in the centre of it all, chanting into a megaphone was a preacher standing in front of a large red crucifix proclaiming that the revellers were all going to burn in Hell. He labelled New Orleans the 'Devil's playground'; knowing what I now knew and looking around at my first, late-night impressions, I couldn't help but wonder if preacher-man might just be onto something.

I'd travelled to a lot of cities over the past two years. I'd seen my fair share of red-light districts, and there wasn't much that affected me any more, but this, *this* street seeped into my bones and I didn't know what to make of it.

A sideways glance at Carter told me he viewed it all quite differently. In fact, he looked positively thrilled as he appeared to mentally catalogue the bars he planned to return to.

'Really?' I commented, watching as he eyed off a girl hanging out of one of the clubs in nothing but a teeny-tiny bikini.

He gave me a wink. 'When in Rome ...'

'I'm sure even Rome has clothes,' I mumbled.

Lincoln, who had been walking behind us with Gray and Ray, laughed. I shot him a hard look and he just shrugged, laughing again.

'I don't think I like this place,' I said.

'It's not all bad, Violet. You must be able to sense that, too?' Gray asked.

'Yeah, well, right now I'm not feeling it.'

He snorted. 'Right now all *you're* feeling like is a prude. You of all people should know that everything has a balance. For all the bad you see here – and you will – there's just as much that's good. And apart from that, we could all do with a few drinks to take the edge off.'

'Hear, hear,' Carter agreed.

'What edge?' I asked.

'You don't feel it?' Gray asked, raising an eyebrow.

I looked at Leila and Ray, who were watching us carefully, and then at Lincoln, who actually shuddered. 'I feel it,' he said, looking unhappy about the admission. 'I don't know how you guys can stay here. It's as if …'

Ray nodded. 'It's not easy, but you learn to push the sensation aside.'

I let out a breath, relieved that I wasn't the only one feeling the urge to turn around and run away. And never, ever stop.

'We aren't welcome here,' I said, finishing what Lincoln had been about to say.

No one replied. There was no need.

A shiver of uncertainty ran down my spine and, as if sensing my concern, Lincoln subtly moved closer to me. And damn him because my soul instantly responded, at once both calmed and ignited.

'Have you been here before?' I asked Lincoln as we dropped back a few paces behind Ray and Leila.

'I have. After my mum died. But things didn't feel like this back then.'

I couldn't help but wonder what he'd come to this place for back then. And if he'd found it.

Reading my reaction, he chuckled, which he had started doing quite a bit over the past couple of days. It worried me, the way he seemed always to know what I was thinking. Mostly because it made me feel like we were still just 'us'. Yet everything had changed.

'How about after dinner I show you one of the reasons people flock to New Orleans?' he asked.

I raised an eyebrow. 'You mean apart from the hard-core nudity and debauchery?'

'Yes,' he said, his eyes twinkling. 'Apart from those.'

'Okay,' I whispered, unable to resist, even though I knew I should. But there was something in me that needed to see this other side to New Orleans. And even more so, that wanted to see it through his eyes.

# chapteR twenty-five

*'For we have already said, That wickedness dwells here ...'*

**Hermes Trismegistus**

Over dinner, Leila and Ray painted a dismal picture. Since they'd arrived, their team had been plucked off one by one, leaving them nowhere to hide. Tonight was the first time they had returned to the safe house in months, too afraid to give up the location without the manpower to defend it. As a result they, along with Roman, had been in constant hiding.

'Why didn't the Assembly send reinforcements?' Lincoln asked. 'How could I not know about this?'

Leila shrugged. 'We sent out what communications we could. We hoped they got through but you can't trust anything here and we suspect that exiles control most facets of technology and communication. We sent word out, but we never heard back – not until this morning when the Academy's navy contact found us and told us you were coming.'

Lincoln, pulling apart his bread roll, listened quietly, but I could tell he wasn't satisfied. I decided to wait until we were alone to ask him.

*Alone. Hell, I need to get a grip.*

'How did they make contact?' Gray asked.

Ray barked out a laugh. 'A military chopper landed on the roof of the building we were hiding out in for the night. They'd locked onto the GPS trackers we keep in our phones. He told us that an evacuation team was headed our way and to have transport ready at the airport within eight hours. We figured it must be something big.'

'It is,' Chloe blurted out. 'I mean, he is. Important, I mean. Spence.' Her cheeks reddened. 'I mean, he's my partner and we have to get him back.' She pushed her plate away – a rice dish called jambalaya that reminded me of paella – and took a nervous sip of her drink. 'What's in this thing, anyway?' she asked, looking at Carter, who had ordered it for her.

Carter's smile said it all. 'It's called a hurricane. Local speciality. Drink up,' he said, while Ray and Leila simply shook their heads.

I moved her glass away from her. 'Maybe stick to water from now on,' I suggested. Chloe nodded just as her elbow slipped off the table.

*Good God. How many of those things has she had?*

'Look,' Ray said, picking the conversation back up with a heavy sigh. 'We understand you want to get your man out of here, but this place is crawling with exiles and their armies. You've brought an impressive team with you, but frankly ...' He shook his head, making it clear he thought we were lacking in numbers.

'Armies?' I asked. 'Do you mean the Nephlim?'

Ray sucked on a long claw of shellfish. 'I do. But it's not just the Nephlim they control. They've turned this place into a turnstile. People come to New Orleans from all around the world to let their hair down and have a good time, and that makes them prime targets – susceptible to influence.'

Lincoln nodded. 'I saw the shadowing on the walk here.'

Leila's eyebrows shot up. 'You're a shadow finder?'

Lincoln nodded again.

'I've never met one before,' said Leila, clearly impressed.

'Neither have I,' Lincoln replied, reinforcing how rare his skill of seeing the marks exiles leave behind on humans really was.

'Humans,' Gray said, putting it together in the same way that I was. By Ray and Leila's silence, we knew we were right. All the trails led here. All to Sammael.

'What about the humans?' Carter asked.

Gray described to Carter the suicidal humans we had encountered in New York, and their commitment to doing Sammael's bidding. With a look of disgust, Carter put down his spoon and rubbed his forehead. Apparently even *he* wasn't immune to everything.

'Do you know where the exiles are?' I asked.

Leila looked me over, then settled back in her seat, showing her first hint of attitude. 'You seem young to be in charge of this mission.'

'I am,' I said, smiling to see that she had no idea who I was.

'What's your strength?' she asked, cutting to the chase.

I shrugged. 'I have a few.'

'How about you give me the highlights?'

*Choices, choices.*

I could feel everyone watching me – especially Carter and Chloe. Leila didn't realise she was asking everyone's favourite questions.

'Well, for one, I don't need direct contact with an exile to strip their power and make them only human.' I let this sink in, watching Leila's poor attempt to hide her surprise, then I added, 'And they don't have to will it.'

Her eyes went almost as wide as Ray's.

'What rank are you from?' she asked, watching me carefully.

'Yeah, purple, exactly what rank *are* you from?' Carter threw in. This was the first time he had heard anything like this from me. Rogues did not share.

My eyes locked with Lincoln's and through them I felt his strength and support. As Grigori, we were partners. Despite what I tried to tell myself, that would never change.

I could feel what he wanted me to do, and I wanted it too. This was not the time to hide. I unclasped and removed my bracelets, revealing the markings that were already swirling like rivers of liquid silver. 'My maker is one of the Sole.'

Leila dropped her fork. Ray stopped chewing, his mouth hanging open. Though I'd never admitted this to Gray, he wasn't surprised. Lincoln held my eyes with warmth and something so much more that I had to quickly look away. Chloe looked in awe. And Carter ... he spat his mouthful of gumbo all over us.

'You've gotta be shitting me!'

I smiled slyly at him. 'Now, now, Carter. Try to be respectful to your superiors.'

His shoulders dropped and his eyes narrowed. 'Aw, hell, Gray. Tell me she ain't that chick everyone's been whispering about the past two years.'

'She ain't that chick everyone's been whispering about the past two years,' Gray deadpanned.

'She's the chick, ain't she?' Carter replied.

'Yeah. She's the chick,' Gray said, trying to repress his smile.

'But you and her ...'

Gray cut Carter a sharp look. 'The only time I ever tried to touch her, she broke my nose and near took my arm off.' He looked at Lincoln. 'I swear it.'

Lincoln knew this too now, but that didn't stop his jaw tightening, as if merely the thought of me being around Gray for the last year – even just as friends – was intolerable.

Carter looked at Gray, before holding up his hands, perplexed, and gesturing towards Lincoln and me. 'And what are those two, then?'

'Partners,' Gray said. Then, obviously deciding that it was a tell-all kind of day, he added, 'And soulmates.'

Carter fell as silent as the rest of the table for a few beats, his gaze settling on Lincoln curiously, but I had seen how Lincoln's shoulders had relaxed, as though hearing the confirmation of our status had helped. Finally, Carter looked back to Gray. 'Mate, I'd be guessing you're lucky she didn't break something a whole lot more important.'

Gray took a deep drink of his beer. 'I've considered that.'

I rolled my eyes, while Lincoln now appeared quite pleased with the conversation. Thankfully things changed direction as Leila and Ray went on to tell us they believed that the exiles' main base of operations was down by an old deserted power plant on the river's edge. If they had Spence in the city, that was where he would most likely be by tomorrow night.

'We'll stake them out at first light,' I said. 'Just Sal, Zoe and us. Everyone else can move over to the military accommodation and start preparing for the incoming Grigori,' I added, glancing at Gray.

Lincoln nodded, confirming he was well aware of Gray's Rogue activation. 'Once we have the lay of the land tomorrow, I'll put in a call to the Assembly to give them our green light.'

'You might not get a message out,' Ray advised.

I caught Gray's eye, wondering if his text had made it, but his relaxed expression indicated he understood my concern but didn't share it.

Lincoln shrugged, also unperturbed by Ray's comment. 'The navy has satellite equipment. We'll be fine,' he said.

We spent the rest of the meal outlining a strategy for the next day, and we even managed to have a few laughs.

Just as we got up to leave, Carter had a rare light-bulb moment, grabbing Gray's shoulder. 'That's why you call her princess, isn't it?'

Gray smiled mysteriously. 'One of the reasons.'

When we were back out on the street, Lincoln said something quietly to Gray, who nodded and then addressed the others. 'Let's get back to the safe house so the others can find something to eat.' His eyes met mine. 'First light, princess.'

I rolled my eyes.

'Must everyone have a nickname for you?' Lincoln asked, a small smile playing on his lips as the others started to walk away. I took a step in their direction and returned his smile.

'It must be because I'm so warm and fuzzy,' I said.

Lincoln laughed and grabbed my hand, pulling me in the opposite direction.

'Where are we going?'

'I told you I was going to show you some of the other reasons people come to New Orleans.'

Intrigued and petrified at the same time, I let him lead me down the busy road, dodging bodies, and then down a significantly quieter side street. 'Is it why *you* came here?'

'No, but it's what I found.'

With that cryptic message worthy of my angel maker he opened a painted black door and pulled me down a narrow staircase, keeping hold of my hand the entire time. My world was suddenly submerged within the sounds of a slow drumbeat, a smooth piano and the overwhelmingly sensual tones of a saxophone.

I paused at the base of the stairs. 'I ... wow.'

'Yeah.' Lincoln squeezed my hand. 'Wow.'

He pulled me into the dark bar, dominated by black furniture and red curtains, towards a small round table in the corner that had a small loveseat wrapped around it.

A waitress in a short black dress and dangling earrings was with us before we sat. 'Can I get you two some drinks?'

'I'll have a beer,' Lincoln said, looking to me.

'Me too,' I said. She nodded and asked to see my identification. I showed her my fake ID, which listed me as twenty-one.

Lincoln noticed it. 'Evelyn?'

I nodded. 'She has a lot of contacts. When we ...' The word *left* lodged in my throat. 'She, um ... she took me to one of her contacts and he's been looking after me ever since.' I didn't elaborate, but I'm sure he'd worked out in the time he'd been trying to find me that I had more than a few aliases and passports. If I needed to, I could disappear quickly.

*But do I need to?*

Our drinks arrived and we sipped slowly while we listened to the sounds of the band rebounding off the walls. I was in overdrive, so fixated on the man sitting next to me that I swear I could feel the rise and fall of his chest with his every breath. Hell, at one point I thought I could hear his heart beating. I really needed to get it together.

'So, this is jazz?' I asked. I'd never really heard it like this – live. No, *alive*.

Lincoln leaned close to my ear. 'No, Vi. *This* is New Orleans.'

And then, forcing myself to ignore the warmth of his breath against my neck, I started to understand.

For all the bad that might be here, this city had a soul.

And with that realisation came the solidification of my role in this fight.

*I'll be damned if I'm going to stand by and watch another soul break.*

We sat in silence for a while, and I watched the musicians do their thing. The trumpet player stood out in his black-rimmed glasses, faded brown shorts and loose T-shirt. He looked awkward beside his band members, who all wore crisp tuxedos, and yet he drew attention from the crowd. He was a trumpet geek and somehow that worked for him, made it real. He wasn't performing. He was at home, doing all he'd ever known or wanted. I recognised the far-off look as something

I might once have had when I held a paintbrush. I hadn't painted since I'd left home.

I envied him.

He was so content, as if through his music it all made sense. It was thrilling to see. And devastating.

My throat tightened, the air surrounding me becoming too thick to breathe.

Lincoln was suddenly standing, pulling me to my feet so I was close to his body. I could feel the heat coming off him, my body zapping it up hungrily.

'Enough?' he murmured, and even over the sounds of the band his voice was clear.

I licked my lips as I looked up at him. His eyes held mine and I was shocked by the realisation that his reflected no fear.

'Linc?' I whispered.

He let out a sigh. 'Vi,' he said softly.

I was lost in his eyes. Engulfed in sun-warmed honey.

'Do you still dread me?'

His left hand encircled my waist and I knew I should be moving away, but I didn't, not even when his other hand moved up to cup my face. All I could do was watch him as he said, 'I stopped trying to deny this love a long time ago.' If possible his eyes became even more intense. 'I'm not afraid of us being together any more. Not one bit. Violet, I ... I breathe you. I live you. I love you.'

I swallowed, locked in his gaze.

He moved closer, so his lips were just millimetres away from touching mine. 'The only thing I dread is another moment of my life without you as mine, the way I'm forever yours.'

Spellbound, I waited for his lips to collide with mine, to take what I knew he wanted, but he held so still. So close. And yet I realised quickly that he might have done all the work to get this far but he wasn't going to close the last distance.

That was my bridge to cross.

My heart hammered so loudly I was sure the entire bar could feel the pulse.

Lincoln breathed heavily, his breath grazing my lips. But he stood his ground.

Desperate to find some kind of control and stop my runaway mind, and body, I blurted what I'd been wondering earlier. 'Why don't *you* have a nickname for me?'

Lincoln smiled, his hand tightening around my waist. And when he spoke his voice sounded raw and not like anything I'd ever heard from him. 'Oh, but I do, baby. I just wasn't sure you were ready to hear them.'

*Them.*

*Oh.*

Lincoln won. I closed the distance. A voice in the back of my mind whispered that I was going to regret it, even as my blood ran hot. My body fitted to his as he made a sound and pulled me closer. Memories of everything right with this world, of being alive, being human, flooded me as I flashed back to the night he'd held me in his arms – me as his, him as mine.

How could something so right be wrong?

*I love you, too. I. Love. You. So. Damn. Much.*

*Enough to let him go?*

*Enough to deny myself?*

*Enough to walk away?*

I gasped, pulling back and throwing up my reluctant emotional walls. Lincoln released me as if he'd known it was coming. He didn't argue or try to touch me again. Instead he reached into his pocket, threw a few bills on the table and gave himself a small nod before looking into what had to have been my ghost-white face. 'Let's get you back,' he said gently.

*But I just don't know if there is any way back from here.*

# chapter twenty-six

*'In order for the light to shine so brightly, the darkness must be present.'*

**Francis Bacon**

I struggled with my thoughts and emotions as I tried to regain some measure of control. The late-night streets of New Orleans were in full swing and the life of the city bled into me. We brushed past such a mix of people, and many of my initial thoughts of horror were dampened by the sights and sounds of laughter, by people coming together both young and old, by the diversity of races. This city was unique not just because of its French–Spanish–American origins but also the adversity its people had been forced to face.

As we wandered, Lincoln allowed me to put a little distance between us again and calmed my runaway mind by explaining some of the history. How when the French owned the land the Roman Catholic Church, keen for converts, had insisted on baptising many of the slaves and teaching them the ways of Catholicism. But the slaves were not so easily convinced and took their true religion of Voudon underground, eventually driving out the French and the Catholics. But it was the combination of these two religions that really birthed what Voodoo is today.

Lincoln led me through the streets of the French Quarter until we came to a huge church in the central square. I pointed to the building next to it, where there was – oddly – a large speedboat wedged into the front porch.

'Hurricane Katrina,' he said. 'The waters came up so high they brought in all kinds of things. The people left that one as a memorial.'

His words and the image of the speedboat triggered something in me. For the first time, I really looked at this city, slowly turning around and seeing the faces of New Orleans. Gypsies rimmed the square, selling their fortune-telling services to gullible tourists while locals sat at nearby tables and worked in overflowing restaurants. The city was alive with activity, but the whispers of past hardships remained in their eyes. I could see it now. But I could also see the light: the passion and strength within that had driven them to fight back, to defend their lives, their families, their homes.

'Tell me more,' I said, pointing to the church.

Sensing I needed to hear and understand all I could, Lincoln continued the lesson, explaining that in the 1830s, Marie Laveau became the first Voodoo Queen. She was a devout Catholic and brought many to the Voodoo religion, performing public rituals right near where we now stood, out the back of the St Louis Cathedral. She took the religion to new heights, declaring herself the Pope of Voodoo and recruiting new followers by introducing prayer and saints.

'Do you think she was under Sammael's control?' I asked.

'I've been wondering about that,' Lincoln replied. 'Much of what she did is still debated. Some see her as a cult leader and a devil-worshipper; others want to see her sainted. Some say she brought the darkest of magic; others say she represented the good in spirits and nature.'

'What do *you* think?'

He shrugged. 'I think there's a chance she was Nephlim. I think she may have used illusion, exotic concepts and extravagance to gain a devoted following. But as much as Sammael might have thought he controlled her, I'm not sure he did in the end.'

'She became too powerful?' I asked.

He nodded. 'Possibly. I think that might be part of why he was so determined to control anyone else who threatened his throne.'

'What are you talking about?'

'There's a lot of history in this city, Vi. Ghost stories always start somewhere. There's the story of Delphine LaLaurie, who tortured and murdered a great number of slaves. She and her husband disfigured them and left them half dead and chained to her stove, and they were only found after the house caught fire.'

He watched my expression change.

'I know … She escaped before anyone could stop her.'

'That's …'

He nodded. 'Then there was the great Sultan's massacre in the late eighteen-hundreds. He kept a mansion in the French Quarter like the LaLauries', but his was famous for parties, opium and a harem of women and young boys. Until one day the house suddenly fell silent. When the authorities went in they found the floors covered thickly with blood and dismembered body parts strewn throughout the house. The Sultan was the only one left in one piece, in a shallow grave in the garden, his hand reaching out as if he'd been buried alive. No one ever found out who was responsible.'

'Sammael?' I asked softly, my fear of and anger towards this exile growing in equal proportions.

'I think so. It makes sense if he saw this land as his. He would pride himself on controlling people, leading them to unspeakable acts, but if any of them became too powerful he would have been quick to erase them. There are many more stories like—'

I grabbed Lincoln's arm. He tensed instantly, knowing what I was telling him.

'How many?' he asked under his breath.

'Six that I can tell, very close,' I responded. I gestured towards a nearby side street. 'Let's lead them down there.'

'Are you sure you don't want to make a run for the safe house?'

I shook my head. We couldn't lead them back to the other Grigori, and to Phoenix. 'But can you ...' I struggled to find the words. I wished it would make a difference if I asked him to fight as my partner and not just jump in the way of every danger I faced. But there was no point. I knew he would. I just had to hope we made it out. We could manage six.

'We can't leave loose ends,' I said instead.

Lincoln looked at me strangely but let it go, giving me a tight nod. 'You don't want word to spread that you're here.'

I shrugged. For whatever reason, Sammael had an interest in me and I wasn't going to make it any easier for him.

'It's clever, Vi. You're a smart fighter,' he said.

I gulped, wishing the praise didn't affect me. But Lincoln had been my first trainer, he was my partner – despite what

I told myself – and no matter what had happened between us, when it came to the fight his praise carried more weight than anyone else's.

A crowd in front of us began to clear, and we saw them. As the street hummed with the activity of partygoers the exiles were obvious, remaining statuesque, their eyes intent and fixed on us.

We ran down the side street, trying to get as far into the shadows as possible. In such a populated area it really would have helped if we'd had some glamour Grigori around to mask the inevitable fight, but we were on our own.

When we stopped and turned, the six exiles – all typically handsome, and dressed in varying combinations of fitted denim and leather to blend with the city's more trendy socialites – were stalking towards us. Their desire for death and blood showed in everything from their hurried, rigid movements to the snarls on their lips and the hunger in their eyes.

We withdrew our Grigori daggers and I pushed out my power, not bothering to delay with so much on the line. My amethyst mist suddenly surrounded me and I heard Lincoln's intake of breath beside me. I ignored it and pushed my power out, willing it to do my bidding.

The mist moved like an extension of myself, growing until all six exiles were within my range and then I used it to shock them immobile. Lincoln didn't hesitate.

He stood in front of the first one, who, draped in leather and wearing heavy eyeliner, looked like he should be the lead singer of a band instead of an exiled angel. Lincoln levelled the point of his Grigori blade against the exile's heart.

'Release him,' he said.

I did, keeping the others easily within my hold. I could feel my power urging me on, as if it wanted me to push more and move into my incorporeal state. But I was all too aware of the warnings I'd received. None more so than from Evelyn. She was adamant that I needed to avoid spending too much time within my Sight – and in particular, giving in to the lure of it. I knew she worried that my corporeal body could separate from me permanently. I feared at times she was right.

So, I held myself in place.

'Choose,' Lincoln ordered the exile. He stood before Lincoln, a dagger at his chest, and only smiled.

'There is no choice left. Humanity as you know it is in its final days.'

Lincoln drove his dagger into the exile's heart, the glistening colours of his power misting the immediate area as he sent the exile to face his judgement. By the time the exile disappeared, Lincoln was facing the next one to deliver the same question.

They had a choice. But not one ever chose this.

*Why?* I wondered for the millionth time.

*Why can't they see?*

Even while they live as men – apart from a few rare exceptions, who take female forms – in our world they have no idea what it is to be human. They don't see the beauty that emotions bring and a physical body provides. When they exile and find human form, only insanity awaits.

All six chose the same end. Lincoln and I were methodical, but we knew each time what answer to expect. As soon as the last one was returned I spun to check no partygoers had stumbled across the scene, just in time to see the four exiles I'd been too preoccupied to sense drop from the rooftops on either side of us.

Before I had a chance to unleash my power again, I caught a fist to the face and a foot to the gut. There was no way around this one but combat.

Again Lincoln didn't hesitate. He faced the two who had landed closest to him while I quickly found my footing and tended to the other two. Of course, just as I thought that this wouldn't be too bad, another two dropped down in front of me.

*Shit.*

The sounds of flesh against flesh echoed from the narrow street as Lincoln and I fought hard. I took down one exile quickly, but the other three boxed me in and I copped it from all sides. I saw the glow of Lincoln's power in my peripheral vision, relieved to see he'd dispersed one of his opponents.

I took a few hard hits to the side of my face, and damn if my temple didn't want to explode as I felt my nose trickle blood. I managed to angle my dagger up and take out one more exile, leaving me with two to deal with.

I saw Lincoln's power erupt again and I quickly divided myself off from one of the exiles now facing me, knowing that Lincoln would pick up the slack. But the one fighting me was tall and had a footballer's muscular and wide build. On top of that, he was old and therefore experienced, which made him fast and strong. With the beating I'd already taken, he was quickly gaining ground on me. When I kicked out hard, causing his arm to snap back, he struck me hard across the side of my face, the force throwing me to the ground. I shuffled backwards.

He shook his head, smiling. And then he stepped on my hand, breaking the small bones instantly and causing me to lose my grip on my dagger.

*I really hate that.*

I kept scurrying back as he prowled over me. 'Like all the rest of them in the end, aren't you? Crawling on your hands and knees? Just as you should.'

I let him talk. They couldn't help themselves, especially if they got one up on me. Their egos simply exploded.

'Will you beg now?' he goaded.

While he told me I was the scum of the universe and that he would take pleasure in feeding my insides to the river rats, I gradually edged back and reached for the arrow resting against my spine.

Lincoln's power erupted one more time and I heard him run in my direction, screaming my name. But I kept my eyes fixed on the exile – who had just stunned me by pulling out a gun.

Exiles have no ethics. It's a well-understood fact for all Grigori that exiles will kill them with no regret, but we hardly ever see guns. Exiles can barely contemplate the idea of giving up a barehanded kill to a human-made weapon. They enjoy the power of blades, sure, but not guns.

My eyes went wide as he cocked the safety, smiling even as he cradled his left arm, which looked broken.

*And will heal in about one minute.*

I knew that if Lincoln threw himself in front of me, the exile would shoot him dead. Desperate to protect Lincoln, I let my eyes dart to him quickly and called out just two words. 'Trust me!'

I didn't have time to look back again. I half expected the exile to already be turning on Lincoln and firing, but instead he maintained his stance over me, kicking me hard on my shin for good measure. I grunted. It hurt like hell and had my vision blacking out for a second, but I was fairly certain he hadn't broken it.

My fingers touched my arrow.

*I just have to get it out and tip it with my blood.*

Suddenly grateful I hadn't bothered with my wrist cuffs since taking them off at dinner, my hand wrapped around the arrow and I moved it down from underneath my shirt, my broken and trembling hand somehow holding me up.

The exile, smiling victoriously, swung his boot out again, this time colliding with the same side of my face that had already taken too many hard knocks. He aimed the gun.

I saw his trigger-finger twitch. But I was already moving. Using the speed that Phoenix had gifted me, and ignoring the pain that shot through my leg and hand, I sliced the arrow across my wrist and threw it straight and true into the exile's chest. The gun went off as I flung my body hard to the left, managing to protect my heart, catching the bullet in my shoulder as reward.

Panting hard, I kept my eyes on the exile the whole time, watching his smile disappear just before he did. And as soon as he was gone, I saw beyond, to where Lincoln stood, exactly where I'd seen him last, when I'd begged him to trust me.

And my heart stuttered to life.

Because he had.

# chapter twenty-seven

*'Things do not change; we change.'*
**Henry David Thoreau**

'Can you walk?' Lincoln asked, his voice controlled but strained.

It was a good question.

The fact was, I was stunned stupid and it had nothing to do with the bullet or various other injuries.

'I think so,' I said, desperately trying to rally. 'You didn't help me,' I blurted, clearly failing.

He paused, looming over me, eyebrow raised. 'You asked me to trust you. I do.' He held out his hand and I took it, still dazed as he pulled me to my feet. He focused his attention on my shoulder and methodically checked the entry and exit wounds until he was satisfied. He gestured to my hand. 'Broken?'

'Yes.'

'There could be more on the way. We need to get back to the safe house,' Lincoln said, keeping his eyes on our surroundings, all while mine stared dumbly at him.

'Were you hurt?' I asked.

He glanced at me briefly, then away.

'What's wrong?' I asked, swaying a little as I adjusted my weight to the leg that hurt the least.

His eyes shot to me then, overflowing with so much emotion that some of it spilled into me so hard I staggered back a step.

I gasped.

Fear. Conflict. Concern. Desperation. Longing ... Love.

He shook his head as if he knew I could sense it all. 'You're bleeding and broken, Violet, and I stood by and let it happen. I'm trying here, but ... Jesus, let's just get you back so I can ...' He closed his eyes and drew a deep, shuddering breath before opening them again, resigned. 'So you can fix yourself.'

I nodded and let him put my good arm around his neck as we jogged towards the safe house. I tried, unsuccessfully, to ignore the pain. But it was starting to become abundantly clear that the real pain was not about to go away. Not unless I was willing to do something about it.

Sneaking the odd glance at Lincoln while he helped support my weight, I didn't know what to make of the night. He'd only been back in my life for a handful of days and already I was starting to question everything.

I'd left for a reason.

*A good reason.*

I'd consoled myself day and night that my motives had been valid. If I'd stayed behind I honestly believed that he would have died, but something ... He was different. Changed in a way that can only occur through time and contemplation.

I paused as we reached the gates to the safe house.

'Are you okay?' Lincoln asked, worry creasing his forehead.

I nodded, but really, I wasn't okay.

*Not even close.*

Because I realised one other thing.

'I've changed too,' I admitted to myself, not noticing I'd said the words aloud until Lincoln's hand brushed the hair back from my bloodied face.

He tilted my chin until my eyes met his.

*Beautifully green, even in the dark.*

'Some things never change, Vi,' he said, his voice husky, his fingers lingering on my face.

I was faintly aware of the blood dripping from my fingers as my arm hung limp at my side. I also vaguely noticed that lights had come on, flooding the area around us, and that voices were nearing. But only one thing held my focus. Kept me grounded.

I stared into Lincoln's eyes and I knew he was the only one who would ever truly see me.

Suddenly, he broke eye contact and everything else came rushing towards me. The light, the people, the noise.

'What the hell have you done now?' Phoenix hissed, pushing others aside until he was in front of me.

I hobbled around to face him. 'I'm fine.'

But of course, he didn't bother listening to me and had already turned on Lincoln, shoving him in the chest. 'You're supposed to protect her! Not bring her back in pieces!'

Lincoln stepped into Phoenix's space, still managing to keep a supportive arm around me. 'She's already in pieces!' he growled, his nose almost touching Phoenix's. 'And we're the ones who did it to her. Or have you forgotten that part?'

Phoenix's jaw clenched at Lincoln's words, but his eyes flashed to mine just long enough for me to glimpse his pain and guilt.

'Phoenix, I'm okay,' I said with a sigh.

'What happened?' Gray asked, moving forward and serving stern looks to Lincoln and Phoenix, which they both ignored.

'Exiles,' Lincoln answered, still glaring at Phoenix. 'Ten of them.'

Gray snorted. 'That all,' he said, pulling me away from Lincoln, who let my arm slide from his as they walked me up the stairs.

'You want me to carry you?' Gray asked.

I saw Lincoln, at my side, shake his head to himself with an almost smile as I shot Gray a furious look. Phoenix stood by the doorway, also smirking. Gray raised his free hand in surrender. 'It was just an offer,' he mumbled.

*I'm no victim. If my legs work, they carry me.*

Steph was suddenly on the other side of me, nudging an increasingly frustrated Lincoln out of her way. I blinked. 'When did you get here?' I asked, worried that she'd been in this city alone.

'They helicoptered me in about twenty minutes ago. Is that a *bullet* wound?'

'Yep,' I said.

Steph shook her head and tried to keep her expression calm. She knew me. Knew I hated the fuss or looking weak. Lincoln was right: some things never do change.

'Well, Griffin will be appalled,' she said.

I smiled, remembering how Griffin felt about the fighting code. 'Speaking of?'

They moved me through the front door and towards the bedroom I was sharing with Zoe.

'He's fine. He's on his way to New York and he'll be heading this way once he's checked in on Nyla.'

'I'm glad he's on his way there. He should stay with her.'

Steph rolled her eyes. 'Do you really expect him to leave the fight to everyone else?'

Enough said.

Gray helped me ease myself down onto the edge of the bed. I looked up at everyone hovering around me, including half a dozen overgrown male Grigori crowding the small room. I was surprised to note that Carter had pushed his way into the throng.

*How have I managed to go from having no one to rooms packed with bodies in just a few days?*

My shoulder was burning alive but I settled a bored expression on them.

'I appreciate everyone's concern, but I'm fine. I'll be good as gold when you all give me a little privacy and I can have a soak in the bath.'

Gray and Carter nodded, grabbing Ray on their way and pulling him out of the room.

Lincoln remained with Phoenix hovering by the doorway, somehow managing to ignore one another. I sighed and looked at my watch. It was ten p.m.

'Lincoln, I'll help her. I'll call you if we need you,' Steph said gently.

*Best. Friend. Ever.*

His eyes cut to hers, as hard as steel but then softened and he nodded. 'I'll be in my room going over plans for tomorrow. We'll move out for recon at first light.'

I nodded and he headed out the door, looking back briefly. 'You know where I am if you need me.'

I heard him walk down the hall and a door close.

'Phoenix, you too,' I said. 'I'm fine. I just need to get cleaned up.'

He studied my face for lies.

I sighed. 'Please. And promise me you won't leave the safe house tonight.'

He tilted his head. 'I'll stay here tonight. We need to talk about Sammael.'

I kicked off my boots. 'We'll talk as soon as I'm healed.'

'That might take a while,' he said before disappearing down the hall.

*Whatever.*

I slumped back onto my bed and Steph closed the door, giving us some privacy.

'Okay, what gives?' she asked, hands on hips.

I closed my eyes, trying to breathe successfully. 'We were attacked. Everything was fine and I was down to the last one when he pulled a gun. I was on the ground and I thought Lincoln was going to throw himself in front of me,' I explained.

'Totally understandable Lincoln behaviour,' Steph agreed.

I nodded. 'Right. But then, I asked him to trust me and he ... he stood back and let me fight. I could've died.'

We were both silent. She knew what I was saying, what a huge thing it was.

'He loves you, Vi,' Steph said eventually, her own voice thick with emotion.

She was a romantic. I knew better. 'It doesn't mean everything will be okay, Steph. Too much has happened.'

She plonked down on the mattress beside me, taking little care to avoid my injuries even when I winced. She put a hand on my knee.

'You're scared. I get it. You've been through *so* much. No one will ever understand what you've been forced to face and sacrifice. But in spite of the fact you've spent the past two years running from him … He. Loves. You. And, honey, that's not his curse like you make it seem. It's his existence. His *choice*. And *he's* entitled to it.' She squeezed my knee. 'At some point you're going to have to let yourself live and take the chances that everyone else does. And that's not because you're Grigori, Vi, that's because you're human.'

She blew out a breath and flung her hands in the air before letting them flop back down. 'Everything is so huge with you. Big moments. Life-threatening sacrifices. World-changing triumphs. But love isn't like that. Love is all the small moments. It's what fills the quiet.' She sat up suddenly, looking down at me. 'Do yourself a favour and just sit in the quiet for a while, and hear what fills it.'

She stood up and walked to the door. She looked at me and smiled. 'And then do us all a favour and listen, because Lincoln isn't the only one who misses you.'

She closed the door behind her. Desperate to concentrate on something else, I quickly refocused on healing my bullet wound, but I only made it far enough to just close the wound. It would need a lot more attention, along with my hand and the rest of me, later, but Steph's words had hit hard, and, driven by some crazy compulsion, I was suddenly shoving my feet back in my boots and slipping down the stairs. I was grateful yet again that my defensive shields helped keep me beneath Phoenix's and Lincoln's radars. Getting caught sneaking out would not go down well, but I needed this.

I grabbed an overcoat hanging by the door to cover the blood more than keep me warm and snuck back out onto the street.

Walking aimlessly, I eventually hit the riverbank and slumped onto a deserted bench overlooking the dark Mississippi. It was surprisingly quiet, and though I could see lights on the other side of the river and hear the far-off sounds of night-time shenanigans, I was alone save the odd passer-by.

I pulled out my phone and dialled, unsure if the call would connect.

Evelyn answered on the third ring.

'Violet?' she said, not because she saw my caller ID but because I was the only person who had that number. Already, I could hear her instinctive concern.

'It's okay,' I assured her. 'I'm okay. I just … Spence got himself into a bit of trouble and I'm trying to get him out of it,' I explained, leaving out all the added extras that would only worry her and Dad.

'Where are you?'

I grimaced. 'New Orleans.'

Silence met me at the other end and I could picture her lips pressed tightly together as she processed all the possibilities. Finally, she sighed.

'How bad?' she asked, though her tone said she already had a good idea.

I swallowed. 'Lincoln's here,' I said, avoiding her question and answering it at the same time.

'Oh. How are you holding up?'

I took a deep breath. 'Mum, why was one of your conditions when you agreed to let me become Grigori that my partner be from the Power rank?' She'd had two conditions, and though I knew why she'd asked to be tied to Lilith's life force, I'd never known why this other condition had been so important.

Mum sighed. 'I've been wondering when you would finally ask that. Are you sure you want to hear the answer? Now? Maybe you should ask me again when you get yourself out of whatever you've landed yourself into there, first.'

'Tell me.'

After a pause, I heard a screeching noise and could tell she was dragging a chair towards her. She took a deep breath. 'I chose that rank because I knew that Powers are loyal to a fault. They're self-sacrificing, and as a result, of all the angelic ranks, Powers are the least likely to exile. More than anything, they are territorial and the strongest of fighters. Their inclination to protect is ingrained in them, and I knew that it would be an asset in your partner.'

My heart clenched, absorbing her words as yet another piece fell into place. 'You knew he'd die for me.'

'Yes. I did.'

I took a few moments to take it all in, Mum allowing me the time. Finally, I sighed. 'Do you know of an exile called Sammael?' I asked.

'He's an exile of light. Very powerful. He had ties with Lilith and we were aware of him, but ... I'm sorry Violet, my memory ...' She trailed off and I could sense her frustration. She hadn't known she would pay this price to become wholly human again, that her memory of her Grigori years would be so greatly reduced. But even so, we both knew she made the right decision.

'It's okay, Mum. I just thought I'd ask.'

'I know this much, Violet – I can feel it so deeply and truly that it goes beyond any memories that might have been taken: you do *not* want to go up against him alone.'

'I'm not alone,' I replied, my voice tight.

'I'm sure you're not. But are *you* sure?'

I said goodbye, promising I'd call again soon, and tilted my head back, closing my eyes. Breathing in and out slowly, I listened to the rhythm. To myself.

When I felt the urge, for once I didn't fight it. I lowered my shields a touch, letting the emotion I worked so hard to keep at bay slither into me.

*God, it hurts so much!*

I wanted to stop and yet, I wanted to let go too.

Concentrating on my breathing, I kept going until I found a kind of medium that I could manage. And then, again, I listened.

Almost immediately, I smelled it.

Strange, the things that mean the most.

I didn't need to open my eyes to know it wasn't a New Orleans smell. No.

*It smells like ho —*

It was the smell of Lincoln's warehouse. Basil. And the

sounds ... Cooking. Glasses clinking. A coffee machine steaming.

I could feel myself smiling all the way to my core. I remembered every little detail about the many days I'd sat at his kitchen bar and watched him cook. The way he'd prepared fresh meals for me and insisted I eat more than two-minute noodles. But also that he'd always kept a packet of my favourite chocolate biscuits in the cupboard even though he never ate them.

The memories fell like a landslide. Running every day. Feeling strong. Needing his friendship. Trusting him. The late-night talks. Dreaming of more. The confidence being around him gave me. The hand-holding. The smiles. The honesty.

And I remembered the feelings of betrayal when I found out what I was and that he'd always known. I'd been so tough on him. I was young. I knew that now. If I could go back and do things differently, tell him I understood and not hurt him, I would.

Finally, I remembered the promises. Him to me, that we would find a way. And then there was my promise to him. The one I told myself was impossible to keep. The one night we'd made love ... I could still feel his fingers combing my hair as we lay in the bed.

*'I want you to know: you're it, everything I want.'*

I remembered how his words had morphed into a long, toe-curling kiss and then he'd said: *'No matter what happens tomorrow – no matter what – tonight was exactly what I wanted and for all the right reasons. For you. Because I love you. Promise me, Vi. Promise me you will always remember that.'*

And I'd stared back into his intense eyes, and I'd promised.

My eyes opened slowly and I found myself staring at something floating in the river that had not been there before.

I stared at it for a time, taking note, before I stumbled to my feet, propelled by a force that was beyond me. Relieved when I hit the cover of the streets and roaming people again, I pulled in a trembling breath and wrapped a hand around my stomach.

I was broken.

I loved him so much but I was so afraid that it would be me who would cause his end.

Tears slipped from my eyes. I couldn't stop them. And suddenly, I was running.

*Yes, I'm broken.*

*But he loves me anyway. And he wants to save me. I know he does.*

*And I love him. So much I can barely contain it.*

My feet moved faster. I knew. I knew now.

*I love him enough …*

I burst through the gates, waving at the guards so they knew it was me as I threw myself through the front door and took the steps three at a time until I barged right through his bedroom door, skidding to a halt, panting like a crazy woman.

Lincoln was leaning against his windowsill, looking over papers. He looked up, startled and then just wary.

The silence beat hard around us.

Finally, making the choice that was more daunting than jumping off any cliff … I leaped.

'I need you to fix me,' I blurted out.

*Because I love him enough … to let him.*

His eyes darkened as he put down the papers and took a tentative step towards me. 'Your injuries?' he enquired.

I shook my head slightly. 'All of me.'

His breath stuttered and he slowly took another step. 'Do you know what you're saying?'

'Yes.'

'What happened?' he asked, looking around as if expecting to see more than just me. 'Did the world end while I was having a shower?'

I shook my head.

'Well, something huge must have happened to change your mind.'

My heart was thudding, trying to jump-start. 'Actually, it was the quiet. I found my life in the quiet.' Tears welled in my eyes. 'And all I could see and hear and smell and feel, was you. Us.'

Seconds felt like hours as he stared at me, straight into my soul that belonged to him. I waited, my heart thumping hard. But when he moved, it wasn't to me; he strode straight towards the door and disappeared.

My hand reached out for the nearby desk to steady myself; without it I would have collapsed to my knees. I heard talking out in the hall, but everything was a distant buzz compared to the deafening truth from which I could no longer hide.

*He doesn't want me*

And I couldn't even blame him. I'd left. I was the one who had taken the knife and severed the ties.

I was having difficulty breathing, my throat had tightened and my vision was blurring at the edges. None of that mattered.

Then suddenly the door was open again and I didn't need to look up to know it was him.

I cleared my throat, hoping I could at least make it out of his room before falling apart. 'I'll leave you to get some rest,' I stammered, my voice sounding as hollow as I felt. Lincoln ignored me, and I looked up in time to see him push the door closed, and turn the lock.

He paused, still facing away from me, his palm pressed flat against the door. 'I won't go back again,' he said, his voice gravelly but also threatening in its own way.

Slowly he turned to face me, while I processed the fact that he was here, the meaning of his words, the locked door. His eyes fixed on mine and burned with such intensity I almost couldn't get the words out. But I did. 'Neither will I.'

His eyes narrowed as if he didn't believe I was lucid. He took a cautious step towards me. 'Say you want this.'

'I want this.'

'Say you need us as much as I do.'

'More.'

'Impossible,' he said instantly. He took in a sharp breath. Another step. Our feet were toe to toe.

'This will be for life. For eternity, human and beyond. More than any commitment, than any marriage. Violet, are you ready to marry me?'

I swallowed, trying to catch my breath, because he was so close. So close to touching me. 'As long as we're together, I'm ready for everything.'

Breathing hard, he leaned in, our lips almost touching, his fingers moving through my hair as his hand wrapped around the back of my head. 'Tell me you'll never run away from me again.'

He wasn't asking me to promise nothing bad would ever happen or that I would walk away from every battle. We knew those promises could not be made.

'Never,' I swore, and then I voiced the words that neither one of us could ask the other for. 'I forgive you,' I said, relinquishing every last piece of me.

His eyes seemed to soften and intensify at the same time.

'I forgive you, too,' he said, right before he pulled me closer, his lips crashing into mine. My cold soul shuddered with desire, and hope filled me for the first time in two years.

Somehow I managed to pull back enough to confess, 'I'm not sure it will work. I don't know if I can ever be okay again. You need to know what you might be signing up for. My soul … the coldness … it might be too late. It—'

He put a finger over my lips, silencing me.

'How about you let me worry about that? You might be able to do a lot of extraordinary things. But, baby,' he smiled knowingly, 'I was made for you and I'm about to find all the little pieces. I'm going to search your entire body. Every. Single. Inch.' His smile grew just as my heart started to seize. 'And I'm going to build the world a queen.'

And then he set about doing just that.

He kissed me thoroughly, lifting me gently onto his bed. First he opened his power to me, pushing at me softly and encouraging mine to work with his and heal my external injuries.

'Relax,' he ordered, his lips never leaving my mouth. I pulled him tighter and let my power go.

He took it all, controlling and manipulating it until we were surrounded by our powers misting the room and it felt like floating in a sea of purple rimmed with green.

Gradually, our clothes disappeared and when Lincoln abruptly stood up I panicked, but he grabbed my hand, pulling me with him and walked us into the bathroom, where he proceeded to wash all the blood from me. He took his time, and when he was certain I was blood-free he dried me off, towelled himself down, and took me back to bed.

Lying on our sides facing each other, he swept the hair off my face and held it back as he pressed his forehead against mine.

'You have to drop your shields. You have to let me in.'

I grinned mischievously. 'That was the plan.'

He mirrored my grin but his eyes remained serious. 'Everywhere. You have to drop your walls completely.'

My smile quickly disappeared and I started to shuffle back, but he held me tight. 'You don't understand, I can't ...'

His hand cupped my face. 'Trust me.'

*Oh, holy crap.*

Tentatively, I started to lower my shields.

Lincoln shook his head, his powerful gaze never leaving mine as he said again, with more emphasis. 'Trust me.'

*I do.*

My shields crashed down around me and I cried out in pain, tears pouring from my eyes. My body convulsed and I started to panic, but Lincoln's hold was firm and he held me down. 'Look at me!' he demanded.

My eyes flashed up even as I screamed again and then he leaned down and he spoke into my ear. 'I love you. Hold on.'

And that's exactly what I did. I screamed as my soul's damage was finally and fully exposed for the first time since that night two years ago. I felt Lincoln's agony that this was what I'd become and I wanted to console him, to tell him I understood. That I forgave him, but the pain was so intense I could only scream.

Piece by piece, he tended to me, his power working its way through me, trying to calm me. Finally, I managed to get enough control that he leaned down and risked a kiss. He must have felt confident I wasn't going to bite his tongue off, because the kiss deepened and I felt small sparks of fire ignite in my body. Sparks of life.

'More,' I said, gasping.

'More,' he agreed.

When finally we came together, understanding was mine.

There was no fighting it any more. We were two halves of one whole. Each fundamentally incomplete without the other.

It wasn't like the first time – all new and explorative. This was real. Understood. Fought for. Against. Lost. Now found. And so much more.

We had suffered life without each other and now it was simple: we would never let each other go again. Ever. We held on tight and dropped all the façades. All the smoke and mirrors of strength and perfection, and it was raw and needy and desperate.

At some point my screams of pain turned into something else altogether as our powers finally merged completely for what we both knew was the beginning of our forever.

His power coursed through me and I welcomed it as he lay back, his body shaking slightly as my power overwhelmed him. I kissed him lightly, soothing him until it settled.

Then his thumb grazed my cheek and he murmured. 'No more crying.'

I smiled, kissing him quickly before whispering, 'The cold has gone. You burned it out of me. They're tears of joy.'

And then a tear slipped down his face too.

Later, we lay silently in the dark, my head resting on his chest, surrounded by a peace unlike anything I've ever known.

It wouldn't be long before morning, and there was much to do with the new day, but it had been the best hours of lost sleep in my life.

Just before we drifted off I told him, 'I know where they are, Linc. I know where they're going to take Spence.'

His hand continued to slowly stroke my arm and I felt him nod, unsurprised. I realised that very little I did ever surprised him.

He kissed the top of my head and pulled me closer. 'First light?' he asked.

I closed my eyes. Bliss. 'First light.'

# chapter twenty-eight

*'Yourself – your soul – in pity give me all,*
*Withhold no atom's atom or I die.'*

**John Keats**

Coffee.

Lincoln.

Naked memories.

Paradise.

'It's like a dream,' I said, stretching out and gratefully accepting the to-go cup. He smiled as he held up a paper bag. I raised an eyebrow.

'It's from a little cafe that opens at the crack of dawn.' He pulled two square pillows of pastry doused in icing sugar out of the bag, smoothing the bag flat to use as a plate. 'They're famous for their beignets.'

He held one out to me and I took a cautious bite. It was still warm and the dough was more like a doughnut than a pastry and surprisingly savoury, but the thick covering of icing sugar more than made up for it. My eyes rolled back and I took a sip of coffee. 'Definitely a dream.'

And I realised, feeling my body and soul in a way I had never imagined would be possible to do again, that it really was. I felt whole, undamaged, warm, content. The pain of the last two years was still sharp and vivid but with my soul bond with Lincoln back in full effect, it had become secondary. The sensation of rightness bubbled up inside me, making a slight humming sound escape from my lips.

Lincoln chuckled, that low, adoring chuckle.

*My chuckle.*

I smiled sadly.

His brow furrowed with concern. 'What?'

'I've just missed that laugh. I'm sorry I left, Linc,' I confessed.

'Shh,' he said. 'I'm sorry I was such an ass when you turned up at the Academy. But things happen for a reason sometimes. Even the hard stuff. I admit I never want to relive the past two years of my life but somehow we've ended up exactly where we always belonged, so that makes it all worth it.'

I nodded, understanding.

I could hear people starting to move around in the house. It was time to get moving and I still needed to talk to Phoenix. I crinkled my nose, looking at Lincoln. 'Do you think we should keep this to ourselves for now? At least until we get Spence back?'

Lincoln laughed so hard he had to grab his stomach.

'What?' I asked, fighting his contagious bouts of laughter.

He took a deep breath. 'Do you have any idea how much noise we, er *you*, made last night? Aside from that little issue of the most powerful Grigori known to this world just *happening* to drop her shields completely. In a city filled with exiles.'

I blushed and bit my lip. 'That was where you disappeared to,' I murmured, remembering the way he had left the room.

Lincoln was still smiling widely. 'I talked to security and had them put some extra hands on external protections.' He shrugged. 'I figured if there was a chance that … I wanted you protected.'

'Oh,' I said, relieved that he had been of sound enough mind to think about such things.

'And …' he added, his smile now dimming a little, 'my guess is, the only reason no one beat my door down to see who was killing you was …'

My smile dropped away altogether. 'Phoenix.'

He was the only explanation. Lincoln was right; with the amount I'd screamed as he'd mended my soul, the whole house would have heard.

*But Phoenix would have felt it.*

I jumped out of bed looking for my clothes.

Lincoln pointed to the chair. 'I stopped by your room and grabbed a few things from Zoe,' he said.

'Thanks. God, we shouldn't have—'

'Yes, we should have,' Lincoln said adamantly.

I shook my head. 'But we should've waited.'

'No. We shouldn't have.'

'But we … and he … It wasn't fair!'

Lincoln grabbed me by the shoulders. 'I'm not going to apologise, Violet. You were hurting. Do you think I was going to let that go on once I knew you were ready? Do you really think Phoenix would've wanted you to go on? He more than anyone would know what pain you've been living in. Christ, Violet, *I* felt it in you last night. I have no idea how you survived the past two years.'

His expression was so haunted that all I could do was nod and fall into his arms. 'Okay. Okay.'

His shoulders relaxed.

'But the whole house heard us?' I asked in a small voice.

The quiet chuckle returned. 'Possibly the whole street.'

I groaned.

He chuckled again.

I found Phoenix on the roof. It was the first place I looked. Maybe it was because of the shared essence that I could easily sense him. Or maybe it was just because it was us, and I knew him.

He was in his usual black pants and had on a lightweight navy sweater that really suited him. His hands were in his pockets and he was looking down towards the now-quiet streets of the French Quarter.

I was sure he knew I was there, but he didn't turn to face me.

We stood in silence for a minute and then I said, 'I'm sorry.'

I could almost feel the effort he was putting into closing off his emotions from me and it made me sad, though I understood. 'I'm not,' he said.

When I didn't respond, he went on. 'It's terrible, isn't it? I'd take so much back, if I could. But also, I'm not sorry in so many ways. Do you understand?'

He'd found me. Phoenix had found someone he wanted to love, someone he did love. It had pulled him apart and hurt both of us, just as my love for Lincoln had. It was still there and its effects had been both terrible and beautiful. But they had been his choices. His will. Griffin had once said it perfectly, when I'd faced my choice to embrace, knowing how hard the decision was and that it must be made of my free will: he'd called it a terrible freedom. Phoenix's love for me had been his own version of this. But he'd found his strength in it as well. His redemption.

I reached out and took his hand and when he wrapped his fingers around mine I could feel our connection. More than friends. More than a past relationship. More, even, than a mutual essence. We were a shared story, a history, and still ... an unknown. We stood together, holding hands, looking out to the world and not at one another as I promised him, 'I understand.'

After a few minutes he cleared his throat and I wondered if he'd been crying but I still didn't look. It seemed like we'd agreed to not allow our eyes to meet.

'What am I going to do?' he asked, not just me, but the universe.

'What do you *want* to do?'

'Apart from slaughter Lincoln, you mean?'

I almost smiled, but it was too close to the truth. 'Apart from that.'

'I want all I've ever wanted: I want to belong.'

My heart clenched to hear the sadness in his voice and because I didn't know how to make that dream a reality for him.

Of course, he knew this and didn't wait for me to come up with some lame response. Instead he changed the subject.

'Sammael wants the ultimate power over life and death. He hates Michael more than any other angel. Michael has thwarted his every plan and Sammael wants his revenge.'

'How, Phoenix?'

'By bringing Michael to battle.'

'But no angel is permitted entry to earth, not in a physical form. There's no way an angel like Michael would do that.'

'I know,' he said. And in just those words, the way he said them, I understood.

'The link between the realms,' I whispered. Phoenix, still holding my hand, squeezed. 'My blood.'

'Your blood.'

By the time Phoenix and I came downstairs, everyone was assembled in the living area, preparing to move out to the navy vessels that would become our base of operations from here on out. Steph was in the corner looking giddy. I was about to force my expression to neutral but then I spotted Lincoln standing near the door to the kitchen, his eyes fixed on me, and there was no way to stop the smile.

*Screw it! They all heard everything last night anyway.*

So, in front of everyone, I strolled towards him, smiling when his eyes widened. By the time I reached him he was smiling too. And then I threw my arms around his neck and kissed him.

Wrapped in melted honey and sunny days, I laughed at the variations of cheers, whistles and calls to 'Get a room' but mostly, I just basked in all that was Lincoln and our love.

*Finally ours.*

When I pulled back and looked over at Steph she was crying like a baby – with a big smile on her face. I winked at her. 'That quiet thing really worked.'

She burst into a snotty laugh and Salvatore put his arm around her, while Gray, standing alongside them, gave them a hopeless look. But when I caught his eye he gave me a quick wink – his blessing. And it meant a lot. He'd held me together the past year and our friendship had come to mean so much more to me than I had ever before let myself acknowledge.

'Can we *please* go and kill some exiles now?' Carter called out gruffly. 'No wonder I never wanted to work with you people. It's like a bloody soap opera!'

I looked over at him, smiling, but in full agreement. It was time to go and get Spence.

'They're out on the river,' I said, surprising everyone in the room except Lincoln.

'That's impossible,' both Ray and Leila stated.

I shrugged. 'You're just going to have to accept that I'm right. And I am. Once we get down to the river I'll see if I can help you see through the glamour they're using.'

'What exactly do you mean when you say they are on the river?' one of the conductors asked.

'They have a big-ass steamboat.'

Ray shook his head. 'There's only one steamboat left in these parts and that's a tourist attraction.'

'The red and white one?' I asked.

'Yes, that's it.'

'Yeah, well there *is* another one: it's grey with blue trim and it's got all sorts of bad coming off it. There's also a helipad on the top. My guess is that's how they'll bring in Spence.'

I looked at Steph, who had pulled herself together and refocused. 'What did you find out?'

She stepped forward. 'Dapper was right. It appears New Orleans is Sammael's city. He *made* it, and as far as he's concerned, that makes him God. We believe he's played many roles in the history of the city. He was one of Marie Laveau's husbands and through her he controlled the focus of religion and worship. But Sammael *is* Voodoo. He used exiles and Nephlim to create illusion and influence human minds, generating belief in all of his magic. He was behind a number of terrible slaughters and massacres and we suspect he was even responsible for the many disasters that have touched this land. The floods, the yellow-fever epidemic, the hurricanes ...'

'But why would he attack his own land?' Carter asked.

Steph nodded, happy with the question. She was turning into such a scholar. 'Because it's sinking. Close to seventy per cent of the city is already below sea level and only protected by the surrounding levies. In just the past seventy years more than seven hundred thousand acres of wetlands have disappeared.'

'He's losing his hold on the land. It's the natural order,' Phoenix chimed in, causing all eyes to zero in on him. I could see his weariness and understood that those who did not know him found it hard to accept that he wasn't like all the other exiles. But for now I was grateful that they seemed willing to listen. 'The land was never intended for the air, but for the sea. It will be returned. It must,' he explained.

'But it's not that simple,' Zoe protested. 'People live here. There's three hundred and fifty thousand in the city alone.'

'It's the natural order,' Phoenix said again, his tone matter-of-fact.

'And since Sammael knows this too, we fear that he'll take matters into his own hands. It looks as if he's trying to rewrite a new history,' Steph added.

'I don't understand,' I said.

'Thank Christ,' Carter muttered, while I noted Gray had his eyes cast down contemplatively.

Steph rolled her eyes at Carter. 'Sammael sees himself as a god, and history credits a great deal of destruction to God. Biblically speaking, when it comes to entire cities; cities that look like they've lost their way; cities like New Orleans ...' She shifted uneasily.

'He's created his own Sodom and Gomorrah,' Lincoln said, and I felt his worry surge through our bond.

Steph nodded.

I wasn't great with my history but I knew enough. 'But those cities were destroyed.'

Steph struggled to hold my eyes as she responded. 'Yes. No one was left alive. And when Sammael has what he wants he'll make an example and ...'

'He's going to destroy New Orleans,' Gray finished, finally joining in the conversation and looking up, his face pale. Looking much like how I felt.

'Okay,' I said, trying to look for the out-clause. 'So what does he want?'

Steph shook her head. 'I don't know. But it will be something finite. He wants to change the way of the world. All I know for sure is that we definitely do *not* want to see that world.'

'But how?' Zoe asked, clearly confused. '*How* would he make a new world?'

Silently my mind ticked over, and I wasn't completely surprised when Phoenix spoke. 'By killing the Weigher of all Souls,' he said, finally freeing the information that, as an angel, he was prohibited from sharing.

Steph snorted. 'What? God? Does Sammael even know if God exists?'

Phoenix raised his eyebrows and wandered over to Steph's laptop that rested open on the coffee table. 'Sammael was once an angel of the Sole, Steph. There is every chance he knows everything.' He sat and started to tap away on the keyboard.

'Oh,' she said. 'But that still doesn't mean he can just go and … kill … God. Does it?'

Phoenix spun the laptop around to face the room and flicked through screens showing different pieces of artwork.

'These are all images of the Final Judgement. In the centre you will see that there is one who holds the scales for all souls. Look closely,' he invited the room. 'Tell me what you see.'

I didn't need to look. I knew my art. I knew these works. But that wasn't why I had the answer. Phoenix had already told me in as many words.

'He has wings,' I said.

Steph looked closer and I heard her gasp. 'The Weigher of all Souls is an angel,' she said.

'The Commander and Chief. The most loyal and ruthless. And above all else, irreplaceable,' Phoenix said.

'Michael,' Gray said softly.

No one disagreed.

Phoenix closed the laptop and stood up, briefly meeting all the wide eyes in the room then settling on mine. 'By killing Michael, Sammael will extinguish humanity's ultimate judgement, thereby removing the greatest of consequences.'

'Heaven and Hell,' Steph said.

Phoenix nodded. 'No human knows what they truly are, what awaits them after death, but the idea is enough to make most people consider the final outcome. Take away accountability, conscience will soon follow, and the world ...' He looked down. 'The world will slip into anarchy.'

'With Sammael at the helm as its new god,' Lincoln said.

# chapter twenty-nine

*'He who does not punish evil commands it to be done.'*

*Leonardo da Vinci*

$f$rom my place, lying on my stomach, wedged between Lincoln and Carter on the roof of the Governor Nicholls Street Wharf, I had a perfect view of the river. I could see both the battleship we had hovering just around the bend and the steamboat glamoured beneath a thick fog anchored in the middle of the Mississippi.

'Once we get your boy, we should just green light the navy boys to blow up the whole damn thing. You know, simplify,' Carter said, still grumpy it had taken him the longest to break down the glamour and reveal the steamboat. Lincoln hadn't needed any time at all. Our powers were once again linked. What I saw, he saw.

Of course, that went both ways.

'There are humans on that ship,' I said, even as I shuddered. Having a connection to Lincoln's power meant that I was again able to see the shadows left behind by exile interference. Almost the entire city was shaded. I'd never imagined that something so tainted was possible.

Mia, lying on the other side of Lincoln, looked appalled. We had teamed her with us since we were in the most exposed position. Mia was a senior Ghoster and her skill-set meant she could produce a 'look away'. It was similar to a glamour, but instead of making us look like something else, she made us look like nothing. If a pair of eyes – exile or human – looked upon us, they would simply not register that we were there.

'Yeah, well, they made their choice. Greater good, purple. Sometimes you gotta make the tough decisions,' Carter pushed.

The worst thing was, as much as I wanted to smack Carter over the head for even considering it, I knew there would be many who would agree with his point of view and I worried that with the high number of soon-to-arrive Grigori, including Josephine, this view would receive more attention.

I shook my head. 'We don't kill people, Carter. That's not our job. Nor our right.'

'Is that what you tell yourself?' he asked, rolling slightly from one hip to the other to reposition. 'You see the line so clear?'

'Of course,' I said, though my voice wavered. There *had* been a time I'd found the choice to return exiles, to take my blade to them, a difficult one.

Carter shrugged. 'Maybe it is. But that doesn't change the fact they went and got themselves human bodies. We call them exiles but you can't pretend there is nothing human about them.'

'We give them a choice, Carter. It's the most we can do. *They* choose,' Lincoln said.

Carter snorted, making me feel uncomfortable because I felt an element of what he was saying had merit and according to him that made me a hypocrite. 'You really think they can choose anything? They're insane. Their choice will only ever reflect that.'

'Either way, Carter, that doesn't change the fact that we will not harm the humans on that ship if we can avoid it,' I said firmly.

'Not to mention,' Lincoln added, 'that unless you were planning to blow up the boat with Grigori shrapnel, it would at best only injure the exiles on board.'

Carter grunted. 'We could always fill it with something else,' he said looking at my wrists.

I flinched and Carter froze when, beside me, Lincoln growled. I could feel the overwhelming anger flow from Lincoln in waves, and from the look on Carter's face, he could too. I hadn't told Carter about my blood, but he'd been privy to a lot of information lately and, with the number of rumours circulating, I wasn't surprised he'd put two and two together.

'Of course, we could always just stick to the plan,' Carter said, looking back out towards the river, clearing his throat. 'It's a good plan.'

I bit my lip to hold back my smile and discreetly slid my hand into Lincoln's. Instantly I felt the tension in his body ease.

Mia shifted closer to the edge. 'Come on,' she chanted impatiently. 'Please, we need to get him back.'

'We will,' Lincoln consoled, and I felt a clear flash of his feelings towards her: warm, protective, deriving entirely from his sense of brotherhood with Spence. And I realised that was why Lincoln had been looking out for Mia the night she was dancing with Gray, and why he had often deferred to her counsel when it came to matters that affected Spence's life.

I tightened my grip on his hand, my heart clenching.

Mia nodded and kept her eyes fixed on the steamboat.

I looked out to the other positions where we had hidden our small teams. It wasn't as easy to sneak up to the river as we had hoped. There was a lot of open land, which made visibility a problem, and the streetcar line divided the river from anywhere we could park surveillance vehicles. So, we had broken into small groups and scattered.

Gray and Salvatore were captaining speedboats currently on standby. Tactically positioned close to the navy Destroyer and on opposite sides of the river, they waited for our signal.

A few hours later, my limbs numb from holding the same position for so long, my phone buzzed.

The text from Phoenix, who was positioned precariously at the top of a nearby electrical cable tower, was brief.

*Incoming.*

We all looked up in time to see the speck in the sky come into focus, the thumping chopper sounds growing steadily louder.

I could hear Mia whispering. 'Please, please, please.'

I did the same internally. If Spence wasn't on this helicopter, we were out of ideas. And that wasn't acceptable. The only thing that made me believe we were right was the knowledge that Sammael *wanted* me to find him.

*He needs me.*

I pushed the thought aside.

'You sure you've got us covered?' Carter asked Mia as the chopper neared.

Mia sent him a sharp look. 'Of course I have!' she replied defensively. It really wasn't a good idea to question a senior Grigori's capabilities, and Carter knew it. 'Do you even *have* a strength?' she added.

Before she finished her question, Carter was suddenly no longer next to me, but lying beside Mia.

She gasped. 'How the hell did you do that?'

I would've rolled my eyes if they weren't fixed on the helicopter as it approached the steamer. 'He has a five-second rewind,' I explained. 'Usually by the time he realises he needs to go back, it's too late. But every now and then it comes in handy.'

'Like the time I blocked that axe from going through your spine?' he offered.

'Like that,' I grumbled, then added, 'Look. They're down.'

We all waited as, beneath the rotating blades, a well-dressed exile jumped out, then another. Then we saw three humans jump down, all wearing business suits. All shadowed. I held my breath for a small eternity and finally, we saw another exile emerge. He was large and dressed in loose pants and a T-shirt. Fighting clothes, like ours.

Spence was draped over his shoulder.

'He's not moving,' Mia hissed.

My phone buzzed again. This one was from Chloe.

*He's alive.*

'She wouldn't say it if she wasn't sure, Mia,' I said, trying to give her the strength she would need. Because we could all see, even if he was alive he clearly wan't in a good state.

'Our boats are on the move,' Lincoln said, putting his phone away.

And that was our cue. We all pulled on the ropes – anchored to the rooftop and threaded through quick-draw D-rings – attached to our waists. Without pause we backed off the edge, plunging quickly to the ground and landing easily.

By the time we ran to the river's edge Gray was pulling up in his speedboat, slowing to give us a chance to leap into the back.

I held on tightly as he lurched forward again, sprays of water spitting into my face. We knew that our boat, or Sal's, which was approaching with the rest of the team from the other side, would be spotted in moments. We had to get on board fast.

As Gray pulled alongside the steamboat Lincoln and Carter shot arrows connected to cables up and onto the deck. Once they were hooked, Mia climbed onto Carter's back and I climbed onto Lincoln; they then flicked the retract button and we were hauled up onto the deck.

'Gotta love the navy boys,' Carter remarked as he threw the one-shot weapon, courtesy of our Grigori positioned within the US navy, to the ground.

On the other side of the boat Phoenix and Chloe boarded, along with the conductors, Milo with Taxi, and Zoe flying solo.

Chloe looked as pale as a ghost, and I was sure it had nothing to do with seasickness and everything to do with whatever she was sensing through her partner bond.

*I need to get to Spence. Now.*

Exiles and humans alike started to run in our direction, the humans carrying automatic weapons and the exiles with swords, or simply smiles.

*Holy hell, there are more than we'd counted on.*

'Linc.' It was all I needed to say. Instantly he was by my side.
*My sentinel.*

'Zoe, your team has the deck!' Lincoln yelled.

I trusted that Lincoln had things in hand as he continued to issue orders. So, I blocked him and everything else out and I focused on my power – the part that sat right at the base of the well within me. The part that made me feel as light as air and frighteningly powerful. Breathing deeply, I urged it forward, beckoning my Sight and leaving my corporeal form behind where Lincoln stood guard.

I could see the boat now from my bird's-eye position – like a pattern or blueprint, shaded and obscured, its evil intent pulsing on the perimeter. And within, I could see auras. The human impressions were not as bright as they should have been, and I knew that this was because they had been tainted by the exiles controlling them.

Auras were always one colour. The exiles were easily spotted: always shades of red. Grigori were different, but each one still a solid colour. Except for me; like so many things, mine was an anomaly. A rainbow.

I instantly registered Lincoln's grass-green aura, but I was momentarily surprised to see that it had changed: still green, but right in the centre a shimmer of colour bled out.

*In his heart.*

*Of me.*

I forced my eyes to move on and continue the search. Phoenix's unique shade of orange-gold caught my attention and then my Sight travelled below deck.

It was only a matter of seconds before I found Spence. His particular shade of azure-blue was almost completely smothered in thick ominous shadow, and beside him was a great expanse of red. Blood-red.

*Sammael.*

Anger saturated me and I harnessed it, feeding my power and pushing it out over the entire vessel until every exile was under my hold. All except Sammael. I wouldn't be fooled again. I knew he was immune to my ability.

Zoe led the way – with Phoenix close behind – as our people pushed through the fighting humans, concentrating on taking out the exile threat as quickly as possible. While Grigori used their blades, I knew that Phoenix would be reaching in and tearing out their exile hearts.

At that moment, with Spence covered in shadow, it was a gruesome tactic I was prepared to live with.

Once they were all taken care of on the top deck I felt Lincoln's power calling to me. For the first time, the lure of holding onto my Sight and remaining in my incorporeal state held little temptation. The feeling was present, but it was simply outweighed by another feeling that was so much stronger.

When I opened my eyes, Lincoln was waiting for me and he smiled, as if he knew exactly how much he had truly fixed me.

Catching my breath, I looked out over the ongoing fight with the remaining humans. Taking out the exiles on deck had given us the advantage for the moment but we were still only a few against many.

'We'll try to disarm the humans and knock them out so we can get them off the boat,' Lincoln said. He didn't need to speak the silent 'but'. We both knew there was a chance things would go wrong.

I nodded once, already looking for the entry to the lower decks. 'I know where he is.'

I grabbed Lincoln's hand and started to push through the throng towards the lower deck, Lincoln pausing only to call out to Zoe that she had control of the deck.

By the time we made it down the stairs Phoenix was at my other side and Carter, Milo and Taxi stormed down the stairs heading in the opposite direction to secure the cabins.

I walked straight towards the wide double doors at the end of the hall. When I reached them, I threw them open, abandoning any further attempts at stealth. Sammael knew we were there. Sure enough, there on the far side of the ship's casino, he stood, waiting, Spence beside him.

We strode across the room, stopping about five metres from them.

'Spence,' I said.

'You're earlier than I expected,' Sammael mused, though clearly unperturbed.

'Spence!' I said again when he didn't respond. He just stood beside Sammael, staring out through blank eyes.

*He doesn't see me.*

'He does not exist in this reality any more. Not entirely,' Sammael said from beside him.

I turned my heated glare on the exile, my senses on high alert as they fought against the onslaught that was Sammael. Beyond powerful; unlike the last time we'd crossed paths he wasn't holding back. He wanted me to know what I was up against.

He looked exactly the same as he had that night at Lilith's estate. Unassuming. Short, slim and bald with light grey eyes hidden behind wire-rimmed glasses. Again he wore an expensive-looking yet conservative suit with a blue tie. The only difference was that this time, his shoulders were back and his eyes proud – he expected to be noticed.

He gave nothing away, taking his time to study first Phoenix and then Lincoln, who were standing on either side of me.

'Would you prefer something more like what you are used to?' he asked, sarcasm leaking into his words as he suddenly morphed into a taller, considerably more handsome – and haired – appearance. 'Humans are so predictable. They all dream of being surrounded by beautiful things.' He smiled, returning to his former self. 'Angels who exile automatically take on beautiful forms. Why would they not, when beauty is so often richly rewarded?' He winked at me. 'But I'll let you in on a secret. I never wanted the beauty. You see,' his tone dropped and became more intimate, 'you can achieve so much more when no one is watching.'

'Give him to me,' I said, keeping my eyes on Sammael and making my threat clear.

'Of course,' Sammael continued as if I hadn't spoken, 'all those angels who abandoned their realm simply thought they could rule this world better.' He chuckled lightly. 'Not me. No, I never wanted to rule *this* world.'

'Then perhaps you should consider leaving it,' I sniped, losing patience.

He ignored me. 'I am going to *make* a better world.'

'A world based on fear?' I asked.

He shrugged, holding out his arms. 'What do you think *this* world is built on? Do you not ever wonder why religion exists? The *point* of it all? Ask yourself: are humans more inclined to conform because they *hope* for Heaven or because they *fear* Hell?'

I didn't respond. Instead I asked, 'What have you done to Spence?'

'How could I deny him? It was a beautiful dance of free will at its worst for him and best for me. Oh, Violet, he *wanted* to find me. He has hunted me for years. Of course, I could have taken him any time, but I needed to be sure everything was in place first.'

When I narrowed my gaze he rolled his, as if disappointed I wasn't more impressed. 'He is absent. Absent in mind, in conscious thought. Adrift, while his imagination has very likely delivered his mind to somewhere ... unpleasant.'

'Release him!' I yelled, pulling out my dagger.

'Violet,' Phoenix – who had remained otherwise silent – warned quietly from behind, causing Sammael's eyes to sparkle with glee.

'Release him,' I demanded, my voice now lowered, but no less intense.

Sammael watched me calmly.

*Too calmly.*

'How have you been sleeping, Violet?' At his taunt I took a menacing step towards him, but he merely chuckled and held his hands up in feigned surrender. 'Agree to aid me and you may take him with you now. I will return him to his previous state as payment for your services once completed.'

'What do you want her to do?' Lincoln asked, his tone even despite the raging protectiveness I could feel through our connection.

Sammael tilted his head, studying Lincoln. 'It is intriguing that even as soulmates and with your powers entrenched within one another, her ultimate powers have been withheld.' He turned his attention back to me, his eyes roaming up and down making my skin crawl. Lincoln took a threatening step forward as Sammael spoke again. 'Why don't you tell him, Keshet? I am sure by now, you know.'

I swallowed, keeping my eyes on Sammael as my grip on my dagger tightened and my free hand fisted even as my body shook with both fear and anger. 'You want to cross the realms.'

Lincoln's power caressed me, reminding me he was there.

Sammael smiled and then suddenly shoved Spence towards us. Phoenix caught him as he stumbled.

'If you want the rest of him ...' He walked casually to the large portside windows and pointed to a tall decrepit building close to the riverbank. 'You will be on that rooftop in the minutes before midnight tomorrow.'

'Even if she decides to go, she's not going up there without me,' Lincoln said.

'Understood,' Sammael conceded. He took out a hand-kerchief and pulled off his spectacles, to clean them. 'Did you ever wonder what might be odd about the rainbow being the sign of the covenant? Interesting, don't you think, that the ultimate bow that can harness the arrow of destruction, Violet, *Keshet*, is pointing *up*?'

*He's talking about me. I'm the damn rainbow.*

My mind spun with his words.

*What the hell am I?*

'I'm a weapon,' I said absently.

He nodded. 'But for all things in this world, there must be …'

'Balance,' I whispered, the gravity of this new understanding gripping at my insides like a determined claw.

'Balance,' Sammael echoed. 'You may be the greatest and most powerful of all warriors for the angels, but in being that, you must also be their greatest and most powerful threat.'

The air left my lungs.

And with that, he vanished.

*Like magic.*

# CHAPTER THIRTY

*'Nature in her most dazzling aspects or stupendous parts, is
but the background and theatre of the tragedy of man.'*

John Morley

**B**ack on the upper deck, Zoe and Carter had matters under control.

Phoenix carried Spence, who remained unaware of his surroundings, across the deck and then Lincoln helped to lower him onto one of the speedboats. A navy vessel pulled up on the other side of the steamboat, and a bridge was set up for the humans – who were either restrained or unconscious – to be carried over, overseen by the conductors.

The trip had been a broken success and we all felt the weight of what was still to come.

I jumped into the speedboat and Gray took off at a much slower pace. 'What will happen to the humans?' I asked Lincoln, who had been on and off his phone sending out orders.

'One of the boats is heading to the Jacksonville navy base. They'll take the humans there and navy Grigori will take charge of them until we can figure out what to do. Best case, they'll all come to their senses with some time,' Lincoln explained.

'Worst case?' I knew I shouldn't ask.

'Almost all of them have broken human laws. If we can't bring them to their senses and work out a way to help defend them, it's likely they'll go to jail.'

*What is happening to this world?*

I felt like screaming but I knew from too much experience that it did jack-all, so instead I considered what I now knew very likely lay ahead.

When we pulled up to the navy Destroyer, I took the hand of the officer who offered it and let him pull me aboard. Even if I hadn't automatically known he wasn't Grigori, his look of confusion as he watched what was no doubt a very unusual day unfold pegged him as pure human.

The young officer looked over his shoulder and then back at me as Lincoln and Phoenix grappled with Spence's uncooperative body.

'Who *are* you people?' he asked quietly, obviously deciding I looked like the one most likely to explain it all. 'You're all, what – twenty, twenty-one?'

I kept my eyes on Spence, ready to jump in and help the guys. 'Actually, I'm nineteen,' I said.

'I don't get it. You're all young, but you've got the resources of the whole US navy at your beck and call, and you lot have got moves I've never seen before.'

I noticed the pair of binoculars around his neck before I crouched down to keep the boarding ladder steady.

*Someone's been paying too much attention.*

I don't know why, but I repeated what Griffin had said to me that first day I'd found out what I was: 'We're the gardeners. We clear the weeds.'

The guy snorted. 'Well, if you're the gardeners, what the hell are we?'

I looked up at him, squinting into the sun and smiled briefly. 'You're the wheelbarrow.'

He laughed. 'Is that your way of calling us a taxi?'

'Might be,' I replied, helping Lincoln carefully heave Spence up the last step.

Once Phoenix and Lincoln were on deck and had Spence between them we started to walk towards our cabins – where we knew we were guaranteed privacy. Officer Wide Eyes chased after me a few steps and called out, 'You have to get some fancy qualifications, or something?'

I looked over my shoulder and called back. 'It's more of a birthright kind of thing!'

'Just my luck,' he said, defeated.

I paused and turned around, letting Phoenix and Lincoln go on ahead. The officer was young and eager. He reminded me a bit of Spence. 'It just might be,' I said.

He watched me closely as I showed him just a touch of the truth, letting a little of the battle, the sacrifice, the loss, and the promise of death fill my eyes until finally he nodded. He saw enough in that moment to understand that this life was not something to be painted in pretty colours. After a small nod, the officer walked back to his post.

Just as I caught up to Phoenix and Lincoln at the doors going inside, Sal and Zoe suddenly came barrelling towards us from the other side of the deck, pulling up quickly when they saw Spence, who was still looking entirely absent. I could see the moment they both registered that we had a serious problem.

Before they started with the questions, Lincoln took charge, handing Spence over to them. 'Take him down to the infirmary. Tell Chloe to stand guard and Mia to sit with him. Maybe one of them can reach him. Then meet us in the war room.'

His final two words sent a shiver down my spine.

Sensing the gravity of the situation, Zoe and Salvatore were consummate professionals, reminding me that they too had grown over the past two years.

I had missed so much. Too much. And I knew that if I made it through this battle, I would make it up to my friends and family.

We collected Steph on our way and found the rest of our team, minus Milo and Taxi, waiting for us in the war room, which turned out to be a large boardroom with the addition of soundproofing.

'I asked Milo and Taxi to watch over the humans, just in case,' Carter told Lincoln, who nodded in both agreement and respect for Carter's judgement.

Lincoln placed a call to the New York Academy and switched to speakerphone as he updated Josephine and Drenson, along with a few other key senior Grigori who were patched in from various locations around the world. A few minutes into the call a new voice came down the phone, and I smiled when I realised it was Griffin, who explained that he had just arrived in New York, and that Nyla was expected to wake up at any moment.

Steph discreetly called Dapper on her mobile phone, and he and Onyx listened in at their end in case they had anything to offer.

The instant Lincoln finished relaying Sammael's threats, Drenson spoke loudly. 'So, Violet is the problem.'

'Who's this dick?' Carter bellowed, causing a few smiles around the room, and a chuckle from Gray.

'I'm the one who controls the resources of the Grigori Assembly and International Academy.'

'I'd be careful with your choice of words, Drenson,' Lincoln said. 'You may be Principal but each Grigori is chosen by something much greater than you and is taught very early on the value of free will.' As a number of faces watched him intently from around the room I realised I wasn't the only one struck by how strong and controlled he was.

*A leader. A general.*

'What do you suggest our ultimate situation is, Lincoln?' Josephine asked, in a clear let's-move-on voice.

Lincoln ran his hand through his hair. 'Griff, she's the key,' he said, addressing Griffin in favour of Josephine. He was making a clear statement to any who could be bothered to read between the lines. His respect rested with Griffin.

*Mine too.*

'Somehow he plans to use her to destroy the angels,' Lincoln explained.

'But what I don't understand is: how? Violet, do you?' Griffin asked.

My pulse raced. This was the moment. I couldn't hide from what I was any longer. There were too many lives at stake and, besides, I was tired of all the secrets. Tired of hiding from what I am.

'My blood,' I said. 'My blood isn't just his key, it's more.' I looked at Lincoln, seeing nothing but strength and support.

Phoenix stood at the back of the room and when my eyes met his he nodded me on softly.

'Most of you already know or assume this, I suppose, but it's time to confirm it. My angel maker is of the Sole. My mother, who was also Grigori, sacrificed her life to him so I could be created. Among my abilities are all five senses and a Sight that enables me to move beyond the confines of my body to any place that I will it and view the blueprints and auras of the world.' I paused, searching out Gray's eyes as people began to gasp. He simply smirked and gestured for me to continue. I wasn't surprised that – despite never having verbally confirmed very much – none of this was particularly news to him.

'In addition to carrying the essence of my maker, who is an angel of light, I also carry the essence of Phoenix, who in giving it to me saved my life and gave me the additional abilities of speed and the capacity to control my emotions, which helped considerably while I endured the past two years with a shattered soul.' My last words broke and Lincoln took my hand.

'Recently, my soul was mended and the bond I share with my soulmate, Lincoln, has been eternally tied.' I felt Lincoln's warmth beside me, and a pang of sadness.

*Phoenix.*

'My markings, as many of you will have noticed, are my version of your wristbands, but they come from within; they flow through my blood and include a part of the angelic realm. It is a poison that helped me kill Lilith when our blades could not. A poison that is lethal not only to exiles,' I said, taking a shuddering breath, 'but also to angels in physical form.

And finally,' I rushed on, needing to get it all out there, 'I can cross the realms and go to a physical space that is created in conjunction with the angels. It looks similar to what any of you would have experienced on your trials when you embraced, but what you saw was illusion – where I go is real.'

'Sammael wants to use your blood to kill angels?' Josephine asked, keenly zeroing in on the most relevant point, her tone appalled.

'Not just any angel,' Phoenix said. 'He wants Michael.'

'And if he can use you to cross the realms ...' Steph said, working it all out and grabbing Salvatore's hand tightly.

I nodded. 'He will go to the physical space that will draw the angels to him in a corporeal form. And he will have his fight—'

'With your blood on his sword,' Griffin finished, a heavy silence following his words. Because it was true.

*And I don't know how to stop him. And everyone in this room knows it.*

'I don't see why we are even entertaining this idea,' Drenson snapped. 'It seems simple enough that Violet is the cause of this mess. If we remove her from the problem, Sammael won't be able to do any of it.' I heard a few murmurs of agreement from the senior Grigori listening in.

'If I thought that was an option, I'd gladly agree,' I responded. 'But Sammael has control over Spence's mind and he won't relinquish it if I don't turn up.'

'So what!' Drenson retorted. 'You expect us to risk the world for your friend? He is Grigori. It's his job to make this sacrifice.'

Carter snorted. 'Right tosser, he is,' he mumbled.

'I've never liked him,' Gray threw in.

My hands fisted. 'Josephine was right when she evaluated me at my testing, Drenson. I *will* put my friends and family above all else. I will fight with my last breath for what is right, but I will not *ever* leave one of them behind if it is in my power to help them.'

'There is something else you need to consider,' Phoenix said, his words spoken with a force that, when combined with the menacing look in his darkened eyes, served to remind the entire room that he was an extremely powerful exile in his own right. 'Sammael already has some of Violet's blood. With his magic it is possible he can create his own gateway, and as Violet is the only other person who can cross over ...'

Griffin's voice came through over the loudspeaker: 'While she could be the world's downfall, she is also our most likely saviour.' I could almost hear Griffin's small smile. 'And if I had to guess, I would venture that, like you, Drenson, Sammael has greatly underestimated the power of Violet's will.'

I looked down, embarrassed by the praise. But when I looked back up I saw a room of warriors watching me with something new in their eyes. The combination of fear and curiosity was still present, but now there was also hope.

In me.

Then, of course, Josephine spoke. 'Violet, I hate to sound unsupportive at this stage. We've had our differences in the past and despite your feelings towards me ... It would be remiss of me to not ask whether you have considered that it might be better if you left others to deal with this? That your presence causes more complication than aid?'

I took my time. A couple of years ago I would have been hurt by what she'd just said. But I'd grown up.

'Josephine, your question is fair. I've faced death and loss, and since becoming Grigori I've had to come to terms with the fact that I don't seem to be quite like anyone else. More than once I've considered the danger that my existence puts those around me in, and those I love the most have paid greatly for those fears. But finally, I am beginning to understand that while I don't have the answers you may need, I do have the only one that matters. *I* was made for this. Yes, there is danger and chaos. But also reason and design. I was created by one who has the most unwavering sense of faith in the goodness of this world. He trusts in me to protect that at all costs. And *that* is exactly what I will do. Can you understand that, Josephine?'

There was silence at the other end, and our room was deathly silent. 'Yes, Violet. I believe you've explained it perfectly.'

I waited for Drenson to argue but he was surprisingly mute.

Looking up at Lincoln, I knew he saw the resolve in my eyes as I became more and more sure of my role in all of this. 'I have to go with Sammael.'

He was silent for a moment, watching me, then said, 'You took Rainer with you to find Nyla.'

I nodded.

'So, you could take me, too.'

I winced. 'Hypothetically, yes, but I kept physical contact with Rainer the whole time. I don't know what would have happened if I'd let go of her. I could have lost her forever.' My voice caught. I'd only just got him back.

I knew what I was looking down the barrel of. This was like history repeating itself. I stood firm. 'I should go alone.'

Phoenix cleared his throat. 'Before you make any final decisions, you might want to take a good look outside and consider the other problem you will almost certainly face.'

Instantly everyone moved towards the windows.

'It's started to rain,' Salvatore said.

'It's not the rain,' Phoenix said gravely.

'The wind,' Gray said, with a faraway, haunted look. 'There was no wind earlier.'

Phoenix had not moved to the window. He knew exactly what the wind was doing. It was a part of him.

'If Sammael believes he will defeat Michael tomorrow night, he will unleash his magic and bring destruction to this city. Even if you manage to stop him ...' Phoenix looked down and when his eyes came back to the room they settled sadly on mine. 'He has an army of exiles of light already here, and thanks to the tournaments he has been controlling he has an opposing army of dark exiles closing in. And it is not just a battleground he has created.'

'Spell it out for those of us who need the kiddie's version,' Carter said, causing Gray to flash him a smile.

Phoenix tilted his head and spoke to Carter. 'He has brought too many exiles to the one place; a place that was never intended to exist. The temptation will be too much for the angels. Regardless of the outcome, of any battle, when it all comes to a head this land *will* be returned to the ocean.' He took a shuddering breath. 'Even if Sammael doesn't succeed, the angels will destroy New Orleans.'

'Would Sammael know that, too?' I asked.

Phoenix smirked, but not in a kind way. It was his darkness pushing through. 'Absolutely.'

Steph had her phone to her ear, listening to Dapper and Onyx. 'Hurricane,' she said.

'A hurricane might destroy the city but it won't kill the exiles,' Gray said.

'It won't matter,' Phoenix replied. 'Once the city is taken by the water, the angels will open a pit and send them all to Hell.'

*This was New Orleans.*

*It had to be a hurricane.*

# chapter thirty-one

*'Why, O Lord, do you stand far off? Why do you hide in*
*times of trouble?'*

**Psalm 10:1**

'**N**o,' I said. 'That is *not* going to happen. I've only been here a couple of days but I've seen this city. These people have been through enough. *They* didn't raise this land from the sea. *They* didn't ask to be punished by tragedy after tragedy. But they have stayed and their homes are here. New Orleans might have started from something sinister but that isn't all it is any more.'

'I agree,' Steph said. 'Exiles might be in abundance but so is human life. They deserve a chance.'

Phoenix shook his head. 'It is a price the angels are willing to pay.'

'Because they're not the ones paying it!' Steph yelled, her hands shaking.

Phoenix closed his eyes briefly and when he opened them they were on me. 'It's the way of the universe. I cannot tell you what to do, Violet. I'm not even sure where precisely to start – but I do know that *this* is your Gordian Knot.' His eyes flicked around the room before returning to me. 'It can only be untied by you.'

*Nothing like a dash of pressure.*

I turned my attention to the small window of the battleship looking towards the city. The wind was causing a carpet of spray across the muggy Mississippi and on the walkways I could just make out people pulling their coats tight and holding onto umbrellas threatening to fly away. Lincoln joined me, seeing what I was, his hand resting on my lower back soothingly.

*How exactly does one stop a hurricane?*

'We need help,' I mumbled.

'Tell us what you need, Violet,' Griffin said through the speaker, reminding me everyone was still listening in.

Nervously, I began to pace, knowing the fate to which I was possibly condemning the entire Grigori population. 'We need everyone.' I turned to Gray. 'Even the Rogues.'

Gray nodded. 'They're already starting to arrive.'

'Tell them the truth, Gray. Tell them what might happen if they come here and fight with us and we don't win. The choice must be theirs.'

'They're Rogues, Violet,' Gray said, his pride for his fellow Grigori clear in his tone and expression. 'One thing you can always trust is that the choice is absolutely theirs.'

'The resources of the Assembly and Academy will be at your disposal,' Josephine offered. 'We will arrive by morning.'

Again, I waited for Drenson to bellow through the speakerphone, but nothing.

'I'll focus on stopping Sammael,' I said, taking a deep breath and glancing at Lincoln briefly, who stood close beside me, emphasising to the room that we were united. 'Everyone else needs to be ready to fight the city's exiles and, somehow … the hurricane,' I said.

As I looked to Phoenix, something passed between us. Understanding and an acceptance to face this burden together. At that moment I realised that it hadn't been for me that he had returned. Not really. He simply hadn't been able to stand aside and let this happen. Aware of it or not, Phoenix was more human than angel.

He nodded once to me and then turned to Zoe. 'Can you gather all your nature wielders? We'll need every single one with any ability to control weather, wind, cloud, water, currents ... all of it. And your telekinetic users.'

Zoe glanced towards me, then Lincoln.

Lincoln nodded. 'Phoenix is one of us,' he said, simply, and through our souls I could feel that he meant it. They would never like one another for any of the reasons that made sense, but Lincoln understood Phoenix. And, oddly, he was grateful to him for loving me. Because, although it almost ended the world as we knew it, and he *did* kill me once, his love had also saved my life. Twice.

Zoe paused for a beat, before straightening and turning her gaze back to Phoenix. 'Consider it done.'

Gray cleared his throat. 'Listen, I know what we did in Santorini, holding back that tsunami, but I was in Miami in 1926 when a category-four hurricane hit and believe me when I tell you – a full-force hurricane isn't like anything you've seen. Even with all of our forces combined ...' He shook his head.

'You're right,' Phoenix answered. 'But with your nature users and telekinetics at my back, you might be surprised what I can do.'

'This is crazy!' Steph yelled against the force of the weather as we stood up on the deck. In the past few hours the wind had continued to fluctuate unpredictably.

'I have to speak with my angel maker!' I yelled back.

'What can you say? He might not be able to help you, Vi!'

'Then maybe Nox and Uri can do something. They can't just let this happen!'

Lincoln suddenly appeared behind us, grabbing us and dragging us back inside.

'What were you two doing out there?' he asked, closing the door behind him.

'I'm going to see the angels,' I explained.

He nodded as if he'd been expecting me to say exactly that.

'And I need to do this one on my own,' I added.

Lincoln's eyes flashed up. 'Does that mean you're going to take me with you tomorrow?'

I nodded, resigned to the fact that for better or worse, we were a team and I wasn't going to try to fight that any more. 'We'll talk about it, but yes. If I cross tomorrow night then we cross together.'

'Thank you,' he whispered, pulling me briefly to his chest. And I knew that it was about more than being in the fight. In many ways, it was our last hurdle of trust.

'Would you give me a minute?' I asked them both, stepping back. 'I need to do this on my own.'

Steph hesitated, but Lincoln gently took her arm and steered her down the hall. 'She knows what she's doing, Steph.'

I heard Steph laugh as they turned the corner and say, 'A little nooky and suddenly you're the voice of reason?'

I didn't hear the response, but I felt it, through what could only be described as a cheeky kiss through our soul bond.

I walked to my cabin and wasted no time, using my abilities to cross the realms.

But when I arrived in the blank expanse of space that I created with the angels, I found myself eerily alone.

I searched with both my Sight and my senses. 'I won't leave that city to die! This is not why I fight!' I yelled into the nothingness. 'They have families and people who love them. The world is a much bigger place than it was when you took down Sodom and Gomorrah. If you destroy New Orleans you will destroy much more than the land and the people on it!'

But there was no answer, and I knew that no matter how long I remained, no angels would talk to me today.

Lincoln sat me down and insisted we eat dinner. I couldn't remember the last time I'd eaten, nor could I stomach the idea of food, but as soon as he put a plate of pasta in front of me, I found myself grinning like a fool.

'You cooked?' I asked, looking down at my favourite pasta dish.

He chuckled. 'No, not exactly. But I did have a long chat with the chef and may have given him an extra incentive to make something special.'

I regarded him suspiciously. 'You paid him, didn't you? How much?'

'Enough to expect that every mouthful is perfect, so eat!' he ordered, avoiding the question.

I twisted a mouthful onto my fork and dove in. 'So good,' I mumbled. I couldn't remember the last time I'd had a proper meal like this.

Lincoln's thumb wiped away a drip of sauce from the corner of my mouth and I blushed as he licked it off his finger, his eyes on me.

I cleared my throat. 'So, do you still own the warehouse?' I asked, watching as he finally looked away from me to begin eating.

'We do,' he said, between mouthfuls.

I straightened. 'We?'

*What have I missed?*

'Yes, Violet, *we*. As in: you and me. Everything I have is yours, which makes us considerably wealthy.'

My eyes widened. I'd always known that Lincoln had inherited a vast amount of money from his mother, but I'd never dared nor cared to try to put a figure on it.

'And once all of this is done, you and I are going to sit down and make some decisions,' Lincoln went on.

'About?' I asked, nervously shovelling in another mouthful of pasta. I hadn't thought that far ahead. Not that it was a problem but I'd built a life, albeit not a perfect one, around being a Rogue, and there was a part of me that was proud of that.

'About a lot of things. For example, where we are going to live.'

I swallowed with a gulp. 'I agree. Let's just ...'

'Save the world first?' he offered with a raised eyebrow.

'Yeah. And then a city.'

When Lincoln left to thank the chef for our dinner, I headed to the infirmary. Despite all the world-ending problems we were facing, things were ... good. Odd how that can happen, I suppose, but I was also sure that nothing would be right in my world if I let down Spence when he needed me most.

'What did you do?' I asked quietly as I held his hand. He stared at me from his bed, seeing nothing, and I was struck by his green eyes – how devoid they were of their usual mischievous spark. My hatred towards Sammael grew. 'You should never have gone after him. *I* should never have left you to deal with my mess. I'm so sorry, Spence. Just hold on, wherever you are.'

I threw my arms around my frail friend who had become my brother and whispered in his ear. 'I've got your back. Now, and always. I'll bring you home.'

I forced a smile and tried to hold his eyes that had begun to wander aimlessly, seeming to focus in on things that I could not see. 'We should go on vacation after all this, don't you think?' I forced a pathetic smile. 'A beach. You can teach me to surf, and laugh when I'm tragic at it. Lincoln can cook and we can bring the whole gang. You can even bring Mia – yeah, I know all about that little secret,' I teased, even though my voice quivered.

I stared at my hand holding his. 'I really made a mess of things, Spence. And something tells me I owe you big time for helping Lincoln when I was gone. But here's the crazy thing: I finally know who I am.' I half laughed. 'I've been searching for so long. Hiding for even longer.' My eyes stung with unshed tears. 'I'm human,' I whispered, my words catching in my throat. 'And I get it now. My flaw is my strength.'

I squeezed his hand. 'I'll fight for my family and friends to the end, Spence. And I'll do whatever it takes to make sure no one else is hurt in the process.'

Lincoln found me as I left the infirmary and then led me to his – our – cabin.

After a shower – one that Lincoln insisted we share for the all-important reason of water conservation – I lay in his arms that night not knowing what tomorrow would bring but realising that, for the first time in my life, I was content and that no matter what lay ahead, we would face it together.

Mia and Chloe were watching over Spence and they would stay with him until this was all over. I would find a way to bring him back to them.

We drifted in and out of sleep for a few hours. I smiled whenever I woke to find Lincoln's hands tracing every inch of my body and encouraging mine to do just the same to his. His eyes held mine, piercing green even in the dark, daring me to question everything we were to one another ever again. It was a dare I knew I would never take. Never wanted to.

Later, when I woke him with gentle kisses to his face and down to his chest, I laughed when he grabbed me in response, pulling my mouth up to his in order to explain – in his own toe-curling way – that gentle kisses were simply *not* going to cut it. I'd never felt so beautiful, or loved, or cherished or ... flat-out *wanted*. Years of imagination had gone into these moments and they did not disappoint. Bottom line: it was hot. *He* was hot.

In the early hours of dawn, exhausted but sated and unwilling to miss a moment, I pulled Lincoln's arm close and snuggled into the crook of it. 'Promise me you haven't made any secret side deals with Phoenix or anyone else that could take you away from me again?'

His fingers played on my arm, weaving some kind of pattern over and over, distracting me. 'I promise. Now, promise me that you won't cross over the realms again without me by your side.'

Although I'd already agreed about tomorrow night, I could sense that this was about an ongoing commitment. I swallowed, part worried that I was risking him, part relieved that he would be with me always. 'I promise, Linc.'

I started to sit up but his hand snaked around my stomach and pulled me back to him. 'You should try to get some more sleep,' he said.

'I can't,' I said. 'Not until this is over.'

He sat up beside me, taking my hand in his and quickly kissing the back of it before suggesting, 'Run?'

*The man knows me.*

I glanced out the small window. The sun was yet to appear on the horizon and rain fell lightly, but the wind had eased for now.

I beamed. 'Coffee first.'

He laughed as he stood up and tossed me a T-shirt. 'Coffee first.'

And it turns out, even when the world might be about to end, a girl can still swoon.

By the time we returned to the ship we could see a number of small aircraft touching down, along with cars pulling up at the dock and new arrivals being efficiently directed to meeting rooms by navy personnel.

*I don't even want to know how the Grigori within navy ranks are pulling this off.*

Our run, it turned out, had been quite the information-gathering exercise. As soon as we boarded the ship, Lincoln disappeared to talk with Gray about what we had seen. Or, rather, sensed.

Now that Lincoln and I were joined again he could sense the exile activity just as acutely as I could. And he wasn't the only one who'd never felt anything like it before.

'They're everywhere, Steph,' I said as she watched me unload and prepare my weapons. I was going fully armed tonight, and I would make sure as many people as possible would be equally prepared. 'The city's divided in two: light exiles are in the French Quarter, and the dark have taken over the Warehouse District. I've never felt so many before – it was like a pulse of power was closing in on us – and they're still flooding in. We saw a few street fights – they're barely bothering to keep themselves hidden from humans.'

She fingered the crate of non-Grigori blades that I'd asked Carter to arrange for me. 'It's odd, almost as if this city entices division,' she said. 'It always has for humans. First the French and the Spanish, then the rivalry between the French and Americans. There have been divides in religion and even between the living and the dead. And now the exiles are breaking the city in half, and something tells me a spot of jazz music really isn't going to help fix things.'

I half smiled. 'I don't even know if exiles hear music. They're so insane they don't see the beauty in what they're trying so hard to destroy.'

It was a thought that I seemed to be having more and more – the ultimate problem of this Gordian Knot, as Phoenix called it, that I now faced. No matter what happened in this battle, unless we could somehow attack the problem of the ever-growing exile population in our world, we would always be just trying to keep up.

Something had to change.

'Well,' Steph said hesitantly. 'Dapper and I think we might have found a small loophole.'

I focused my attention on her. 'What?'

'We think the angels might have stepped in once before and stopped Sammael from destroying the city.'

'When?'

'Hurricane Isaac. It came after Katrina and according to all of the weather warnings was supposed to be much bigger. If it had reached its potential over the city it would have destroyed it.'

'But it didn't.' Clearly.

'No. Suddenly it changed direction. No one knew why, but it was drawn out to sea.'

'The angels,' I said, more to myself than to Steph.

But she nodded anyway. 'We think so.'

'So, they could do it again, if they chose to. I just need to figure out a way to convince them.'

*Sure. Because changing the minds of divine beings is soooo easy.*

I sighed, taking out my Grigori blade and glancing at Steph. 'So, tell me about the wedding.'

Her brow creased and she scrunched up her nose. 'Don't try to distract me. I know what you're about to do.'

I shrugged and sliced my blade across my markings, holding my wrist above the non-Grigori blades. As my blood trickled onto each of them they became instantly lethal weapons. After I'd touched them all with my blood, I healed the wound and picked up one of the daggers, holding the hilt out to Steph.

'You shouldn't need it, but just in case; I need to know you're protected.'

'Er ... Vi ... I ...' Steph stuttered, her horrified eyes fixed on the blade. 'I can't fight like you guys.'

'And you won't need to. If an exile attacked you he would know you're human, and that's your advantage. Let him come at you and then cut him any way you can. My blood will do the rest. Just ... don't hesitate, okay?'

'We're having an outdoor wedding,' she said quickly. 'Did I tell you that? Salvatore's mother wasn't happy about it at first but Father Peters agreed to it and I really liked the idea. Oh, and you should see the dress I've chosen for you. It's perfect, not disgusting-typical-bridesmaid. It's—'

'Steph!' I cut her off, fully aware of who was distracting whom now.

She swallowed, nervously taking the hilt in her hand. 'Okay, Vi. Cut. Don't hesitate. Got it,' she said, her hand and voice shaking equally.

I nodded. 'Good,' I said. 'And when they tell you it's time to move out of the city, promise me you will go.'

She nodded solemnly. 'I'll run like my ass is on fire.' After a beat she added, her voice now less sure, 'Vi?'

I met her eyes and, seeing how they glistened, sat down beside her. 'He'll be okay, Steph. Zoe will be by his side and they're a great team. They'll have each other's backs and they'll be on high ground.'

She nodded, a tear slipping down her cheek. 'I know. It's just ... it feels like I'm so close to happiness and everything I've ever wanted. I'm scared.'

I pulled her towards me, my arms encircling her protectively. 'Me too,' I told her, holding tightly until finally Steph sniffed and said, 'And he looks so damn delicious in a tuxedo.'

Relieved to hear the familiar sass in her voice I grinned and sat back. 'More importantly, tell me about *your* dress.'

# CHAPTER THIRTY-TWO

*'Nearly all men can stand adversity, but if you want to test a
man's character, give him power.'*

**Abraham Lincoln**

apart from a moderate storm pattern, the weather stations
showed no hint of the impending natural disaster – evidence
that Sammael wanted to keep his intentions hidden from both
humans and exiles. When the hurricane hit, no one would be
ready and despite our attempts to notify the right people and
arrange an evacuation of the city, we were getting nowhere fast.

'We have no proof,' the conductors pointed out again. 'We
have people in power but they cannot arrange for an entire
city to be cleared on no notice with no verification. And on top
of that, we're out of time.'

I glared at the Grigori pair, hating how they appeared so
unaffected, but Lincoln listened calmly and sent them on their
way. When he looked at me and registered my frustration
he simply said: 'We pick our battles. It's a conductor's job
to look at it objectively. Our best hope is to concentrate the
official resources we *can* draw on to evacuate as many of the
surrounding suburbs as we can. Within the city now, people's
best chance for survival will be to stay in their homes.'

I dropped into the chair beside him. 'I'm scared,' I whispered in a rare admission.

'I know.' He turned and knelt beside my chair, his hand going to my face. 'I wish you could see what I see when I look at you. The warrior you have grown into. How strong you are both inside and out.' The corner of his mouth lifted. 'How beautiful.'

'I don't know that beauty is going to help us here,' I said, even though the compliment sure hadn't hurt.

'I don't just see the beauty on the outside, Vi. I see all of you, and you're luminous.'

Before I could respond, Zoe barrelled into the room. 'Linc, we're running out of room up there!'

We both stood. 'What do you mean?' I asked.

She huffed, out of breath but with a tinge of excitement in her eyes. 'Come and take a look for yourself,' she said, turning tail and heading for the upper deck.

With a quick glance at one another – part intrigue and part disappointment that our brief moment together had been so, well, brief – we followed.

The sight that met us was staggering. Hundreds upon hundreds of Grigori covered the large deck of the navy vessel. Steph stood on a podium flanked by navy guys who looked more miffed than anyone else as she called out orders, sending Grigori this way and that as she, along with Gray and the conductors, allocated newcomers to groups.

Lincoln and I stood, holding hands in the midst of the chaos. 'How many?' I asked Zoe, who was looking around wildly.

'Almost two thousand, last I heard,' she said, before darting off.

'Look,' Lincoln said, pointing to the helipad, where a Black Hawk chopper had just touched down and Josephine, followed by Drenson, Adele, Seth, Decima, Hakon and Valerie were offloading. I beamed when I saw the last person to step off the helicopter. He had the same dusty brown hair, though for the first time it looked in need of a trim, and was wearing one of his usual navy button-down shirts and tidy black pants, which, despite his recent travels, looked freshly pressed. But, as always, it was his light grey eyes that drew me in and had me exhaling with relief to see him.

Griffin.

The Assembly members moved right into the fray, a number of senior Grigori quickly closing ranks around them, and I knew it wouldn't take long for Josephine to assume control. The question was: would that be the best thing?

Lincoln started to walk in their direction, but instead of following him I felt a pull behind me and I turned to look back over my shoulder. Phoenix stood at the bow of the vessel, hands in his pockets, looking out to the river as the sun highlighted the streaks of silver and opal in his hair. I was overcome by his loneliness. Phoenix's shoulders stiffened and I knew he had sensed me, but he didn't turn.

Lincoln gently took my arm, pulling me back in his direction. 'You can't give him what he wants, Vi, but that doesn't mean you're to blame for his sadness.'

I bit my lip and nodded. 'I know,' I said.

But I wasn't sure I did. I wanted peace for him. Desperately.

We made our way towards the Assembly. Josephine spotted us first. Her eyes went straight to our joined hands, and for a brief second it actually looked like she smiled.

*Probably a muscle spasm.*

'I see most of the troops have arrived,' she said, looking around.

I ignored her and threw my arms around Griffin, who pulled me tight. 'She's awake,' he whispered in my ear.

I pulled back, my stomach twisting with the news that Nyla was back.

Griffin braced my shoulders. 'She's still adjusting and hasn't said much yet.'

I nodded.

'But she asked me to give you a message,' Griffin said, and my heart missed a beat as I waited nervously to hear that she hated me for bringing her back. 'She said to tell you that the bond was worth it.' Griffin gave a quick nod to Lincoln before looking back at me. 'But it seems you've already figured that out.'

I nodded, my breath leaving me in a hurry.

Griffin's eyes softened and he smiled crookedly. 'And she said to tell you: thank you.'

I bit down on the inside of my cheeks trying to halt the tears, but then Drenson spoke and that worked even better.

'I can't believe we've lowered ourselves to this level,' he said, looking at the large group of Rogues to his right and then settling his unfriendly gaze on me. 'Though I suppose once you start letting in the trash, more inevitably follows.'

'Feel free to leave,' I hissed, taking a threatening step in his direction.

Drenson's eyes narrowed, moving beyond me to Lincoln. I didn't need the bond to know Lincoln would be showing nothing but complete support for me. Drenson's ever-quiet partner, Adele, took a step closer to him. I couldn't help but wonder if it was a display of support or because of a fear that he might try to challenge us. Individually Lincoln and I were powerful. But together …

Josephine, no doubt sensing the building tension, raised her hands in a placating gesture. 'Rainer and Wilhelm have remained behind to run the Academy and tend to Nyla. You've called for the full resources of the Academy and Grigori from all corners of the globe, and you have been answered. More would have come if not for the flow-on effect that the exile tournaments have left in their wake,' Josephine explained.

'We appreciate you mobilising so much support on short notice,' Lincoln said.

'And now that you have us all here, I wonder, do you have any idea what you are doing?' Drenson asked, his tone mocking.

As his voice had risen, the entire deck had quietened and were now listening in.

'We are doing everything we can to stop Sammael and help the people of New Orleans,' Lincoln said levelly.

'And you expect us to what? Put our trust in her?' he spat, pointing at me. 'A child who has shown time and time again that she has no place among us?'

'If you are very lucky,' Lincoln responded, his voice low and flat. 'What is it that bothers you, Drenson? That she is powerful, or that she is more powerful than you could ever hope to be?'

*And that is how to make an entire navy Destroyer able-to-hear-a-pin-drop silent.*

'I'll remind you who you are talking to,' Drenson ground out, his face red with fury, and possibly embarrassment as he regarded Lincoln as if *really* seeing him for the first time.

Lincoln simply delivered a blank look. 'I'm fully aware of who you are.' He waited a beat before adding, 'And who *we* are.'

This reply only served to further Drenson's rage but before he could carry on with his attack, I spoke up.

'I can assure you, Drenson, that *we* know what we are doing,' I said, feeling the eyes of an army at my back. 'Perhaps after this is all over – if we survive – it will be *me* who will have the pleasure of returning that question to you.'

Drenson bristled and Josephine surprised me by calmly smiling. 'And as interesting as that promises to be, let's settle for focusing on the problem at hand, for now. I've read through your battle plans,' she said, addressing Lincoln. 'As per your request all Grigori have been given the option to stay or go – no surprises, they have all chosen to stay and fight.'

I couldn't hide my surprise.

'Try to remember, Violet, that every Grigori has a purpose. It appears you have finally accepted yours, just as all the Grigori who surround you have previously accepted theirs.' She turned her attention to Lincoln while I absorbed the truth in her words and felt rightly chastised. 'You have your forces divided into five teams. I see you have left the nomination of leaders blank. Do you have a proposal?'

'You're not going to appoint them?' Lincoln asked, warily.

Josephine smiled while Drenson sneered. 'This is still your mission.'

Lincoln looked at me.

*Hell.*

I shrugged, passing it straight back to him. This was definitely his department.

He turned back to the Assembly and stepped up onto a nearby platform looking out over the two-thousand-strong army.

'Team one,' he called out loudly enough for the Grigori to hear him clearly. 'You are all glamour users and will be led by the conductors to keep our battle from human eyes. You will remain elevated where you can, and be armed accordingly. It will be impossible to contain everything, but the conductors will instruct you on the priorities. They will be waiting for you in the eating hall below deck after this.'

Lincoln stood tall, never wavering in his authority. 'Team two: you are our front-line fighters. All gifted warriors, you will have the privilege of being led by the two greatest warriors of our history – Seth and Decima.'

There were a number of cheers, and when Lincoln looked to them, both Seth and Decima gave a vacant nod of approval.

'Team three,' Lincoln continued. 'You are a team of Rogues and your cunning will be our key to attacking the exiles and fortifying around our own people, who will fight Sammael's hurricane. I ask that you follow the leadership of your fellow Rogues Gray and Carter.'

Again a few hoots went up, some in agreement, others arguing, but all in all they took it well. Carter threw me a wink, and for the life of me I'd never seen the man look so damn proud of himself.

'Team four: you are our heavy lifters and telekinetics. You will work hand in hand with team five and follow their ultimate directive. When you are not working with team five, you will be on the ground fighting. You will be led by the Academy Vice, Josephine, and by Griffin Moore.'

Josephine looked intrigued, but she nodded Lincoln on all the same. As I expected, Griffin simply accepted his place and would do his part.

'Finally, group five: your contribution to this battle will be the most vital. You are some of our most gifted Grigori – our nature users.' Lincoln paused and took a deep, calm breath. 'If he will agree, I ask that you be led by Phoenix. I'm sure you all know who he is and that he is an exile. What you may not know is that he is only here with us because he sacrificed his own angelic nature in order to save the only Grigori ever made by one of the Sole. He is an exile, he is human, and he is our ally.'

I looked towards where Phoenix had been standing alone. He was closer now, listening to Lincoln, his hands still in his pockets. Gradually all eyes on the vessel moved in his direction.

Phoenix finally looked up and out to the crowd, as if making a decision. He pressed his lips together briefly before speaking. 'Some of you will die. Perhaps all of you. I will not lead you to your death – but I will go and I will stand at the helm to fight for the life of this city. If you choose, you may follow.'

His words were so ... Phoenix. A complication.

One by one the nature users walked towards him, moving to stand behind him.

Lincoln nodded to Phoenix and then they shared a flash-smile. I looked at Lincoln for an explanation, and he bent to whisper in my ear. 'I just made Josephine and her entire team answerable to a dark exile.'

I tried not to smile as I quickly looked to Josephine, who

once again threw me completely by simply flashing me her own, knowing, smile.

'I really hope she doesn't try to kill Phoenix before the fight even gets started,' I murmured.

'We move out in three hours,' Lincoln announced. 'Be ready and well-armed. We will have additional weapons set up in the weaponry below that have been ... enhanced,' he said, glancing at me and winking. 'Our base of operations will remain here but if the hurricane manages to ...' His words trailed off, but everyone knew what he was going to say. 'There will be a secondary base that has been set up at a nearby sports dome south-west of here. This will also be where we send any people in need of help. Maps will be provided.' He looked out over the masses of Grigori before him.

We were going to war. We all knew it. There was nothing more to say. Lincoln clearly felt this way, too, simply nodding and repeating, 'Three hours.'

The crowd began to disperse, heading off with their teams to find weapons. Lincoln wrapped his hand around mine and I could tell he was keen to slip away and start our preparations, but Gray was in front of us before we managed to do so. He crossed his arms and looked every bit the big bad warrior as he stared down at me. 'I still don't like you two going up there alone.'

I shrugged. 'You'll get over it.'

His eyes narrowed and he turned to Lincoln. 'I see you haven't done anything for her attitude.'

Lincoln laughed. 'I like her attitude.'

'You bloody well would,' Gray said before clasping Lincoln's hand and turning worried eyes back on me.

I started to squirm, not ready for this discussion.

*The one where people figure you're about to die, so they say something nice.*

Gray took my hand and kissed the back of it. 'I've been honoured to follow you.'

I snorted. 'You don't follow me, Gray. You don't follow anyone.'

He smirked. 'Princess, I've been following you since the day you showed up in my city a year ago. You just never realised.' He dropped his head fractionally. 'And my service remains yours, eternally.'

I froze, my eyes fixed on Gray's retreating figure as he walked away.

*Rogues most* certainly *do not serve anyone, ever.*

'Are you really that surprised?' Lincoln asked softly.

*Ah, yes. Yes I am.*

Attempting to thaw from the shock I could only manage to stare at Lincoln's amused eyes. He seemed to have no trouble hearing my unspoken response.

Once I had my faculties back under control I glanced around and caught Josephine's eye again. She'd been watching, and I could almost see her mind ticking over, making me wonder, yet again, if she was playing another angle.

'Onyx is right,' came a familiar voice from behind me, 'There is never a dull moment with you.'

I turned to see Dapper leaning against a steel wall, watching me with a knowing smile. I knew why instantly.

*He can see my aura. Our auras.*

'Why?' I asked Dapper, noticing that Onyx was there too, standing apart and talking quietly with Chloe. Grigori were here to play their part in the fight, but Dapper and Onyx were not able to fight and yet had willingly entered this city knowing it was likely a one-way ticket.

'I heard that a lot of Rogues were going to be here and I figured you could use someone with some extra healing abilities on standby.'

I nodded, pressing my lips together to fight back the tears. Rogues rarely still had their partners, which made healing a problem. Dapper's help would be very much needed.

I glanced over to where Onyx and Chloe were still talking, their body language awkward yet a genuine bond evident between them. 'What's the story between those two anyway?' I asked.

Dapper was watching them too. 'Oh, it's one of violence, death, regret and forgiveness.' He turned back to me. 'You know the type.'

I already knew that was all he was going to say. 'I have an idea,' I said, smiling as Onyx sauntered towards us.

'And why did you come?' I asked, looking at Onyx.

He waved a hand in the air, feigning nonchalance. 'It might have something to do with that family thing we talked about the other day.'

Dapper rested his hand on Onyx's shoulder and squeezed. For Dapper it was a major PDA.

Lost for words, I stared back at Onyx knowing, no matter what was in our past, he was now and forever my family.

'I see you have the fire back in your eyes,' Onyx said, glancing at Lincoln, who was talking to a nearby group. 'Looks like things are finally how they should be for you.'

I nodded. 'I'm surprised *you* don't have any gloating to

do,' I said, still half expecting a sly comment to follow. But then I followed Onyx's line of sight to where Phoenix stood talking with some of the Rogues.

'Apparently I'm turning into a bit of a girl.' Onyx gave a tight smile. 'Besides, I've already collected on all the betting pools.' But his quip fell short of his usual flair.

I nodded, looking awkwardly at my feet as I said, 'He could use a friend.'

When I looked up again, Onyx was giving one of his dramatic eye rolls. 'Oh, please. I've seen what Phoenix does to his friends and it isn't pretty.'

'You're not the only one who's changed, Onyx,' Dapper said softly.

Lincoln joined us then, halting our conversation. He shook hands with Dapper and Onyx and I could tell he was just as humbled by their presence as I had been.

After a brief chat to bring them up to speed – which Steph had mostly taken care of – Lincoln turned to me. 'Vi, we only have a couple of hours left.'

I nodded. 'I'll be ready.'

Lincoln kissed me quickly and then rested his forehead against mine, speaking just to me. 'I know, I have to go and take care of a few things but come and find me soon. I was hoping we could have a bit of time together, just us, before ...'

I nodded, wanting nothing more, before turning into the fray and getting on with business. As I walked away I wondered if it would always be like this: battle waiting as we joined hands and got on with the job, sharing brief kisses when we had the chance.

*Could I be so blessed?*

# CHAPTER THIRTY-THREE

*'The belief in a supernatural source of evil is not necessary;*
*men alone are quite capable of every wickedness.'*

Joseph Conrad

By 10 p.m. the full moon, weighted with the promise of devastation, had risen above the steeple of St Louis Cathedral, and almost two and a half thousand Grigori had taken up position along the riverbank of the Mississippi.

Spotters had alerted us to a number of tournament fights that had already broken out within the city. The largest was happening within the old abandoned power plant on Market Street. Ray and Leila had led Gray and his team to deal with that and we left the other, smaller, battles to go on, knowing that tonight we had to be smart.

Sammael's plan was becoming clear, but the tournaments were one piece of the puzzle that still left me confused. All of our intel told us he was a purist – that he believed in the division between light and dark and that light would prevail – but then why bring them all here, knowing that even if the battle and the hurricane didn't end them, the angels most definitely would? Was it simply to ensure his plan for devastation worked?

The conductors and senior Grigori had advised that Sammael would use the river to build the strength of his hurricane, so Phoenix and his team had taken up elevated positions along the river. We wouldn't be able to stop all of the destruction caused to the outer wetlands and suburbs, but our military alliances had stepped up and covered as much ground as possible in the afternoon, evacuating many of those areas.

The river's edge would be the place we would make our stand.

Of course, the always-statistical conductors also highlighted that it was suicide. This information, however, did not stop any Grigori from arming up – not even the conductors.

Steph had stayed by Salvatore's side until he had left with Zoe and their team. I could see the fear in her eyes but, even more, her strength and acceptance that this would be her life if she was going to commit to being by this man's side. Steph, Dapper and Onyx remained with the navy, who had anchored their ships with the intention of pulling back into the city on foot. They had taken Spence and Chloe with them and would push back as many of the city's residents as they could along the way.

Drenson had made his unhappiness known to all in the final hours before we headed out, and now I observed as he and Adele stalked up and down the pavement on the edge of the French Quarter. He was using each return lap to glare at me.

Josephine and Griffin stood nearby shouting out orders to a number of their team members, positioning them where they could gain the best advantage.

'You have a lot to answer for, you know!' I yelled over the wind.

Lincoln took my hand, trying to pull me back, but I wasn't having it. This might be my last chance to say something.

Josephine, who was head to toe in fighting leathers, turned to meet my fierce expression.

'I take it you are talking about Drenson. And I remind you that it is none of your business. You chose not to be a part of the Academy. Remember?' She raised her eyebrow, knowingly. 'Or has that changed?'

'I've never *not* cared about the Academy, Josephine, but I refuse to let go of who I am in order to become one of your puppets.' The wind picked up and I was grateful I'd tied my hair into a braid. 'Does he even know how to fight?' I blurted.

Josephine laughed, though she sobered quickly. 'He is Grigori, Violet. He may choose an administrative role now, but he has faced many battles, of that you can be assured.'

Josephine's words sank in and left me feeling reprimanded. I had passed my judgement on Drenson without really knowing him. His clear dislike for me had caused a defensive response from the beginning. I let go of Lincoln's hand. 'I'll be back in a minute,' I said, walking towards Drenson and Adele. As I approached, Adele cast her eyes away from me and meekly scurried off.

*What is it with her?*

Drenson walked around the corner, out of sight, and I followed, realising that Josephine was right. Who was I to criticise Drenson? Maybe we'd just started off on the wrong foot.

As soon as I turned the corner, Drenson whipped around and had his hand around my neck. He pushed me back into the wall and squeezed, his face less than an inch from mine.

'You are like a parasite that will not go away,' he hissed. 'Do you really think you can take my place?'

I shook my head. 'I don't want your place,' I gritted out as I fought for breath.

'And you will never have it!' he returned, his grip tightening to the point where I couldn't talk even if I had something to say. I was going to have to fight back.

I closed my eyes briefly, feeling a surge of sadness and bitter justification. My instincts had been right. Drenson saw me as his enemy and his need for power was dangerous for all Grigori.

I opened my eyes, resigned to engaging in a fight with the head of the Assembly, but I never got the chance. All I saw was Drenson being thrown so far he hit the wall on the opposite side of the street. And then Lincoln's hand was at my throat, tilting up my chin, checking for damage.

'I'm fine,' I assured him, blinking in disbelief – because it hadn't been Lincoln who had thrown Drenson off me. It was Josephine.

Josephine's hand was wrapped tightly around Adele's upper arm as she watched Drenson collect himself from the ground, shaking her head in barely contained anger. 'Why didn't you fight back?' Josephine asked, briefly looking over her shoulder at me.

I exhaled, taking another deep breath. 'I have enough enemies to fight tonight already.'

Adele looked pale as Josephine released her. She made her way hesitantly to Drenson, who had slumped back to the ground.

'Thank you,' I said to Josephine.

'Keep him away from her,' Lincoln said, his tone deadly clear.

Josephine opened her mouth to say something, but her attention was caught and I turned to see Drenson, now awake, huddled close to Adele, whispering.

'I hope you are everything they believe and more,' Josephine said, and I detected a note of tiredness in her tone that I had not heard before.

'Who are *they*?' I asked.

She tilted her head to the sky and back at me before crossing the road. 'He will not bother you again.'

'She's so strange,' I murmured as Lincoln collected his backpack of supplies from where he'd dumped it on the ground and hooked his arms through its straps.

'She wants us to be strong,' Lincoln said, leading us towards the riverbank. The wind was so forceful now it felt like we were walking into a wall.

'Us?'

'Grigori. All of us. She wants us to triumph, and most of what she does is done for that reason. I think it's hard for her to consider that though she has always been the strongest leader, that may be changing.'

I shook my head, frustrated. 'It isn't about who's the strongest, Linc. It's about who's trusted. Who will be followed.'

He nodded, smiling.

'What?' I asked.

His lips twitched. 'Nothing. I just realised I'm not your teacher any more.'

I smiled in return. Because maybe that was true.

Lincoln's phone beeped. Then again. Then mine. Then they both started to ring. We both answered.

'Violet, you've got incoming,' Gray yelled, out of breath like he was running. 'I don't know what the bloody hell happened but a huge group of dark exiles stormed through, taking out every light exile in sight. Hell, we barely made it out of that damn power plant!'

Lincoln was talking quickly on his phone, looking down towards the French Quarter. He put his hand over the mouthpiece and spoke to me. 'It's Mia. She said there are thousands of light exiles marching down the streets of the French Quarter. They're headed this way.'

'Violet, where are you?' Gray yelled.

'We're on Canal Street, almost at the river,' I replied.

'We're almost there. They're headed right for you. Get out of there! Get out!' The line went dead.

Lincoln had my hand and started to pull but my feet were rooted to the spot as I looked from left to right. Canal Street was wide – three lanes each way and streetcar tracks through the centre. The road was straight and flat and I could see clearly as, via the dozen side streets on each side of the dividing road, exiles began to pour out.

*Thousands.*

*And thousands.*

Lincoln and I stood right in the middle of their battlefield.

As light and dark faced off from opposite sides of the street, Lincoln and I tried to move back towards the river. My heart thudded seeing the sheer number of exiles in the one place.

'Linc,' I said, my hand trembling in his.

'Just keep moving,' he said levelly, adjusting his backpack.

But the wind was lashing like crazy and pushed me so hard I stumbled. Lincoln caught me, but it had been enough. The eyes of nearby exiles turned.

A group of at least twenty dark exiles started to run towards us. I braced for the impossible onslaught.

*How can it have come to this? I have to get to Sammael! I have to save Spence!*

Fury took the place of fear and I grabbed my dagger.

'Look!' Lincoln yelled, pointing to our left.

Gray and Carter barrelled out of a nearby side street, their troops close behind. Their team of wayward Rogues worked seamlessly as one tight unit, taking down exiles as they moved through.

'Gray!' I screamed.

He looked around frantically, and the moment he spotted us he started to shout out orders.

'Get to them! We protect them at all costs!'

Gray's team hit the onslaught of exiles just as they reached us.

'Go!' Carter yelled, putting his body between the exiles and me.

My mind raced. I knew I needed to run, to stay alive until I could face Sammael, but I couldn't just leave them.

Lincoln grabbed my arm. 'We have to!' he shouted, his face looking as pained as I felt.

Indecision bit at me.

'Gray!' Lincoln yelled. 'Mia's got the rooftops!'

I looked up, seeing he was right. Grigori scampered along on the edges of many of the buildings edging the street. The conductors' team were in charge of putting up a force field to keep the battle hidden from human eyes as much as possible, but while they were doing that they could also help out with other things.

Gray ordered his team back, trying to give the high-placed warriors a clear shot, but they were boxed in.

I unleashed my power, sending it out towards the river end of the road. I could feel as my power spread to a few, then a few more, then twenty, then thirty and finally, close to forty exiles. It was the most I'd ever held at one time.

Holding my concentration, I squeezed Lincoln's hand. He knew exactly what I needed.

'Gray!' he yelled. 'Clear the path!'

Gray's Rogues charged forward, taking out the exiles who were under my control, and as we ran, arrows tipped in my silvered blood started to fly. Exiles around us dropped to the ground briefly before disappearing.

Gray's team then moved into a defensive position, creating a wall around Lincoln and me.

'How far have you got to go?' Gray asked Lincoln as we ran.

'Right there,' Lincoln said. Fifty metres away stood the tall building that marked the end of Canal Street and the edge of the riverbank. It stood at the border of the French Quarter and the Warehouse District and smack bang in the middle of what had now become the division between the exiles of light and dark.

'Doesn't anyone ever get tired of the symbolism?' Carter grunted, looking up.

I took in the building, which was about forty storeys high. 'You've got to be kidding me,' I said. Sure, I'd noticed that the building was an odd shape from the steamboat last night, but I hadn't even considered that it would continue on like this on the other side. 'It's a cross.'

'Yep, pointing to the sky,' Carter said.

*Of course it was.*

'Get them to the doors!' Gray shouted, and our convoy pushed forward.

As we neared the entrance to the building, the exiles stopped pursuing us.

'Are they scared?' I asked, baffled by their restraint.

Lincoln watched them retreat. 'They don't look happy about pulling back.'

We watched as one exile tried to get closer to us but failed to cross an invisible threshold. 'It's a force field.'

The exile continued to push in his attempt to get closer to us, but it looked as if someone had put him on a treadmill. Gray saw the same thing and gave us a nod. 'You'll be protected from them in here. But hell knows what's waiting for you inside. You should take a few of the Rogues with you,' he suggested.

But the battle was only growing and we could hear screams coming from the riverbank where we'd left Josephine and Griffin's team.

I shook my head. 'Go back and help the conductors' team. We'll be okay.'

Grudgingly Gray nodded and then working with Carter, they split their team in two and scurried down a side street where they could re-join the battle on their own terms.

Lincoln and I made for the front doors, which stood open, torches alight with fire on either side. 'What do you want to bet that this isn't really a dilapidated abandoned building inside?' I asked.

'Nothing I want to keep,' Lincoln replied as we stepped into the empty white-marbled foyer.

'Wow,' I said, looking around. Apart from the outer walls, there was nothing in this building except a set of cables in the centre of the room reaching from the ground to the ceiling forty-odd storeys above.

As we watched, a glass elevator made its way smoothly down the cables, stopping in front of us. We could see that it was empty, but even so, when the doors slid open I tensed.

'Vi?' Lincoln prompted, his voice gentle, and I knew what he was asking.

*Anything.*

He'd do anything I needed right then. He'd turn around and walk out; he'd run; he'd fight. Anything.

I licked my dry lips. 'I love you, Linc,' I said, throwing every last piece of my heart deep into the words.

'Don't you dare say goodbye, Vi.'

I stared ahead at the elevator waiting for us. 'I'm not saying goodbye. Just that I get it now, that saying: *A life without love is no life at all.* It's true. And now, live or die, I know I've really experienced life. With you.'

I held out my hand and his slid smoothly into its rightful place.

'I love you, too.'

We walked into the elevator and the doors closed automatically. As we began our incline, Lincoln turned to me. 'And you and I *will* experience everything this world has to offer and then we will grow old together, with our family.'

I swallowed hard at his words. It seemed like a fantasy to even contemplate being here and together for so long that, as Grigori, we would grow old together.

*How many years would that take?*

*Family? Does that mean he wants to have children?*

*What would that mean?*

*Can we even …*

Sensing my runaway mind, Lincoln squeezed my hand, bringing me back to the here and now.

The elevator slowed and finally crested right through the ceiling and stopped on the open rooftop. When the door opened we were assaulted by heavy winds and rain sheeting sideways, and I raised my hand to protect my eyes.

'Glad I'm not afraid of heights,' I said as we got out, trying to keep our balance as we walked along the glass rooftop. Lincoln quickly wedged his backpack between the elevator and a supporting pylon while I noted, somewhat desperately, that there was no railing or wall surrounding the roof perimeter. If the wind pushed us too far in one direction, we could easily plummet to our death.

At the tip of the eastern arm of the building's cross, closest to the river, Sammael – dressed in a modern black suit with shiny lapels, sans tie – stood in the centre of a large pentagram drawn in what looked a lot like blood with white stuff scattered over it.

'Blood and salt,' Lincoln said. 'A life pentagram.'

Sammael smiled, hearing us despite the wicked wind blowing at this height and the rain that now sheeted down. Two exiles stood at each point of the pentagram, though I suspected their purpose was more to do with security than any ritual. More curiously, four women stood behind him. And they were not exiles. They looked like gypsies but I could sense that they were Nephlim. Possibly his own progeny.

'Salt represents this earth, you see,' Sammael pronounced, adjusting his belt and exposing the long sword sheathed at his side. 'All rituals require unions. Blood, life, earth and sacrifice. With my power and your blood – the life force of angels – I can cross the realms and he will meet me.' He stood tall, despite his short stature. Proud.

'Why the tournaments? Why bother with the elaborate setting? Was it just to get your kicks?' I asked.

Sammael's expression changed to one of amusement. 'It is the dawn of all tomorrows and I will be god to all who survive. Let's just say I'm trimming the fat.'

And finally, I understood. He wanted them all gone. That was why he had lured such a vast number of the strongest and most competitive exiles to the same place at the same time. It ensured his end result and reduced the competition. Through our bond I could feel Lincoln's disgust.

Sammael's enjoyment only seemed to increase as he gauged our reaction. 'I must admit, I expected you to bring more bodyguards with you. However, since you have made it so easy for me, perhaps I should just allow my exiles to take out your partner now and we can bleed you after.'

My eyes flicked to the exiles now edging in our direction. I grabbed Lincoln's hand and he didn't hesitate to open his power to me, giving me whatever I wanted to take.

My amethyst mist, now speckled with Lincoln's colours, surrounded us, and with a determined will I sent it out to do my bidding.

One by one, as my eyes remained glued to Sammael's, I brought the ten exiles under my control and held them still. To drive my point home I stripped the power from one, then two, then four of the closest exiles, releasing them as they dropped to their knees screaming. Now only human.

'I wouldn't say I've made it *so* easy,' I said, trying to hide the fact that even I was surprised it had gone so smoothly. I still had the other six well under my control and I was tempted to just get it over with and return them for judgement, but until I had Spence I needed bargaining chips.

'I've seen that trick before,' Sammael said, feigning boredom, though I noticed a telltale twitch at his jaw that suggested otherwise. 'Release them,' he said.

I did as he commanded, watching as the stunned exiles turned fierce eyes first on me and then on the four – now humans – who had been reduced to nothing more than rodents in their eyes. Before I could blink, they grabbed the four men and threw them straight off the building. My stomach turned over while I did my best to keep my expression neutral.

Sammael smiled, knowingly. 'Consequences, Violet. Aren't you tired of them?'

# chapter thirty-four

*'I know indeed what evil I intend to do, but stronger than all my afterthoughts is my fury, fury that brings upon mortals the greatest evils.'*

**Euripides**

'**Y**ou said you would release Spence's mind!' I yelled into the wind, keeping my feet wide apart for balance. 'I'm here! Release him!'

Sammael produced an oversized silver chalice with intricate designs etched into it. It hummed with an energy I instantly recognised. Lincoln squeezed my hand, letting me know he had made the connection too.

*He has a tabernacle.*

The first tabernacle I had come across had been in Jordan, and in an offering of exile and Grigori blood it had produced the ancient scriptures once hidden away by angels.

I now understood from where Sammael was drawing the extra power that would help him cross the realms. A relic from the time when angels walked on the earth – imbued with their power.

Sammael looked at his watch. 'We only have minutes left. Fill it.'

The women standing behind Sammael stepped back, as if moving into position. I noticed then that their eyes had changed since I first looked. The whites and irises had been replaced with pure black. They were Nephlim, but they were also something else.

'It's too big. She'll bleed out!' Lincoln yelled.

'Release Spence first!' I yelled at the same time.

'Violet,' Lincoln cautioned, but we both knew I had to do this.

Sammael's eye twitched. He really didn't like to negotiate. A gust of wind whipped across the rooftop but his shirt barely ruffled while Lincoln and I struggled to keep our feet planted. It became clear that Sammael had some kind of protection within the pentagram.

'Know that if you do not give me your blood my witches will find him and take it back. I will make sure he exists locked in a reality of pain and nothingness for hundreds of years.'

I shivered at his warning.

*So, that's what these women are. Exile-made witches. The real Voodoo.*

'I believe you. Now release him.'

Lincoln's phone rang. I saw Chloe's name on the screen and watched as he answered and listened.

'He's alert. He's demanding she give him a dagger.'

My heart skipped and I let out a chuddering breath as I nodded.

*He's okay.*

'Your blood!' Sammael roared.

I let go of Lincoln's hand and pulled out my dagger, walking into the pentagram, careful to avoid the lines of blood and salt. Lincoln had been right: the chalice was large. I wasn't sure if I would be able to stand after I had filled it with my blood. But I'd made my deal with the devil and I sliced my wrist open, carefully wiping the blade against my sleeve until it was clean as my blood – swirling with silver currents – gushed into the silver tabernacle.

I could feel Lincoln's anxiety at my back as I bit the inside of my cheek to distract me from the pain. Sammael's eyes lit up with greed as he watched my blood drain into the chalice.

When the chalice was finally full, Sammael held out his hand.

'Dagger,' he ordered.

*Oh, shit.*

'Now!' he yelled when I hesitated.

My mind raced with options. Fight him? Refuse him?

*But he could take Spence's mind again as easily as he had returned it.*

Give it to him?

*What could he use it for, anyway? A Grigori blade could kill exiles, but not angels. And I've already made sure to wipe my blood off the blade.*

I clenched my jaw and held out my dagger. He snatched it and pushed me back and out of the pentagram. Lincoln caught me when I stumbled weakly and I felt his healing soothe me instantly as he closed the wound on my wrist and helped replenish some of my strength.

Using my Grigori blade, Sammael opened a small wound on his palm, hissing in pain as he did so, and allowed a few drops of his blood to mingle with mine. Then he passed the chalice to his witches and threw my dagger off the edge of the building.

In a trance-like fashion the witches separated most of the blood into two small bowls and returned the main chalice to Sammael before resuming their places.

The full moon was at its peak, and in the distance the bells of St Louis Cathedral began to chime over the rain and the battle cries below. Lincoln continued to pummel his healing and strength into my depleted body as two of the women stood opposite one another, each holding a bowl containing my blood stained with Sammael's. Gracefully, in perfect sync, they threw the blood high into the air. Unaffected by the winds, the two streams arched and joined high above our heads, and then remained suspended as my blood, red and silver, turned to glistening shades of black. I bit back my gasp.

*A black rainbow.*

The air around us began to still. Gravity started to distort. And a slight vibration surrounded Sammael.

'What is that?' Lincoln asked from beside me, his hold on my arms tightening as he stared at the black arch.

I stared ahead, inevitability and fear mingling to create a bitter taste in my mouth. 'He's done it. The realms are crossing.'

Sammael heard me, his eyes alight as he pulled a long sword from the sheath at his waist and poured my remaining blood over the blade.

When he stepped towards the suspended arch of blood that would be his gateway, the hunger and victory in his eyes was maniacal. 'His last thought will be of you. The knowledge that the very thing he created was the thing that delivered his end.' His voice lingered over the final word.

Sammael stepped through the gateway, disappearing from this world. The arch of blood instantly dropped to the rooftop floor, and his human witches collapsed a moment later.

*However he plans to return, it will not be through this gate.*

Lincoln checked the witches.

'Are they ...' I started.

He shook his head. 'Unconscious. Maybe in some form of coma.' He stood back up. 'Vi, what was Sammael talking about when he said "the very thing he created"?'

I looked around us. Chaos had closed in. Below, I could see the war between light and dark exiles. There were too many. Thousands. Their battle had migrated to the river, using the open land along the embankment for maximum fighting space. I could hear their screams carrying in the wild wind and knew that many of our Grigori brethren were paying the ultimate price.

*We're losing.*

*This is the beginning of the end.*

Small explosions sounded nearby and the rain shot down like sheets of glass. I studied the place where Sammael had disappeared as I answered. 'I've always known,' I said, realising now that it was true. 'I just wasn't ready to believe it.'

'What?'

I held out my hand for Lincoln. He took it without question and I looked deep into his green eyes, hoping I might have the chance after all of this to tell him all the things that my heart wanted to scream from a very different rooftop. 'I know who my angel maker is,' I said. Lincoln watched me, holding his balance strong against the weather, his eyes flickering as he tried to make sense of my words ... and then widening when he did.

'Oh,' he said.

I mirrored the thought and pulled my katana from the sheath at my back, checking my arrows and that my secondary dagger strapped to my thigh was in place. 'Are you ready?'

'Always,' he said simply.

With my love at my side, with my angel maker waiting for me, and with death already at the party, I crossed the realms.

I escorted Lincoln through the cross-over, knowing I was risking it all, considering that everything I wanted was held clasped in my sweaty hand. But this was my life. His too. And we would take this chance together.

Even so, I tightened my hold.

The moment we made the transition the wind vanished, the rain stopped and we were in another place, an uncharted space.

'The desert?' Lincoln asked, looking around first in wonder, then in panic. 'Vi, there's nothing … anywhere.'

I shook my head. 'The space can be anything. For some reason I almost always conjure a desert, but now that we're here, I can …' I smiled. 'Watch.'

I closed my eyes, willing this image away and for the truth of this space to reveal itself to me. I opened my eyes when I heard Lincoln gasp.

'Oh my God,' he said.

The desert was gone.

Darkness enveloped us.

Lost souls glittered in the space beyond. And hundreds of rainbows lit the nothingness before us. Bridges to a cosmos of possibilities.

My angel maker stood at a distance, another at his side. My maker's expression remained calm, his sword gripped loosely in his right hand. The angel beside him was startlingly identical to my maker, though I instinctively knew that he was his opposite in every way.

*Like Uri and Nox. The ultimate balance of light and dark.*

And behind them ... an angelic army wearing silver armour over white linen and holding imposing swords were mounted on a field of proud white horses. The vision so otherworldly, so ... heavenly, it almost brought me to my knees.

Sammael's back was to us as he stood facing them on foot, his sword at the ready. His glasses and shoes were gone and he was now in grey linen pants with an untucked white shirt.

I wasn't sure if he knew we had crossed over. But my angel maker's eyes looked beyond him – even as Sammael shouted his challenge – and deep into mine, searching, knowing.

*Did he always know it would come to this?*

*I think he must have.*

Tentatively I released Lincoln's hand, hesitating before letting him go completely and flinching with relief when he remained beside me when we finally broke the last contact.

'A challenge is my right in this place!' Sammael yelled. 'Would you set your army on me or prove your worth? *You* who are so mighty, favoured above all others, and so worthy of all praise!'

It wasn't difficult to play the conversation forward. Angels were prideful creatures even though they claimed to be emotionless. Not one would hide from a forthright challenge, nor would they relinquish the chance to defeat a mighty foe such as Sammael.

Sensing what I was about to do, Lincoln leaned close to my ear. 'Our connection is altered in this place. I don't think I can heal you here,' he whispered desperately. 'You're still weak from the blood loss. Let me do this.'

I turned to him and cupped his face in my hand. 'You will. You'll be with me every step of the way, but we both know it has to be me.'

Tears welled in his eyes but did not fall. His Adam's apple bobbed as he swallowed thickly and gave a short nod. 'Be smart. Be ruthless. And keep our connection open. If I can help, let me,' he said.

I nodded and my heart swelled. This, more than anything, was Lincoln's great sacrifice. His willingness to let me take the ultimate risk, knowing there was a great chance I would not survive, was an act of love beyond anything I had believed possible. Using my control and will of this space in time, I altered my katana as I approached, lengthening the blade to match that of Sammael's.

'You challenge my maker, and so, you challenge me!' I called out, causing Sammael to spin in my direction. 'If you wish to fight him, you must first defeat me.' I pulled my extra weapons – my arrows and thigh dagger – from their sheaths and threw them to the side, keeping just my sword that matched his.

The statuesque angels did not react to my intrusion. Sammael, however, while clearly unsurprised to see me, was caught off-guard by my proclamation.

'You cannot fight me,' he said, laughing loudly. 'I have my greater power here. I am unstoppable.'

I flexed my grip on the hilt of my sword and used my will to change our surroundings into a full oval arena with a hard dirt ground, Roman style.

I shrugged. 'I have great power here, too.' I gave him a taunting smile, knowing that this would be the best way to lure him into engaging with me.

'Are you going to let the human fight for you?' he questioned my maker. 'Are you so pathetic?'

My angel maker tilted his head, unperturbed. 'She is a representation of me. I see no reason why not. If you cannot defeat her, you certainly should have no right to challenge me.' But when his eyes swung briefly to mine, I glimpsed the sadness and I understood then that, though my angel maker was entirely angel – emotionless and aloof to matters of the heart – in his own way, he cared for me.

Sammael responded by turning his sword and leaping in my direction. Laws of gravity and force did not work the same way in this place and as much as I was able to bend this piece of the universe to my will, it was quickly apparent that Sammael could control elements of it as well.

I spun, keeping myself grounded, remaining tactical as all of my training – first with Lincoln, then Griffin, Nyla, Rainer and Gray – came to my aid. Our swords clashed with such ferocity that sparks flew each time they collided.

As Sammael reared his sword back to strike at my side, I raised mine to meet it and, risking a one-handed hold, took the opportunity to strike out with my free hand, hitting him hard across the face.

He blinked from shock and stumbled back. I didn't delay, moving forward and kicking out in an attempt to disarm him. He dodged my efforts and instead managed to slice his sword at my arm, causing a deep gash just below my shoulder.

I winced, staggering to the side. I could feel Lincoln's power surging through me, giving me strength even though our healing connection was not working.

Our swords rose again. Sammael's technique was flawless as little by little I lost momentum and he gained the upper hand. When his blade sliced into my thigh I cried out, falling to one knee before I could steady myself. He didn't hesitate to pounce, kicking me so hard across my face I first flung back then forward onto all fours as blood flowed from my mouth and I spat teeth onto the ground.

I could feel Lincoln pacing the arena and the army of angels watching impassively while Sammael steadily beat me to death. I tried to get back onto my feet, but he kicked the side of my head with his booted foot.

And he laughed. The laugh of madness.

Determined, I staggered back to my feet, somehow still gripping my sword. I parried a few strikes and with all my remaining strength I swung out, my blade skimming his chest but little else. Sammael, enraged by the small incision I'd made, stormed forward in response. His sword collided with mine; the weight was like a mountain and when he drew back for another strike I knew my reaction was too slow.

The blade burned its way through my stomach and my scream was bloodcurdling.

I fell.

He had bettered me. Life was pouring out of me, my mind drifting towards an inevitable end. And I was tortured to realise there was so much I had yet to do. So many things that had been put on hold. Strangely, in that moment as I struggled to find air to fill my failing lungs, I wished for a canvas, for one more chance to paint and see the world in colour.

'GET. UP!'

His voice was so strong that even in my haze, it was loud and fearsome.

'GET. UP. *NOW*, DAMN IT!' Lincoln bellowed.

And then I felt it through our connection. It rocked me to my core and beyond.

Decima had told me I could not win against Sammael if I fought with no heart. She was right. And Lincoln was showing that as he pushed everything we were, *are*, into me. Our strength, our purpose, our friendship, our loyalty, our passion, our loss, and most of all our love. And I realised that it couldn't be about *risking* it all.

That was the whole point.

It was about fighting to *keep* it.

Fighting for our life together, our love to go on. Fighting for our right to free will. To be human. To be flawed. To be fragile and foolhardy. To have the chance to make every mistake but then somehow learn to get it right.

If Sammael defeated me, his sword would rise above my angel maker and all of those rights would be lost. The world would be forever changed.

He grabbed my hair, pulling me to my knees and holding me out to the angels as a sacrifice. I remembered the way Lincoln had taught me to slow down and control my movements – to be economical and see the fight coming. I closed my eyes. I would only get one move in before my body gave out on me. My sword returned to its slightly shorter katana blade and I dropped it to the ground between my knees.

'She will be your warrior no more!' Sammael yelled.

I breathed deeply.

In.

Out.

Focused.

He yanked my braid hard, baring my neck and his body pulled away as he drew his sword wide for the final, sweeping blow. My eyes closed, I felt his strike race towards my neck. At the final moment I dropped my head, as if in prayer, and the sword sliced through my braid, releasing me. I spun on one knee, lifting my katana as I lunged forward.

The blade pierced Sammael's lung, perilously close to his heart. Caught off-guard, he dropped his sword and froze.

Keeping one hand wrapped around the hilt of my katana still lodged in his chest – not a killing blow, yet – I quickly filled my other hand and rose, my stance deceptively steady.

Unnatural silence surrounded us as Sammael's wide eyes watched my blade.

'That is not a Grigori blade,' he said, but his eyes did not match the confidence of his tone.

'That's true,' I conceded, as I sharply twisted the blade. It might not have been a Grigori dagger but that didn't mean it didn't hurt like a bitch.

'And it does not hold your blood,' he growled, gaining sureness even as I continued to hold him still.

I managed to raise a blood-filled smile. 'That's true, too,' I admitted.

Sammael's lips twitched.

His eyes narrowed.

He planned his next move.

He was already too late.

The arm resting loosely at my side drew back and then swiftly forward, jamming Sammael's own sword – the one that had landed at my knees – into his stomach.

'You dropped something,' I said. And he knew instantly that it was over. For he had ensured that his sword had well and truly been covered in my blood.

*Yeah, consequence is a bitch.*

And because of everything that was at stake, and just … because, I didn't wait for him to fall, or disappear, or even be taken away by the angels. Instead, I pulled both blades back and wide and in one final show of speed and strength, I scissored them straight through his neck.

Sammael and I fell to the ground together.

But he would never rise again.

# chapter thirty-five

*'There is a certain greatness in the angels; and such power
that if the angels exert it to the full, it cannot be withstood.'*

**Saint Augustine**

**S**ammael was gone.

Given the extent of my injuries I should have been close
behind. And yet, my lungs continued to fill and my heart
continued to beat.

Lincoln skidded to the ground beside me, pulling me into
his lap.

'Vi, I ... I ... I ...' he stuttered, his trembling hands
sweeping over my face frantically. 'There's so much blood,
Vi,' he said, his voice thick.

'It's okay,' I said, my breathing evening out. 'I know.'

Our powers did not work the same way in this place. He
could not heal me.

'We need to get you back,' he said, looking up at the
angels. 'We need to get her back!'

'Linc,' I said softly, causing his wild eyes to come back
to mine. 'Breathe,' I said, lifting my arm up. 'Good.' I smiled
weakly. 'Now, help me up.'

He shook his head. 'You shouldn't move.'

'It's okay. Trust me,' I said.

With a furrowed brow he took my waiting arm and helped me slowly to my feet so that I could face my maker.

'Are you strong enough to cross the realms?' Lincoln asked.

Before this moment, I would have answered no. But something had changed in me. An acceptance of everything that I am and can be. I nodded, my bloodied hand cupping his face. 'This first,' I said, leaning into him and pressing my lips to his.

His kiss was gentle and powerful all at once and even as his lips trembled with his fears, his touch was sure and claimed me in every way. He pulled back, his forehead resting against mine. 'How are you standing?'

I smiled. 'I'm not – you're standing for both of us.'

When he stared back at me in utter confusion, I turned to the angels, looking until I found him. He was mounted on a white horse in the front line, Nox beside him. 'Tell him, Uri,' I said, looking at my guides.

Uri grinned – a rare display of emotion. 'It is beyond his comprehension.'

I laughed, grimacing as pain shot down my side. They were the same words Uri had given me the first time we'd met and I'd asked for an explanation. 'Try,' I suggested.

Uri looked at Lincoln, his eyes dancing with secrets. 'You are strong. Made of a Power. Your destinies have always been entwined. But destiny must also be chosen. It was never a matter of *if*, but rather when and how. Like all things of greatness, when used to cause harm your union brought devastation. You have both fought against your souls and it was as useful and painful as hiding from air when it is the very thing most fundamental to your survival.'

Lincoln glanced at me.

I shrugged. Grimaced. 'He likes being cryptic.'

'Comprehension is always in the eye of the beholder,' Uri continued. Cryptically. 'When she first came to me to embrace I sent her on a journey and told her that even though her powers would be plenty even the greatest bringers of justice will only find salvation in ...' He looked to me.

'Surrender,' I finished, then turned to Lincoln. 'I thought it meant giving up my life to be Grigori. That it meant fighting and surrendering to Lilith. Or even losing you. In the end I hated it that every time I saw Uri he reminded me that I still had to find my surrender even at times when I felt I'd given everything.' I swallowed back the tears. 'But it wasn't about giving or sacrificing, not really. It was about letting go. Surrendering my heart. To myself and thereby, to you.'

'And through your surrender, you find your salvation and your ultimate power,' Uri said, turning to Lincoln. 'For she may be our Keshet – our rainbow – but *you* are what brings her light. Why do you think you had to wait so long for her?'

Lincoln had waited years until he was appointed his partner. Me.

*It always had to be us. Not just me. Us.*

'All this time, you wanted us to be together?' Lincoln murmured.

'Of course. Your power is in your balance, in your surrender to your purest emotion of love. Humans strive for love – it is the one thing they give the most and yet fear they receive the least. You are strange creatures. And yet, it is your ability to love this way that makes you capable of the extraordinary.'

I shook my head, knowing that it would have been easier if they'd just told us all of this in the beginning, and yet I understood. It was all of the mistakes, the separation, the friendship, the fear, the determination and the love built not just on simply loving but on thousands of moments shared and missed. Our choices and our consequences are ours and could only be reached through our own journey.

I looked at my angel maker. His eyes were lowered and his expression grave.

'Why so sad?' I asked, as Lincoln steadied me when I swayed. We had defeated Sammael. Surely he was satisfied.

'Judgement must come to pass.'

My stomach sank and I shook my head.

*New Orleans.*

'No. No. We know you've saved the city before. You can turn the hurricane back out to sea. We stopped Sammael. Now you can do it again!'

'We are angels, child. Our function is finite.'

'What? You're just going to wipe out the entire city?'

'The land is intended for the ocean. Life will be reinstated beneath the water in time to come.'

'And all the people who live there now are just supposed to die? What will they do?'

Stoically, he replied, 'What they always have. They will panic, they will mourn and they will fight back. Eventually, they will move on, speculate, learn and, in time, forget. It is the way of humanity.'

'But I'm supposed to be your rainbow, the *symbol* of this covenant that protects us, that promises faith in humanity!'

'And you have done your part and more in protecting the masses. You will continue to do so.'

'But it's not enough?' I asked, my legs giving out as Lincoln caught me.

'We need to get her back!' he said urgently.

My angel maker ignored him as we continued to stare unblinkingly at one another. 'Right?' I pushed.

His chin lowered slowly. 'It is the way it must be. We cannot deny the opportunity to right what was wronged and rid the world of so many of our exiles. You will understand in time.'

I shook my head. 'No! No amount of time will ever make this right. This is because of exiles, *not* humans. The time of punishing humans for suffering the choices of angels and the insanity of exiles is over!' I stood taller as my angel maker raised an eyebrow at my outburst.

But I held his gaze, letting him see the truth.

With Lincoln and I joined as we were, and with everything I now knew, I was complete. And I was capable.

'I can see what you are thinking,' he said.

'Is it possible?' I asked.

He considered me, glancing briefly at Lincoln as if seeing him for the first time. It probably was the first time he'd bothered.

'You have proven that much is a possibility. But even so, there will be a price.'

'There always is, Michael. There always is.'

My angel maker, the commander of all armies, the greatest of all the Sole angels and according to some, one and the same as Jesus, gave me a small and knowing smile, raising his chin slightly, as if basking in his name. And I watched, stunned, as a solitary tear crept down his cheek.

'I never asked for you to fight him,' he said with a touch of defiance.

'With my blood on his sword, would you have won?' I asked.

'It is likely.'

The angel, identical to Michael, standing at his side, chuckled lightly.

I almost did a double-take. It was such a strange thing to see an angel so animated.

'But not certain?' I pushed Michael.

'Not certain,' he conceded.

I shrugged. 'Well, that wasn't a risk I was willing to take. Not when it seems you're kind of important to the end game.'

'You are of great importance, too.'

'Yeah, well, we're about to find out exactly what I can do.'

He bowed his head. 'You will not have much time to act once you return.'

I understood. For now time was halted but once we returned, the city of New Orleans would still be crumbling around us.

I turned slightly to the angel standing beside Michael. He was garishly dressed in snug black pants, a silver shirt and lightly tinted sunglasses, and when I looked straight at him, he was striking in a way Michael was not. I couldn't take my eyes off him and yet, when I hadn't been looking at him, I wasn't drawn to him at all. As if he were somehow hidden in plain sight.

'If you stand at the side of the Prince of the Elect, am I right in assuming you are the Prince of the Malign?'

He nodded, his eyes brimming with mischief.

I watched curiously. 'But you're an angel? All about function and all that?'

'To an end,' he said, his voice unnervingly similar to Michael's.

I raised an eyebrow. 'Do I even want to know your name?'

'Oh, everyone knows *my* name, at least, one or two of them. But I prefer that you simply think of me as the one who shines brightest.' He smiled.

Michael cleared his throat, cutting him off. But when they looked at each other, their eyes shared a brotherhood and fondness that was distant yet true.

*Light and dark. Elect and Malign. United, as has always been.*

I marvelled at the complexities of life as I moved my hand into Lincoln's. He sighed with relief that it seemed I was ready to get moving. I started to turn but then looked back at the angels, feeling an overwhelming sadness in the knowledge that one day some of them might choose through pride and ego to exile in an attempt to take charge of my world.

'Now that we have created this space, can you return here any time you wish?' I asked.

Michael nodded. 'If we were to wish.'

I squeezed Lincoln's hand as I absorbed Michael's words, a seed of an idea already blooming in my mind. I smirked at Lincoln and he smiled back, shaking his head as if he already knew what I had in mind.

*He probably does.*

'Can we please go now?' he asked.

I nodded, knowing that my plan could wait.

I started to concentrate on crossing us back over when the angel beside Michael spoke up.

'Aren't you going to ask?' he called out.

'Ask what?' I replied.

'About God!'

'Oh. No. I don't need to,' I threw back.

'Why?' he asked, genuinely intrigued. '*Everyone* asks.'

I looked up at Lincoln, whose expression suggested he was about to take on the Prince of Malign angels himself if he didn't let us get going soon so he could heal me.

'Nah,' I said, keeping my eyes on Lincoln. 'I know where heaven is and I'm going there now. I'm not stupid enough to waste my time sweating the small stuff.'

And then the oddest thing happened.

As Lincoln and I crossed the realms I was sure the last thing I saw was thousands of angels laughing. And the sound ... soul churning, like a choir of harps, a sole trumpet rising above, heralding a new era.

# chapter thirty-six

*'What lies behind us, and what lies before us are tiny matters*
*compared to what lies within us.'*

**Ralph Waldo Emerson**

the winds assaulted us the instant we returned to the rooftop. Lincoln put his arm around my waist and half carried me to the elevator.

The hurricane was in full force, the battle below at its height and all around us the city was crumbling. The riverbank was overflowing and far out I could see the waters moving in, taking the land bit by bit, and I knew that the angels would not stop this until they had their reason.

'I need to get closer!' I yelled as I stumbled.

Lincoln put me down on the ground, helping me all the way when my legs gave out. 'Concentrate,' he ordered.

I nodded, drawing into my weakened power and opening myself up to our connection. I felt his power, strong and ready, surge into me, charging me like a battery so that together, we could heal my wounds.

Once satisfied, he rocked back on his heels and brushed the hair out of my face. 'Better?'

'Better,' I said, sitting up and then standing. I was ready.

Lincoln grabbed the bag he'd left lodged by the elevator. He pulled out a long cable rope.

'The power is down; we're going to have to jump,' he instructed, already tying the rope to a metal support beam and then to his belt. I loaded up with the extra katana I'd packed in the bag and my spare dagger. Carefully, I nicked the edge of my wrist, noting the large scar that now lived there, and edged the blades with my blood, swiping Lincoln's from his waist and giving it the same treatment before he could stop me.

He grabbed it back, resting his hand on my wrist to close the small wound before fighting against the wind as he walked over to the edge of the tall building.

He held his right arm out and without hesitation I stepped into his embrace and we backed off the edge of the building.

Propelling into a war zone in a shower of glass as windows exploded under the hurricane's force, Lincoln expertly guided us down, and the moment our feet touched the ground we unsheathed our weapons and ran towards the river.

We worked quickly and relentlessly as we charged through the battlefield. Exiles had lost whatever hold on reality they once had and were attacking Grigori and exiles alike, all while dragging innocent humans in for the slaughter.

I saw two exiles beating a group of human men who were trying to defend two women and their young children. Lincoln saw at the same time and we risked the quick detour, running down the street now ankle-deep in water, grabbing the exiles and pulling them off the men before dispensing with them.

The men scrambled to the women and children protectively. 'What the hell's going on?' they screamed over the hurricane.

'Run!' I yelled. 'Get as far away from the river as you can! Run and don't look back!'

The men didn't hesitate, lifting the children and starting to move away. 'What about you?' one of the women yelled, looking back. 'Come with us!'

I shook my head and smiled at the little girl in one of the men's arms. She couldn't have been older than four or five. 'Please, run!' I told them again before Lincoln and I took off.

We returned a number of exiles as we moved, and though it was plain to see how extreme things had become I found my eyes barely believing the scene of unrestrained combat and devastation.

I spotted Gray in the middle of it all with Carter fighting at his side. They were both covered in blood and their team was heavily outnumbered. I could see them screaming frantically at something and I followed their line of sight. Milo and Taxi had been separated and pushed into the ocean of exiles. They were surrounded.

'Up there!' Lincoln yelled.

But my gaze was fixed on Milo. And I could hear my shrill screams as I watched, helpless, as three exiles ripped his limbs apart. Out of nowhere a dagger flew through the air and then another, taking out the two exiles beating Taxi, and freeing him long enough for him to move out of immediate danger.

Gray and Carter now fought with their fists, having given up their weapons to save Taxi.

'Violet, we can't stop!' Lincoln yelled, pulling at my arm. 'We can't help them from here!'

I knew he was right and tried to shake myself out of my mind spiral.

*Milo is dead.*

I looked to where Lincoln pointed. It was one of the riverbank buildings, only two storeys high. On the top Grigori were panned out – all with their arms raised as they tried to push back the wind and rain.

'Let's go,' I said, letting him lead the way as we took down as many exiles as we could. We couldn't stop to help Gray, but as soon as I moved into an elevated position I yelled his name and as he turned I threw him my katana, which he caught and tossed to Carter in one movement, just in time for Carter to swing the blade straight through an exile's neck. I yanked my arrow from my back and javelined it, watching as it sailed into Gray's hand. Knowing exactly how the weapon worked, he had no sooner split it in two than he drove the pointed ends into the eyes of the two exiles lining up for a killing blow. Gray swung his attention back to me, his determined eyes locking with mine briefly as he nodded me on before throwing himself back into the fray.

*At least they're armed.*

We ran for the building's outside stairs, Lincoln mowing down everything that blocked our path. His clothes were torn and blood had caked thick over his arms and neck, but he was relentless. A warrior in every way, he moved lithe and sure, carving his dagger with effective precision. I let him take the lion's share in an effort to conserve what energy I had left. I knew that Lincoln would get us there.

And I knew what I had to do when he did.

We reached the base of the stairs and hit a wall of exiles fighting each other. Lincoln glanced at me and I nodded; we both knew that the exiles could sense the Grigori up there – our nature users – and wanted to take the fight to them. That was something we could not allow. Those Grigori were the only thing holding the hurricane at bay right now.

Lincoln leaped into the fight, quickly taking out two exiles as he did, but another five promptly rounded on him.

I'd just stepped towards him, ready to back him up, when a strong hand gripped my neck from behind and dragged me beneath the shadow of the stairs, throwing me against the wall. My head hit the brick hard and I felt the trickle of warm blood run down my neck.

Blinking until my vision held, I looked up expecting to see the insane eyes of an exile, but instead I was met with the vicious intent of Drenson.

'Adele is dead!' he snarled, his hand wrapped around my throat holding me against the wall as the other moved his dagger firmly over my heart. 'All of this is your fault! I'm the head of all Grigori and I *will* end this now!'

My eyes darted right, to where Lincoln was still fighting off a horde of exiles. I could hear him screaming out for me between hits and knew he was feeling me through our connection. I tried to calm my thoughts and my body so that he wouldn't lose his concentration, and I looked back at Drenson.

'I'm sorry about Adele,' I rasped, struggling to speak with his hand tightening around my neck. I considered my options but he had me. Anything I did would cause the dagger to slide right in.

'You should be! Without her voting favour it's only a matter of time before I lose my seat. It was enough to have that bitch Josephine control me at every turn, but not *you*!' he spat. 'I have hundreds of years ahead of me; I won't live in shame while you steal everything that is mine!'

A figure dropped from above into a crouched position, landing a few metres behind Drenson – as if it had fallen from the sky. I couldn't make it out but even if it was an exile, it couldn't make my situation any worse, so I kept my eyes on Drenson so as not to draw his attention to it.

'I know how to stop this!' I said.

'Even more reason to finish you,' he hissed. And just as his arm flexed and he made his move, I saw the glint of silver and then Drenson's eyes cloud over, his arms losing their grip and falling limp along with the rest of his body as he fell to the ground face down. A Grigori dagger was embedded between his shoulderblades.

Spence stood over him.

His fierce, warrior eyes looked up at me sharply. 'Always got your back, Eden.'

I threw my arms around him and squeezed tightly before letting him go.

He delivered a roguish smile and gestured knowingly to the stairs. 'Do what you have to do,' he said, giving me a nod before bending down and reefing his dagger free. 'Chloe and I will make sure the building is protected.'

I saw her then, running up behind him, out of breath.

I shook my head. 'Don't worry about us. Go and help Gray and Carter. They're a hundred metres up the road and need to get out of there.'

Without another word, Spence grabbed Chloe's arm and they ran.

And I knew it was time to do exactly what I was put on this earth to do.

I called out for Lincoln and turned in time to see Griffin

and Josephine's team jump into the fray where Lincoln was still fighting, freeing him to come with me.

'Where were you?' he asked as we ran up the stairs.

'Dealing with Academy politics,' I replied.

On the low rooftop – and neighbouring rooftops along the river – the nature users continued to fight the storm, calling on their strengths and pushing back with all they had, but the hurricane was just too powerful.

At the front, calling out orders and holding the weight of the wind, stood Phoenix, looking every bit the unearthly creature he was. His black shirt was ripped and flying in the air. Wind encased him and I gasped.

'He's channelling the hurricane. Pulling the power to him and trying to send it back out to sea.'

'It'll tear him in two!' Lincoln yelled as we watched Phoenix's body being brutally lashed by invisible whips of air. Zoe stood beside him, her focus on the rising river. It had already lifted over the levies and was now pouring into the city streets even as she and those beside her worked at creating new currents to send it away.

I looked around frantically. We were heavily outnumbered; there were at least twice as many exiles to our Grigori. My knees weakened at the thought.

Lincoln grabbed my shoulders to steady me.

'What now?' he screamed over the wind and rain, over the cries of madness below.

I turned and ran towards Phoenix, getting as close as I could before the wind pushed me stumbling back. I regained my balance and screamed his name as I felt Lincoln behind me.

Phoenix turned slightly, his shoulders sagging in relief as he kept the winds rippling and swirling around him. He knew where I'd been; that Sammael had been defeated.

'You need to leave!' I screamed, pushing closer again.

'A little busy right now!' he called back, somehow managing a small smile.

'Phoenix, look at me!' I cried.

He glanced over briefly, his strained expression filled with knowing. There was blood running from his ear and down his neck.

*Jesus, how much more of this can he take?*

'You always worried you were becoming a new kind of angel, but can you finally see?' he called out. 'You were always becoming the best kind of human.' His eyes met mine, and for a few magical beats all the mayhem around us went away and his calm brown eyes met my hazel ones and understanding passed between us. He knew what I was going to do.

'This is your destiny!' he yelled.

Tears fell and I shook my head. 'There's still time! You can get away,' I called out, ignoring Lincoln, who had braced my shoulders from behind as if he knew I might do something crazy.

Phoenix held my gaze and it felt in that moment as if he were holding me together. 'You are exactly where you are supposed to be and so am I.' He managed a smile. 'It's time for the final act.'

'No!' I screamed at him, angry now. 'You'll die!' I couldn't stand by and let him make this choice. This ultimate sacrifice.

'Listen to her, Phoenix,' Lincoln called out. 'You don't have to do this.'

Phoenix's eyes lingered on me before moving to Lincoln's. 'Promise me!'

Two words that could have meant anything, but which Lincoln and I both knew were solely about me.

Lincoln didn't hesitate. 'Always.'

Phoenix nodded once then looked back across the river to the suburbs being ripped apart, the land sinking into the ocean, and then back to me. He knew he was the only one strong enough to hold the wind. But I didn't care. Right at that moment, I honestly didn't. I wanted him to be safe. He deserved his chance.

'Do it!' he mouthed and then turned his face back to the storm, his arms wide as he gave it everything he had. And the sheer fortitude in his eyes transferred to me and I found myself nodding even as my throat closed in.

My hand went out and Lincoln moved to my side and grasped it. 'Open everything, Linc. This is going to hurt.'

'Take whatever you need,' he replied without faltering, squeezing my hand and opening our soul bond, bringing me new strength beyond anything I'd ever experienced.

I pulled it all within, adding it to what already lay inside me, and then I lifted into my Sight, hovering above my physical form. I concentrated on the scene below, taking one, then ten, a hundred, a thousand, as far as I could push, my Sight travelling with little more than a thought as I cruised first along the river and then the main square of the French Quarter, down Bourbon Street and finally to Canal Street, looping back down to the river and sucking every exile within the circle into my power. It was more than I'd ever tried or contemplated trying to hold before tonight.

All the while, I tried to exclude Phoenix; tried to keep him free of my power, but in the end it was impossible. The power that had always beckoned me was too strong. Unleashed as it was it consumed me, leading the way.

I knew I had only enough control for one final choice.

I made it.

I tore from each and every one of them what they had given up any right to have. The power coursed through me, my body shaking as I gave the last. My all.

And every single exile under my power fell.

# chapter thirty-seven

*'Neither shall they say see here or see there, for behold, the
kingdom of God is within you.'*

*Luke 17:20*

**W**hen I opened my eyes, I was cradled in Lincoln's arms
while he shielded me from the wind and torrential rain.

His eyes were fixed on mine.

'Did it work?' I gasped.

He nodded in awe. 'They're all down.'

'Phoenix?' I asked, my voice breaking. But, really, I already
knew.

'Phoenix too,' Lincoln said.

I stumbled to my feet, despite Lincoln's attempts to stop
me, and faced the storm.

'Michael!' I screamed at the top of my lungs. '*Michael!*' My
hands fisted at my sides.

'Over there,' Lincoln said in my ear, pointing me to the
corner of the rooftop.

A lion stood proudly at the edge, his front paws mounted
on the surrounding wall – the wind neither a deterrent nor
bother. And with one almighty roar that sounded and felt

like thunder, the rain stopped and the hurricane pulled into a gentle tornado and travelled back out to sea.

Cheers sounded out from the rooftop and below, but only tears fell from my eyes as I watched my lion walk over to where Phoenix lay.

My lion – my angel maker, Michael – gently leaned over Phoenix and nudged his face, giving him a small nurturing lick, as a lion would his cub. And with a final look back at me, his eyes as blank as ever, he took off, bounding in great and mighty leaps all the way to the edge of the rooftop and beyond as Grigori watched in wonder.

'Vi, you're bleeding,' Lincoln said, sounding worried.

My hand went to my face and I looked down to see the streaks of blood that my eyes, nose and mouth had left behind. My power was gone. I couldn't feel it at all. I couldn't feel the senses. I couldn't feel the lure of my Sight. The well that sat deep at the base of me was empty. And still, none of it mattered as I staggered over to Phoenix, collapsing at his side.

My hand trembled as it ran over his face.

'I'm sorry! I'm so, so sorry,' I cried.

Slowly, his dark brown eyes opened and lifted to meet mine. He stared at me for what was probably just seconds but felt like a brief lifetime. And in his eyes I found everything I needed at that moment. Acceptance. Forgiveness. Relief. And … humanity. I had killed him. Not today. Perhaps not for many tomorrows. But immortality was his no more.

No longer a malign angel.

No longer a dark exile.

Phoenix was human.

Just like every other exile in the nearby radius.

And yet, in those final seconds before the world around me went black, I saw something new in his eyes. Something that looked an awful lot like hope.

It hurt. Everywhere.

I'd moved in and out of consciousness for what seemed like a very long time; opening my eyes, seeing Lincoln, feeling his closeness and then slipping back under all too soon.

I could hear chatter here and there.

'She might not make it—'

'Yes, she will.'

'I'm just saying you should be prepared.'

'No need … Get this joker out of here.'

And then, later …

'We should consider moving her.'

'Is it safe?'

'We can't know, but it has to be better than keeping her here.'

'Get a plane ready.'

And then, moving. Lying in a bed and then being cradled in the arms of the sun. Warm. Loved. Safe. I sunk in.

People came and went. Again I heard them talk. Sometimes I even knew who they were.

Griffin sat with me often. I thought I heard him cry. But then he got on with it, letting me know that he was looking after things. That the clean-up was well in hand. All the exiles in the city of New Orleans had fallen. My range hadn't been much more than a dozen city blocks but since they'd all been in that area for the battle, it had worked a charm.

The Grigori had started to detain the now-powerless exiles immediately, with assistance from the navy. A number of the exiles had taken their own lives before they could be stopped and many had fled but were being pursued.

Griffin marvelled at how the events of that night had changed the face of the fight. There were still many exiles out there to fight and the guarantee of more to come, but the playing field had been significantly evened.

All the while Lincoln stayed by my side.

I wanted to open my eyes and tell them I would be okay. But I couldn't. The darkness held me even while light surrounded me.

Eventually, I became aware of loud noises. Then I heard a familiar voice.

'Honestly, you'd think they'd give a guy a break. It's like fricking Fort Knox getting in here.'

'Yeah, a few of the Rogues have taken it upon themselves to add a little extra security.'

'A little!' he scoffed. 'I almost peed myself.'

I heard Lincoln chuckle. 'It's good to see you.'

'Yeah, well, I got sick of waiting for you to come and visit me.'

'Sorry, Spence.'

*Spence.*

'No sweat. I would've been here sooner but Mia and Chloe are worse than the pit bulls guarding this room.' I heard his voice change, soften. 'How's she doing?'

I heard Lincoln sigh. 'I can't feel her like I usually do. She's weak but she's holding on. I try to help the healing along but it's like something is blocking me.'

'Maybe she just isn't ready,' Spence said simply. I felt a hand at my forehead. 'Is it terrible that there's a part of me that wishes we'd never figured it all out? That we'd been somewhere on the other side of the world when that war had gone down and the angels had just dealt with it like they were going to.'

'No. I've had that thought myself. Doesn't mean we'd change things, though.'

There was a pause before Lincoln added, 'What you did … Drenson. How are you dealing with it?'

I could almost hear Spence's shrug. 'Not like I look back on it with regret, if that's what you mean. It was him or her, which meant there was no other option. And it helps that no one locked me up.'

'I agree.' Another pause, and then, 'But?'

Spence sighed. 'Yeah. Just wish he hadn't been such a dick, I suppose.'

'Yeah. Me too.'

'So, what happens if she wakes up?'

'When,' Lincoln corrected.

'When,' Spence confirmed.

'That's up to her.'

'What if she wants to go back to London? Stay with the Rogues?'

'Then that's what we'll do.'

I waited for Spence to make some kind of barbed comment, but none came. Instead, he just said, 'Fair enough, man. I hope you two get your chance at happiness. You deserve it. Call me if there's any change.'

'You got it.'

Time passed from there. I could hear machines beep. And more people as they came and went. Steph was a constant. She talked about her wedding and deliberated over candles or lanterns, sit-down dinner or cocktail-party receptions, honeymoon locations and music until I would sense her slump beside me, and sob as she begged me to wake up.

Dapper read books to me. Ancient tales intended for few to hear. Onyx came with him, throwing in his own biased recollections of particular events. And all the while I lay still, wishing I could heal myself, but my power remained dormant. Or gone.

I heard Phoenix come and go. Unlike the others he didn't speak to me, but when he was there he always held my hand.

'I know you still love her,' Lincoln said, his tone matter-of-fact.

'I'll always love her. But she has always and will always love you. I won't ever stand in your way again.'

'That might be wise since you're significantly easier to hurt nowadays.'

I felt their smiles.

'What are you going to do now?' Lincoln went on.

'Wait for her to open her eyes and say the words we all need to hear her say.'

The darkness pulled me under after that.

Finally, dreams started to flit into the darkness. Growing up with Dad. Silly moments, such as making him a Father's Day painting and breakfast in bed only to realise when I snuck into his room that he'd already left for work. And other things; the look of desperation on his face when he'd come to collect me from the hospital after a teacher had attacked and very nearly raped me. I'd never seen how badly that broke him at the time, but watching it now I saw the love, and the agony of not knowing what to do or how to help.

I dreamed of my first day at a new school after the court case and meeting Steph. She was like a blast of fresh air and I knew from day one I had a friend for life.

Then there was the first time I met Lincoln. The self-defence course that delivered me my very own guardian angel. He watched over me, and in my dream I saw in a new light how he cared, how he worried. I saw our friendship grow and the conflict in his eyes when it became so much more and his care turned to torment.

I dreamed of the night he first kissed me, feeling once again the overwhelming passion and sureness that this man was my other half; that we were absolutely meant for one another. How right I'd been.

And then suddenly I was outside his warehouse discovering the truth, feeling the sting of betrayal. But this time, I saw so much more. I saw his pain and fears for me and us. I saw my innocence drift away and my rage and I wished, not for the first time, that I'd found it in my heart to be more forgiving, and yet I knew that the path had been the one I'd had to travel to reach this day of understanding.

The dreams kept coming. Life and death, and love and loss. All painful and beautiful. All real.

I felt Lincoln's hand, warm and wrapped around mine.

'Come back to me, baby. Please come back to me.'

This time when I tried, my eyes cracked open and I saw him beside me, ruffled and beautiful.

'I never left,' I whispered. My throat was dry and my body ached all over.

Lincoln jolted then looked at me, his entire body sagging in relief.

'Hey,' he rasped, his fingers trailing along the curve of my chin.

'Hey.' I tried – and failed – to smile. 'Where?' I croaked.

'We're back in New York. We moved you here about a week ago.'

'How long?'

'Two weeks since the hurricane.'

I nodded. 'New Orleans?'

He smiled, going along with my two-word vocab. 'The city was saved. The outer areas closer to the ocean are gone but the navy managed to evacuate many people. Lives and homes were lost, but nothing near what would've …'

Then I felt something. It wasn't my power but it was powerful. 'Someone's here,' I whispered.

Lincoln looked around, shaking his head. 'Just us.'

'No,' I replied, waiting. Sure enough, a few moments later I could see him. Michael.

'Am I dying?' I asked.

Lincoln immediately moved to stand between Michael and me.

Michael raised his hands gently. 'I have come to take you *both* somewhere, but rest assured you will be returned.'

'Can't this wait?' asked Lincoln. 'She's only just woken up. The doctors haven't even seen her yet.'

'Do you fear she may suffer a medical emergency while under my care?' Michael asked.

*Wow. Did he just crack a joke?*

I smiled weakly, reaching up to take Lincoln's hand. 'As long as we're together,' I said.

Michael nodded. 'I would not dream of anything other,' he said, and suddenly the pain was gone from my body and Lincoln and I were in the place that I could only call ... other, standing in a field facing Michael. But not just any field.

*A field of white lilies beneath a violet sky and a glowing golden sun.*

It was warm, like home. Like love.

'My painting,' I whispered.

'Your heart,' Michael corrected.

And I agreed.

Lincoln held my hands in both of his, looking at the field with a sense of contentment and understanding.

'Your souls are bound in every way?' Michael asked Lincoln

Lincoln turned to him and nodded. 'Every way.'

Uri and Nox appeared behind Michael. They were wearing their usual contrast in clothing and yet they seemed more relaxed than usual, closer together rather than so far apart.

'You have finally surrendered?' Uri asked.

I nodded. 'My self.'

Uri bowed his head.

Michael took a step towards us. 'We would offer you a final binding, if you choose to accept.'

'I think we are already quite final, Michael,' Lincoln said.

'That is true, but symbolism has its place, too. It comes after but still carries weight. Join your left hands.'

Lincoln and I did as Michael asked, not sure what was going on but trusting that it was right.

A light pressure began to build and then something akin to an electrical current ran through our hands causing us both to flinch. When I looked down I saw a new marking. Intricate, like the designs on my wrist markings, again with tiny wisps like feathers, but so much finer. A ring on my wedding finger, and another on Lincoln's. Matching in design, but whereas mine was purple with a shimmer like stars in the night, Lincoln's was silver, just like my wrists.

We looked to Michael, who seemed pleased with the result.

'In Hebrew,' he said, 'amethyst means *dream stone*.'

Michael, commander of all armies, the greatest of the Sole angels, bowed. 'May your dreams be many.'

Lincoln bowed his head in return. 'Thank you.'

'Will I ever see you again?' I asked.

'If you need me, yes.' He tilted his head in that way of his. 'So, it is unlikely. You know who you are and what you can do.'

I smiled. 'I am you. Like you are me.'

Michael nodded once. 'We do not run. We do not quit.'

My smile widened. 'And what of fairytales?'

He raised his hands, palms up. 'Life, child. Is life not the greatest fairytale of all?'

I nodded in understanding. 'What about if you need me?'

His eyebrow twitched. 'There is always that possibility.'

I rolled my eyes at his inability to admit he might just want to see me. I guess only time would tell, though I did realise one thing. 'I can't come back here, can I?' I was a danger to them, and we could no longer deny it.

'It is your space to command and it will not be taken from you, but no, it would not be wise.'

Somehow this space had become a part of me, and already I mourned its loss, but I knew that this was right, and what I wanted to do. It was the idea that had first come to me after facing Sammael and now it was time to make it happen.

'It's your space now,' I said before I looked off into the distance and closed my eyes, smiling.

First, I returned it to its true form of nothingness, with its searching souls glimmering in the distance and countless smatterings of rainbows connecting what might be. Then I thought of my senses – the gifts that the angels had given me. Why had I been given all five? Why had that been necessary?

*Perhaps ... for this.*

I breathed deeply and brought forward the conflicting sensations I'd always felt in my blood and bones. Rivers of cool; lands of warmth. I thought of the sounds of birds flying and trees blowing in the wind. I drew on the smell of flowers, in particular white lilies and all they invoked, and then the flashes of morning and evening. And finally, the taste of apple.

Slowly I opened my eyes. Before me was a vast meadow of rolling hills with a carpet of white flowers and trees in the distance, birds circling and swooping. The rainbows shone brightly, casting light, and in the centre … a tree bursting with ripe red apples.

Beyond my field there was still the great expanse of nothingness. I had not created a new world or even a new city, but it was a start.

I smirked, gesturing to the apples. 'Feel free to help yourselves.'

'You take great assumption by thinking this is something we would desire,' Michael said flatly. 'If we would desire anything.'

I nodded. 'Rest your pride, Michael. Rest your pride and maybe we can all evolve.' Maybe this could be a place where angels could indulge and experience time in a physical sense. Angels might be the higher beings but that didn't mean they could not learn.

# chapter thirty-eight

*'There is a sacredness in tears. They are not the mark of weakness, but of power. They speak more eloquently than ten thousand tongues. They are messengers of overwhelming grief ... and unspeakable love.'*

**Washington Irving**

**D**isoriented, I opened my eyes. My groggy mind took a few moments before it allowed the memories to flood in. I looked at my left hand to see the violet ring and then to the end of my bed where Lincoln sat in a chair, watching me.

'When was the last time you slept in a bed?' I asked, smiling.

He shrugged in response.

'I see.'

'How are you feeling?' he asked, moving closer.

'Okay. Physically, I feel like I'm mending.' I frowned as I combed my fingers through my now considerably shorter hair. 'But my power ... I still can't feel it like I normally can.' I tried to hide my concern but of course he saw right through me.

Lincoln brushed the loose strands of hair back from my face. 'I know. I can't heal you like I should be able to. Griffin thinks you probably burned out. It might take a little time for everything to come back online.'

I exhaled, but not fully. There was a part of me that worried I had lost it for good. It made me realise just how much I'd come to embrace my power and role as Grigori. It is who I am.

I'd been out of it for a couple of weeks and I knew that not all the news waiting for me would be good. It couldn't be. I took Lincoln's hands in mine.

'Milo?' I whispered.

He shook his head.

'Who else?'

Lincoln's eyes glassed over and he swallowed thickly. I felt the tears slip down my cheeks.

Later that night, Chloe sat on the edge of my bed while Spence and Lincoln moved back to give us some space.

'Someone's *got* to talk to those Rogues out there,' Spence said to Lincoln. 'Steph almost lost her shit with them earlier when she tried to visit. And they made us leave all our weapons with them like they own the place or something.'

I bit back a sad smile, confused by the Rogues' uncharacteristic behaviour.

'You know they don't care what I say,' Lincoln said plainly.

Spence crossed his arms. 'Then who the hell will they listen to?'

Lincoln looked at me, and my chest started to hurt even more.

'Are you sure this will work?' I asked Chloe.

She nodded. 'We were there. Spence and I were running along the rooftops, trying to get to them. We saw you with Phoenix and then what happened below. Spence tried, Violet. He leaped right off the roof and into the fight. He did everything he could.'

I held back the tears that seemed to have been streaming for the past twenty-four hours.

'Are you sure you want to see this?' Chloe asked tentatively.

'Show me,' I said.

Two days later, I laid a white rose on Milo's gravestone. The Grigori who had given their lives had been brought back and buried in a special Grigori graveyard just outside Manhattan. Given that most of us have outlived our family by the time we die, the graveyard had been established to keep us together.

More than two hundred Grigori had died in the battle, making it the largest loss in Grigori history. Many senior Grigori from all corners of the world and a large number of Grigori still too young to be gone had given their lives.

Drenson and Adele had been given headstones like everyone else. I had placed a flower on each of their graves. Sure, Drenson had tried to kill me but I understood how heady a thing power is. Drenson had been unable to fight the lure. Did that make him unaccountable? Of course not. Did that make him evil? I don't believe so. Mostly it just made him an ass who had lost control and paid the price. His judgement would come, but not by my hand.

I passed by Seth's and Decima's headstones, feeling a sense of relief for them. In many ways I think their end was their gift. They were ready, and to go out fighting seemed only right.

Finally, I stopped at the last grave, grateful that Lincoln had seen to this while I was asleep. It was white marble and sat beneath a weeping willow tree, separate from the rest, as I knew he would wish. After all, his life had always been lived apart.

I stood at his grave for many hours.

Sometimes I cried. Sometimes I just shook my head wishing it wasn't true.

Mostly, I prayed.

Stupid, I know. Me? I still didn't even know the truth of it all. Whether there was a god and if there was if it was even a god I cared much for. But still ... I prayed for his peace. I prayed for his happiness and I prayed that he knew how much he had done for me. That at that craziest, darkest time of my life, he had been there for me and somehow managed to drag me through day after day.

He had been my saviour when I had least accepted that I needed one. He had been my friend. And I would do anything to have him back. But he was gone.

It was fast, at least. Chloe had shown me that much with her gift. He had stepped in the way of a younger Grigori's fight. He had saved the girl's life and pushed her aside, leaving himself wide open for the exile, who had not hesitated to drive his sword right into his chest. Spence had leaped into the fight at the same moment, but he'd been too late. There was nothing anyone could have done.

Lincoln stood quietly to the side, where he had been for hours, waiting patiently, but now he joined me, saying softly, 'It's time.'

I nodded, brushing my hands across the marble headstone. 'Mondays and Thursdays will never feel right without you,' I whispered.

I placed the last dozen roses, all white apart from one red. Because he stood apart, and because he would always carry a place in my heart.

'Love you, Gray,' I said. 'Thank you for dancing with me.'

'How are you holding up?' Lincoln asked as we rode the elevator back up to the Academy.

I took his hand while my other hand tucked my hair behind my ear. I just couldn't get used to it being short. 'I'll be okay,' I said. And it was true. Dealing with the losses, especially Gray, was going to hurt for a long time, but I knew that they had not died in vain, and that helped. 'What's happening now that Drenson's gone?' I asked. 'Has Josephine taken over?'

Lincoln shrugged, helping me out of the lift as I still hobbled with aches and pains. At least the worst of the bruising on my face had settled.

'I'm not sure. The Assembly and senior Grigori have been convening all week here and at the main headquarters around the world. There's supposed to be an announcement today and Josephine told me to be there.' He checked his watch. 'It's already started.'

I nodded. 'Then let's go.'

But he simply smiled and backed me into the wall beside the hall doors.

'What?' I asked, grinning.

He took a few strands of my hair in his fingers and I couldn't help the wave of self-consciousness. Lincoln had always liked my long hair. He leaned in close, kissing me lightly just below the ear. 'Have I mentioned how damn sexy your hair is?'

When I started to shake my head he stopped me by kissing me again, on the lips this time.

'Just when I thought you couldn't be any more stunning, you prove me wrong.' He watched my reaction until he was satisfied that my embarrassment had gone and then planted a quick kiss on my forehead. 'You know you're incredible, right?'

I blushed. Only Lincoln could have made me suddenly love my new hair in just two sentences.

He pulled me away from the wall as he chuckled, that laugh he reserved just for me, as we pushed open the doors to the hall.

I had never seen the grand hall so full. With many Grigori having returned here after the battle at New Orleans, the Academy was over capacity, but everyone seemed to be happy enough to squeeze in.

Lincoln and I began to worm our way through, looking for familiar faces or just somewhere to stand so we could hear the Assembly's decision.

As we weaved, people around us were quick to give us space, which at first I appreciated, until I realised they were moving too quickly than was merely polite. The chatter died down suddenly and whispers began as a walkway opened before us and every set of eyes was trained in our direction.

'Linc,' I murmured, 'do you know what this is about?'

'No idea,' he said, though he seemed considerably less surprised than I felt. He really had a knack for that.

'Why is everyone looking at us?'

'They're not looking at us, Vi. They're looking at you,' he said softly.

*Oh, great. Hang me out to dry, why don't you?*

I spotted the group of Rogues to our right, Carter at the front. Relieved to see him I made my way over, ignoring the following eyes, and flung my arms around him. He pulled me tight and I bit my lip to hold back the tears.

'What did he say to you?' I asked. In the vision Chloe had shown me, it was Carter who'd caught Gray's body as it fell and had his ear to Gray's mouth for his final words.

Carter squeezed me one last time. 'I tried,' he rasped. 'I was too damn slow.'

He was talking about his ability to rewind. He hadn't been able to get to Gray in time to stop what happened.

'I know,' I said, my hand on his shoulder. 'Of course I know.' Carter loved Gray too. He would've done anything to save him. 'What did he say?' I asked again.

His eyes came up to meet mine briefly before he leaned in to whisper in my ear. 'He said, "Purple's the colour of royalty. Protect her always."'

I heard the reverence in Carter's voice and pulled back. As I did, I was further stunned to see Carter and all the Rogues standing behind him drop to their right knees and bow their heads.

I looked behind me where Lincoln was watching on with calm acknowledgement. He held out his hand to me and, with one last look back at the Rogues, I took it.

'You bring us together, Vi,' Lincoln said as I accepted his strength to keep me balanced and limped through the centre of the room.

One by one, Grigori began to kneel and bow their heads.

When I reached Spence I almost leaped on him, so relieved to see a familiar face. But he simply said, 'Don't be afraid,' before he too, took to his knee.

I passed Chloe, Salvatore and Zoe and I bit my lip when even Steph dropped down. Until finally we reached the front of the room, where Griffin and Nyla waited for us and the Assembly sat in their great chairs.

Griffin smiled. 'Good to see you up and about, Violet.'

'It's good to be upright,' I said, smiling back. I glanced between him and Nyla. 'Are you …' I asked Nyla, unable to finish the question and dreading the answer.

'Honouring Rudyard with every day of my life? Yes,' she answered. And though I could see the sadness in her eyes, I could also see the acceptance. She and Rudyard had fought and loved side by side. Their bond had been as epic and complete as the one I shared with Lincoln, but she was here and she would mourn his loss even as she fought as if he were still by her side.

I nodded, admiring her great strength even as I hoped I would never have to make the same choice.

Nyla glanced at Griffin. 'And I have a new partner of whom I know Rudy would have approved.'

I smiled now for them both. It was a perfect partnership. And Griffin deserved to have a loyal and strong warrior by his side. No one had heard from Magda since she disappeared from Lincoln's warehouse two and a half years ago. It had taken time for Griffin to get over Magda's betrayal and I knew that deep down he hoped he would never see her again. Because if he did, he would have her brought to justice for her crimes.

'Then it was worth the wait?' I asked Griffin.

'The best things usually are,' he said, gesturing to my ring finger.

I leaned a little closer, dropping my voice. 'Any idea what's going on?' I asked, my eyes darting about nervously.

His smile broadened and with Nyla mirroring his actions they both knelt. 'A new era.'

I swallowed tightly and looked up at the Assembly. As I did, Rainer and Wilhelm stood and knelt, followed by Valerie and Hakon. I glanced at the empty chairs of Seth and Decima – Seth's chair now pure white ivory and Decima's a perfect black ebony in a fitting tribute – and then to those formerly held by Adele and Drenson. Beside Drenson's empty chair stood Josephine.

She looked out around the room before settling her gaze on me.

'Leadership is a privilege,' she announced, and I braced myself for whatever she had up her sleeve. 'As old as time, we may implement structures and elect the people we believe to be best at this role, but in the end, the greatest leaders will never wait to be elected. They will not conform, they will not abide. Nor will they campaign or protest.' For the first time, Josephine's smile seemed genuine. 'They simply ... *are*.' Josephine stepped forward and in front of the entire hall of

Grigori, the Vice – and acting head – of the Assembly knelt before me.

Slowly I turned to look around the hall, still silent as every single one of them balanced on one knee, though now with raised heads to watch on. Beside me, Lincoln lifted my hand to his lips and kissed it once before also dropping to his knee.

Stunned, I wanted to shake my head, to tell everyone to stop being crazy. They didn't need to kneel to me. I hadn't done anything other than try to save the people I loved and fight for what was right. Everyone in this room had done the same. I was about to say as much, when I remembered how Steph had explained the levels of regard for Grigori. Kneeling was the highest sign of respect, and I realised I could not throw that back in their face.

Studying the crowd, I understood now that this was my role. I was made by the Sole. I was the Keshet – the rainbow. The sign of the covenant. I was created to lead. And I had been empowered to do so by my angel maker, by my soul connection with Lincoln and by my humanity.

'Stand,' I said, surprised how steady my voice came out.

The room silently stood as all eyes watched me.

'Next month I will be twenty,' I said, smiling when I heard a few chuckles skitter through the room; some of the Grigori in the hall were well into their hundreds. 'I'm still a child in many ways,' I agreed. 'But I have seen a lot in these past few years. I have learned much. I have been broken, have died and been revived and fought some truly horrific foes. And I have been lucky enough to have friends and family who have sacrificed greatly in order to stand by my side. New Orleans was a victory but the cost was terribly high, and there is not one of us in this room who has not felt a great loss. Thank you for honouring me in this way. It means so much, but please, honour those we have lost. And let us try to work together. Let us be brave, be flawed and yet always be strong. Let us be human and fight for our right to free will. I promise you that I will stand with you and fight by your side until my very last breath. But it is I who will serve you.'

Before the great hall of my Grigori peers, I knelt and bowed my head while all around me, Grigori raised their daggers to the sky in salute.

'Violet Eden,' Josephine said, 'you have been elected the new head of the World Assembly. The vote was unanimous.'

I stood and turned to Lincoln who, in typical Lincoln fashion, seemed to be taking all of this in his stride. 'Whatever you decide is the right choice for us,' he said, simply.

I closed my eyes briefly, considering this choice. 'If I am the head of the Assembly, do I choose the remaining Assembly members?'

Resigned to what this might mean, Josephine nodded. 'It will be left to your discretion as your first act. Grigori law states that you may nominate your Assembly at the commencement of your leadership, however, following that, any amendments would be by a vote of your peers.'

I nodded.

'Then,' I said, looking over the room, 'I nominate that Seth's and Decima's chairs be filled by the Rogues. We have had division among the Grigori for too long now and there is no reason for it. Both Rogues and Academy Grigori bring skills to our everlasting wars. We must learn to work together or we are no better than the exiles. If they will accept, I nominate Carter and Taxi, two Rogues whom I know and trust with my life.'

The Rogues began to whistle and cheer as Carter and Taxi stepped forward looking dumbfounded.

'Is this a paying gig?' Carter asked when he reached me.

I laughed. 'I'm sure you'll be well provided for.'

He nodded uncertainly. 'You sure you want to do this, purple? There's probably a few other people who might be better suited to this than us,' he said as Taxi nodded.

I smiled. 'That's exactly why you two are perfect.' I gestured to Seth's and Decima's seats. 'They were great warriors. Like you.' It was bittersweet to not see Gray take one of those chairs, but I knew he would agree with my choice, and he would smile if he could see the way Carter and Taxi stood tall as they took their places on the Assembly.

I settled my attention on Rainer and Wilhelm as well as Valerie and Hakon. 'Your seats are yours for as long as you choose to keep them, but know that things will not go on the way they did under Drenson.'

All four nodded and took their seats, reassuming their places as Assembly members.

My eyes met Josephine's. 'You have been running things from the sideline for too long,' I said.

She remained silent, like a prisoner waiting to hear her sentence.

'You wanted me here. You brought me back to Lincoln. Why?' The question had been bugging me since she arrived in New Orleans.

'I hoped that you really were what my instinct whispered.' And in our world of interfering angels manipulating and creating choices of both light and dark, only to then dangle free will over us all, I understood what she was saying.

'Do you regret your choices, knowing that I now hold this power over your future?'

Josephine took a deep breath and let it out. 'All I care about is the cause. So, while there are many things in my life that I regret, this is not, nor will it ever be, one of them.'

I watched her closely, but I also turned to Griffin for confirmation that she was giving nothing but truth. On his small nod, I turned back to her. 'You are a good Vice, Josephine. But you will have to accept your place if you are to maintain your seat. The days of your rule are over.'

'You would still allow me to hold my seat?' she asked tentatively.

'If you can mind your place, then yes. You are a warrior who believes in Grigori more than any other person I know.'

'Then I would humbly maintain my position,' she responded, sitting down, and I noticed Carter roll his eyes as she did. They would make an interesting team.

I turned to Lincoln and pulled him close so I could speak quietly into his ear. He listened, absorbing my words. And when I pulled back he was smiling with pride and a tinge of excitement that solidified my decision. I smiled back and turned to the hall.

'You deserve a *great* leader. And I believe that, with Lincoln beside me, I can be that leader for you.' I walked over to where Griffin and Nyla stood. 'Some day,' I added. 'But you need strength today, and someone who will lead with not only courage but also experience and integrity. And I ... I need some time to become the leader you all deserve. I promise you that I will return, but today I abdicate my chair and pass my seat of power to a person I would follow without a second thought: Griffin Moore.'

Griffin's face filled with restrained emotion as Nyla discreetly took his hand, giving him her support.

I approached Griffin and grabbed his hands in mine. 'I thought we might do a trade,' I explained. 'You can have my job until I'm ready, and in return, if you would trust us, Lincoln and I would very much like to go home.'

Griffin pulled me into a tight embrace. 'I'd be honoured. And I look forward to the day that I will stand aside so you can take your rightful place.'

'I know that,' I assured him.

Griffin, still holding Nyla's hand, walked up to the middle two chairs and turned to face the hall. As they took their seats, the entire hall behind me erupted into applause and cheers.

# CHAPTER THIRTY-NINE

*'To see a World in a Grain of Sand*
*And a Heaven in a Wild Flower*
*Hold infinity in the palm of your hand*
*And Eternity in an hour.'*

**William Blake**

**I**'d been waiting for him.

It had been a few days since Griffin became the head of the Assembly, and things were gradually settling down. Steph's wedding plans were going full-steam ahead. The term 'duck and cover' was being used with particular regularity within Academy walls and, well, let's just say no one was warrior enough to escape the wrath of bridal-Steph.

Tonight, everyone was at Ascension enjoying a night off and a joint bucks-and-hens night for Steph and Salvatore, who had decided that after recent events it would be more fun to be all together. They had been right.

After watching Dapper and Onyx bring out a huge pre-wedding cake, I had taken the opportunity to slip away for some fresh air. Watching all of my friends smiling and dancing helped put things in perspective. And perspective, I have discovered, proves this: life goes on.

But it is a different life now.

As I sat on the Brooklyn Bridge, Phoenix finally showed up.

He sat beside me, his legs dangling over the edge like mine.

'It's strange not sensing you,' I said. My powers had been returning gradually, gaining in strength and accuracy every day. It wouldn't be long before I was 'all systems, go!'. But even then ... my days of sensing Phoenix were over.

He half laughed. 'Everything is strange.' A gust of wind blew my hair back. 'Especially that,' he said, marvelling.

'Wind?'

'Wind,' he confirmed.

I nodded. I could imagine that feeling the wind without being able to mingle with it would take some getting used to.

He hesitated for a moment before giving me a familiar smirk. 'It suits you.' When I looked at him blankly, he added, 'Your hair. It's bad-ass and beautiful at the same time.'

I blushed and looked down.

He laughed, fully this time. 'And that's weird too. Not feeling your emotions even though I can see them.'

'Do you miss it?'

He shrugged. 'Are you well?' he asked instead.

'Getting there,' I responded, accepting the subject change.

We were silent for a time, watching the cars stream by below, their brake lights leaving trails of red in their wake. Yes, life goes on.

'I could try to do something,' I blurted out suddenly. 'Speak with the angels.' I hadn't seen them since I'd woken up the second time and I wasn't sure if I would ever see Michael again, but surely someone would answer me if I called to them.

'Thank you, but I don't want you to do that.'

I looked at him for the first time. His dark eyes sparkled, and his hair, still stunning with shades of black and purple, seemed ... quietened. It struck me that he was different in more ways than one. He was human, yes. But he was ...

'You look young,' I said, smiling.

He laughed darkly. 'Not for long.'

I sobered. He was right. Phoenix would live a normal human life now, he would grow old and die. Because of me.

'I'm so sorry,' I whispered.

His hand went to my face, his touch filled with unsaid words, and he gently tilted my chin until our eyes met. 'I'm not.'

I saw the truth in his eyes. *Felt* it. 'But you'll die.'

'One day, yes. But I think this might well be the first time I have looked forward to living. I've always been different. Not quite angel enough, not quite human enough. I've been searching for my place, and now I've found it.'

'You *want* this?'

He smiled. 'Didn't you? I get it now. It's different from just being half here as an exile. And best of all, without my powers, I don't leak emotion all over the place. A girl hasn't thrown herself at me once since I changed.'

I looked him up and down, and I couldn't stop my smile. Phoenix was a gorgeous example of a man. 'I wouldn't count on that becoming the rule,' I said wryly.

He shrugged, but his eyes stayed glued to mine, searching for the memory of past times, when we had been more to each other. And of course it was there. The memory was bittersweet and I would carry it with me forever. I could tell the moment

Phoenix found it too, from the ripple of pain that showed in his expression. He looked away.

'Maybe. But maybe there's a chance one of them might actually want me for … me.'

I swallowed. 'I'm sorry, Phoenix.' And this time I was apologising for something more personal. And he knew it.

'Me too.'

I blew out a breath. 'What now?'

Phoenix swung his legs in time with mine. 'We both know the answer to that.'

My chest suddenly tightened and tears slipped from my eyes. Because he was right.

I bit down hard on my lip. 'You'll always know where I am. If you ever …'

He nodded. 'I'll know. But you need to get on with your life.' He gestured to my wedding finger. 'And I need to find a life that won't hurt the people I care the most about.' He looked back into my eyes and then away, running his hand through his hair and rubbing the back of his neck. 'Don't look like that, Violet. Please. Seeing you sad … I had to watch you these past two years and it ripped me apart.'

'I wish things had been different.'

'No, you don't. Not really. You and I were destined to come together. I was destined to share my essence with you, and I think you were destined to change me so completely that when it came to making my ultimate decision, I was ready. I thought that with you I would belong and that I would find my place in this world. But it wasn't *with* you so much as through you. I understand that now.' He half laughed again. 'Turns out you weren't the only one with a Gordian Knot to slice through.'

I nodded quickly, trying to hold back more tears.

He cleared his throat. 'That doesn't mean it doesn't hurt like hell to see that marking on your finger, but it means I can accept it.'

I took in a shuddering breath, absorbing Phoenix's words – both his understanding and his forgiveness.

After a few minutes of silence Phoenix stood and pulled me up and into his arms. I gripped him tightly, knowing that this would be the last time.

'I hope you have the most amazing life. You deserve it,' I said. 'And I hope that when she finds you, you will finally see the truth you have always denied.'

'You sound like *them*, speaking in riddles,' he admonished. '*Who?* And *what?*' he said with a smile.

'The one. And, how incredible and deserving of true happiness you really are.'

His arms tightened around me and then his mouth moved close to my ear. 'That certainly *is* something to look forward to.' He lingered, breathing in and out slowly, before whispering, 'I'll always be with you. Even though we'll be forever apart.'

Phoenix was right. I carried the essence of his angelic being.

*He will always be with me.*

I held onto him for what felt like seconds but was probably much longer. Our lives had collided with an almost obliterating force, but we had taught each other to survive, to fight, to be strong and inevitably to act with our hearts and consciences. Our future was not together, but our history would be forever entwined.

Eventually, he brushed the hair back from my face and looked at me for what I knew was the last time. 'Say the words I came to hear,' he said softly.

I almost whimpered, but he deserved them. So did I.

And so did Lincoln.

I took a deep breath and cupped his cheek in my hand. 'Goodbye, Phoenix.'

His smile was painted with both pain and relief as tears slipped down his face to mirror my own. 'Goodbye, lover.'

The wedding was perfect.

Grigori glamour users put a dome of cover over Central Park and the nature users went crazy. Steph, on Dapper's arm, walked down an aisle rimmed by white daisies; the same white daisies that went as far as the eye could see – Zoe's gift to the happy couple.

Steph was breathtaking in a vintage Chanel dress that showcased her slim figure in the most delicate Chantilly lace and intricate beading, while her veil remained short and understated. Her parents, too wrapped up in their own lives, had not made the trip to celebrate her day but had insisted on paying for it. Much to Onyx's horror, Steph had returned most of the money to them. Minus the cost of the dress.

Zoe and I played our roles as bridesmaids, each wearing a dusty-blue silk dress that flowed to the ground, cutting a slim elegant line with a low and open back. Zoe tipped her hair with gold and with her smoky eye make-up looked divine.

I had let Steph style my hair, as she had always been the expert on shorter styles, and the end result had a 1920s glam feel about it. I loved it.

Lincoln and Spence got off considerably easier in the duties department as groomsmen. Salvatore, no surprise, was the most relaxed groom imaginable.

They spoke their vows in both English and Italian. And when Father Peters proclaimed them husband and wife, the applause was thunderous as their love was felt by all of the two hundred guests.

As the day moved into night the glamour users continued to keep the full sit-down meal, band and dance floor hidden from human eyes.

Just before the reception began, I slipped away for a few minutes to collect my wedding gift for Steph. It wasn't perfect, considering I had wanted to have it ready before the ceremony started, but still …

'Are you ready for this?' I asked sternly. 'You need to know what you are walking into, and if you can't handle it, don't come.'

He looked at his feet and nodded. 'I've messed up, Violet. I know it. But I want to fix things. Starting right now.'

I smiled and pulled him in for a hug. 'Right, we better get you and your perfectly tailored tuxedo in there, then.'

He followed me through the invisible wall of glamour, and once I told him what to look for, his human eyes gradually adopted.

'Don't pass out,' I cautioned. 'Breathe.'

He nodded quickly, and slowly the colour returned to his face. We stood on the side of the dance floor and I gestured to the middle, where Steph was dancing with Lincoln. They were speaking close to one another, smiling and laughing.

I walked into the centre of the floor and tapped Steph's shoulder.

'I think I'll cut in now,' I said.

Steph pouted. 'But I want to keep dancing.'

Failing at holding back my smile any longer, I stepped aside. 'And I have the perfect partner for you.'

Steph's line of sight cleared and she gasped the moment she saw her brother, standing there with a proud smile on his face.

'Sorry I'm late, sis,' he said.

Steph ... well, Steph is one of the good ones. She doesn't hold a grudge. She isn't cold. No. She simply burst into tears and flung herself into her brother's arms.

'Whoa!' Jase laughed, stumbling back. He would have gone down too, if Salvatore's hand hadn't steadied them.

Jase stepped back and quickly put his hand out to Salvatore. 'Welcome to the family, man. You got the best of us.'

Salvatore shook his hand, smiling as he gestured to the wedding party. 'And welcome to ours.'

Steph looked over to me, delight shining in her eyes as she mouthed, 'Thank you.'

I smiled as I mouthed back, 'You're welcome.'

Lincoln slid his arms around me from behind. 'So, that was your top-secret mission?'

I admit I was feeling pretty damn smug. We'd waged a silent war over the past week over who could come up with the best wedding gift.

*What? I never said maturity had to dominate in all areas of my life!*

'Yep,' I said, pulling his arms tighter as we watched Steph and Jase dance, both of them laughing as they goofed around. 'How did yours end up?' I asked.

*Me? Gloating? Never.*

Lincoln looked at his watch and then whispered in my ear. 'Look up.'

Just as I did, silver and gold fireworks erupted from all over the place, flying right up to the edge of the glamour dome before exploding within until the entire dome was illuminated in a completely unearthly and beautiful way.

'How?' I asked.

Lincoln shrugged behind me, his fingers gliding up and down my bare back, making me shiver. 'A little help from telekinesis and the conductors. How did I do?' he whispered into my ear as I watched on in awe.

I feigned nonchalance, at both his words and his still-wandering hands. 'It's okay, I guess. But family trumps everything,' I said.

Sliding his hands around my waist, he turned us both slowly on the spot, and pointed to the bar.

'Yes, baby. Family trumps it all.'

Mum and Dad raised their glasses of champagne towards me – and just like Steph, I burst into tears. I hadn't seen them for more than a year

As they walked towards us, I turned to Lincoln. Before I could speak, he kissed me, then said, 'We might have been married by angels, but that doesn't mean you have to miss out on a few wedding gifts yourself.'

'I love you,' I said, just before my father whisked me up into a bear hug.

'There's my girl,' Dad said, almost squeezing the life out of me.

He put me down and Mum pulled me tight. 'You're everything and more than I could ever have dreamed.' She then held me back at arm's length and looked me over. 'Even without my Grigori gifts I can see what they all see.'

'Who?' I asked, smiling with confusion.

She looked around. 'Everyone, sweetheart. Everyone.' She cupped my face with both of her hands. 'You're empowered. And that makes you luminous,' she said, using the same word Lincoln had used, not so long ago.

Dad looked down at Lincoln's hand, which was joined with mine, and gestured to the markings on our wedding fingers.

He raised his eyebrows at Lincoln. 'Missed a call, did I?'

Lincoln swallowed beside me and, in a rare display of nerves, suddenly seemed to be struggling for words.

Dad maintained his stern face and spoke levelly, which only made it worse. 'What? You don't believe in tradition?'

Lincoln cleared his throat.

I elbowed Dad in his side and he finally gave way to a smile. 'So, I'm guessing they don't have phones in the angelic realm?'

Mum and Dad started to laugh as they took in Lincoln's freaked-out expression. I couldn't help it; I busted up, too. It turns out we all have the same twisted sense of humour.

Lincoln forgave us. Eventually.

Three hours, a few too many glasses of champagne and way too many dances later, Lincoln and I slid into the car we had waiting. Steph and Salvatore had already left, headed on their honeymoon to the Amalfi Coast in Italy.

'Ready?' Lincoln asked as we settled into our seats, bound for the airport.

I nodded. 'It'll be strange going back and Griff not being there.'

Lincoln pulled me into the crook of his arm. 'True, but Spence and Chloe will only be a couple of days behind us, and Steph, Sal and Zoe won't be far behind.'

I smiled at that. We hadn't asked any of them to come with us but Spence hadn't hesitated, stating plainly that now that I'd got my shit together there was no way he was going to miss out on the fun. Which pretty much translated to: he figured he'd get more fighting action with me around.

He was probably right.

I'd already placed my bet with Onyx that Mia would be close behind. Judging by the way she and Spencer were currently dancing, I was confident it was money in the bank.

'And Dapper and Onyx will be back and forth,' Lincoln went on.

That was true too. Griffin had recently put Onyx in charge of a new task force for the Academy, to help the transition to human lives for the many exiles who had been stripped of their power in New Orleans. Onyx was the only one we knew who had previously gone through the transition, so he was the perfect choice to run a kind of halfway house.

I snuggled into Lincoln's welcoming arms.

The driver turned to us. 'JFK airport, was it?'

Lincoln nodded. 'That's right.'

'You two headed home or going away?' he asked, in a friendly voice.

'Home,' we said together.

'Oh, yeah? Where exactly is that?' he added.

I took in another deep breath. Sun. Honey. 'Actually,' I said, meeting the green eyes I would love until the end of time. 'I'm already there.'

The driver gave us a nod of understanding and turned his attention back to the road.

Lincoln smiled, pulling me closer. 'It's midnight,' he said. Then he leaned over and kissed me, and the world was just as it was intended to be. We would fight again. I was no longer naive. Terror would strike at its leisure and darkness laced in misery would test and threaten all we had. But not today. Today was ours.

'Happy birthday, baby.'

I smiled, realising I'd spent my entire life wishing my birthdays away and this time I had actually forgotten. It wasn't as if they'd ever represented anything I wanted to celebrate. For the first seventeen years it had only been a reminder of my mother's death, and for the past two, just a marker of time spent alone.

Lincoln reached behind him, revealing a black velvet box and a large envelope. My brow crinkled as I took them. 'What's this?' I asked, turning the envelope over in my hands.

'Open the box first,' he said, tucking a wayward strand of hair behind my ear.

I bit down on my lip when I looked inside and saw a divine platinum necklace holding a solitary lily pendant; a diamond nestled in each of its delicate petals.

I tilted my head to allow Lincoln to fasten the chain. He took full advantage of the moment, peppering my neck and shoulder with goosebump-inducing kisses.

'I love it.' It was the perfect symbol of our love.

Lincoln sat back, smiling proudly and gestured to the envelope. 'Open it.'

I did. The words took a moment to sink in. My hand went to my mouth and beneath it I could feel my uncontrollable smile as I reread the words over and over: *You have been accepted into the Fenton Art Course.*

It had been my seventeenth birthday when my world had changed. I'd been headed towards a future that I thought I wanted, and it included a place in the prestigious Fenton Art Course. Of course, my path had altered since then, and between the heartache and blood loss, well, art had been lost to me as well. But I missed it every day. It was a part of me. Part of my humanity.

The course started next month.

I sank into the arms of the man I loved, knowing that the inclinations I'd once felt to run or quit were far behind me, and that in their place was a simple readiness to face whatever lay ahead, with my partner at my side, and to appreciate the good moments for all they could be. I inhaled deeply – a new memory logged – and at that moment I realised that birthdays would forever more be one of my favourite things.

# angel hierarchy

### the sole

Violet Eden (G)
Violet's Angel Maker
Sammael (EL)

### seraphim

Uri (AL)
Nox (AD)
Lilith (ED)
Griffin (G)
Josephine (G)
Drenson (G)

### cherubim

Nahilius (EL)
Rudyard (G)
Beth (G)
Adele (G)
Hakon (G)

**1st choir**

### thrones

Phoenix (AD)
Jude (EL)
Becca (G)
Evelyn (G)
Wilhelm (G)

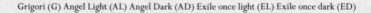

Grigori (G) Angel Light (AL) Angel Dark (AD) Exile once light (EL) Exile once dark (ED)

## POWERS

Lincoln (G)
Nyla (G)
Gressil (ED)
Nathan (G)
Decima (G)

## DOMINATIONS

Onyx (once ED)
Spence (G)
Gray (G)
Archer (G)
Rainer (G)
Carter (G)

2ND CHOIR

## VIRTUES

Salvatore (G)
Morgan (G)
Valerie (G)
Milo (G)
Taxi (G)

## PRINCIPALITIES

Irin – The Keeper (EL)
Kaitlin (G)
Max (G)
Seth (G)

## ARCHANGELS

Zoe (G)
Olivier (EL)
Mia (G)
Father Peters (G)
Ryan (G)

3RD CHOIR

## ANGELS

Magda (G)
Samuel (G)
Hiro (G)
Chloe (G)

# acknowledgements

**W**riting this series has changed my life. Big words, I know, but very true. Discovering Violet's character marked the beginning of my writing career, literally changing the direction of my life and for that, these books will always be so close to my heart. I guess you could say that while I discovered Violet, it was Violet who really discovered me. So it is bittersweet to say goodbye to her.

There are many people to thank. First of all, Selwa Anthony, my agent, who was the first to see something special about these characters and this story: thank you for all that you have done, and continue to do, since you first read *Embrace*.

To my publishers, Hachette: wow, it really does feel like an end to an era. Special thanks to Vanessa Radnidge, the best publisher a girl could ask for and an absolute joy to work with. To editor Kate Ballard, who has worked tirelessly on the books since day one: thank you, thank you! Also, to editor Claire de Medici and proofreader Pam Dunne: thank you for all of your work and contributions that have helped to make this book all that it can be.

Much gratitude to Publishing Director Fiona Hazard and Children's Books Sales & Marketing Director Chris Raine, who have stood firmly behind this series from the outset. A huge shout out to Airlie Lawson in international rights: you are amazing! And to Christine Fairbrother in marketing and Theresa Bray in publicity: thank you for the many, many things that you have done to bring these books to readers!

To my family and friends – you are the best support and I am so grateful to you all for enduring the countless hypothetical conversations, the over-analysing and the cover dissections. Thank you all for your kindness, generosity and support. Special thanks to my first readers: Mum, Harriet and Kylie – I can't tell you how much I appreciate your feedback!

Huge thanks to my husband, Matt, and our girls, Sienna and Winter. Committing to write these books has taken a lot of time, yes, but also a big piece of mind and heart space. Sometimes it is exhausting, and not just for me but also for those who have to live with me! So, thank you for always understanding and never criticising, even when anyone else would have. I love you guys!

Finally, to the readers around the world who have taken this journey with me: thank you for giving your time to these characters and for trusting me to tell this story. I have my fingers crossed that come the end, you will feel it was time well spent!

# Discover a thrilling world
# of angels and romance

# OUT NOW

WWW.ORCHARDBOOKS.CO.UK

Read on for an exclusive
extract of

the new psychological thriller

by

Jessica Shirvington

# PREFACE

I am a liar.

Not compulsive.

Simply required.

I am two people. Neither better than the other, no superpowers, no mystical destinies, no two-places-in-one-time mechanism – but two people. Different in ways fundamental, even though at the most basic level I look the same. My physical attributes, my memory and my name follow me. For the past eighteen years, everything else, *everything*, about me is different. Twenty-four hours as the first of me. And in the blink of an eye, twenty-four hours as the second of me. Every day, without fail, it goes on...

I've never told anyone. By the time I was old enough to figure out everyone didn't have two lives – by the time *that* little shock settled in – I didn't know where to begin. *How* to begin. And society, both of them, didn't want to know.

When I was a child, I didn't realise I was different from everyone else. But I'm pretty sure I've always been this way – this two lives way – which means I was probably born twice, was a baby twice. No surprise I'm glad I can't remember that. Being torn from one set of arms and thrust into another every twenty-four hours? Well, it doesn't matter how much they love you… Can anyone say, issues?

Practice makes perfect though, and I like to think of myself as a pro. I've ironed out the kinks; identified the major pitfalls and how to avoid them. I manage. I know who I need to be in each of my lives, and I try not to confuse my brain with the 'infinity questions' anymore.

I've learned to accept that in one life I love strawberries, while in the other my taste buds cringe at the flavour. I know that in one life I can speak fluent French, but even though the memory of the language comes with me, in my other life I must not. Then there are easier things to remember, like Maddie, my gorgeous little sister in one life, and my not-so-great big brothers in my other.

Above all else – though I try not to think about it – I know which life I prefer. And every night when I Cinderella myself from one life to the next a very small, but definite, piece of me dies. The hardest part is that nothing about my situation has ever changed – the only thing I can be certain of is the fact that my body clock is different from everyone else's. There is no loophole.

Until now, that is.

# COMING SOON...

PB: 978 1 40833 173 6   £6.99
eBook: 978 1 40833 174 3   £5.99

# IF YOU LIKED EMPOWER, YOU'LL LOVE

Stunning romance and relentless suspense – discover the first incredible book in **THE GODDESS WAR** trilogy.

From the bestselling author of **ANNA DRESSED IN BLOOD**.

WWW.ORCHARDBOOKS.CO.UK

From the bestselling author of **KNIFE** comes
an extraordinary story for older readers

**OUT NOW**

R J ANDER...    ...ing author of ULTRAVIOLET
ANDERSON

**ULTRAVIOLET**
EVERYTHING YOU BELIEVE IS WRONG

**QUICKSILVER**
EVERYTHING YOU ARE IS A LIE

Pbk 978 1 40831 275 9   £6.99
eBook 978 1 40831 371 8   £6.98

Pbk 978 1 40831 628 3   £6.99
eBook 978 1 40831 629 0   £6.98

## ONCE UPON A TIME THERE WAS A GIRL WHO WAS SPECIAL.

## THIS IS NOT HER STORY.

## UNLESS YOU COUNT THE PART WHERE I KILLED HER.